Andrea Laurence is an award-winning contemporary romance author who has loved books and has been writing stories since she learned to read and write. She always dreamed of seeing her work in print and is thrilled to be able to share her books with the world. A dedicated West Coast girl transplanted into the Deep South, she's working on her own happily-ever-after with her boyfriend and five fur-babies. You can contact Andrea at her website, andrealaurence.com.

*To the Dedicated Soldiers of My Street Team
Andrea's Army of Awesomeness—*

I can't list all of you individually, but know that this dedication is for you! Thank you for all the hard work you put in to help make each of my books a success. It may not seem like a lot, but every review you write, every bookmark you hand out, every post you share with friends...makes a difference. I am happy to reward all of you with books and goodies because it's worth every penny to have you on my team. Thank you for your support and friendship. You're awesome. *(Obviously!)*

Prologue

"Do you want to get out of here?"

Amelia Kennedy turned and looked up into the cool blue eyes of her best friend, Tyler Dixon. Of course he would be the one to save her. "Yes, *please*." She got up from the banquet table and accepted his hand, happily following him out of the ballroom, through the casino and out to the glittering lights of the Las Vegas Strip.

Just breathing in the cool desert air made her feel better. Why had she thought her high school reunion would be fun? It was just a room filled with people she never liked, gloating about how great their lives were. Even though she couldn't care less about what Tammy Richardson—cheerleader and all-around stuck-up brat—had done with her life, hearing Tammy brag had some-how made Amelia feel less enthusiastic about her own achievements.

It was ridiculous, really. She co-owned her own company and was very successful, but the lack of a ring on her hand and toddler photos on her phone made her the odd girl out tonight. This entire trip was a waste of her precious vacation time.

Well, not the whole thing. It was worth it to see Tyler. They had been best friends since the ninth grade, but recently they had both gotten so busy they were lucky to see each other once a year. The reunion was a good excuse.

They stumbled down the sidewalk hand in hand with no destination in mind. It didn't matter where they ended up. Every step they put between them and the reunion improved Amelia's mood. That, or—if her softening knees were any indication—the tequila was finally kicking in. A low rumble caught their attention, and they stopped outside the Mirage to watch the periodic eruption of the volcano out front.

They leaned against the railing, Amelia resting her head on Tyler's shoulder and sighing with contentment. She really missed spending time with him. There was just something about being with Tyler that made the world seem better. There was a comfort and ease in his arms that she'd never found in another man. Although they'd never dated, Tyler had set the bar high for her future relationships. Maybe too high, considering she was still single.

"Feel better?" he asked.

"Yes, thank you. I just couldn't look at any more pictures of weddings and babies."

Tyler wrapped his arm around her, chasing away the January desert chill. "That's what happens at reunions, you know."

"Yeah, but I didn't expect it to make me feel like such a…"

"Successful, talented businesswoman in control of her own destiny?"

Amelia sighed. "I was thinking more along the lines of a relationship failure on the fast track to a house with too many cats."

"Quit it," he said in a stern voice. He turned toward her and tipped her chin up so she had to look him in the eye. "You are amazing. You're beautiful, talented, successful... Any man would be lucky to have you in his life. You just haven't found one worthy of you yet."

That was a nice thought, but it didn't change the fact that she'd been on a fruitless quest for Mr. Right since she'd come of age. "Thanks, Ty," she said anyway, as she wrapped her arms around his waist and buried her face in the lapel of his suit.

He held her tight, resting his chin on the top of her head. It was a simple hug. One they'd shared a hundred times before. But tonight, somehow, it was different. She was suddenly very aware of the movement of his hard muscles beneath his shirt. His cologne tickled her nose, so familiar and yet so enticing in the moment. It made her want to bury her face in his neck and inhale the warm scent of his skin. Run her palms across the rough stubble of his jaw...

A wave of heat licked at Amelia's cheeks, and she realized it had nothing to do with the flames shooting across the water beside them. There was a warmth curling in her belly, a need building inside her. It was a familiar arousal, but one she'd never associated with Tyler. He was her best friend. Nothing more.

But in that moment, she wanted more. She wanted him to show her how beautiful and talented he thought she was with his hands and his mouth instead of his words. It was a dangerous thought, but she couldn't shake it.

"Do you remember graduation night?"

"Of course," she said, pulling away to put an end to the physical contact stirring the blood in her veins. She couldn't forget that night. They had suffered through family parties, and then they'd snuck off together to camp in the desert. Amelia had driven them out to the edge of town, where they could finally see the stars. "We drank wine coolers and stayed up all night watching for shooting stars."

"Do you remember the pact we made?"

Amelia thought back to that night, the details blurred by a combination of time and fuzzy navels. She remembered them pinky swearing something. "What was it about? I don't remember."

"We agreed that if we weren't married by our ten-year reunion, we would marry each other."

"Oh, yeah," she said, the moment flooding back into her mind. In their eighteen-year-old brains, twenty-eight was nearly ancient. If they weren't married by then, all hope was obviously lost. They'd sworn they would save each other from a lonely middle-aged existence. "Twenty-eight sure doesn't feel the way I expected it to. I still feel young, and yet sometimes I feel like the oldest, most boring person I know. All I do is work. I never have adventures like we used to have together."

Tyler studied her face, his light brown eyebrows drawing together in thought. "Do you feel up for an adventure tonight? I guarantee it will cheer you up."

That was exactly what she needed—the kind of night that would make for a great story. "I am definitely up for an adventure. What did you have in mind?"

Tyler smiled and took her hand in his. The touch sent

a surge down her spine, and she knew she'd agree to anything when he smiled at her that way. Then he dropped to one knee, and she realized she was in for more than she'd bargained for.

"Amelia, will you marry me?"

One

"Amelia," Gretchen pressed, "tell me you didn't elope in a Las Vegas wedding chapel."

Amelia took a deep breath and slowly nodded. Her stomach was turning somersaults, but she managed to get the words out anyway. "I did," she admitted. "The details are a little blurry, but I woke up married to my best friend."

"Wait." Bree held up her hands in disbelief. "Did you just say you're married? *Married?*"

Amelia looked at her two friends and coworkers, not entirely certain she could repeat the words. It had been hard enough to say them the first time. She actually hadn't admitted it aloud until that very moment. The past few weeks it had all seemed like a fuzzy dream, but with Gretchen and Bree staring at her as though she'd grown a second head, it was suddenly very, very real.

"My high school reunion didn't go the way I planned,"

she explained. "I thought going back to Las Vegas would be fun, but it wasn't. Everyone was passing around pictures of their wedding days and their kids..." Her voice trailed off.

The sad state of Amelia's love life had hit her hard that night. She'd been in the dating scene for ten years with nothing to show for it but a string of almost-but-not-quite relationships. It wasn't for lack of trying—she put herself out there time after time, but with no luck. She refused to settle for anything less than a timeless love, and it seemed just out of her reach.

Her hectic career hadn't helped matters. She'd spent the past few years since college focusing on building the business she and her partners had founded, From This Moment. Running a wedding facility was a stressful job, and her area of expertise—catering—was no small task. Between menu tastings, prep work and wedding cakes, the wedding day itself was the least of her troubles. She loved her job, but it left little time to seriously dedicate herself to finding the love and family she'd always fantasized about.

She was only twenty-eight. Hardly old-maid material. But then she'd gone to the reunion and found that her schoolmates had left her in their familial dust. Even dorky Dave Simmons had come with his wife, and she'd been certain he'd never find a woman. Not even having Tyler there—equally single—helped. He was single by choice, too happy to play the globe-trotting CEO to have the burden of a serious relationship.

"I was feeling sorry for myself. My best friend, Tyler, kept bringing me drinks, and eventually we decided to blow off the party and go down to the Strip."

"Skip to the part where you eloped," Gretchen pressed,

with an odd mix of wonder and glee on her cherubic face. She enjoyed living vicariously through others.

Amelia shook her head. "It's kind of a blur, but Tyler reminded me about this stupid pact we made on graduation night. We swore that if we weren't married by our ten-year reunion, we would marry each other."

"You didn't!" Bree said, her large blue eyes growing wider by the minute.

"We did." She couldn't believe it either, but they'd gone through with it. When Amelia woke up the next morning, the giant diamond ring on her hand and the naked man beside her in bed had confirmed her worst fears. The night before had not been just a vivid dream. It had really happened. She was married to her best friend.

"We did it for a laugh, you know? In high school, the two of us were always coming up with crazy ideas. I think Tyler was trying to cheer me up, offering to marry me so I wouldn't feel like the single one at the reunion anymore. It seemed like a brilliant solution at the time."

"It always does," Gretchen noted, as though she'd had her share of impetuous experiences.

"What the hell kind of liquor were you drinking?" Bree asked at last, sliding away the bridal magazine she'd been reading to plan her own upcoming nuptials.

"Anyway," Amelia continued, pointedly ignoring Bree, "the plan was to annul it as soon as we can. He lives in New York. I live here. It's obviously not going to work long-term."

Work? What was she even talking about? Of course it wasn't going to work. She'd just married her best friend from high school! *Tyler.* She knew everything there was to know about him and she was certain Tyler was not husband material. He worked too much, he traveled constantly and he had a bad habit of falling off the face of the earth for weeks at a time. She loved him, but she couldn't count on him. And yet, here she was. Married to him.

"So far the annulment plan isn't panning out the way I'd like. Turns out you can't annul a marriage in Tennessee just because it was done on a whim. New York may have better laws, but if not, that means a full-on divorce. Either way, Tyler has been traveling too much to start the process. I've only gotten a few texts from him in between stops in Belgium, Los Angeles, India... I haven't even spoken to him on the phone since I left Las Vegas."

"So do you think he's really busy, or is he avoiding you?" Gretchen asked. "I would think that might be an awkward situation to deal with. I can't even imagine sleeping with one of my guy friends from high school. If the sex was bad it would be hard to face him later. If the sex was good...that might be even worse."

"The sex was amazing," Amelia confessed, quickly clamping a hand over her mouth. Had she really said that out loud? She shook her head. The words had spilled out because they were true. Tyler had been the most talented and attentive lover she'd ever had. Their wedding night had easily left her top five encounters in its dust. She wasn't entirely sure what to think about that.

"Well, then," Bree noted with a smile twisting her lips. "Do tell."

"Oh, no," she said. "I've already said too much."

"Maybe he's dragging his feet in the hopes of getting some more of that sugar," Gretchen suggested.

"There's no more sugar to be had. That was a one-night thing and we both know it," Amelia argued, even as she felt the untruth of her words. She wanted more, she just knew she shouldn't. "He's just busy. He's always busy."

Tyler obviously wasn't that concerned with fixing this.

In the few texts she'd received, he'd told her to relax. If annulment was off the table, there was no rush, so unless she was madly in love and needed to marry someone else right that minute, it wasn't a big deal. He, of all people, knew about her relationship struggles and knew that the odds of that were extremely low.

But it was a big deal to her. Especially considering the extenuating circumstances. She couldn't even wrap her brain around that, so she continued to ignore it. It wasn't a pressing issue…yet.

"So you're really just going to walk away from the man that gave you the greatest orgasms of your life?" Gretchen frowned. "I don't think I could do that, even if I couldn't stand the guy. You and Tyler love each other, though. It's not much of a hop from friends to lovers, is it?"

"It is a huge hop over a massive chasm, I assure you." Amelia knew for certain they shouldn't go there again. Tyler had been her best friend since ninth grade, but she had never really allowed herself to consider anything between the two of them. For one thing, there was no way she wanted to risk their friendship in an attempt to take it to the next level. If it failed—and the odds were that it would—she'd lose the most important person in her life.

For another reason, there was a big difference between being friends and being lovers. Being friends was easy. She tolerated Tyler's jet-setting, bossiness and extended radio silences just the same as he tolerated her romantic drama and pickiness. It wasn't a big deal because as friends, it didn't impact them directly. Dating someone magnified those personality quirks, and suddenly they were deal breakers.

Her raw emotional state at the reunion had apparently forced all those concerns out of her mind. The next thing she knew, she was on the verge of consummating her marriage. In that moment, nothing mattered more than peeling away Tyler's clothes and getting a taste of the forbidden. His hard body and sure touch had been an unexpected surprise, and she hadn't been able to get enough of him. Even now, the mere thought of touching him again sent a thrill through her body, awakening parts of her that should never, ever throb with need where Tyler was concerned.

Since she'd gotten home from the reunion, their night together had haunted her. The marriage could be undone. But the memories… Those couldn't be erased. The way he'd touched her. The way he'd coaxed pleasure from her body as though he'd studied his whole life for that moment… She could never go back to the blissful ignorance they'd once had. They had eaten the forbidden fruit.

A chime like a kitchen timer went off on her phone, rousing her from the mental spiral she'd just dived into. It was a new text. She frowned down at her phone when she saw the name. Speak of the devil, she had finally gotten another text from Tyler. Unfortunately, it didn't address her million questions or make up for the weeks of waiting he'd put her though since they'd married. All it said was, Are you at work?

He must be ready to talk about all this at last. Perhaps his jet-setting had abated for a few days and he was finally able to move forward.

Yes, she replied to his text. She would be able to call him back after the staff meeting was over. At that point, she could go into her office, shut the door and have the much-needed discussion to put this behind them. Natalie, the wedding planner and office manager, would arrive any moment with coffee, as she did every Monday morning. Not even Amelia's latest life catastrophe would throw off Nat's schedule.

On cue, Natalie pushed open the door of the conference room and stopped in the doorway. She had the cup holder clutched in her hands, four paper cups held tightly in place, as usual. But there was a strange look on her face. Her normally calm expression was pinched, her mouth tight. Something was wrong.

"What's the matter, Natalie?" Bree asked.

Natalie turned from Bree to look at Amelia, her long dark ponytail sweeping over one shoulder. "There's an incredibly hot guy here to see you, Amelia. He says that he's your, uh...*husband*."

Someone gasped. Amelia wasn't sure which of them it was. Probably her. She launched up out of her chair, her expression no doubt panic-stricken. He couldn't possibly be here. He'd just texted her and hadn't made any mention of being in Nashville. Natalie was surely mistaken. "What does he look like?"

Natalie's brow shot up. "Five minutes ago, I didn't think you had *a* husband, period, much less so many that you wouldn't know who he was immediately when I mentioned him."

"Tall, dark blond hair, bushy eyebrows, icy blue eyes?"

Natalie nodded slowly. "That would be him. He's waiting in the lobby with a shiny wedding ring on his hand. Have I missed something?"

"Oh, yeah." Gretchen snorted.

Moving into the room, Natalie set the drinks on the table and then crossed her arms over her chest. "You're married? To the guy in the lobby?"

"Yes," she admitted.

"Amelia—the one who's had her wedding planned since she was five? Amelia—the one who just a few weeks ago was complaining that there was no one special in her life? I mean, you *are* the same person, right? You're not a pod person that just looks like Amelia?"

She wished she could blame her rash behavior on alien influences, but it was all her doing. Natalie was right to be surprised. Amelia quite literally had had a wedding planned for twenty-three years. Her files of cartoon drawings and magazine cutout collages had evolved into Pinterest boards and spreadsheets, but the content was basically the same. And considering she had never been engaged, it was an excessive level of detail. She occasionally updated the color palette, but the rest was the same. She'd always fantasized about a big wedding with hundreds of guests, tons of good food, dancing and all the elegant touches she adored. All she needed was the love of her life to slip into that Armani tuxedo and make her dreams a reality.

To throw all that away so she could get walked down the aisle by Elvis and marry her best friend was... unthinkable. But Vegas seemed to have that power over people. "It's a long story. They can fill you in." Amelia started toward the door.

"Do you at least want your coffee?" Natalie asked, holding up the paper cup with her white chocolate–caramel macchiato.

Amelia started to reach for it, and then she caught a whiff of the strong aroma. Her stomach immediately started to turn, making her wince and step back. "Ugh—no, thanks. Maybe later. I just can't face it right now."

Turning quickly, she disappeared down the hallway. Natalie's voice easily carried the distance. "Will someone *please* tell me what the hell is going on?"

Tyler Dixon waited longer in the lobby than he expected to. When the dark-haired woman disappeared down the hallway to deliver his message, he was certain Amelia would come rushing out to him immediately. She would run and jump into his arms, greeting him with a big hug and a kiss on the cheek the way she always did.

Glancing down at his Rolex, he started to wonder if he'd miscalculated. He'd known she was here, even before she'd texted him back—he'd recognized her car in the parking lot. That meant she was either angry and making him wait for ignoring her, or she was avoiding him because she was embarrassed by the whole sex thing.

He didn't know what she had to be embarrassed about. With a body like hers, walking around naked could be considered a public service. Sure, they'd crossed a line, but they could work through that. They'd weathered rough patches in their friendship before.

It probably had more to do with him not calling her back. His schedule had been pretty hectic since the reunion, but it had to be. He'd bought some raw diamonds and taken them to India to be cut. He'd hit an auction in Belgium and picked up an antique sapphire brooch formerly owned by French royalty before the revolution. He'd closed a huge deal with a Beverly Hills jewelry designer to provide diamonds for their pieces. Whenever he'd thought to call her, the time zones were off. She wouldn't have appreciated getting those calls at 2:00 a.m.

This was why he didn't get in serious relationships anymore. He'd gotten burned with Christine and learned his lesson. He knew that most women didn't appreciate his schedule, even if they appreciated the money that resulted from it. At first, his diamond airline status and exotic travels seemed exciting, but it didn't take most women long to realize that meant he was always on the go. No, he wouldn't be able to go to that work thing with you. No, he couldn't talk about your crappy day when he was ten times zones behind and busy working.

Amelia had never minded his schedule before. Had that changed along with their marital status?

What was the rush anyway? She hadn't found Prince Charming in the ten years leading up to now. Certainly she hadn't found him in the past month while he'd been gone. He loved Amelia, but she wasn't known for her successful relationships. He'd only met one woman in his whole life who was as high maintenance as she was, and that was his ex. He'd known that about Amelia going into this, but she was his best friend and he would do anything to make her happy. Apparently.

They'd take care of the divorce. That was why he was here at his first opportunity. Despite what Amelia might think, Tyler wasn't deliberately dragging his feet. Although, if he was honest with himself, there was a part of him that was sad that he'd never get to touch those soft curves again. He'd always been happy to be Amelia's friend, but he wouldn't mind spending a little more time exploring her body before they went back to being just friends. He'd only had one brief taste, and that wasn't nearly enough for a woman like her.

But in the end, he knew their friendship would outweigh his erection. Amelia was the most important person in his life and he wouldn't risk that, even to make love to her again. She wasn't just his best friend; she was a driving force in his life. As a kid, he'd been a nobody lost in the chaos of his large family. At school, he'd been just as invisible. Amelia had seen him when no one else did. She'd seen his potential and lit a fire in him to make something of himself. Over the past ten years he had built up his own company, dealing in precious gems and antiquities. He lived a lifestyle he never could've imagined as a poor kid growing up in Vegas. Amelia had made him believe he could do all those things.

No, he wouldn't risk his friendship with her for the greatest sex ever had in the whole universe.

Tyler looked up to see Amelia watching him from the doorway. She didn't run and leap into his arms, but at this point, he was no longer expecting an enthusiastic greeting. He was just happy she hadn't left him standing out here indefinitely.

She took a few hesitant steps into the room, not speaking at all. She looked amazing today. There was a glow about her that lured his gaze to travel over her body, admiring the fit of her sweater dress. The dark purple tunic was gathered beneath her ample breasts and flowed to her knee. She was wearing black leggings and boots with it that enhanced her shapely legs.

The deep V of the dress's neckline displayed an amethyst pendant he'd sent her for her birthday. The fat teardrop gemstone fell just at her cleavage, drawing his eyes to her breasts. Amelia was petite in many ways, but the Lord had blessed her with enough assets for three women.

He knew he shouldn't look, but the memories of their wedding night rushed into his brain, and he couldn't turn away. In an instant, he could see her naked body sprawled across the hotel bed. His palms tingled with the memory of running his hands over every inch of her flawless porcelain skin. Tasting those breasts. Hearing her cries echo through the room.

The lobby was suddenly very warm. It was a cruel trick of the fates to give him a woman so desirable for a wife, then not let him keep her. And he couldn't keep her. He had to remind himself of that. They'd only disappoint one another and ruin their friendship.

"Hey, Ames," he said, finally meeting her gaze.

She swallowed hard, watching him warily. With her big dark brown eyes, she almost looked like a doe, easily spooked by any sudden movements. He hated that. She'd never looked at him with anything other than adoration and love before. He supposed getting married had ruined that. This was just his first taste of what it would be like to be in a real relationship with his demanding, high-maintenance best friend. The honeymoon was barely over and he was already in trouble. He definitely shouldn't have waited this long to talk to her.

"What are you doing here, Tyler?"

Apparently they were skipping the pleasantries. "I came to talk to you."

Her arms crossed over her chest, her breasts nearly spilling from the dress with the movement. "*Now* you want to talk? What about the past few weeks when I've tried to get hold of you and you just blew me off? When I wanted to talk to you, all this didn't seem to matter. Am I just supposed to drop everything to talk to you now because you've decided you're ready to deal with this mess?"

Tyler's lips twisted in thought, his hand rubbing over the rough stubble on his chin. Now did not seem like the time to try to convince her it wasn't a big deal. She had always been a very emotional person, her temper as easily lit as the flames of her red hair. He'd seen her unleash that fury on past boyfriends and he didn't ever want to be the recipient. "I'm sorry I didn't get back with you. I needed to take care of a few things."

"And I needed you to talk to me!" She took several steps toward him, a strand of auburn hair falling from its clip to frame her face. A red flush rushed to her cheeks and décolletage, marring her pale, creamy skin. "We're *married*, Tyler. Married! You can't just keep ignoring this. As much as I'd like to pretend this never happened, we've got to deal with it. Talk about it. Of all the times to ignore me for business, this is the wrong time."

"I know." He held out his hands in an appeasing gesture. It hurt him to hear how distraught she was over their situation, but there was nothing to be done. Business was a priority over a fake marriage, even with his best friend. "I should've called, I know. I'm sorry. I hopped a flight out here as soon as I could so we could deal with this in person."

That seemed to calm her down. Her hands fell to her sides, the tension in her shoulders relaxing. Even then, there was a concern lining her eyes. Something was wrong. More than just her irritation with him. He knew Amelia better than anyone else on the planet. A thousand miles apart, he could detect that she was upset over the phone. In person, it was hard to ignore that something wasn't right.

She crossed her arms over her chest, and he noticed she wasn't wearing her wedding ring. He could feel his own wedding band encircling his finger. He didn't know why, but he'd worn it faithfully since the ceremony. Somehow it felt tighter and more irritating when he knew he was the only one wearing it. "Where's your ring?" he asked.

"It's at home in my jewelry box. Until five minutes ago, no one knew I was married, Tyler. I can't strut around here with that giant rock on my hand and not get a million questions."

She was right about that. Subtlety was thrown out the window after you moved past a couple carats. Her ring was a flawless eight-carat D-color cushion-cut diamond. He'd purchased it a few weeks before the reunion and had been taking it, and a selection of other jewels, with him to

LA for a potential buyer. The reunion had only been possible because he could fit it in on his way. When they'd scrambled for last-minute wedding rings, he'd pulled it from the hotel vault. They'd agreed that when the prank was done, she'd return it.

"I've wanted to keep this whole situation pretty quiet," she continued. "The fewer people that know, the better. What's an adventure to us is a ridiculous mistake to others."

That was probably true. He slipped his own ring off and dropped it into his lapel pocket, noting how his finger suddenly felt naked. It was amazing how easily he'd adjusted to wearing that ring. He'd only gotten close to putting one on the one time, years ago, and since then he hadn't given much thought to it. "Is there any way we can go somewhere to talk?" He glanced down at his watch. "It's still early. I'll take you out for pancakes, my treat."

Her face fell into another frown, this time with her delicate brow furrowing. "I can't right now, Tyler. I'm supposed to be in a staff meeting. You may be able to work whenever and wherever you want, but I'm not a jewel dealer that zips around the country whenever I please. I run a business with partners that count on me. And on Mondays, we have a standing meeting."

"I'm sure they'd understand. Come on, Ames. It will be like senior ditch day all over again. We can have eggs and sausage and pancakes. Maple syrup. I caught a dawn flight from LaGuardia and came straight here without eating anything. I'm starving."

Amelia's eyes narrowed for a moment, then widened with a touch of concern. Her free hand flew to her mouth. "Shut up about the food," she said.

"What?" What did he say that was so offensive? Breakfast was hardly an unpleasant concept.

"I said, shut up, *please*." Her eyes were squeezed tightly shut, her muscles tense as she fought for control. It concerned him. He wanted to run to her, do something, but he didn't think the gesture would be welcome.

After a moment, she took a deep breath and seemed to recover. "I can't talk to you right now, Tyler. You just show up out of the blue with no thought to my schedule. I'm not fifteen anymore. I *will* meet with you, but you've got to respect the plans I have. I can meet you for lunch if you want."

He nodded, knowing she was right. His schedule was flexible, but to assume the same of hers was inconsiderate. "Whatever you need to do, Ames. I'll take you for barbecue, if you want. I haven't had some good ribs in a long time."

She started to nod, then froze as a look of panic spread across her face. "I—" she began, then turned on her heel and dashed around the corner.

Tyler started to follow her but stopped when he heard the unpleasant sound of retching. Apparently barbecue was not terribly appealing to her.

She returned a moment later, her face flushed and her eyes watery. "I'm sorry about that."

Why was she apologizing? "Are you okay? Did you eat something bad?"

She shook her head, a somber expression in her eyes. "No," she said. "I'm fine. I'm just…pregnant."

Two

This was a bad dream.

This was not how her life was supposed to go. Not how this moment was supposed to be. Her first child was supposed to be a blessed occasion. She was supposed to be joyous, not nauseous. Telling her husband the news should be a gloriously happy moment.

Gloriously happy were not the words she would use to describe the look on Tyler's face. His square jaw was slack, his pale blue eyes wide with panic. Not even his expensive suit could keep her superconfident, successful best friend from instantly transforming back into the startled, unsure teen on his first day at a new school.

She still remembered the day her father, the principal at El Dorado High School, had walked into her freshman English class with a new student in tow. She'd pointed out an empty seat beside her and befriended the new boy. It was the best decision she'd ever made. Tyler was the best friend a girl could have.

Today, looking at that same lost expression on his face, she didn't know what to do. Hugging him seemed awkward considering the state of their physical relationship and the legal ramifications of their marriage. She didn't have any words of comfort or wisdom to offer. If she did, she'd say them to herself. She was still reeling from the morning's dose of unexpected news.

She was pregnant with Tyler's baby. She just couldn't figure out how something like that could be possible. From the moment she'd seen the two pink lines on the pregnancy test this morning until she'd announced it to him, it had felt surreal. She loved Tyler more than anyone else. She'd known him since she was fourteen. But having his baby had never been a part of her plan. And Amelia had big plans.

Apparently, it wasn't part of his plans, either. Before she made her announcement, his gaze had drifted over her body, bringing a flush to her cheeks. It didn't take much to realize that he was mentally reliving their night together. She understood. Seeing him standing there in his tailored suit with that charming smile had made it hard for her to remember she was supposed to be irritated with him.

Now all he could do was stare at her midsection, looking desperately for some kind of evidence that she was wrong. She wished she were wrong, but she hadn't needed that test to know the truth. It had only confirmed what the past few days' misery had made abundantly clear.

"Say something," she pressed at last.

Tyler cleared his throat and nodded, her words snapping him back into the moment. "I'm sorry," he said. "I wasn't expecting..." His voice trailed off.

"I don't think either of us was expecting *any* of this. Especially me being pregnant." Or her throwing up into the lobby trash can. "But what's done is done. As much as I'd like to go back in time and change things, we can't. Now we have to figure out what we're going to do."

She needed his input desperately because she didn't know what to do. In any other scenario, Tyler would've been the one Amelia ran to for support and advice. If she'd found herself pregnant by another man, he'd be the first person she called in a panic. He would be the one to talk her down and tell her everything was okay. But it was his baby, and somehow that made everything more difficult.

"So do you still need to go to your meeting?" he asked.

Now that the baby was out of the bag, so to speak, the meeting didn't seem as critical. Her stubbornness had really been more from irritation about his disregard for her plans than anything else. She loved Tyler, but sometimes he forgot he wasn't the CEO of everything and everyone. He'd steamroll people if they let him. Amelia was one person who never let him.

The meeting wasn't her number one priority at the moment. She could catch up on the high points later. It was more important to talk to Tyler about what they were going to do. She needed a story, a plan, before she faced her friends again and had to tell them what was going on in any depth whatsoever. They'd be like a firing squad, lobbing questions at her that she didn't have any answers for. Yet.

"No, let's just…" She eyed her office, and her gaze strayed to the open doors of the wedding chapel just beyond it.

The white-and-gray chapel was so elegant. Beautifully detailed, yet understated enough not to upstage the bride or her chosen decor. Since the day construction was completed, Amelia had envisioned herself getting married in that same chapel wearing a strapless ivory Pnina Tornai gown. She could easily picture sprays of white and pink roses filling the room with their delicate fragrance. The rows of friends and family crying happy tears.

That was the way her big day was supposed to be. Not at 1:00 a.m. in the Li'l Chapel of Love with the pink bismuth–colored upholstery and dusty silk flower arrangements. She'd been wearing a black cocktail dress, for chrissake. Married in black! No old, no new, no borrowed, no blue. It was blasphemous. And obviously very bad luck. The whole thing made her want to curl into a ball and cry the tears of a five-year-old who'd had her dreams destroyed.

Her office was a convenient place to talk, but the sudden urge to get as far away from the chapel as possible nearly overwhelmed her. "Just get me out of here," she said.

"You got it."

She moved quickly, slipping into the coat she'd hung nearby. She should tell the others she was leaving, but she didn't dare stick her head back in the conference room. She'd text Gretchen once they were on the road and let them know she'd be back later.

They walked out of From This Moment together, Tyler holding the door for her like he always did. He led her through the parking lot to a black BMW parked out front.

"Nice rental," she said. Whenever she flew somewhere, she usually ended up with some tiny compact car, not a luxury car. That was the difference between her and Tyler, with his jet-set lifestyle and wealthy business associates.

"It's okay," he said, opening the door to the passenger side. "I wanted an Audi, but they didn't have any available."

"Aw, you poor thing," she muttered as she climbed inside. Such a hardship. The leather interior was soft, and the car smelled brand-new. Fresh from the factory. She hadn't experienced that in a long time. She was still driving the little crossover she'd saved up for after graduation. It was ideal for hauling catering supplies, but it was more practical than posh.

It must be nice to have money. She'd never really had a lot. Her father was a math teacher turned high school principal and the sole breadwinner in the family. He did okay, but she'd never considered her family to be more than middle class. As an adult, every penny of her own had gone into making From This Moment a success. Tyler had had even less when they were kids. He was one of six kids in a family that could barely feed two despite his parents' best efforts.

Driving a brand-new BMW around had been a pipe dream when they were kids. Tyler had done well for himself over the years. No one was prouder than she was of everything he'd accomplished. If he could get his eyes off his smartphone and stay in the country for more than a day at a time, he would make some woman a great husband one day. She just couldn't fathom that person being her.

"Where are we headed?" he asked.

"There's a coffee shop a few blocks up, if that's okay."

"Sure." Tyler started the car, pulled out of the parking lot and headed in the direction she'd pointed. A nearby commercial district had restaurants and coffee shops where they could sit down and talk. Considering the state of her stomach, she would pass on the food, but she could get some hot tea. And maybe, if that went okay, a scone.

They didn't speak in the car on the way there, which was odd for them. They always had a million things to catch up on. They could talk for hours about anything and everything. Now, as she feared, there was tension between them. Sex changed things, as she'd known it would. She'd never wanted their relationship to cross that line for that very reason.

She sighed and looked out the window instead. There would be plenty of things to say, but she could tell neither of them was ready to say them. He'd just found out he was going to be a father. That needed time to sink in. Tyler had never mentioned having an interest in a family—at least, not since he'd broken up with Christine. After that, he'd focused 100 percent on business. This had to be an unexpected blow for him. Amelia had always known she wanted children, but it had still been a shock for her.

Eventually, they arrived at the small independent coffee shop. He opened her door, helped her out and then followed her inside. Tyler bought them both drinks and got himself a giant cinnamon roll while Amelia found a plush couch in the corner away from the others in the shop.

Tyler came over a few minutes later with their things on a tray. He put the drinks on the coffee table and sat beside her. His knee barely grazed hers as he did, but even that simple touch was enough to awaken her nervous system. It was the first time they'd touched since that night. Being in such close proximity to him again was confusing. Her body remembered his touch, aching to lean closer to him and feel his hands on her again. Her brain knew it was a bad idea, but she didn't want to act childish. It was a simple touch, an innocent one. Just because her libido lit up like the skies on the Fourth of July didn't mean it meant anything.

Amelia busied herself preparing her tea and distracting herself from Tyler's nearness. She added a pack of raw sugar and stirred it, waiting for him to say something. She'd already said enough. Now it was his turn.

"So," he began, after a few bites of cinnamon roll and a sip of his coffee, "do you want to tell your parents first, or mine?"

She tried not to choke on her tea. That was not where she'd expected him to go with this. "Tell them what, exactly?"

"That we've gotten married and we're expecting a baby."

She shook her head furiously. He must still be in shock. "Neither."

Tyler frowned at her. "We have to tell them eventually. We can't just show up at their house with an infant and say, 'Here's your grandchild.'"

"I know that," she argued. "We will have to tell them about the baby eventually. I meant about the wedding. I don't see why anyone needs to know about it if we're just going to file for divorce anyway. I'd rather my father not know what we did, to be honest. You know how he is. The only reason he let me go to college in Tennessee was because my grandparents live here. He's just waiting for me to get into some kind of trouble so he can point out he was right."

Tyler nodded thoughtfully. "I understand your concerns. I wasn't planning on telling my family about the wedding, either. I mean, I came to Nashville so we could get the ball rolling on the divorce. But…everything is different now."

She flinched. "How? How is everything different now?"

"We're going to have a baby together," he said, as though it were the most obvious thing in the world. "I know we've got to work out the logistics, but starting a family is a complicated thing."

"A f-family?" she stuttered, a feeling of dread pooling in her stomach.

"Well, yeah. I mean, obviously, since you're pregnant with my child, the divorce is off the table."

Amelia's face flushed as red as her hair, and Tyler knew immediately that he'd said the wrong thing. Or at least, he'd said it in the wrong way. He knew he was right about what they needed to do. Convincing her would take more finessing than just blurting it out the way he had. Amelia didn't take well to being told what to do. *Good job, Dixon.*

"Divorce is off the table," she mimicked with a bitter tone. "You act as though you're the only one with any say in the matter. I know you're Mr. Big Shot and you're used to your word being law, but you aren't the boss of me, Tyler. You can't bully me into staying married to you."

"Of course I'm not the only one with a say," he soothed. "And I'm not bullying you. As if I even could. You're the most stubborn woman I know. But we have a child to consider now. What about the baby?"

The baby. Tyler could barely believe he was saying those words out loud. After his engagement with Christine had ended, he'd told himself that he wasn't going through all that again. The joy and high of love weren't worth the inevitable crash and destruction at the end. He'd shelved the idea of anything more complicated than sex and focused on his work. Business came a lot easier to him than romance.

That meant that any idea of marriage or family had been put to bed, as well. He'd been okay with that. How were a wife and a family even possible when he was jet-ting from one place to another and working long hours? He had five siblings to carry on the family name and give his parents the grandchildren they craved. No one would miss his genetic contribution to the world.

And yet, faced with the eventuality of a family, he found the idea didn't bother him as much as he thought it would. The image of a rambunctious toddler with wild red curls running through the coffee shop formed in his mind. It was so real, he could almost reach out and snatch the giggling child up into his arms. He suddenly wanted that, down to the depths of his soul. When Amelia had told him, he'd been startled, of course, but now he knew what had to be done.

Tyler had been given the chance to have the family he hadn't realized he wanted, and perhaps he could keep his heart from being destroyed a second time. He was having a child with his best friend. That child needed a stable, loving home, and he and Amelia could provide that. Why would they divorce now?

Amelia's gaze fixed on his. "What *about* the baby?" she asked. "You know I'm not the kind of woman that would insist on getting married to someone I didn't love just because I got pregnant. Why would I insist on *staying* married to someone I didn't love just because I got pregnant?"

Tyler tried not to be offended. This wasn't about him, and he knew that. And he knew that she loved him. She just wasn't *in* love with him. He wasn't in love with her, either. But they could make this work. They had affection, mutual respect and history. Some shotgun marriages started with less. "I know that our marriage and our child are not what you have down in your big notebook of life plans. But don't you think it's at least worth giving our relationship a try, for our baby's sake?"

"Why can't we just be friends with a baby? We can raise it together. If you're in Nashville, it makes things easier, but we can do it. We don't have to be married to have this baby. We don't have to pretend that our wedding night meant more than it did just because I got pregnant."

She made it sound as though they'd just had a random hookup. It might not have been love, but it certainly ranked higher in importance than picking up some girl at the bar and taking her home. It had been an amazing night, one that had haunted him the past few weeks as he'd traveled the globe.

As much as they might want to forget it, they'd made love. And it had meant something. He wasn't sure exactly what, but he knew he didn't want to just be friends with a baby. He wanted the benefits, too.

"Okay, fine. Let's set the issue of the baby aside for a moment. I just want us to sit down and seriously talk all this through. It's too important to make a rash decision."

"You mean like eloping in Vegas in the middle of the night?" she snapped.

"*Another* rash decision," he corrected. "Let's not compound the issue. We have time to figure this out, so let's do it right. What's so horrible about the idea of us staying together?"

"I know that the concept of failure is something you're not comfortable with, but I don't think you understand what you're asking of me. Of us. This is about a hell of a lot more than just creating a happy home for our baby. You're asking me to choose you as the man I want to be with for the rest of my life and potentially compromise my ability to find my real soul mate. I love you, Tyler, but we're not *in love*. There's a difference."

Tyler couldn't help flinching with the sting of her sharp words this time. He was asking her to settle for him. He hadn't thought of it that way, but when she said it like that, it was painfully obvious that he didn't meet her sky-high standards. That was okay, though. He was used to being the underdog in any fight; he actually preferred it. That was just a detail. His parents had struggled his whole life, but they'd always put their kids' needs first. Not loving Amelia wasn't a good enough reason for him not to make the sacrifice and provide a stable home for their child. "People have married for reasons other than love for hundreds of years and it's worked out fine."

"Well, I don't want to be one of those people. I want love and romance. I want a husband who comes home every night and holds me in his arms, not one that texts me every other day from his latest hotel room."

Tyler sighed and took a sip of his coffee. This was bringing back uncomfortable memories of his last fight with Christine. Nothing he did was ever good enough for her. She'd wanted him to be successful and make lots of money, but she'd also placed all these demands on his time. He couldn't win, at least not playing by her rules. Maybe with Amelia it could be different. If they both made the effort, he was certain they could find something that worked for them. If that meant she had to fall in love with him, he would work to make that happen.

Staring into the polished wood of the coffee table, he asked, "Do you think loving me is a total impossibility?"

She scoffed. "That's a ridiculous question, Tyler."

His head snapped back to look at her. "No, it's not. Tell me—do you find me physically repulsive?"

"Of course not. You're very handsome, obviously, or we wouldn't have made this baby to begin with."

"Okay. Am I obnoxious? Pretentious? A jerk?"

Amelia sighed and leaned back against the cushions. "No. You're none of those things. You're wonderful."

Sometimes Tyler didn't understand women. And Amelia in particular. But he'd decided they were staying together for this baby. If he knew nothing else, he knew how to sell something. He was going to market himself like one of his finest gemstones until she couldn't resist saying yes.

"So I'm good-looking. I own my own business and make good money. I'm fun to be around. You've trusted me with all your secrets. You enjoy spending time with me. The sex was pretty awesome, if I may say so myself... I must be missing something, Amelia. Is there a crimson *F* stitched to the front of my shirt, because you refuse to see me as anything but a friend? If there was another person on the planet exactly like me, you'd date him."

Amelia frowned. "You're talking nonsense."

"No, I'm not. Tell me your top five must-haves for a man you could love. Seriously." He knew the list was probably closer to a hundred must-haves. After each of her relationships ended, she'd add a new thing or two to the list.

She thought about it for a moment, holding up one hand to count off on her fingers. "Smart, a good sense of humor, compassionate, ambitious and honest."

He twisted his lips in irritation. If he'd asked her to name the five things she liked best about him, she might have recited the same list. "And what on that list do I not have? I'm all of those things and more."

"Maybe, but you're not around. I'm not going to sit at home alone with this baby while you hopscotch around the planet."

"What if I said I could be better about that? Maybe having a wife and a family will give me something to come home to."

"We're still not in love," she argued.

"Love is overrated. Look what it got Christine and me—a bunch of heartbreak. I'm not saying it will work. We might end up being totally incompatible, and if we are, we end it and you can go back to your quest for the White Buffalo. But why can't we at least try? Pandora's box is open. There's no going back to where we were."

She sighed and shook her head. "I don't know, Tyler. I can't…lose you. You've been the person in my life I can always count on. You're my rock."

"You're not going to lose me, no matter what." A wicked smile curled his lips as a thought came to mind. "We've slept together and the world hasn't ended. I'm still here. And since I've seen you naked, I've got even more incentive to stick around. I've touched and tasted every inch of your body, and if there's the potential I'll get to do it again, I'm not going anywhere."

Amelia's eyes widened, her cheeks flushing. "Tyler…" she chastised, but he wasn't hearing it.

"I know you're attracted to me. You just have to admit it to yourself."

"Wh-what?" she sputtered. "What makes you say that?"

"Oh, come on, Amelia. You can't blame that whole night on tequila. You were wildly passionate. You couldn't get enough of me, as though you'd finally let the floodgates open and allowed yourself to have something forbidden. It was the sexiest thing I've ever witnessed," he added, and it was true. He hadn't lusted over his best friend in the past, but since that night, he couldn't get her out of his head.

He placed a hand on her knee and leaned in close. "If that night was any indication, we might have a chance. So why not see what could happen if you opened your mind to the possibility of us? Forget about Tyler the friend and think of me as the hot new guy you're dating."

That, finally, made Amelia smile, and relief washed over him all at once.

Her eyes narrowed at him, her lips twisting in deep thought. "Okay, fine," she said at last. "We'll give this relationship a trial run. I will *date* you, Tyler, but there are some ground rules I want to lay down first. Number one, no one is to know we're married, or that I'm pregnant. Especially not your family. Did you tell anyone?"

"No," he said quickly. He'd never thought their marriage would last as long as it had. His family loved Amelia, but he wouldn't get their hopes up for nothing.

"Okay. My three coworkers found out this morning, but they're the only ones and that's how I want it to stay. Number two, I'm putting a time limit on this so it doesn't drag on too long. You've got thirty days to win me over. And I mean it. I want to be wooed, Tyler. I want romance and passion and excitement. You're not going to get off easy because we're friends. I'm going to be harder on you because you should know what I want and need."

A wide grin broke out across his face. Tyler never backed down from a challenge, and this wouldn't be any different. He could win her over in thirty days, no problem. He knew her better than he knew himself. She just had to let him try. "That's fair."

Amelia turned to look across the coffee shop and survey her surroundings. She sighed heavily and shook her head. She seemed disappointed by everything that had happened. Worn down. He didn't like seeing her that way. If there was one thing he loved the most about her, it was her optimism when it came to love. She believed—really, truly believed—in the power of love. But she didn't believe in them. He would change that. To make it happen, he would lift her up, make her smile, make her believe this was the right choice for them both, even if he wasn't entirely sure of it himself.

"All I've ever wanted," she said softly, "was a marriage like my grandparents have. They've been happily married for fifty-seven years, and they're just as in love today as they were the day they got married. That's what I want, and I'm not going to compromise that for anything or anyone."

Tyler took a deep breath, wondering if she was on the verge of changing her mind. He knew all that about her. She'd always talked about her grandparents and how she wanted a love like theirs. That was a high bar to set, but he was up to the challenge. If she didn't fall in love with him, it wouldn't be for lack of effort on his part.

No, he wouldn't even allow the negative thought. Amelia would fall in love with him. There could be no doubt of his success.

"At the end of thirty days," she continued, "we'll decide how we feel about each other. If we're in love, you'll propose again—properly—and we'll announce our engagement to the world. I want to get remarried with the big ceremony and all our family and friends there. And if one of us doesn't want to continue, we quietly agree to end it."

"And then what? Are we just supposed to go back to how things were and pretend it never happened? That will be pretty hard with a child."

"If we divorce, we make the best of things. I hope there won't be any animosity between us. We stay friends, okay?"

"Okay." Tyler knew failure wasn't an option, but he was comforted by the idea that he would have her friendship no matter what. She was notoriously picky when it came to men. He refused to become just another guy thrown onto the reject pile with the rest. "Anything else?"

"I think that's it," she said with a smile that betrayed she already knew it was too much.

"Okay, then, I have one demand of my own." If she was only going to give him thirty days, he needed to make them count and get every advantage he could. That meant proximity. There was no way this was going to work if they went to dinner a couple times a week and went to their separate corners when it was done. He couldn't disappear to Antwerp or work eighteen-hour days. If they wanted to figure out whether they could cut it being married, they needed to go all the way. "I want us to live together the whole time."

He watched Amelia frown into her lap with dismay. "My apartment isn't really big enough for two people. It's just a one bedroom, and my closet is already overflowing."

Tyler had zero intention of living in her tiny little apartment with her. There was a difference between proximity and being locked in a cage together for thirty days. He was certain only one of them would make it out alive. "I'll get us a new place," he said simply.

"I have a lease."

"I'll pay the fee to break it."

She sighed, obviously irritated with his ability to shoot down her every concern. "And what if at the end of thirty days, we're not in love? I'll be pregnant and homeless."

He sighed. "You will be nothing of the sort. If we don't work out, I'll help you find a new place that's big enough for you and the baby. I'll buy you whatever you want."

"You don't have to buy me a house, Tyler. I'll just keep my apartment for the month, stay with you, and we'll figure out what to do about it when we've made a decision about us."

He chuckled, knowing there wasn't much sense in continuing to argue about this when that wasn't how it was going to end. "Fine, but you've got to get used to the idea of someone else helping out. You're having my child and I'm taking care of you. That point is nonnegotiable. Have we got a deal or not?"

"It's a deal. Congratulations, Tyler," she said, holding out her delicate manicured hand to shake on their agreement. "You may now date your wife."

Game on.

He took her hand, shaking it for only a moment before pulling her knuckles to his mouth to kiss them. She was soft and warm against his lips, reminding him of how he'd spent an entire night kissing every sensitive curve. His skin prickled where it touched her, the sudden rush of need to have her again rocketing through his veins like a shot of adrenaline.

Amelia's reaction was just as potent. Her lips parted softly and she sucked a soft gasp into her lungs. Her eyes fluttered closed for a moment as his lips pressed to her skin and she leaned in to him.

He was going to enjoy this challenge. Pulling her hand to his chest, he leaned close. The air was warm and charged between them, her eyes widening and her pupils enlarging as he neared her. Her breaths were short and rapid, and her tongue moistened her lips on reflex. She wanted him to kiss her. Winning her over might be easier than he thought if she reacted to him so easily.

He pressed his lips to the outer shell of her ear and whispered in a low, seductive tone, "What do you say we seal the deal with a real kiss?"

When he pulled back, he noticed that a smile had lit

Amelia's eyes and curled her lips. She moved ever so slightly closer to him, placing a hand on his cheek.

"Sorry," she said with a shake of her head. "I don't kiss on the first date."

Three

Amelia watched a flicker of emotion cross Tyler's face before he leaned back and sighed. He seemed tired. The familiar blue eyes she'd looked into a million times were lined with fatigue, and the muscles in his neck and shoulders were tense. She didn't know if it was the early flight, the stress of their marriage or the pressing worry of impending fatherhood that had him tied in knots.

She wanted to reach out and rub his shoulders to loosen him up, but she realized that probably wouldn't help. She might be the reason he was exhausted, as she was refusing to play by his rules and making everything harder than he probably thought it needed to be.

"If you won't let me kiss you," he said at last, "will you at least let me buy you another cup of tea?"

"No," she said, shaking her head. She didn't want anything else in her stomach. Right now, she felt okay, but she didn't know how quickly the balance could tip. "I could actually use some air. This coffee shop is a little stuffy." The combination of the heater and the smell of roast coffee were verging on overwhelming. Amelia loved the scent of coffee, but her tolerance was limited today.

She could also use a little breathing room from Tyler. She should've known he would shoot out from the starting gate at the proverbial sound of the gun, but she hadn't prepared herself for the sudden assault. Nor had she been prepared for her body's response to him.

"How about a walk?" Tyler suggested. "I know it's a little chilly today, but the sun is out."

That worked for her. Amelia always thought better when she moved anyway. Of course, that meant she might take three steps and realize she was a fool. If she was honest with herself, she already knew that. As she watched Tyler devour the last of his cinnamon roll and toss their empty cups into the trash, she felt the worry pooling in her already tumultuous stomach.

She had very nearly kissed her best friend just a moment ago. She'd covered her weakness with a joke, but for a second, it had been a very real impulse. The skin of her knuckles burned where he'd seared her with his mouth. Her heart was still thumping at double the speed. The goose bumps continued to stand tall across her arms. Fortunately, she was able to hide all that beneath her blouse and the jacket he was currently helping her into.

Kissing Tyler shouldn't be a big deal considering she'd let him do a hell of a lot more only a few short weeks ago. But this time she was stone-cold sober, and she still wanted him. She supposed she should be happy about that fact. That was the path they were on now. She'd agreed to date him. Move in with him. They were having a baby—

the best thing she could do was fall in love with Tyler. That would make everything easier.

But if she knew anything about relationships, it was that none of it was easy. Amelia wasn't the kind to slip and fall in love. She was too analytical, too driven to find just the right guy. With over seven billion people in the world, the odds of running across the one who was meant for her were astronomical. Yet every day, happy couples came into From This Moment, ready to get married. Were they settling, or had fate really brought them together?

Fate had certainly thrust her and Tyler together. Did that mean he was the one she was meant to be with? She didn't know. But whether dating him was a good idea or a bad one, she'd given her word to try. And almost immediately, she'd found her body was on board with the plan, even if her mind was resistant.

It was official—her life had spun out of control. Could she blame her reaction to him on pregnancy hormones?

Tyler opened the door of the coffee shop and they stepped out onto the sidewalk. It was a beautiful day. The sky was a brilliant robin's-egg blue with no clouds to be seen. There was a cool breeze, but the warmth of the sun on her face made it worth the chill. Winter had been rough this year, pounding them with uncharacteristic snow and ice storms. Her coworker Bree had even been trapped in a Gatlinburg mountain cabin by a wicked winter storm just a few weeks before Amelia went to Las Vegas.

The weather in Nashville was usually pretty mild, but she was certain today was the first time she'd seen the sun since November. Having a taste of it made her look forward to the summer. She couldn't wait for flowers, ice cream trucks, sandals, cute pedicures and spending a little time cooling off in her bikini at the pool of her apartment complex.

Wait, she thought. Summer might be very different this year. For one thing, she'd be four or five months pregnant, so the bikini was probably out. And based on their discussions, she wouldn't be living at her apartment much longer. She was moving into a place with Tyler. At least for thirty days. After that, who knew?

Tyler tugged his leather jacket over his navy blazer. They were barely half a block down the road when she felt his fingers reach for hers.

They held hands a lot—in a goofy, best friend sort of manner. She and Tyler had always been physically affectionate in a nonthreatening way. At least, nonthreatening to her. The guys she'd dated had never cared too much for the male best friend she talked about all the time. They'd never believed her when she insisted they were only friends. Perhaps they'd seen something in the two of them that even she couldn't see.

Amelia laced her fingers though his until they were palm to palm. As much as she didn't want to admit it, holding his hand felt different somehow. Maybe it was the soft shudder that ran through her when his warm skin pressed against hers. Perhaps it was the occasional whiffs of his cologne that drifted past her nose. Or her sudden awareness of his body so close to hers. It was most likely that all three were combining to remind her of that night together—the one when she'd realized what he was hiding under those expensive suits, and that she couldn't wait to explore every hard, muscular angle of it.

"This area has built up a lot since I was here last," Tyler said, oblivious to where her thoughts had strayed.

"Yes. None of this was here when we first bought the land to start building From This Moment. Fortunately, it filled in with a nice residential area and some higher-end shopping centers. I wish I could afford to live closer to work, but we found a good spot between two really expensive residential areas, so it's not happening. There's not even an apartment complex anywhere around."

"It's nice. I like it. Close to the interstate, but not too close. Nearby shopping and restaurants. Not too congested. What do you think about looking for a place around here?"

Amelia turned to look up at him with a frown. "Did you miss the part where I said it's really expensive?"

"Did you miss the part where I auctioned off a thirty-one-carat canary diamond at Christie's auction house last month?"

He had mentioned it, but she hadn't thought much of it. He was constantly buying and selling stones. "But it's not like you made pure profit. You've got what you paid for it originally, company overhead, insurance, fees to Christie's... If you got it recut, there's that expense, too." There had been a time in Amelia's life when she'd known nothing about the world of jewels and gemstones. There had also been a time where she hadn't owned any jewelry worth more than fifty dollars. Tyler had changed all that.

Every year on her birthday, or for Christmas, he sent her something. The large teardrop amethyst around her neck had arrived on her twenty-sixth birthday. She also had sapphire earrings, a ruby-and-diamond tennis bracelet, an emerald ring and a strand of pearls. She never dared to ask how much he spent. She didn't want to know. She just bought a small fireproof safe to store it and increased her jewelry insurance policy every year.

"Of course I have expenses," he argued. "My point is that we don't have to rent a tiny place in a cheaper neighborhood on the other side of Nashville. If you'd like to live around here and be closer to work, I'll have a real estate agent start looking."

The average home in the area ran about half a million. A good number of them were twice as much. She couldn't imagine what the rent would be on a place like that. "You can look," she said with a tone of disbelief, "but I doubt you'll find something that works in this area. We don't need a four-thousand-square-foot mansion with a five-car garage and an indoor pool."

He shrugged, leading her down the sidewalk as though discussions of multimillion-dollar real estate transactions were nothing to him. "You don't know that. I live in Manhattan. Real estate is at such a premium that some people live in apartments the size of a dorm room. The idea of a ridiculously large house—with private parking—sounds awesome to me. Why not? You might like having an indoor pool."

"Get real, Tyler," she said with a wry chuckle. "We may only live in this place for a month. Even if we stay longer, we need at most a three-bedroom house with a decent yard. Maybe a good-size kitchen so I can cook. And that's only if we like the place enough to put in an offer to buy it. Right?"

"Right," he said, looking thoughtfully off into the distance.

Amelia knew him well enough to know he wasn't paying any mind to what she said. He'd pick whatever caught his fancy, regardless of price or practicality. All she knew was that if he picked a massive house, he'd better hire a housekeeper to go with it. It would be a full-time job keeping it clean, and she already had one of those.

They paused at an intersection, waiting for the light to change. "I'll see what I can find. But like you, I'm not going to compromise, either. This isn't just about finding a place to stay for a few weeks or months—it's about finding a home where we can start our life together. It's the house to which we'll bring our child home from the hospital. It's where he or she will take their first steps."

Tyler had only known about this baby for an hour, but it didn't matter. It was still an almost abstract idea in her mind, and yet he'd already revised his entire strategy to accommodate and care for his surprise family. He couldn't just settle for a house to spend the next few weeks. He wanted a home for his family. He wanted to take care of her and their child. She didn't understand how he could roll with the punches like that.

"You know, you don't have to be so confident and positive about everything. You're allowed to be upset and scared by the prospect of what's happening. I threw a grenade at you and you're just standing there holding it with a smile. I know that you don't want to be tied down, and a family wasn't on your radar. I'm freaking out. Tell me you're freaking out, too, so I'll feel better."

Tyler turned to look at her with a frown. "What good would it do to get upset? Worrying just wastes valuable time. When I'm feeling uncertain, having a plan to go forward and executing it is the only thing that makes me feel better. No, a child wasn't what I was expecting or wanting. Yes, a part of me wants to get in my car and disappear. But I won't do that to our child. I have an obligation to step up and take responsibility for my actions, and I'll do whatever it takes to make it work."

It wasn't a romantic declaration, but she'd asked for his honesty and gotten it. Having Tyler's child wasn't her plan, but she knew she would be hard-pressed to find a better father for her baby.

"You're only thinking short-term, Ames, but I have no intention of us getting divorced in thirty days. Successful people plan for success, so I'm going to find the perfect house for us. We'll rent until we're sure we love it, and then we'll see if we can convince the owner to sell it. It will be the place where you and I will raise our family."

His words should've been reassuring, and yet she felt a cold chill run through her as the concept started to sink in. He wasn't resigned to his obligation or even optimistic about their future together. He was treating this like a challenge to be overcome.

Until that moment, she hadn't fully realized that she'd waved red in front of a bull. Laying down a thirty-day challenge to Mr. Overachiever wasn't very smart if she didn't want to be with him in the end. Whether or not his heart was in this, he would likely get his way, be it with the house, their child or their relationship.

She felt a sudden pressure against her chest; the air clamped down in her lungs. Suddenly, a thirty-day trial period had just changed to the rest of their lives.

What had she really agreed to?

"I'm serious about us making this work, Ames. Our baby deserves it," Tyler said. Before he could elaborate, he noticed a bit of the color draining from her face. She was fair complexioned, but she was approaching the shade of a sheet of paper. "Are you okay?"

She grimaced a little but didn't answer, making him wonder if she was battling morning sickness again. "Are you going to be sick?"

"No," she said with a shake of her head. "Suddenly, I'm just a little tired. I didn't sleep well this weekend and it was a big wedding with three entrée choices. I think it's just catching up with me."

He had witnessed two of his older sisters' pregnancies, and their biggest complaint was always exhaustion.

It started earlier than you'd expect. Taking her elbow, he led her to a bench around the corner.

Tyler sat her down on the wooden seat and crouched at her knee. He looked up at her, realizing for a moment that he was in the same position he'd been in when he'd proposed to her on a sidewalk along the Las Vegas Strip. The memory made him smile despite his concerns for her. He wasn't sure what had made him remember their teenage pact that night, but it had seemed like the perfect remedy for her frown. In that moment, he would've done anything to cheer her up. He'd never dreamed that their adventure would ever go this far. He'd never even expected them to consummate the marriage, much less have a baby together. Would he have gone through with it if he'd known? That was a question with an irrelevant answer, unless someone had invented a time machine he didn't know about. He returned his focus to her.

"Can I get you anything? A bottle of water? Or do you need something to eat? There's a convenience store across the street. I can bring you anything you want."

"Stop fussing," Amelia said, although her eyes were pinched tightly shut as she spoke. "I'm fine. I just need a minute."

"Are you sure I—"

"I'm pregnant, not helpless, Tyler. I just needed a little break from walking around."

Tyler ignored her, jogging across the street to the store and returning with an ice-cold bottle of water. He pressed it into her hand.

Amelia sighed but twisted off the cap to take a sip anyway. "Are you going to be like this for the next eight months? 'Cause I don't think I can take you hovering over me all the time. It reminds me too much of my dad."

"Hey, now," Tyler argued in an offended tone. "There's

a big difference between trying to take care of you because I want to and doing it because I think you're incapable of taking care of yourself. I'm not your father. And you're not your mother."

Visiting Amelia's home when they were kids had been an eye-opening experience. In Tyler's home, everyone pitched in. Both his parents worked. The older kids helped take care of the younger ones. The boys and the girls all did their share, equally. That was the only way they could get by, day to day.

Then he went to Amelia's house and watched with surprise the way Principal Kennedy fawned over and protectively guarded his wife and daughters. He treated them as though they were delicate and helpless, a perception Amelia's mother worked hard to create. She was fragile and often ill with headaches or other ailments, although Amelia insisted there was nothing actually wrong with her. It didn't matter. Amelia's father took care of everything. He made all the decisions, earned all the money. He hired a cleaning woman to come a few days a week and relieve her mother of that burden. The two Kennedy girls were expected to do nothing but be pretty and shop, just like their mother.

It had made Amelia crazy growing up. She was far from helpless and fragile—she had a spine of steel. She was smart and independent, but her father never gave her enough credit for anything she did. He expected her to marry well and carry on the way her mother had.

And he supposed she had done that, even if she hadn't meant to. Tyler was successful. His business in gemstones and antiquities was amazingly lucrative. The markup on diamonds was insane. A quick trip to his suppliers in India or Belgium would set him up easily with a stash of high-quality stones at an amazing price. On any given day, he could have a quarter of a million dollars in precious gems tucked into his lapel pocket. If Amelia wanted to quit her job, he could take care of her and their child for the rest of their lives.

But he knew she would never allow that. He wouldn't even suggest such a thing for fear of bodily harm. She wasn't her mother. Not even close. "You might not like it," he continued, "but I've got a vested interest in your welfare. For one thing, I haven't had a chance to get a life-insurance policy on my wife yet." He grinned wide and was pleased to see her reluctantly smile and roll her eyes at his joke.

"And for another," he said, getting to his feet and sitting beside her on the bench, "that's our kid you're hauling around in there. It's my job to make sure both of you have everything you need to stay happy, healthy and safe. You can complain all you want and it won't make any difference."

Amelia searched his face for a moment, looking for something he didn't understand. Then she nodded and placed her hand over his, squeezing gently. "Thank you for that. I'm sorry for being difficult today. I feel as though my whole life has been hijacked and shifted off course. I've gotten used to being on my own and taking care of myself. It may take a while for me to adjust to anything else. But I do appreciate it. You. No matter what happens between us, I know you'll be a good father."

Tyler watched a bright red lock of hair slip from its clip and curl around the curve of her heart-shaped face. The peachy tones of her skin had returned, beckoning him to reach out and caress her velvet-soft cheek, pushing the hair behind her ear. Today, he would do it because he could.

He reached out to her, letting his knuckles softly graze

across her cheekbone as they swept the errant curl away from her face. The pale peach of her skin was replaced with a rosy pink as her cheeks flushed. Her dark eyes watched him, but she didn't pull away from his touch.

"I've always wanted to do that," he said.

"Really?" she said, her voice betraying the disbelief that reflected in her eyes.

"Absolutely. You've got the most beautiful hair I've ever seen. It's like liquid fire."

"Tyler," she began, hesitating, "I know I can be difficult in a relationship, and you know that better than anyone. Part of me has begun to wonder if I'll ever…" Her gaze dropped into her lap. "Do you really think you can fall in love with me in thirty days?"

Tyler didn't want to lie to Amelia, but he knew he had to. If he told her that he had no intention of ever falling in love with her—or anyone, for that matter—it would all be over. If he wanted to succeed for their child's sake, he had to play along and keep those dark secrets inside. He couldn't let his own doubts spill over and taint Amelia with his negativity.

As it was, he was stunned by her fears. How could a woman so smart, so beautiful, so talented have any doubt that a man could love her? At least, a man capable of opening himself up to loving someone?

"Are you kidding me? You are incredible in a hundred different ways. Your cooking is the best thing I've ever tasted. You tell better dirty jokes than any guy I've met. You're strong of will and spirit. You care so deeply for others that I don't know how you don't get your heart crushed every day. You amaze me in a new way every time I'm with you."

Amelia listened to him speak with silent tears welling in her eyes. He couldn't bear to see her cry, ever. He opened his arms to her and pulled her tight against his chest. She rested her head against his shoulder, allowing him to press a kiss into the silky strands of her hair.

"I didn't want to make you cry, but you need to know how important you are. I measure every woman I date against the bar you've set, and each of them has fallen miserably short. You're the best thing that ever happened to me. You need to think like a winner and erase all those doubts. Then you need to ask yourself, how could I *not* fall in love with you?"

When he finished speaking, she sat back and looked up at him. She studied his face with a curious expression that wrinkled her delicate nose.

He didn't know what she was thinking, but he was hyperaware of how close she was. The scent of her body lotion perfumed the air with tropical flowers. He breathed it into his lungs and held it there, remembering that scent from their night together. The muscles in his neck tensed as the memories rushed into his mind and flooded his veins. It would be so easy to touch her. Kiss her. And he wanted to, first date be damned.

As though she'd read his mind, Amelia reached up and rested her palm against his cheek. Then she leaned into him. She closed the gap slowly, her eyes focused on his until their lips touched and their eyes closed. Her mouth was soft and hesitant against his own. He tried not to push too hard or too fast, applying just enough pressure, but letting her take the lead this first time.

It was hard. The sweet, gentle kiss was enough to start a hum of electricity traveling through his body. Tyler wanted to tug her against him and drink her in. He wanted to caress her silken tongue with his own and press his fingertips into her ample flesh. But he knew she was testing the waters. If he pushed too hard, he would lose valuable time trying to coax her back to this place.

She finally pulled away and he reluctantly let her go. Tyler opened his eyes to find her looking up at him with a dreamy smile curling her lips. She took a deep breath and sat back, tugging down at her tunic. "I've, uh…" She stumbled over her words. "I've really got to get back to work."

"Okay."

Tyler swallowed hard, trying to suppress the heated need she'd built up inside him. His every muscle was tense, his fingertips tingling with the need to touch her. It would have to wait. But not for too much longer. She'd kissed him. That was an important first step on the road to success.

He stood and stepped back, helping her get up from the bench. They walked to his rental car and made their way back to the wedding facility she owned with her friends. Once there, he parked the car and came around to open the door for her. Amelia got out but didn't get far. Before she could escape, he leaned in, pressing a palm against the car and blocking her exit.

"So I'll let you know when the real estate agent finds us a place and I can arrange the movers to pack your apartment. In the meantime, can I take you out to dinner tomorrow night?"

She looked up at him with surprise in her dark eyes. "So soon?"

Tyler had to laugh at her. She really had no idea what she'd done. His beautiful wife was a smart woman, but the terms of their agreement weren't the most intelligent choice she could've made. He had been willing to take their romance slow, but she'd cranked up the dial on the intensity when she'd set her time limit.

He leaned in to her, pinning her with his intense gaze. "You've given us thirty days to fall in love, Amelia. Do you really think I'm going to let a single day go by without seeing you? Touching you? Hearing the melodic sound of your voice?"

Her gaze dropped to the pavement to avoid his eyes, her teeth nervously chewing at her bottom lip. "I understand that," she argued, "but I have a job to do. So do you. You know I pretty much spend Thursday, Friday and Saturday in a kitchen. I can't run off on a date with you every night."

He understood that. They both had responsibilities. He just wasn't going to let her use them as an excuse. She'd agreed to a test run of their relationship, but he knew this would be a battle to the finish. She wouldn't give in easily, and neither would he. "That's fine. That's why we'll spend our nights together at our new place. And during the day, I may very well be by your side, too."

"What?" Her nose wrinkled in confusion. "In the kitchen with me? At work?"

Tyler nodded. "Whenever I can, I'm going to be where you are, Amelia. If you're baking a cake, I'm going to be washing the pans. If you're dicing vegetables, I'll be peeling carrots and taking out the trash. You insisted I be present, not zipping around the world, so for the next thirty days, I'm your shadow. You only get a reprieve today while I make all the necessary arrangements."

Her mouth dropped open and her auburn eyebrows knit together, but she didn't say anything. She hadn't thought this through, and the consequences would come back to haunt her. She'd be begging him to take a business trip before too long.

"Don't you have a job to do? Aren't there precious gems to be sold? Diamonds to be cut?"

He shrugged nonchalantly. "I have plenty of work, I assure you. But I have a flexible schedule and employees that can handle some things. I can conduct business where and when I want to. That's the beauty of what I do. Right now, I'm more interested in focusing all my attention on you. So again," he pressed, "dinner tomorrow night?"

Amelia drew her mouth closed and nodded. "Okay. About seven?"

Seven was perfect. That was his lucky number—an omen of his success on the horizon. He pressed a soft kiss to her lips and stepped back to give her some room. "It's a date."

Four

"She's ba-a-a-ck!"

Amelia winced the moment she crossed the threshold into the lobby and heard Gretchen announce her arrival. She'd been hoping they would have clients in this morning. If someone was booking a wedding with Natalie or taking a tour, her friends couldn't fuss over her. No such luck.

Bree and Gretchen spilled into the hallway. Natalie popped her head out of her office, her headset on. She held up a finger to wait and then continued her phone conversation.

Amelia went on into her office so she could hang up her coat and stow her purse away. She grabbed her tablet in the hopes they would talk about what she'd missed at the staff meeting, but she knew the conversation would be about anything but work.

She carried her half-empty bottle of water with her to the conference room. By the time she got there, her three partners at From This Moment were assembled there, waiting, although not patiently. Bree looked as if she was about to burst with excitement. Gretchen had wicked glee lighting her eyes. Natalie seemed concerned, as she was prone to be. She was suspicious about love in general, and marriage was a bridge too far in her opinion. At the moment, Natalie was probably the smarter of the two of them.

Amelia sat down in one of the chairs. "So what did I miss this morning?"

"Please." Bree groaned. "You are going to tell us everything that's going on with you and that guy, right now!"

"Yes, and start from the beginning," Natalie said, "since I missed the discussion this morning."

With a heavy sigh, Amelia repeated the tale about the high school reunion gone awry. She went into as much detail as she could, hoping she wouldn't have to repeat the story again. She left out the part about it being the most incredible sex of her life and tried to focus on how she ended up married to her best friend while on vacation.

"So," Natalie began with a furrowed brow, "did he just come to town so you can start the divorce proceedings?"

"Pretty much, although I'm not sure we're going to do that just yet."

Bree's eyebrows shot up. "What does *that* mean?"

"It means," Amelia began, "that we're going to date for a month and see where it goes. It's a lot easier to get married than it is to get divorced, so we're going to put more thought into the latter than we did into the former."

"You're going to date your husband? This is all just so wrong," Natalie said with a slow shake of her head.

"Is he moving here? Doesn't he live in New York or something?"

"Yes, his company is based out of Manhattan. He has more flexibility with his work than I do, so he's going to rent a place here for a month." Amelia hoped they didn't ask what they would do after that, because she honestly didn't know. Could Tyler stay in Nashville long-term? She couldn't leave. Amelia was From This Moment's caterer. A wedding without food was…a tacky Vegas elopement. She sighed.

As it was, they would have to figure out what they would do while she was on maternity leave. They would cross that bridge when they got there, she supposed. She hadn't even dropped that bomb on her friends yet.

"You and Tyler never dated before, did you?"

Amelia took a sip of her water and shook her head. "No. We've only ever been friends. You know how I am with men. If we'd dated, we would've broken up by now. It was always more important to have him in my life than to act on some physical impulse."

"Natalie said he was hot. Like, *Chris Pine* hot. How could you go all those years without so much as kissing him?" Gretchen asked.

The simplest answer was that she just hadn't allowed her mind to go there. Yes, he was handsome. All the things they'd talked about in the coffee shop earlier were correct. He had a lot of the attributes she valued in a prospective partner. But in the end, he was just Tyler. That canceled out a lot. "We did kiss once, in tenth grade. This stupid girl dared us at a party in front of everyone."

"And?"

"And—" she shrugged "—it was awkward. I only have a sister, but I thought that might be what it was like to kiss your own brother. Zero chemistry. A very uncomfortable experience. After that, it was easier to keep things platonic."

"Tell me it was better the second time around," Gretchen groaned.

"It was. A million times better." Amelia should've taken into consideration that their first kiss had been with an audience of their peers. On a dare. They'd been fifteen and she had braces. Neither of them had had much experience to go on. It had been a recipe for disaster, but what a difference a dozen or so years could make! "I honestly couldn't believe I was kissing the same person. Even knowing it was Tyler and I shouldn't be doing that, I couldn't stop myself."

"What happens in Vegas…" Gretchen said, as though that explained everything.

And in a way, it did. The lights and the alcohol and the heightened emotions inspired you to move out of your comfort zone and do something exciting for a change. Unfortunately, not everything that happened there stayed there. The consequences had followed her home.

"What did Tyler say to change your mind about getting divorced all of a sudden?" Bree asked as she thoughtfully twirled her long blond hair around her finger. "You've already had a month to think about it, and I was pretty sure you were set on that when you left."

And now they came to the part she was avoiding. "I was. We were. But um…things changed. I, uh…"

"You're pregnant," Natalie stated. There wasn't an accusatory tone to her voice, just quiet resignation. She gave Natalie a lot of grief for being uptight, but she was very observant. She saw everything, even the things people tried to hide.

Amelia couldn't respond so she just nodded, thankful that Natalie had saved her from saying the words aloud a second time today.

"Wait, what?" Bree nearly shrieked. "You're pregnant

and you haven't mentioned it yet? How could you leave that massive detail out of the story?"

"One bombshell at a time, okay?" Amelia frowned. "I just found out and I'm still a little shell-shocked by the whole thing. I mean, it's as though my whole life has gone irrevocably off course. You think it's bad to marry your best friend on a whim? Find out you're having his baby, too. There's no pretending it didn't happen anymore. There's no annulling it and sweeping the memory of it under the rug."

"That's why you're trying to stay together," Gretchen noted, the pieces finally clicking together for her. "What will you do if it doesn't work out? Get divorced and work out a custody arrangement?"

"Yes. It will be okay, though. We've agreed that no matter what, we'll stay friends."

"Um, Amelia," Natalie said, "you don't really think that's going to happen, do you?"

"Of course it will," she insisted. They'd been friends for fourteen years. They could do it. Of course, that had been without sex and emotions and custody agreements in the way.

"I'm not trying to upset you," Natalie clarified, "but you need to be prepared for this. At the end of the month, you two might break up. And it may go okay for a while, but eventually things are going to fall apart. You'll try for the good of your child, but it will get hard. I've seen it happen. He'll show up late to bring the kid back from his weekend and you'll get irritated. You'll want the baby for a holiday that's supposed to be his and you'll argue about it. Make the most of these thirty days, Amelia. If you don't have a husband when the time is up, don't plan on having a best friend for much longer after that."

She hadn't thought about that at all. She was certain

they would be okay, but she had seen it happen to other people. If she thought sex might ruin their friendship, shared custody and a strained relationship would certainly do it.

Natalie reached out and placed a hand over Amelia's. The supportive gesture made tears threaten in her eyes. She never cried. Hated to, actually. She always saw it as a weak feminine gesture her mother used to manipulate her father. But in the moment, all the emotions and worries of the past few weeks came to a head and before she could stop them, teardrops started spilling over her cheeks.

"Damn hormones," Amelia lamented.

"Aw, honey, it will be okay." Bree got up and snatched a tissue from the other side of the room to give to her. "Everything is going to work out, I know it."

"It absolutely will," Gretchen chimed in. "No matter what happens with Tyler after the thirty days are up, you're going to be a great mom. We're going to throw the greatest baby shower in the history of baby showers. And I'll paint a mural in the nursery. We can even turn the extra office into a playroom with toys and a crib so you can bring the baby to work. Bree's getting married soon—we could have babies all over the place before too long."

Bree's eyes widened a touch and she choked on the last sip of her latte. "Um, yeah," she said with a rough cough to clear her lungs. "Babies all over the place."

Amelia had to smile through her tears. She really did have amazing friends. Gretchen was right. No matter what happened with Tyler, things would work out. Neither the marriage nor the baby had been planned, but she would make it through this. "Thank you, guys. I feel a lot better, now."

"That's what girlfriends are for," Natalie said with a

soft smile. "You know we're always here to celebrate, commiserate or eviscerate. Whatever you might need."

"Okay. For right now, all I need is to keep this quiet. Please don't mention it to anyone. Really. No Facebook posts, no offhand comments when clients are here, no telling my mom I'm at the obstetrician if she calls and I'm not around. We're keeping all of this a secret until we decide what we're going to do. You guys are the only ones that know."

"Sure thing," Bree said. "I won't tell a soul."

"Me, neither," Gretchen agreed. She looked up at the clock on the wall and sighed. "We'd better get back to it. I've got the future Mr. and Mrs. Edwards coming by to pick their invitations on their lunch break."

All four of the women stood and started back to their various tasks. Mondays were Amelia's Fridays. She was off the next two days, so she needed to get things in order for the upcoming weekend. That meant submitting her grocery order to the food suppliers. She also needed to email the finalized reception menu to a couple doing a '50s rockabilly-themed wedding. There wasn't time to sit around and mope about her situation for long.

Life went on. And so must she.

Tyler was pretty certain today might qualify as one of the longest days of his life. Probably because he hadn't slept since he arrived in Nashville and the two days had blurred together into one. By the time Tyler rang the doorbell of Amelia's apartment to pick her up for their dinner date Tuesday night, he had been awake for forty hours straight.

He'd learned early on that sleep was for the guy who came in second. He'd accomplished a lot since he dropped Amelia back at the chapel. He'd made arrangements to manage his business dealings from Nashville. He got some of his employees to take on more business travel to free up his calendar. There was still a trip to London on his schedule in a few weeks, but he would play that by ear. He really needed to be there for the Sotheby's auction. Perhaps he could talk Amelia into joining him for that trip.

Work handled, he met with a real estate agent and toured half a dozen potential homes. He was pretty certain he'd found the one, but he wouldn't decide until Amelia had seen it. He'd also turned in his rental car and picked up something more suitable for the next few weeks.

With the logistics in place, he directed his attention toward more romantic pursuits. He made dinner reservations and set out in search of a nearby florist that carried her favorite flower. She'd said she wanted romance and that she expected him to know exactly what she would like. Well, mission accomplished.

Amelia opened the door of her apartment. Before she could even say hello, her gaze dropped to the bouquet of roses in his hands. Not just any roses—green beauties. They were a pale-green-and-ivory rose with darker green edges. The flowers reminded him of tiny cabbages, really, but she'd always loved them. Her favorite color was green after all.

"Wow," she said. She looked up at him with a wide smile brightening her face.

"I was about to say that same thing." Amelia looked amazing. She was wearing a plum-colored dress that popped against the ivory of her skin. It almost looked like strips of fabric wrapped around her body. It had cap sleeves with straps crisscrossing over her collarbones. It molded to her shape, making her incredibly voluptuous figure even more outrageous. She had the kind of dangerous curves that required two hands or a man could lose control. "You look beautiful tonight."

"Thank you. This is a Herve Leger bandage dress I saved up to buy, and I've never had the opportunity to wear it. It's on the snug side to begin with, so I figured I should wear it tonight while I can. If I could get away with it, I'd wear it every day until I hit my second trimester, but it's just not that practical."

Fashion before comfort with Amelia, always. "I would vote for that. I wouldn't get anything done staring at you the whole time, though."

"You're sweet," she said, a rosy color rising to her cheeks. "I can't believe you remembered my favorite flower."

"Of course I did," Tyler said as he held the bouquet out to her. "For you."

"Come in," Amelia said as she took a few steps back into her apartment.

He followed her into the cozy one-bedroom corner unit she called home. Golden overhead lighting shined down from an antique-looking fixture. It illuminated every detail she'd worked hard to put in place. It was a cute little apartment, spacious by New York standards, and very much Amelia. The furniture was shabby chic in style, mixing older, worn antiques with a few newer, brighter pieces. There was a mishmash of throw rugs, embroidered pillows and candles scattered around the space.

She had always had a keen aesthetic eye, be it for fashion, furniture or food. Even back in high school, when Tyler's daily uniform had included jeans and a T-shirt, she had always gone above and beyond when it came to her style. To her, decorating an apartment was like getting her place dressed up to go out. He couldn't be bothered. He wanted things to be functional and not too fussy. Like his clothes.

He watched Amelia disappear into the tiny kitchen and put the green roses in a tall crystal vase filled with water. She had been right when she said there wasn't room for him to live here with her. It was comfortable, welcoming, but not really big enough for more than one person. And she certainly would have difficulty raising a child here, too. There was no room for a nursery. No yard to play in. A couple toys on the floor could create a treacherous obstacle course.

"What?" she asked, coming toward him with the vase in her hands. "You look disgusted about something."

"Not disgusted. I was just thinking of how small your place is. Reminds me of the first apartment I rented when I moved to New York to apprentice at Levi's jewelry store."

"It suits me just fine." She placed the flowers in the middle of her square white dining room table. "It's quiet, I have reserved parking and the price is good. I'm really not home that much anyway."

"Well—" he frowned "—no matter what happens with us, we'll need to find you a new place. Either you'll move in with me or we'll get you something bigger for you and the baby." He raised his hand to halt her protest. "Don't start. You and I both know you'll need more space when the baby comes."

Amelia shrugged and scooped up her purse. "I had been thinking about getting a townhouse before all this started. But there's no sense in worrying about it now. We've got time to figure out things like that."

"Absolutely. Right now, we need to focus on not missing our reservation."

"Where are we going?"

"The Watermark, downtown."

Amelia smiled as she picked up her jacket and followed him outside. "Nice choice."

He escorted her to the parking lot, but Amelia stopped abruptly at the curb. "What's the matter?"

"Where's your BMW?"

"I'd only rented that for a couple days. I turned it back in when I realized I was going to be staying awhile." Reaching into his pocket, he pulled out his keys and hit the button to unlock the doors of the white Audi SUV parked beside hers.

"I see you finally found a place that would rent you an Audi. I bet you're happy now."

Tyler held open the passenger door and helped her inside. "Actually, I bought it," he said before slamming the door shut.

By the time he got in on his side, Amelia was shaking her head. "You're from another planet, you know that?"

"Why?"

"Because," she argued, as they pulled out of her apartment complex, "you buy luxury cars on a whim—with cash, I'm certain. You think a mansion in Belle Meade is a reasonable suggestion. You gave me an eight-carat engagement ring for a spur-of-the-moment wedding in Vegas. That's not normal, you know?"

Tyler smiled and focused on the freeway stretched out ahead of them. "I worked hard to be abnormal. Would you prefer I have a dead-end office job and scrape pennies together for the monthly payment on my practical sedan like everyone else?"

"No…" she said thoughtfully. "I suppose it wouldn't make a difference. Even when you were broke, you were abnormal. Just abnormal with less money."

He chuckled. "I'm not sure if I should be offended or not."

"Don't be. I've kept you in my life this long with you the way you are. If you're abnormal, then I guess I am in my own way, too."

Tyler had to heartily agree with that assessment. For whatever reason, he had lasted in Amelia's life far longer than any other man. Probably because they weren't dating, so she didn't try him on like a pair of shoes and cast him aside when he didn't fit just right. When they'd crossed the line in Vegas, he'd known he was putting their friendship at risk. Despite their long-standing relationship, adding sex to the mix could potentially land him in the discard pile. Even with their agreement to remain friends no matter what, that was still a very real danger.

That was why he'd come to Nashville fully anticipating they would file for divorce and pretend that night in Vegas never happened. He'd never dreamed they might continue their romance, much less stay married.

The wild card in this scenario was their baby. It was Amelia's anchor; it might be the only thing that would keep her from bolting from this relationship like every other one before it.

Might be.

Tyler had agreed to Amelia's thirty-day arrangement for their child's sake. He would put everything he had into convincing Amelia to love him. Everything but his heart. His wasn't any good to anyone anymore. It had been irrevocably broken, and he didn't dare expose it to more damage.

If she fell in love with him, everything might work out, but even then, Tyler wasn't holding his breath. He was fighting an uphill battle with Amelia. Even if he did everything right, she could find fault in him. No one was perfect, not even her grandparents. It made him wonder how much of their idealistic marriage was truth and how much was fantasy built up in Amelia's mind.

Tyler slowed the Audi and pulled to the curb outside the restaurant. He handed over the keys to the valet and rounded the car to escort Amelia inside.

The interior of the Watermark was dim, with pot lights illuminating the tables from the exposed beams overhead. The hostess escorted them to a white linen-draped table for two near the window. Amelia chose to sit on the side with the long white leather banquette, and Tyler sat opposite her. A server quickly took their drink orders and disappeared, leaving them to look over the menu and admire the view.

Tyler knew he should be looking at the impressive cityscape or deciding on his appetizer course, but he found himself distracted by the view directly in front of him. A square glass-and-chrome candleholder in the center of the table cast a mesmerizing glow across Amelia's face. It highlighted the subtle cleft in her chin and soft apples of her cheeks. Her skin looked peaches-and-cream flawless, nearly glowing with radiance.

It took everything he had not to reach across the table and brush his thumb over her full, coral-painted lips. They looked soft and shiny with some sort of gloss that made them shimmer in an utterly kissable way. He wanted to kiss her again tonight, and keep doing it until every drop of that gloss was gone and her lips were bee-stung from it.

That was how she had woken up in his hotel room the morning after their wedding. Her red hair had been everywhere, her mascara had been smudged and her lips had been pink and swollen. She'd looked like a woman who had been well and truly loved the night before. Tyler's whole body stiffened as he thought of being able to make love to her again. It was a masochistic thought, one that wasn't likely to get him through dinner without discomfort, but he couldn't shake it. Once they'd crossed the line in Vegas, he couldn't force himself back.

"Have you ever eaten here before?" he asked to distract himself with conversation.

She shook her head, oblivious to his thoughts. "No, but I've been dying to get into their kitchen. The executive chef here is well-known for his amazing creations. I'm certain nothing we eat will be bad."

"So I chose well?"

Amelia smiled. "You chose very well."

"All this rich food won't be too much on your stomach, will it?"

She shook her head, making the sleek auburn waves dance over her shoulders. "I hope not. But really, I've only had trouble early in the day. By midafternoon I'm starving. I'm anxious to try the duck. It is so hard to find well-prepared duck. What about you?"

"I'm thinking the cobia. Or the lamb."

"Ooh…" Amelia's dark brown eyes lit up with excitement. "Get the lamb and let me try some. You can try my duck, too, if you want."

"Sounds good," he said with a smile. Very few things got Amelia as excited as food. The old saying about the way to a man's heart being through his stomach was just as true with her. Whenever they were together, he went out of his way to find someplace they could eat that would be new and exciting for her.

She was a fashionista at heart, but her first love was cooking. He hadn't been at all surprised to see her go into a culinary program. She had been bringing him food all through high school, using him as a guinea pig when she wanted to try out a new recipe. It was almost always good. And beautiful to look at. Rarely was food both, and that was where her talent really came into play.

Tonight was where his talents came into play. He was a successful jeweler because he knew exactly what the client was looking for, even if they weren't entirely sure. He had the ideal night planned for Amelia. After two hours of talking and dining, including a decadent chocolate soufflé to share, they strolled through the trendy downtown area known as the Gulch. They wandered together, hand in hand, looking in shop windows and listening to the live music streaming out of some of the bars. The conversation flowed easily, the way it always had with them, not stifled by the fact that this was a real date.

By the time they returned to her apartment, Tyler was confident they'd had a successful date. Amelia was smiling and laughing, relaxed for the first time since he'd arrived in Nashville. It was a good night. But it could be better.

He walked her to her door, hesitating as she unlocked it. He wanted to go in pretty badly, but he wouldn't. Thirty days didn't seem like long, but it was long enough not to rush.

"Dinner was great," she said as she turned back to face him. "I had a nice time."

"Me, too." Moving closer, Tyler rested his hand on her waist.

Amelia didn't pull away or stiffen at his touch. Instead she looked up at him with a soft, inviting smile. He accepted the invitation, leaning down to cup her face in his hands and capture her coral-painted lips with his own.

She melted into him, pressing her ample curves against the hard wall of his chest. As his tongue glided across her lips, she opened her mouth to him. Her own silky tongue met his, a soft moan muffled in the back of her throat.

The sound conjured memories of their wedding night. His body instantly stiffened, his palms tingling to touch her. He moved his hands back to her waist, letting them roam over the stretched fabric that clung to her every curve. Tyler boldly cupped the swell of her rear and pressed her hips against the hard ridge of his desire.

The growl deep in his throat made Amelia chuckle softly against his lips and pull away. Her hand caught his, moving it back to her waist. Her eyes were closed, her breath fast and shallow. He understood. That was enough for tonight. He withdrew his hand, placing one last soft goodbye kiss on her lips.

"I want to take you somewhere in the morning."

"I suppose you aren't going to tell me where."

He smiled wide. "What's the fun in that?"

She sighed and shook her head. Although she acted exasperated by him, he could see the glint of excitement in her eyes. When that was there—the way it had been on that sidewalk in Las Vegas—he knew he had her intrigued. That was key to getting her to go along with whatever harebrained idea he'd come up with.

"I'll pick you up at nine."

Five

"So seriously, where are we going?"

Tyler shook his head. "Ames, I haven't told you the past three times you've asked. What makes you think I'm suddenly going to change my mind?"

She sighed and crossed her arms over her chest. "I'm your wife. It's now my job to nag at you until I wear you down and you do what I want."

He chuckled and slowed the SUV to turn off the main commercial thoroughfare and into a large, sprawling subdivision. "I thought we were trying to date. You're not supposed to pull those tricks out of the bag until later."

"Tricks?" she replied in mock outrage. "What about those tricks you pulled on me last night? Those flowers, that restaurant…"

"That kiss," he added.

Amelia didn't reply to that. Instead she turned and looked out her window to watch the houses they rolled past. She wouldn't give him the satisfaction of knowing he'd made an excellent impression on their first official date. She'd had a better time with him than she had on half the dates she'd been on in the past year. Perhaps the fates knew better than she did. Or maybe they were just having fun messing with her head.

The houses they passed were large. On meticulously groomed lots. And not far from work. That was when everything clicked into place. They were going to look at a house. But here? Despite her attempts to dissuade him, he'd apparently sought out a place in Belle Meade. They were obviously not on the same page when it came to the real estate market.

Finally, Tyler turned into a driveway that was barricaded by a large iron gate. He punched in a code and the gate opened, revealing the incredible estate hidden beyond it. They drove down a narrow lane lined with trees and hedges, then circled around a courtyard fountain, stopping in front of the double-doored entrance of stacked stone stairs.

Thoughts of denial swirled in her mind as she looked up at the house. Correction—*mansion*. This was no three-bedroom starter home. To buy it would cost several million dollars, easily. The rent was probably high enough to give her heart palpitations. Was this what he'd envisioned when he'd talked about a home where they could raise a family together? She couldn't even fathom it.

"Tyler..." she said in a warning tone as she looked out the window.

"Just wait until you see the inside," he said, holding his hands up defensively. "It's amazing."

She bet it was. The Biltmore House was nice, too, but she wasn't moving in there anytime soon, either. "Did you already rent this place? Without asking me? That's really not the best way to start out. A woman likes to have a say in where she lives."

"Of course I know that. I did not rent it yet, but I was confident enough that the real estate agent gave me the key to bring you here today. When we're done, I'll either return the key or sign the lease."

Amelia didn't wait for his assistance to get out of the car. She opened the door and stepped onto the cobblestone driveway. The cream-and-gray-mottled brick of the mansion's facade seemed to sprawl on forever, broken up by large arched windows and tall square ivory columns. The house was beautiful, but ridiculously large for a family of two and a half.

"Whose house is this? And why on earth would they rent it out to strangers?"

"Apparently some musician had the place built, then ended up going on a world tour and never moved in. The real estate agent seemed pretty confident that if we liked the place, the owner would entertain an offer."

She sighed and shook her head. It was a rock star's house. She'd never fathomed she'd step across the threshold, much less ever live in the home of a rock star. "Let's go inside and see it before you sign your life away, hmm?"

Tyler offered his hand to help her up the stairs, then escorted her through the entrance to the large marble foyer. Amelia was stunned by the size and luxury of the space. There was very little furniture and nothing on the walls, but the details of the house itself were amazing. There was intricate crown molding, carved stonework and sky-high ceilings with shimmering chandeliers dripping crystals from their golden branches. A split staircase of dark, polished wood encircled the room and met at a second-floor landing.

"I don't think the two of us combined will ever have

enough stuff to fill a house this big." The expansive rooms were so empty, their steps echoed through the space.

"I'm only going to have the movers bring down my personal things from my apartment. It's a lot more modern, and I don't think much of the furniture would work here anyway. We'll need to go shopping for some of the basics to get us through the next month—a bed, a couch, that sort of thing. Then, if we decide to keep the place, we'll start looking for the rest. I want you to decorate however you want to."

Amelia fought the frown threatening to pull the corners of her mouth down. They'd agreed to date only two days ago, yet he was moving forward with the intention of them living here forever. Her head was still spinning, but Tyler was a master of rolling with the punches.

As it was, they'd put the cart before the horse and were scrambling to build a relationship to go with their marriage and their baby. Thirty days was really not enough time to fall in love, but she'd known she had to pick a deadline to put an end to this madness. This would either work or it wouldn't, and now they would know in a month. She couldn't take the uncertainty any longer than that. Tyler didn't seem to acknowledge that failure was even an option. It rarely was in his eyes. It didn't matter if it was a jewel auction or a game of cards with friends—he had to win. This time, she'd made her future the prize he was out to claim.

"I don't know, Tyler... This place is intimidating. As much as I enjoy decorating, I wouldn't even know where to start."

"I know," he admitted. "I had an interior designer do my place in New York. You're welcome to pick stuff for the house, but we can hire a decorator if you need help."

He reached down and took her hand in his. "Come on," he said with a gentle tug. "I'll show you the upstairs first."

They went up the stairs to the second floor, where he led her through a labyrinth of bedrooms and bathrooms. There was another family room and a large open bonus room that was bigger than her whole apartment.

"I was thinking we could turn this into a game room. Maybe get a pool table and a couple of pinball machines. What do you think?"

She thought this house was way too much space for them. It was too big for five or six, even, but she kept that to herself. "That would be fun."

"And through here," he continued, "is the movie theater."

Amelia stopped. "You're kidding, right? Why on earth would we need our own movie theater?"

Tyler grinned wide. "Nope, I'm not kidding. I think the real estate agent officially called it a media room, but it's all the same to me. This is one of the reasons I really love this house."

Amelia walked ahead of him into the windowless room with dark burgundy–painted walls. There was a large screen on the far wall with a projector mounted in the ceiling overhead. The floor was a staggered incline with two rows of leather media chairs that could seat eight people. One row was a step down from the first so everyone had a prime view. It was the craziest thing she'd ever seen.

"When I started looking for a place to rent, I wanted more than just luxury. I wanted functionality. With this, it made me think about how much we both love movies. You and I have wasted hours of our youth watching films together. I think we were at every Saturday matinee for four years. Having a place to screen our own movies in comfort seemed like a good investment for the future."

"It's amazing," she said, nodding blankly. "If you can afford it, why not? I'm sure we'll get a lot of enjoyment out of it."

Tyler continued on with the tour, heading downstairs to show her the luxurious master suite with a bathtub she could swim in. Amelia followed, only half listening to what he had to say about the house. Her mind was being pulled in ten directions, her chest tight with anxiety over this whole situation.

Things seemed to get more complicated minute by minute. Eloping with Tyler had been a mistake, but a correctable one. Getting pregnant was a curveball, but women had children every day with less suitable fathers. She could handle it. Tyler would be a great father, even if they didn't have a romantic relationship. Moving in together, temporarily or otherwise, was a big leap for her. But this place... It was like moving to an alien planet.

She'd known her best friend was a strategist. He always looked at every angle before making a decision, routinely kicking her rear in chess and rarely making a wrong move on the game board or in life. He didn't just win, he won intelligently. Still, it was hard to believe Tyler had pulled all this together in a day's time. He'd bought a car, found an amazing house he knew she'd love... She had no doubt he had movers on standby both here and in New York, just waiting for the call that he'd signed the lease on the house.

What did she expect? She'd laid down a challenge—thirty days to fall in love. Tyler was taking it seriously and would tackle it with the same drive and commitment that had gotten him from an old, overcrowded apartment to a multimillion-dollar mansion in ten years' time.

She would be hard-pressed to fight him off, especially when his opening volley included a mansion with a movie room. He was playing to win. What would he do next?

"I saved this room for last because I think it's going to be your favorite." He led her through what would probably be the living room to the kitchen. That was where her heart stopped and her worries vanished in an instant.

It was a chef's dream. Gorgeous cherry-stained cabinets, gold-flecked granite countertops, ornate tile work on the backsplash, professional stainless-steel appliances... It was gorgeous. She couldn't help rushing past him into the space to look more closely. The kitchen in her apartment was average. Nice, but nothing special. The one at the chapel was large, sterile and industrial, for cooking for hundreds of people at once. Neither of those places had anything on this.

She opened the deep drawers for pots and pans, sliding out built-in spice racks. The massive gas stove had two ovens, six burners and a grill in the center. There were two farm sinks on opposite sides of the kitchen, one beside a full-size dishwasher and the other with a small drawer dishwasher for quick washes of glasses. The French doors of the refrigerator opened wide, revealing enough space for countless platters and large serving dishes. There was even a warming drawer built in beside the stove.

It wasn't just a beautiful kitchen, it was a well laid-out one with all the latest amenities. She knew better than anyone how important it was to have the space designed properly to get work done with the fewest steps possible.

Amelia could cook up a storm here. She could throw some of the most amazing dinner parties ever thrown. Maybe an engagement party for Bree and Ian. They'd gotten engaged right before her reunion and had yet to have a party. Thoughts of gatherings with champagne and canapés started spinning through her head, but a glance at Tyler's smug grin brought everything to a stop.

She'd fallen for it, she realized with a silent curse. What was better than a movie room? The kitchen of her dreams. He knew exactly what he was doing, bringing her to this house and seducing her with stainless-steel appliances. He knew better than anyone that the route to her heart went through the kitchen. She'd underestimated how easily she could be had by someone who knew her every weakness.

Amelia wasn't ready to lose herself to the fantasy quite yet, though. Even if they did rent this place and move in, she couldn't get attached to any of it. In four weeks, everything could be different.

Tyler was confident they could build a successful relationship, but they had a steep hill to climb. She'd take a great love in a camper over a so-so romance with a mansion.

"Well, what do you think of the place?" he asked.

"You've done well, Tyler," she said with a polite smile. She ran her hand over the cool granite countertop. "I can't believe you turned up a place like this in a day. This kitchen is amazing. It's a shame you're the worst cook I've ever met."

He smiled and ran his hand through the messy strands of his dark blond hair. "Well, honestly, I have no intention of ever doing anything more complicated than making a bowl of cereal in here. But when I saw it, I knew how much you'd love it. This is all for you, really."

His pale blue eyes were focused on her with unmatched intensity as he spoke. She could feel the truth of his words and the depth of what they really meant. He could've rented a lesser house with average amenities, but he'd wanted to find the one that would make her eyes light up and her heart flutter with excitement. The kitchen had done that, easily. And he knew it.

Looking around her, it was obvious that her life had taken a very surreal turn. Tyler would rent this house, she was certain of it, and they would be living here by the weekend.

The flowers, the dinners, the granite countertops... She'd demanded Tyler woo her, and he was doing a damn fine job. She could already feel her resolve weakening, and it was day two. What would happen over the next twenty-eight days?

The mere thought scared the hell out of her.

"I didn't say anything because it's a temporary arrangement." Tyler rolled his eyes as his brother Jeremy needled him. He shouldn't have answered the phone when he saw his brother wasn't accepting his text at face value.

"Moving to Nashville doesn't seem temporary."

"I never said I was moving, just that I would be here for a while. I kept my apartment in New York," Tyler argued. "And I'm not moving my business. I'm only telling you so someone knows where I am." He'd chosen to text his younger brother Jeremy so someone in the family knew where he was if something happened. He had his cell phone, of course, but at least one person needed to be able to find him in an emergency. He regretted the decision now. Jeremy wouldn't accept the fact without the justification.

"What's going on that would make you drop everything and run to Nashville? Wait..." Jeremy hesitated. "Amelia lives in Nashville, doesn't she?"

"Yes," Tyler confirmed, feeling anxiety pool in his

stomach. The conversation was unraveling faster than he'd like.

"Is she okay?"

"She's fine. She just…needs me for a little while."

A long silence followed. "Needs you? Cut the crap, man. What's going on? I'll tell everyone you've moved to Nashville if you don't tell me why. Your life will be hell."

Tyler sighed. Better Jeremy know than the whole family. "Okay, but you can't breathe a word to anyone. I mean it."

"Of course. I'm not the blabbermouth in the family. I never even told anyone about that trip to Tijuana where you got arrested."

Tyler frowned at the phone. "I've never been to Mexico, Jeremy."

"Oh, that must've been Dylan," Jeremy said. "Crap, I just told a secret. It's normally not a problem, though. I've kept that secret for five years."

That didn't make him feel better, but he didn't have a choice. "Okay…I'm going to stay in Nashville for a few weeks because Amelia and I got together at the reunion and we're trying to make it work."

"You hooked up with Amelia?" Jeremy asked with an edge of incredulity in his voice. "Finally! I thought you guys would never—"

"We're married," he interrupted. "And she's pregnant."

"Holy crap!"

"I'm telling you, Jeremy, no one can know." That was Amelia's first and most important rule. It couldn't get out.

"Okay," Jeremy said. "It's safe with me, but when Mom finds out, she's going to kill you."

Tyler hung up the phone and shook his head. That hadn't been how he'd wanted that conversation to go, but it actually felt good to get that news off his chest. At least he had one semireliable person to talk to about all this. If all went well, when the rest of his family found out, it would be good news and no blood would be shed.

His phone rang again, and this time it was the moving company. There was no time to dwell on this. The clock was ticking.

The next few days were a blur of activity that made Amelia dizzy just thinking about it. Tyler signed a short-term lease on the house, and his moving companies went to work packing up both their apartments. The real estate agent referred them to an agency that provided domestic contract work, and they hired a part-time housekeeper named Janet, much to Amelia's relief.

After they left the agency, Tyler took Amelia to brunch, and they went furniture shopping to pick out the few things they needed in the interim, including a king-size bed and a desk where Tyler could work.

It was a good thing Tyler had the money to make all this happen, because Amelia certainly didn't have time to do it all. She'd spent all day Thursday baking, filling and crumb-coating a five-tiered wedding cake. Although chefs tended to specialize in culinary arts or in pastry arts, Amelia had studied both. That came in handy when she and her partners had decided to open From This Moment and did pretty much everything themselves.

By Friday afternoon, the cakes were iced, covered in her famous marshmallow fondant and stacked high on the cart she would use to move the cake into the reception hall. Today's cake was a simple design, despite being large in size. All she needed to do was load a pastry bag with buttercream and pipe alternating tiers of Swiss dots and cornelli lace. The florist was bringing fresh flowers for the cake Saturday afternoon.

Leaning back against the stainless-steel countertop to eye her accomplishment of the day, she came to the sad realization that soon she would have to let the cakes go. Cakes took hours. There were some days when Amelia was in the kitchen working on a cake until two in the morning. On more than one occasion, she'd just stayed over and slept on the chaise in the bridal suite.

Those days were coming to an end. They'd need to bring in help anyway to assist her late in the pregnancy when she couldn't power through a sixteen-hour day on her feet in the kitchen, and to bridge the gap of her maternity leave. That would be much easier if they started contracting out the wedding cakes.

Reaching for her tablet, she brushed away a dusting of powdered sugar from the screen and made a note to talk to Natalie about that. When that was done, she loaded her piping bag and started working on the final cake decorations.

"That's a big cake."

Amelia looked up from her work to see Tyler standing in the doorway of the kitchen. She was surprised to see he'd shed his suit today and was wearing a snug-fitting green T-shirt and a pair of worn jeans. It was a good look for him, reminding her of the boy she knew in school. "That's an understatement. It weighs over a hundred pounds."

He whistled, strolling into the kitchen to stand beside her and admire her handiwork. "Pretty impressive. Does it taste good?"

She frowned at him. "Of course it does. It's my special lemon–sour cream cake with a fresh raspberry-and-white-chocolate buttercream filling."

"No real chocolate?"

"This is the South," she said. "Chocolate is for the

groom's cake, which, fortunately, I do not have to make. The groom's aunt is making him one that looks like Neyland Stadium at the University of Tennessee."

Tyler nodded thoughtfully and eyeballed the bowl with leftover raspberry filling. "What are you going to do with that?" he asked.

Amelia sighed and went to the other side of the kitchen to retrieve a plastic spoon. "Knock yourself out," she said, holding it out to him. She waited until he'd inhaled a few spoonfuls of icing. "What brings you by today, Tyler? I really need to get this finished. I've got several hours of prep work ahead of me for tomorrow when I'm done with this."

He swallowed and set the bowl aside. "By all means, continue working. Primarily, I came by because I haven't seen you yet today."

Amelia smiled and climbed up onto her stepladder to pipe the top tier. "Once we're living in the same place, that won't be a problem any longer."

"Speaking of which, I also needed to let you know that you have a new address." He reached into his pocket and dangled a set of keys. "These are yours. I also have a gate opener for your car."

"Wow, your people move quickly. Is everything really out of my apartment?"

"Yep. I even had Janet go by and clean once everything was gone."

Amelia nodded thoughtfully and went back to piping the cake. She was keeping her apartment for another month, but the odds were that she wouldn't move back. As they'd discussed, she would either stay with Tyler, or she would get a new place big enough for her and the baby. He'd been right—her apartment was too small. It was easier to just get everything out now instead of having to go back and get the rest later.

"Janet also went to the store with the list you put together and stocked the pantry and refrigerator with food. And she got all the necessary cleaning supplies to keep the house shipshape."

Amelia was going to like this Janet. While she loved to cook, cleaning was at the bottom of her list. The industrial washing machine in the kitchen made it easier to clean up here, but keeping up with cleaning her apartment had always been a burden. She'd developed a process of immediately cleaning up anything she did as she did it to avoid having to deal with it later. She'd never lived with anyone else, but she assumed that would make it exponentially harder to manage.

"Sounds great. Hopefully I'll get to see what the house looks like before I collapse facedown in the mattress tonight." She had a long list of things that had to be done before she went home today.

"Don't you have anyone to help you in the kitchen?"

At that, Amelia chuckled. She added the last flourish to the top tier and climbed down the steps. "Not really. We bring in a crew of servers the day of the wedding, but I'm pretty much on my own until then."

"What about the other girls? They don't help you?"

Amelia pushed the cart with the cake over to the walk-in refrigerator. Tyler rushed ahead of her to pull the door open and she slid it inside. "It's Friday afternoon," she said, stepping out and shutting the door behind her. "Natalie is in headset-and-clipboard mode, counting down to the wedding. She's probably meeting with the officiant and the musicians right now to go over the schedule. She will be coordinating the rehearsal, then the rehearsal dinner. Bree will be with her, taking pictures. Gretchen is currently in the reception hall setting up tables, laying out linens and doing all the decorating she can do in advance. When the rehearsal is over, she'll start decorating the chapel and lobby. They would help me if they could, but we all have things to do."

"What a circus," Tyler observed with a shake of his head. "I don't recall our wedding being this complicated."

"Yeah, I know," she replied, her tone flat. "Unfortunately, the circus is necessary for a beautiful, smoothly run wedding day. We've got it down to a science."

Amelia picked up her tablet and pulled up her task list for the afternoon. At the top of the list was prepping a hundred servings each of filet mignon, chicken breast and salmon to marinate overnight. She pulled out a large plastic tote and started mixing up the steak marinade.

She kept expecting Tyler to make noises about leaving, but he continued to hover a few feet away. Whereas she normally didn't mind company, he was a distraction. A glance at his smile, a whiff of his cologne, and she'd likely slice off her thumb. Dumping in the last ingredient in the marinade, she turned to him. "Tyler, honey, you don't need to stand around and look at me. I'm sure you have something more important to do today."

Tyler leaned against the counter beside her and shook his head. "No, I don't. I'm here to help you. I'm no chef, but I'm another set of hands. Tell me what you need done."

That was the sexiest thing she'd ever heard. She resisted the urge to throw her arms around his neck and let him take her against the industrial refrigerator. Fridays were a day for work, not play. Instead she took a deep breath and decided where they should start first.

"If you insist." She pointed to a sink on the opposite side of the kitchen. "Scrub up in the sink and grab an apron off the shelf. When you're ready, glove up and grab the beef tenderloins from the refrigerator so we can get them broken down into portions."

If he was going to be a sexy distraction, he could at least be a useful one.

Six

"If I never see another potato, it will be too soon." Tyler opened the front door of their new home and held it for Amelia to step through ahead of him.

"You were a trouper. Thank you for all your help today." She looked down at her watch. "Home by eight. I think that might be a Friday-night record."

He followed her into the kitchen, where she dropped her purse on the breakfast bar and slipped out of her coat. She hopped on one foot, then the other, pulling off her shoes with a happy sigh.

"All your things are in the master suite," he said. Tyler had had to make a command decision when the movers arrived, so he'd given her the nicest room on the main floor and hoped that at some point they would share it.

Amelia followed him, shoes in hand, down the hallway to the master suite. The new bed dominated the formerly empty space, with a green-and-gold embroidered comforter in place. They continued into the master bathroom, where a door led to the walk-in closet.

"All your clothes are in here," he said. "Everything that was in your dressers is in the built-in armoire here. All your shoes are in the cubbies there."

Amelia slipped her sneakers into an empty slot in the shoe display and nodded. "Thank you for taking care of all of this. Since it's all handled, I think I might take a bath in the big whirlpool tub. It might help me relax after a long day. Just not too hot, right?"

He remembered his sister saying something about that because she'd found out she was pregnant with his niece right before her fifth-anniversary cruise. *No drinks, no hot tubs! What a vacation,* she'd lamented. "I think so. I know hot tubs are bad, but they keep the temperature up. The bathwater, especially with the jets running, will cool over time."

"I'm more interested in the jets than the heat anyway. I'll go online on my phone and check first. I've got quite a list of things to talk about with my doctor when I go to my first appointment."

Tyler paused. "When is your first appointment?"

"Tuesday afternoon."

"May I come?" he asked, hesitantly. He was teetering on the edge of wanting to be involved in the process and not wanting too many of the less-appetizing details.

Amelia nodded. "I don't think the first one will be very interesting, but you're welcome to join me and ask questions. We're both new at this."

"Great. Thanks. I'll, uh…" he took a few steps toward the hallway "…let you take your bath now."

Tyler slipped from the room and went back out into the kitchen. He had set up his temporary office in the keeping room off the kitchen. Turning on his laptop, he settled into the new office chair. He was exhausted. He really couldn't understand how Amelia worked that hard week after week. As a steady stream of emails downloaded into his inbox, he realized he wasn't in the mood to deal with any of it. Instead he closed his email program and started playing a game.

Even that was hard to focus on. He could hear the water running in the master bath. It seemed to take an eternity to fill the tub, but eventually the water stopped and the soft hum of the jets started. He lost multiple rounds of solitaire, his mind more interested in imagining Amelia stripping out of her clothes. Dropping them to the floor. Clipping her hair up so it didn't get wet. Lowering her body into the warm, churning water, inch by inch. Rubbing her body with a slick bar of fragrant soap until bubbles formed across her skin.

A prickling sensation traveled down his spine, every muscle tightening with anticipation for something it wouldn't have. He suddenly felt constricted by the clinging cotton T-shirt and jeans he'd worn today. Especially the jeans. Tyler swallowed hard and squeezed his eyes shut, but it wasn't enough to block out his imagination. Nothing could drive the image of her wet skin and steam-flushed cheeks from his thoughts.

Their date had brought his need for her to the forefront of his mind. Their wedding night had been weeks ago, and although he would never forget that experience, his hands could no longer feel her skin, and his tongue could no longer taste her. The kiss on her porch had refreshed everything, making it hard for him to focus on anything else. Not even long hours working in the kitchen had helped with her so nearby.

About fifteen minutes into her bath, Tyler leaped up from his chair and marched toward the staircase. Maybe a little distance would help. He might take a shower of his own. Or bury his head under a pillow and smother the fantasy.

He was halfway up when he heard Amelia's voice. "Tyler?" she shouted. "Tyler, help!"

His heart jumped into his throat. He spun on his heel and sprinted back downstairs, not stopping at the closed door of the suite. Instead he charged in, fearful he would find she'd slipped and hurt herself, or worse. She was still in the bathroom. He headed that way, his loafers skidding across the tile to a stop.

Looking around the bathroom, he couldn't spot an immediate problem. No blood, nothing broken. The air was heavy with steam and a tropical scent she must've added to the water. Amelia was in the tub with the jets turned off. She was watching him with large, surprised eyes, her hands protectively attempting to cover her nakedness in the clear water of the bath.

"Yes?" he asked, breathless. "Are you okay? What's wrong?"

Amelia bit her bottom lip. "I'm sorry, I didn't mean to send you into a panic. Nothing is wrong, at least nothing serious. I'm fine."

Tyler took a deep breath of relief, feeling his fight-or-flight response dwindle away. It was replaced with a different kind of tension as his eyes shifted over the uncovered patches of her ivory skin in the water. Nothing scandalous was visible, but it didn't need to be. He had an excellent memory and could easily fill in the blanks without fail. Damp strands of red hair were plastered to her neck, a rosy flush painted across her cheeks. "What do you need?"

"There's no towels," she admitted with a pained wince. "I'm an idiot and I didn't grab one before I got in. I didn't want to drip water all over while I hunted for one. Do you know where they are?"

Towels. Yes. That he could do. "Sure thing." He turned and opened a narrow door that hid a linen closet. He pulled out a fluffy yellow towel that had come from her apartment and carried it back over to the tub. "Here you go."

"Thank you," she said with a sheepish smile. "I'm sorry to scare you."

"No problem. Let me know if you need anything else." He turned and started walking out of the bathroom.

"Tyler?"

He stopped and turned. "Yes?"

Amelia had stood in the tub and quickly wrapped the towel around her. "Would you like to watch some television with me tonight? I was thinking we could pile up in the new bed and watch something together. I know the list I left for Janet had popcorn and chips, if you'd like some."

Tyler was a little surprised by the invitation, but he was more surprised by the seemingly shy expression on her face while she asked. It was almost as if she was a teenager again, asking if he'd like to sit with her at lunch or something. She was his best friend. Of course he'd like to watch television with her. He hadn't suggested something like that because...things were different now. They had shared a bed on several occasions throughout the years, but lying beside one another in bed now felt more complicated than it used to. Feelings had been unleashed between them.

The last thing he wanted was to lose the parts of their friendship he cherished the most as their physical relationship changed. Perhaps once they made the decision to cross that bridge again it wouldn't seem like such a big deal any longer, but for now, they were in limbo.

Married. Having a baby. Yet dating as though none of it had happened.

"That's a great idea. Are you getting out of the tub already?"

"Yes. I'm not very good with sitting idle, even when it feels nice."

"Okay, well, while you're getting dressed, I'll see what I can find in the kitchen for snacks."

A smile lit up Amelia's face, distracting him from the sight of the tiny towel wrapped around her curves. It was a contagious grin, and one spread across his own face just as easily.

Tyler left the room so she could put on some clothes and started to hunt through the kitchen. Fortunately, Janet had put everything in very sensible places. He found a box of microwave popcorn on a shelf in the pantry. Score.

About ten minutes later, he strolled cautiously back into the bedroom with two cans of soda, a roll of paper towels and a large bowl piled high with movie-theater butter-flavored popcorn.

He found Amelia dressed—thankfully—and sitting on the bed cross-legged. Her hair was still clipped up on top of her head, but she'd removed her makeup, leaving her skin clean and fresh. She was wearing her pajamas— a pair of pale blue cotton lounging pants with a matching tank top. The top had thin spaghetti straps and a lacy edge that gave the impression of modesty where there was none. There was no disguising Amelia's assets in anything short of a turtleneck.

Tyler went around to the other side of the bed and unloaded the contents of his arms into the space between them. Currently, the only television in the house was from Amelia's apartment. He'd opted to put it in the bedroom, since they really didn't have much in the way of living room furniture for now.

Amelia flipped on the television, then piled the pillows up behind her. She accepted the can of soda from Tyler, resting it between her thighs since they also didn't have nightstands yet. "Ooh," she said, looking over at the bowl of popcorn. "That looks like the really buttery, nasty kind. I love it."

Tyler chuckled. "I would've thought that such cheap, pedestrian fare might offend your refined palate."

At that, she snorted. "People like that make me crazy. Whenever I watch those cooking competitions and the chefs are whining because they have to use canned ingredients or something, I just roll my eyes. The average working mom does not have the time to deal with freshly preparing a meal from scratch every night. Real people eat canned foods sometimes. And microwave popcorn," she added, shoveling a handful into her mouth.

They flipped through the channels, finally agreeing on a mermaid mockumentary on the Discovery Channel. They heckled and joked, laughing throughout the show and polishing off all their snacks. It was just like old times, Tyler thought with an overwhelming sense of relief.

Tyler didn't have much time for dating, but when he did, this was always what he was missing from his other relationships. He liked to keep things light and fun, but for some reason, the women were always so serious, as if he was the Lombardi Trophy in the Super Bowl of marrying well. Those women wouldn't dare to be seen without makeup or to be silly with him, but he supposed in the end it didn't matter what was lacking. He wasn't going to fall in love with them. If he wanted friendship and compatibility, he would go to Amelia.

Looking over, he realized Amelia had drifted to sleep beside him. Her red-gold lashes rested against her cheeks, her pink lips softly parted. She must have been exhausted. He felt an ache in his chest as he looked at her lying there. All those other poor women had been doomed before they'd even started. He hadn't really needed them for anything but a sexual release when he had Amelia in his life. His ex-fiancée, Christine, had known that. Even though he'd loved her, even though he'd proposed to her and wanted to start a life together, she'd felt like a third wheel. Maybe she had been.

Through a strange turn of events, it seemed Amelia was going to be the woman in his life. Fortunately, she was the one woman with whom he knew it was possible to have it all. They had the friendship. The sexual compatibility was there. He hadn't stopped wanting her since he'd allowed himself to think of her that way.

As for love, she just had to be open to loving him. He had twenty-six days left. If she loved him by then, that would be as good as it could possibly get. They would stay married, raise their child together... Tyler could be happy with that. He didn't need or want love for himself. In the end, it just made things harder.

Tyler slowly lowered the volume on the television and turned it off. He picked up the empty bowl of popcorn and eased toward the end of the mattress, trying to slip out of bed without waking her. He failed.

"Stay," she muttered into her pillow without opening her eyes. "This house is too big and I don't want to be alone down here. Please."

With a sigh, he put the bowl on the floor and switched off the lights before he climbed back into bed.

"Yay." Amelia yawned, snuggling up next to him and immediately falling back asleep.

Tyler wished he was so lucky. The scent of her per-fumed skin so close to him and the soft heat of her body pressed against his made sleep impossible. He shut his eyes and tugged her close. If he couldn't sleep, he could at least lie contented with her in his arms.

It was going to be a very, very long night.

Amelia was burning up. She woke up in the middle of the night with an unfamiliar warmth pressed against her back and an arm draped over her. It took a full five to ten seconds for her to remember where she was and who was touching her.

Tyler. She'd asked him to stay with her tonight.

That she didn't mind, but at the moment, his internal furnace was making her back perspire. It was like sleep-ing with a hot water bottle. Turning her head to look over her shoulder, she found him on his side, snoring softly near her ear.

She eased ever so gently away from him. The move-ment was enough for him to mumble and roll onto his back, liberating her. She sat up in bed, looking down on him as he slept. The poor guy was still wearing his clothes from today. Those jeans couldn't be comfortable, but she knew he would rather be uncomfortable than get into bed without them and make her ill at ease.

Reclining onto her elbow, she looked down at him. His face was perfectly relaxed in sleep, something he never seemed to be anymore. There was no tension in his square jaw, no crinkles of thought around his eyes. Just peace. She wanted to reach out and touch his cheek to feel the rough stubble of his perpetual five-o'clock shadow. She wanted to feel his soft lips against hers again. But she wouldn't. He'd worked hard today, and she wouldn't wake him up for something so trivial.

As if he'd heard her, his eyes opened and he looked at her. There was no confusion or dreaminess in his gaze. Only a powerful need that hit her as surely as if she'd been punched in the stomach. Without hesitation, his palm went to her cheek. His touch was a match to a forest in drought. It started a pleasurable heat spreading like wildfire through her whole body.

"Amelia?" he asked, his voice gruff with sleep.

"Yes," she replied to his unasked question.

He buried his fingers into the hair at the nape of her neck and tugged until her mouth met his. Neither his hands nor his mouth were gentle, and she didn't mind. She liked the rough feel of his stubble against her cheeks and the sharp press of his fingertips into her flesh.

His tongue thrust into her mouth and slid along her own, making her core pulsate with the anticipation of more. She wanted to be closer to him, to touch him again. He had been right before—once they'd crossed that line there was no sense holding back any longer.

She threw one leg over his hips and straddled him. The move put her sensitive center in direct contact with the throbbing heat of his desire. The thin cotton of her pajama pants did little to dull the sensations that shot through her when they touched.

Amelia was desperate to liberate him from his jeans. Her palm slid along the hard muscles of his stomach, seeking out the button of his fly and stroking him through the denim.

Her fingers had barely brushed the button when in one swift move, Tyler rolled them across the bed. Amelia found herself with her back to the mattress and him between her thighs. His palms sought out her wrists, pinning them over her head. All through this, he never stopped kissing her.

When he finally let her mouth free, it was to taste her throat. Still holding her wrists with one hand, he used the other to gently tug her tank top up and over her head, leaving it tangled around her wrists with her breasts exposed. He didn't hesitate to capture one hardened pink nipple in his mouth, drawing on it until Amelia cried out and bucked her hips against him. His teeth and tongue worked her flesh, sending pleasurable shock waves through her whole body.

"Let go of my hands," she whispered.

"No," he answered between flicks of his tongue across her sensitive skin.

What did he mean, *no*? "Please," she begged. "I want to touch you."

"I know," he said, looking at her with a wicked smile curling his lips. "But if you do, it will be all over. I can't take it." His mouth returned to her breast, effectively ending the conversation.

All she could do was writhe beneath him, drawing her knees up and thrusting her hips forward to rub agonizingly against the hard ridge of his jeans.

He growled low against her sternum. "Two can play at that game." He glided his palm over her hip and under the drawstring waistband of her pants. His insistent fingers easily found her moist center, stroking hard.

Amelia cried out, the sound echoing through the mostly empty bedroom. "Tyler!" she gasped as he rubbed her again and again. She felt herself start to come undone, but the more desperate she became, the more he eased back, leaving her teetering on the edge.

At last, he let go of her arms, but it was only to sit back on his knees. He whipped his T-shirt over his head and threw it to the ground. With the use of her hands back, she did the same. His hands gripped both sides of her pajama pants, tugging them and her panties down over her hips and to the floor.

Standing at the end of the bed, he stopped to look down at her. Only the moonlight from the nearby window lit the room, which made Amelia feel a little less self-conscious about being sprawled out in front of him like this. That, and the look on his face. It was as though he was in a museum admiring a piece of art. A piece of art he wanted to devour.

Without looking away from her, he unzipped his jeans and slipped out of the last of his clothes. Crawling back up the bed, he covered her body with his own. Without hesitation, he found her entrance and moved into her.

Amelia gasped, her body tightening around the sudden invasion. He filled her completely, leaving her biting her lip and pressing her fingers desperately into his shoulders.

"Amelia," he groaned at her ear, slowly withdrawing and filling her again. "I never imagined..." he began, his voice drifting away. Shaking off a shudder that made his whole body tremble between her thighs, he started moving in earnest.

Rational thought slipped away as only the physical drive inside of her remained. Amelia wrapped her legs around his waist and tried to absorb every wave as it washed over her. "Yes" was all she could say. It was an encouraging plea, a desperate demand and an enthusiastic consent all rolled together at once.

And then it happened. The dam broke inside of her. A sudden rush of pleasure swept her up and carried her away. She cried out, bucked her hips against him, clung to him, all the while aware of his soft, encouraging words in her ear.

Her own release had barely subsided when she felt

Tyler tense in her arms. He surged forward like never before, pounding hard into her body before roaring loud into the night.

Amelia held him until it was over. She expected him to distance himself, to roll away the minute it was done, but he didn't. He stayed there, inside her, examining the curves of her face.

"What is it?" she asked after a few minutes under his intense scrutiny. She brought her hands up to smooth the unruly strands of her hair. "I probably look a fright."

His gaze met hers and he smiled softly. "No, of course not. You look perfect. The sexiest thing I've ever woken up to. I just…never imagined being with you would be like this. If I'd known…" His voice drifted away.

Tyler never finished the sentence, but he didn't need to. Amelia knew exactly what he meant.

Seven

Thank goodness it was Saturday.

For some, Saturdays were days for barbecues, college football games and relaxation. For Amelia, Saturday meant all-day wedding chaos, but today she was grateful for it. Her mind had to stay focused on work, so there was zero time to sit and analyze what they'd done last night. Well, aside from fifteen minutes in the shower when she washed the scent of him from her skin and tried to ignore the memories of making love to Tyler only a few hours earlier.

Amelia had not intended on that happening so soon. They were dating, but it was still early on, despite moving in together. None of that had seemed important at the time. She'd gotten caught up in the moment. The fuzzy edge of sleep had blurred her thoughts. When he'd touched her, all she could think about, all she'd wanted, was to fall into his arms again. So she'd gone with it.

In the end, sleeping with the man who was technically her husband was hardly newsworthy. The reality seemed more complicated than that when your husband was your best friend and you were starting an impromptu family together. Of course, this whole process would be easier if she stopped fighting it. The thirty-day challenge wasn't supposed to be a battle; it was supposed to be a trial run. And Tyler was doing his part. He'd done everything she'd asked of him so far, and then some. His every action seemed to be motivated by his thoughtful nature. He was kind. He cared about her and what was best for her and the baby. They didn't always agree on what those things were, but marriage was about compromise.

For once in her life, maybe she just needed to relax and let things happen. Something wonderful could come from it if she allowed the universe to unfold as it should. That was a tall order for Amelia, but she'd think on it. The alternative, as Natalie had pointed out, was unacceptable. She couldn't lose her friendship with Tyler over this.

Once she stepped from the shower and dried off, she had to let that line of thought go and get ready for work. It took a little longer than usual, but she was still adjusting to the new house and trying to figure out where everything was. Since she now lived so much closer to From This Moment, she would still get there well before eight, even when it took five minutes to find her blow-dryer.

Tyler had still been asleep when she got up. When she finished in the bathroom, she moved quickly through the bedroom to the kitchen so she wouldn't disturb him. She wanted to get out the door before he noticed. Yes, she was being a chicken, avoiding an awkward conversation, but she had a good reason to leave.

As she rounded the corner into the kitchen, she realized it was a pointless exercise. Tyler was sitting at the counter hunched over his tablet, reading, with a mug of coffee in his hand. He still had on the rumpled clothes he'd slept in, his dark blond hair wildly standing up in several different directions. Instead of looking messy, the look was charming. An intimate portrait of the man behind the suit. It made her want to come up behind him and wrap her arms around his neck, plant a kiss on his rough cheek and tousle his hair.

Even though they'd had sex, that somehow seemed too intimate. Instead she turned her attention to a tall glass beside him with something greenish brown in it. She was certain it would look unappetizing even if she wasn't having her daily battle with morning sickness.

Amelia knew there was no avoiding a discussion before she left. Maybe he would want to ignore last night's encounter, as well. That seemed like a topic for after noon, at least. With a deep breath, she continued on into the kitchen.

"Morning," she said as cheerfully as she could without sounding suspicious. She opened the door to the pantry and started nosing around for something quick and easy she could take with her for breakfast. Eating was not high on her priority list at the moment, but when the nausea faded, she'd be starving and up to her elbows in twice-baked potatoes for the reception. She picked up a high-protein granola bar with chocolate chips. A bundle of bananas was sitting on the counter. One of those would slip easily into her purse for later.

"Good morning," Tyler replied, his voice low and gruff from sleep. He looked up from his screen. "I already made your breakfast. I hope you don't mind. I know you're the chef, but I thought you might be in a hurry this morning."

Amelia turned around and noticed he'd slid the tall

glass of green sludge closer to her. "Thanks," she said, although she didn't feel very grateful. Her stomach rolled unpleasantly as she neared it. "What is it?"

"It's a pregnancy smoothie. I found the recipe online. It's got cocoa and peanut butter, which you like, plus bananas to soothe a queasy stomach, milk for calcium and spinach for the iron and folic acid needed for healthy fetal development."

She eyed the glass with suspicion. It sounded like a good idea. Maybe it tasted better than it looked. Even if it didn't, Tyler was looking at her with such a pleased and hopeful expression, she'd have to drink it anyway. Lifting the glass to her nose, she sniffed it. It smelled like peanut butter and bananas, mostly. Nothing to make her recoil. Bringing the straw to her lips, she found it tasted the same. The spinach seemed to disappear, adding nutrition while letting the other flavors shine.

"Mmm," she said, swallowing a large sip. "This is pretty good. You can feel free to make me one of these every day."

"Absolutely," he said with a smile. "Taking good care of our child means taking good care of you. I'm glad to do it."

Amelia fought a small twinge in the back of her mind as he spoke. She recognized the feeling as the pang of jealousy, but that didn't make any sense. Who was she jealous of? Their baby? That seemed silly. She should be happy that Tyler wanted them to have a happy, healthy child. And he most likely wanted her to be happy and healthy, too. Amelia was just being oversensitive. She would blame the hormones.

"And after what I experienced yesterday," Tyler continued, "you're going to need all the good nutrition you can get. Are all of your days like that?"

She swallowed another sip and set down the glass on the shiny granite countertop. "Just Thursdays, Fridays and Saturdays. Saturdays are the worst. I have no idea when I'll get home tonight. I probably won't get back until one or two a.m., so don't wait up. What are you doing today?"

Tyler set down his tablet. "I'm going to the estate auction of a country-music singer. She died last year, but her lawyers have finally gotten her estate settled. Her heirs just want to liquidate for cash."

"Who is it?" Amelia asked. There were a lot of country-music stars in Nashville to choose from.

"Patty Travis. That woman was the country-music equivalent of Liberace. She spent almost every dime she earned on jewelry, and her famous roster of lovers over the years bought her even more. It's almost as good as the Elizabeth Taylor auction a few years back. I'm hoping to snap up a few nice pieces."

Amelia frowned at Tyler. "That's why you really came to Nashville!" she accused at last.

He opened his mouth to argue but must have decided against it. "I came to Nashville," he said, seeming to choose his words very carefully, "to see you and work out the details of the divorce we're not getting. It was my first opportunity to come, and I was able to make the time because, yes, I was planning on coming to this auction and I could do it all in one trip. You'll notice I arrived a full five days ahead of the auction so I could devote the time to you. I didn't intend to spend those days renting a house and moving here."

"That's true," she said, carrying her mostly empty smoothie glass over to the sink. She took one last sip and rinsed it out. "Do we need to schedule an auction here in

Nashville the week of the baby's birth so I'll be certain you're in town?"

"Very funny," Tyler said without laughing.

"I'm not entirely kidding." Amelia walked back to the counter and planted her palms on the cool stone. "It took over a month to nail you down about our elopement. If Patty Travis's estate wasn't having an auction this week, it might have taken even longer. I know you've reorganized what you can to make the thirty-day arrangement work out, and I appreciate it. But what are we going to do after that? Even if we stay together, I'm going to spend most of my time in this huge house, alone, while you trot around the world chasing flawless gemstones."

"You could come with me, you know."

Amelia snorted. As alluring as the idea might sound, it would never work. "I have a job, too, you know."

"Do you not get vacation time?"

"It's not a question of benefits, Ty. I am part owner of the company. If I'm not there to do my share, everyone else has to scramble to fill my space. We were lucky when I went to the reunion that the wedding that day was light appetizers and we were able to bring in a contractor. My maternity leave is going to be a huge impact to the business. Traveling with you is impossible."

Tyler frowned. She could tell he wasn't used to someone shooting down his great ideas. He needed to understand that From This Moment wasn't just some job she was keen to cast aside once she had a rich man to take care of her. It was her career. Her passion. A rich husband only seemed to be complicating the issue.

"What if I could arrange the trip to depart on a Sunday night and come back on Thursday or Friday?"

"That would still be pushing it. It would have to be really important. And somewhere I'd like to go. I'm not getting a bunch of shots with weird side effects so you can haul me to India when I'm four months pregnant."

"What about London?" he asked with an optimistic tone.

Damn it if he didn't pick the perfect location right out the gate. Amelia had always wanted to go to London. "Yes, I would like to see London, but timing is key. And," she added, "that wasn't really my point, Ty. In a few more months, I'm not going to be able to travel anywhere. After that, I'll have an infant. More than stamps in my passport, I need you to *be here*."

She looked down at the clock on her phone. "Just think about it. We can talk later. I've got to get to the chapel. Good luck at your auction."

Tyler nodded thoughtfully and waved a hand at her. "Okay. Hope the wedding goes well. I'll see you tonight."

Amelia picked up her purse and went out the door. Tyler could be aggravating at times, but when it came down to it, he knew her better than anyone else. He could use that against her to get his way. Dangling a trip to London was just cruel because he knew how badly she wanted to go. But if she agreed to one trip, he'd find a reason she had to take another. And another. Then after the baby was born, they might as well just bring in a full-time caterer to replace her.

She might be softening on compromising for their relationship, but her job was her dream and she wouldn't lose that. Even so, the whole drive to work she was taunted by thoughts of a proper English tea with fresh scones and the potential to lick clotted cream and strawberry jam from Tyler's bare chest.

"I told you not to wait up for me."

Amelia stumbled in the door around two-thirty in

the morning, her eyes glazed with fatigue and her purse weighing so heavily on her shoulder it could've been filled with concrete.

Tyler frowned and got up from his laptop, where he'd been working. He hadn't intended to stay up, but work had beckoned and the later it got, the more he worried about her. He knew her job was important to her, but she worked too hard. He had seen that same expression on his mother's face when she'd come home from a double shift at the manufacturing plant—bone tired. Too tired to sleep, sometimes. He would make her a cup of tea and sit up talking with his mother until she finally relaxed enough to go to bed.

"You should've called me to pick you up," he chastised gently. "You look exhausted enough to wrap your car around a light pole. Who will cater for them then?"

She shrugged and dropped her purse on a stool in the kitchen. "It's not a long drive home now. I'm fine."

Tyler came up behind her to help her slip out of her jacket. "I thought you had help on Saturday nights."

"I do. There's the waitstaff and a couple people that help cook, like Stella. She was a godsend tonight. Normally it's not a problem. I thrive on the adrenaline rush of the kitchen chaos." She climbed onto the next stool and slumped against the counter. "But lately, I just don't have it in me. A couple hours in and I have to sit down and take a break."

"You're pregnant, Ames."

"So? The baby is the size of a blueberry at best. It shouldn't be giving me this much grief so soon."

"That's not how it works. My sisters complained about the exhaustion far more than anything else. It starts earlier than you'd think."

"I need to get a baby book—*The Moron's Guide to*

Procreation or one of those *What to Expect When Your Body Is Taken Over by a Tiny Alien* books."

"I think we can manage that," he said with a smile. Amelia was really tired if she was getting this crotchety. "Would you like some chamomile tea?"

Amelia sighed, shaking her head and then stopping. She looked up at him with hope beaming in her big doe eyes. "Do we have any hot chocolate?"

"I don't know, but I'll look." Tyler went into the pantry, scanning for the tiny packets of instant mix, but came up empty-handed. He spied a bar of milk chocolate on the shelf and decided to improvise. It had been a long time since he'd made hot chocolate for his little brothers after school. Once his older sisters had gotten part-time jobs, Tyler had been the one at the apartment when the school bus dropped off the little ones. He'd been the one who had made sure they'd done their homework and given them snacks. Hot chocolate had been one of their favorites. Back then he'd made it with bottled syrup, but this would work.

"From scratch?" she asked as she watched him put a small pot of milk on to boil.

"Only the best for you," he said with a grin. He broke up small pieces of the chocolate and dropped them into the heating mixture of milk, vanilla and cinnamon. A few minutes later, it had come together into a frothy brew that he poured into a mug for her. "Here you go. Be careful, it's hot."

"Looks yummy. Thank you."

Tyler rested his hands on the granite countertop and watched her sip the cocoa with a blissful expression on her face. In that moment, he realized just how much he enjoyed making her happy. Over the years, he'd always liked sending her pretty gifts for her birthday or Christmas. That was fun because he knew she would never buy anything like that for herself, and jewels were his business. Seeing her wearing something sparkly and decadent seemed like the perfect treat.

But lately, even before the reunion, their relationship had started to feel different. With their hectic schedules, they rarely saw each other in person, but as life had started encroaching on their technological interchanges, he'd found the idea of it was bothering him more than it used to. He missed talking to Amelia on the phone. Finding emails and texts from her. When he'd arrived in Vegas for the reunion, he couldn't believe how much he'd missed the sight of her. He hadn't even wanted to go to the party. Tyler would've been just as happy ordering room service and spending hours talking in his hotel room.

Now that they were spending almost all their time together, he certainly couldn't miss her. But he still found himself feeling the same little thrill every time she walked into the room. Doing little things like making her breakfast and helping her cut up beef tenderloin gave him a warm feeling in the center of his chest that was more satisfying than giving her some expensive bauble.

She looked at it as being fawned over or taken care of, but that wasn't how he thought about it. He wanted to do things for her because he…cared about her. She was his Amelia. Of course he wanted to do what he could to make her life better. If cocoa made her happy, he'd make it. If this kitchen and a private movie theater that seated eight made her smile, he'd rent this house at twice the price. If marrying her would make her feel better about being single at the reunion…apparently he'd do that, too.

She was the most important person in his life. He'd never expected that she would also be his wife. But now that she was, and the clock was ticking, he was having a hard time envisioning his life without her. He didn't want to go back to just seeing Amelia every now and then. The baby would bring them together more often, but somehow even that wasn't enough. He wanted her here. With him. Every day. This was one challenge he couldn't fail at.

"This was very good," Amelia said, draining the last of her cup. "You're better in the kitchen than you give yourself credit for."

Tyler shrugged and rinsed her mug in the sink. "I am just painting by numbers when in the presence of Michelangelo."

At that, Amelia snorted and burst into exhausted giggles. "I'm more like Bob Ross painting happy little trees, but thank you."

"You should give yourself more credit, too."

"Maybe later," she said with a yawn. "I'm about to fall out with all that warm, chocolaty milk in my tummy."

Tyler wrapped his arm around her shoulder and walked her toward the bedroom. "All right. Come on, let's get you into bed before you collapse on the kitchen floor."

They walked down the hallway to the master suite. There, he sat Amelia down on the bed and knelt in front of her to take off her shoes. He unlaced her little sneakers and slipped them off with her socks, revealing dainty, pink-painted toenails.

"Thank you," she said, pulling her shirt up over her head and throwing it to the floor beside him. "I'm so tired, my feet seem as if they're a million miles away. In a few months, they might as well be. I'll have to get some slip-on shoes."

"You don't need them," Tyler argued. "I'll be here to help you."

"Tyler?"

He sat back on his heels and looked up, catching a glimpse of her large ivory breasts held in the tight confines of her white satin bra. He swallowed hard at the sight of them and focused on her eyes, trying not to look at the temptation on display in front of him. Amelia wasn't trying to tempt him—she was exhausted. "Yes?" he said, clearing his throat.

Her brow furrowed in thought, her eyes glazing over slightly. Even this discussion was tiring her out. "What if thirty days come and go and we don't fall in love?"

That was a good question, and one he hadn't really allowed himself to consider. Having a winning attitude in life had gotten him far. He'd accepted her challenge, never doubting he would be successful. But this was the first time he wasn't fully in control of the variables. No matter what he did, it was possible that Amelia wouldn't fall in love with him. Then what?

That was too deep a conversation for three in the morning. "You mean you're not mad for me already? After last night?"

She shrugged coyly. "I'm getting there. Maybe we should try again tonight to see if it makes a difference."

Tyler chuckled. As much as he'd like to, he didn't relish the idea of Amelia falling asleep in the middle of it. He stood up, planting a warm kiss on her forehead. "Tomorrow night," he promised. "Tonight, all you need to do is slip out of these pants and get to bed."

She nodded slowly, fumbling at the waistband of her black slacks. "Are you staying in here with me?" she asked. "I'll keep my hands to myself."

Last night he hadn't given her request a second thought. Now her question was plaguing his mind with unproductive fantasies about what might happen at the end of their time together. He'd always avoided a relationship with Amelia because he was certain it would end badly, like all the others before him. Now, because of the baby, he hadn't allowed himself to consider any other alternative than them being successful. There was no way he would be sleeping anytime soon. Tossing and turning was more like it. Amelia needed her rest, and that meant he needed to sleep in his own room tonight.

"No," he said, stepping away as she slipped off the last of her clothes.

Amelia slipped under the covers and Tyler pulled the comforter up as if he was tucking a small child into bed. She pouted a little, but the soft pillows quickly lured her into the twilight before sleep, wiping worries from her mind. "Good night, Tyler," she said as her eyes fluttered closed.

"Good night," he replied, looking down as she drifted off to sleep. Tyler couldn't make himself walk away, like he should. He just stood there, watching the soft rise and fall of her chest and the faint smile that curled her pink lips in her sleep. She was the most precious thing he'd ever had in his life. And soon, they would have a child—maybe with the same rosy cheeks and flash of red hair.

Failure was simply not an option. That had been the motto of his life since he was eighteen years old and decided to get into the jewelry business. He hadn't had a family legacy or a lick of experience, but that hadn't stopped him. He had drive. Ambition. A fire that pushed him to succeed in everything in life. It was a passion Amelia lit in him.

That same passion would carry over into their relationship, as well. At the end of thirty days, Tyler would be successful in making Amelia fall in love with him. He might not be in love with her, but it didn't matter. He wasn't the one hell-bent on a perfect love. He just wanted a happy family, and he didn't intend to let this woman and their child slip through his fingers.

Eight

"I can drive, Tyler." Amelia frowned at him as she stared down his new Audi with disdain. "You don't even know where my doctor's office is."

"You can tell me," he said as he opened the passenger door for her to get in. Why would she rather ride in her old SUV than his brand-new luxury vehicle? He had heated leather seats. Individualized climate controls. It was like floating on a cloud to their destination.

She crossed her arms over her chest. "How can I convince you that pregnancy is not a disability? I'm perfectly capable of driving my own car to the doctor's office."

Ah, it wasn't the car. It was him driving it. Too bad. His willingness to do whatever made her happy went only so far. He was going to take care of her whether she liked it or not. "If I had truly thought that about you, the acrobatics in bed last night would've persuaded me to believe otherwise."

Amelia's eyes grew wide, then a smile chased away her irritation. "Quit it," she scolded.

"I will, but how can I convince *you* that letting other people help you isn't a crime?" He stood looking at her expectantly until she finally gave in and climbed into his car. "See?" he said. "That wasn't so bad, was it?"

She didn't respond. Once he got in the car and they started out toward the doctor's office, she turned to look at him again. "You make me crazy sometimes."

He gave her a sly smile in return. "Ditto, sweetheart. You know, you gave me this big, looming deadline to steal your heart, but you fight me at every turn."

Tyler's thoughts drifted to her concerned question from Saturday night. She hadn't broached the subject again since then, but he hadn't been able to put it aside in his own mind. If she didn't love him at the end of thirty days, it wouldn't be for his lack of trying. But would their friendship survive it? He'd insisted everything would be fine and dismissed any concerns because he didn't intend to lose, but could they be friends with a baby? Could they go back to where they came from, knowing what they knew about each other? "How am I supposed to woo you when you won't let me do anything for you?"

"We must have different definitions of wooing. I don't consider it very romantic to drive a woman around everywhere against her will and treat her like a fragile flower."

"That's your problem," Tyler noted. "I don't think you know what love is really about."

"What?" She looked at him with wide eyes as she scoffed at his suggestion. "Love is my business."

"Food is your business. Love is your obsessive ideal, but you don't really understand it. You think love and romance is just about those big gestures—expensive gifts, fancy dinners and moonlit declarations of undying devotion."

"What is wrong with all those things?"

Tyler sighed. "Nothing is wrong with them. It's just that none of that lasts. Flowers die, food gets eaten, words are forgotten. Fifty years from now, when we're sitting in our favorite chairs watching our grandkids play, that's not what you'll remember about our life together. You'll remember the little things, the things you don't give me credit for doing now because they don't fit your ideal."

"You get credit for everything you do," she argued. "I just feel helpless when you drive me around and carry things."

"That is your hang-up, not mine. I'm just being nice. But I could go bigger if you want me to. Would you like me to buy you a new car? That would be a big romantic gesture."

"You are not buying me a car. No way. I don't care how much money you have just lying around, it's a ridiculous suggestion."

"See?" he said, with a shake of his head. "I can't win."

At that, Amelia chuckled. "You're married, Tyler. You'd better get used to that."

That was certainly right. He wished Amelia didn't question the motives of every little thing he did. Somehow being nice seemed to get him in trouble, although he didn't really mind it. He didn't do it on purpose, but he got a little thrill when Amelia got irritated with him. A becoming flush would rush to her cheeks and a flash of emotion would light up her dark eyes. She was a beautiful, passionate woman. He'd had the good fortune to share her bed the past two nights and had taken full advantage of that fire in her. That didn't mean that he didn't enjoy winding her up and watching her spin in the daytime.

He hadn't wanted to push their physical relationship too hard. They'd come together suddenly that first night in the house, and he could tell she was apprehensive about it. Their night together in Vegas had been fueled by raw emotions and alcohol. The second by the delirium of sleep and fierce desires. Since then, he'd thought she'd want some space, but it had been the opposite. She seemed to have abandoned all her reservations about their physical connection. Which he didn't mind at all. But somehow it didn't feel as though they were making relationship progress. It just felt like sex.

What universe was he living in where just having sex with a beautiful woman was somehow less than fulfilling? He was turning into a teenage girl.

Speaking of girls, the doctor's waiting room was crawling with women when they arrived. They checked in, then found a pair of seats among the sea of other ladies waiting. Tyler wasn't certain he'd seen that many women together at once. Young ones, old ones, pregnant ones, ones with babies in carriers... At the moment, he was the only man and feeling very out of place.

"Maybe I should—" he began, but stopped when another man came in with a pregnant woman.

"Are you trying to punk out on me?" Amelia asked with a teasing smile.

"Well, I just wasn't sure. I didn't know what the protocol was for this kind of thing."

Amelia patted his arm, reassuringly. "Daddies can come. Relax. You may just have to look the other way when there are lady parts involved."

"Lady parts?" he asked with a frown.

"I know you're familiar with them, but this is a whole new ball game. Just remember, if you're uncomfortable seeing them, just think how uncomfortable I am putting them on display and subjecting them to various...things."

Things? Tyler swallowed hard. There was a lot to this baby-having business he hadn't considered before.

"Amelia Kennedy?" the nurse called from the doorway.

Amelia got up and slung her purse over her shoulder. Despite his trepidations, Tyler followed her to the doorway, pausing only when the nurse smiled at him and held up her hand to stop him.

"Sir, we're going to take her back to change, get her health history and do a quick pelvic exam. If you'd prefer, I can come back for you when that's done and the doctor is ready to do the ultrasound and chat with you both."

"Absolutely," he said, looking visibly relieved.

Amelia smiled and patted his shoulder. "Saved by the nurse. It shouldn't be long. Read some parenting magazines."

Tyler nodded blankly and returned to his seat. About a half hour later, the same nurse returned and waved him over. He followed her through a maze of corridors, finally stopping at an exam room with a closed door. She knocked softly and entered.

He paused just as he crossed over the threshold into the domain of the female. Amelia was lying back on the table with her feet up. She had a paper sheet draped over her, but his eyes still widened as he took it all in. "The nurse said we were going to do an ultrasound. I thought that meant rubbing gel on your stomach."

"That's for later trimesters," the doctor explained, gesturing toward a stool where he could sit by Amelia's side. "A transvaginal ultrasound gives us a better picture of what's going on early in the pregnancy."

Amelia took his hand and tugged until he sat down.

"We're watching the television screen. Stay north of the sheet and you'll be fine."

Tyler nodded and watched the screen intently as the blurry gray images swirled around. A black circle came into focus and inside it, a tiny gray blob that looked a little like a pinto or kidney bean.

"There's your baby," the doctor announced.

Tyler watched the screen with a touch of disbelief. It didn't look anything like a baby. And yet, his focus narrowed in on the image as if everything else in the room ceased to exist. Up until this moment, the baby had still been a vague concept to him, a challenge he had to face head-on. He'd accepted its existence and had planned how he would care for it when it arrived, but it was still an idea. Suddenly seeing it on the screen made it a person— a tiny little person that he and Amelia had made.

"Wow," Tyler said.

Amelia turned to him and smiled. "Look what we did." Her cheeks were flushed pink and she had glassy tears in her eyes.

Truthfully, he was fighting the same reaction himself. Tyler gripped her hand tightly as the doctor took size measurements and put information into the system.

"What is that little flicker of movement there?" Tyler pointed at the screen. For the most part, the baby was still, but a small section seemed to be pulsing.

"That is the heart beating," the doctor said. "It looks good, too. Nice and strong, considering how early it is."

"Can we hear it?" Amelia asked.

"It's too early to pick up with the Doppler, but it should certainly be audible when you come back in four weeks for your next checkup. That will give you two something to look forward to. Laura is going to print out a couple shots of the ultrasound images for you to take home and show the grandparents," the doctor said. "It's your baby's first picture."

A soft sigh slipped through Amelia's lips as she watched the blurry image. The expression of awe on her face had faded to a faint sadness. Maybe Tyler only noticed it because he knew her so well. It was no surprise that the doctor's words would distress her. A lot of these early milestones in the baby's development would go uncelebrated by friends and family. The excitement, the hugs, the discussion of baby showers and nursery furniture… There would be none of that, at least for now. At some point they would make the happy announcement of her pregnancy to their parents, but would it be tempered by the news that they weren't marrying or even in love?

Little Bean's grandparents would have to wait awhile before they got to learn about his or her existence, much less see the ultrasound photos. Everything would stay under wraps for at least another twenty-two days while he and Amelia figured out what they were doing.

"Okay, we're done here," the doctor said. He helped Amelia sit up and scoot back on the table. "You can go ahead and get dressed, then Laura will bring you back to my office, where we can go over the new-pregnancy packet and you can ask any questions you might have."

They thanked the doctor and Tyler waited outside while Amelia redressed. The meeting with the doctor was pretty short. All their questions seemed to vanish when they were put on the spot, but the doctor laughed and said that was common. That was why they sent parents away with all the paperwork that would answer the questions they remembered once they got home.

When they got back into the car to leave, Tyler noticed Amelia flipping through the massive package with a wide-eyed expression of panic. "There's a lot of stuff in here to read."

"We'll go over it tonight. What do you say we go by the bookstore and pick up some of those baby books you wanted? Then we can get some Chinese takeout, and we can spread all of it across the bed and go through it together. How does that sound?"

"Better," she said with a soft smile. Amelia might be worried about what they faced, but the idea of tackling this together seemed to soothe her concerns for the moment. "Thank you. There's just a lot to think about."

"Sure. But we can handle it. Humans have done it for thousands of years, and most of them without books or handouts to help them. It will be just fine." Tyler tried to think of a distraction, and the weight of the box in his coat pocket reminded him he had a gift for her. He'd had it for a couple days but hadn't found the right time to give it to her yet. "I've got a surprise for you."

She set the paperwork aside and looked at him suspiciously. Amelia wasn't big on surprises, good or bad. "Will I like this surprise?"

"I think so. I bought you something at the Travis auction the other day."

Amelia's nose wrinkled. "I have enough jewelry, Tyler. I know that's your business, but I don't know what to do with all the pieces you've already given me."

"It's not jewelry." He pulled the long, narrow box from his lapel pocket.

"It looks like jewelry," she argued as she took it from him.

Tyler watched her open the box, revealing the delicate silver spoon inside. It had a long, thin handle with a grip designed to look like a crescent-shaped man in the moon. A small diamond was embedded in the eye of the moon. "What do you think?"

Amelia's brow knit together as she examined the box, but no words came. She lifted it, turning the spoon in her fingers and examining the excruciatingly detailed handle.

"It was a gift to Patty from Elvis Presley when she had her first son, Martin. I thought you might like it. You said I wasn't allowed to get any furniture or things like that until after we make it out of the first trimester, but this is a little thing. I hope you don't mind."

"No, I don't mind. It's beautiful." She ran her fingertip over it and placed it back in the box. "Thank you."

He noticed a hesitation in her. He'd noticed it a lot lately. She seemed to second-guess everything he did outside of the bedroom. "But?" he pressed.

"Well," she said with a smile, "I just never dreamed I'd have a baby born with a silver spoon in its mouth."

"These are super yum. I vote for Tasty Temptations."

Amelia turned to look across the conference room table at Gretchen. Between them was an assortment of platters and dishes, food courtesy of the five catering companies they'd interviewed today. Each company had been asked to bring menus, customer references and a sample each of an appetizer and a main course. They were also each asked to replicate one of Amelia's trademark dishes in case a customer requested something specific while she was gone.

"I don't know," Bree said. "We've used Bites of Nashville a couple times, like when Amelia went to Vegas. I feel like they should get priority."

"The only thing I'm loyal to is this little cheeseburger." Gretchen was enamored with a tiny Kobe beef slider by

Tasty Temptations. It had tomato aioli and a tiny, fresh-baked yeast bun.

That was all nice, but Amelia didn't feel charitable. None of the catering companies had really blown her away. "They were okay," she said.

"Okay? Come on, Amelia." Natalie groaned, putting her tablet down on the table beside a platter of Bellinis with assorted toppings. "I'm as big a stickler for perfection as anyone, but you're unreasonably nitpicking. Every company we saw today was great. They were professional and the food was tasty and creative. Chef on Wheels replicated your gorgonzola-and-cracked-black-pepper tenderloin flawlessly. I couldn't tell you hadn't made it."

Amelia frowned at her coworkers. Maybe the hormones were making her oversensitive, but she couldn't help it. Flawlessly? Why should she be happy that someone had been able to copy one of her featured dishes so easily? "I'm sorry, but I'm not that enthusiastic about being supplanted. It's hard to think about someone coming into this place and doing my job. Taking over my role. We'll see how you guys like it when we interview your replacements."

"You know we could never replace you," Bree soothed. "You make the most amazing cream puffs on the planet. But remember, you're the one that got pregnant. We wouldn't be going through this if you weren't going to be out for weeks at a time. And before that, you're going to need help when you're in your third trimester and can't stay on your feet for sixteen hours straight."

"That's not going to be for months," Amelia argued.

"We've got to start the process now, even though you're still perfectly capable of doing the job." Natalie put a hand on her shoulder. "Think about this with your businesswoman cap on, okay? If one of us was going to be away for weeks, we'd need to get a backup set up as soon as we could. Right?"

Amelia sighed. "Yes, I know. You're right. It's just hard."

"Frankly," Natalie continued, "we need to have a backup on standby for all our roles. With your pregnancy we have advance warning, but the blizzard snapped up Bree with no notice at all. Fortunately, we had Willie to fill in, but there's nothing like that for the rest of us."

"Maybe this will help with the vacation issue," Bree said. "We're all pretty burned out, but we're booked solid until the end of next year. We need to be able to take time off. I'm going to want to go on a honeymoon after Ian and I get married. Gretchen has been dying to go to Italy for years. I'm sure there's something you'd rather do than sit behind that desk and work every day, Natalie. Even if one of us just wants to lie on the couch for a week and binge on television, we can't as things stand now."

"How about this?" Amelia offered. "Instead of bringing in a catering company, why don't we hire someone else to help in the kitchen? I didn't realize how much help I could use until Tyler pitched in last weekend. We bring someone in, and then I can spend the next few months getting them trained and comfortable. Maybe we keep Bites of Nashville or one of the others on standby for big events, but there's always someone from our team here."

Natalie thought over her suggestion and nodded. "That's not a bad idea. That way we always have one of our people with eyes on the product. Any ideas on a candidate?"

"I was thinking about Stella."

"From the serving team?" Natalie asked.

Amelia nodded. On wedding days, a restaurant agency provided them with a team of servers to work the front and back of the house with her. Stella was one of the employees who was consistently sent over. She preferred working in the kitchen and had told Amelia she was about to graduate from culinary school in the spring. "She's finishing school in May. That will give us all summer to get her up to speed. By the time my due date comes, she'll do fine with smaller projects and managing the outside caterer if we need one."

"Okay, I'll get her information from the agency and we'll bring her in for a chat." Natalie started tapping on her tablet, capturing the important information. "Now, in the meantime, we still need to pick a backup caterer. I want to have someone on standby."

"Yeah," Gretchen said with a sly grin on her face. "One of us might up and go to London on short notice or something."

Amelia's head snapped up in Gretchen's direction. London? Why would she say London? She and Tyler had discussed that very possibility two weeks ago, but she hadn't said anything to them. Not even in casual discussion. "Is someone going to London?"

Bree snorted into her hand. "You are, dummy."

Amelia's eyes widened in surprise. "I am? Since when?"

"Since Tyler came by last Friday," Natalie informed her. "Before he went into the kitchen to help you, he stopped by my office and asked about the possibility of taking you on a business trip with him. I thought it was nice of him to check before he broached the subject."

Amelia felt the heat of irritation rise to her cheeks. Tyler had the ability to coax an emotional response from her faster than anyone else, for good and bad reasons. She should've known he was up to something. Things had been going too well. It had been over a week since

the doctor's appointment, and it had been smooth sailing. They'd enjoyed their evenings together, read baby
books together, argued about names and laughed together. "Well, it would've been nice if he'd said something to *me* about it! Anyone care to tell me when I'm
going to London?"

"Sunday," Natalie replied.

It was Thursday afternoon. "*This* Sunday? You're kidding, right?"

"No, he told me the date." Natalie looked down at her
tablet. "Yep, March 8. That's Sunday."

Amelia gritted her teeth together. This was *so* like
Tyler—doing whatever it took to get his way without considering what she wanted or how she felt about it. "I'm
gonna kill him. We'll need a backup caterer because I'm
going to be in jail for fifteen to life."

"Are you mad?" Gretchen asked. "Seriously? Your
husband wants to take you on a spur-of-the-moment trip
to London and you're upset about it? I can't get a guy to
take me on a spur-of-the-moment trip to Burger King."

"I'm not mad because he wants to take me to London.
I'm mad because he went behind my back and set it all
up without asking me first."

"That's because you would've said no," Bree pointed
out.

Amelia sat back in her chair and crossed her arms over
her chest. "So what? It's irresponsible of me to leave on
short notice. I just took off time for my reunion, and as
we've discussed, I'll be out again in the fall. I shouldn't
take off more time just for the hell of it."

"Tyler said he'd have you back Thursday night," Natalie reasoned. "Technically, you wouldn't miss anything.
We're not doing the cake next week. They're ordering

a cupcake display from a local vendor. But I think you should take the rest of the weekend off anyway."

"Why?"

"You'll be jet-lagged, for one thing," Natalie said. "You're not going to feel like working when you get back."

"You also need to spend some quality time with Tyler," Bree added. "The clock is ticking down on this relationship trial run of yours. You guys have been so busy worrying about renting a house and dealing with baby stuff. Going someplace romantic might be nice. Go and try to enjoy yourself. Roam the streets of London and let yourself fall in love."

In love? Things had been going well, but somehow the thought of that still seemed ridiculous. Amelia did love Tyler, but she was pretty certain being in love was not going to be an option. There were only two weeks left. They were comfortable together, yes. And the sex had been...noteworthy. But love? Amelia had never been in love, but she figured it would take a lot more than a stroll along the Thames to get them there.

Nine

"I think I might be sick."

Tyler snapped to attention, moving to Amelia's side as they stood on the curb in front of Sotheby's auction house. Her color looked okay, her cheeks pink from the chill of the early-March London air. "What? Are you nauseated again? There's a trash can over there."

Amelia smiled and took his hand. "Sorry, I didn't mean I was really sick. The idea of all those diamonds and millions of dollars changing hands was just enough to make me ill."

"Oh," he said with a chuckle as relief washed over him. Amelia had seemed to be doing better with her morning sickness, especially since they'd arrived in London, so he'd been surprised by her sudden declaration. An auction of this caliber could be intimidating to a first timer. Some of the world's greatest jewels and antiques passed through the doors of this auction house, along with the ridiculous amounts of money that went with them.

"I thought maybe the chocolate tea at the Landmark Hotel had turned on you. We ate so much I was miserable through half the auction."

"Oh, no," Amelia argued. "That food was amazing. The one at Fortnum and Mason yesterday was good, too. French macarons are my new favorite thing and I plan to master them the moment we get back home. I think they'd make a lovely item for a dessert display, especially in the wedding colors."

They'd arrived in London early the previous day. The jet lag had been rough on them both, so he'd taken her on a quick drive around the city and they'd had a classic tea before checking into their hotel. Today they'd tried the tea at their hotel before coming to the auction. They were eating their way through London.

"I just love the idea of having afternoon tea," she continued. "That's usually when I get peckish, so it's perfect. A scone and tea is preferable to the soda and candy bar I typically end up eating. I don't know why Americans don't have teatime. It makes us seem so uncivilized, somehow."

"I just spent two hundred and twenty thousand dollars on a diamond-and-pearl tiara from the nineteenth century. That seems pretty civilized to me."

Amelia shook her head and tugged him down the street. "Maybe if you wore the tiara while having tea."

Tyler laughed, following her. Looking the way she did today, he'd follow her anywhere. She was wearing a stunning cobalt-blue wool jacket that came down past her knees to keep her warm. The bright color popped against her fair skin and fiery red hair. Combined with the pregnancy, she was damn near glowing. Beneath her coat, she was wearing a more muted dress with a gray-and-blue geometric design. She'd paired the outfit with sapphire earrings he'd sent her for Christmas the year before. Seeing how radiant the color was on her, Tyler regretted passing up a brilliant sapphire choker that had been auctioned off earlier that afternoon.

"Where are we headed?" he asked when they'd traveled several blocks away from Sotheby's and in the opposite direction of their hotel.

"You're going to take me for a ride on the London Eye."

"I am?" The giant Ferris wheel overlooking the Thames hadn't been in Tyler's plans at all, but he didn't mind going. He'd never ridden it. His past trips to London had been focused on jewels and finding a good chip shop. "I thought we were going to dinner after the auction."

"We will, but I'm not hungry yet after that big tea. We'll eat after you take me on the Eye."

"Okay," Tyler relented, raising his hand to hail a cab. It was probably a good night to ride the Eye anyway. London had remarkably clear skies for this time of year, so they'd have a nice view. By the time they got there, it would just be sunset, when the sky would glow orange and the lights of the city would start to illuminate. It would actually be a great romantic opportunity if not for the herd of other tourists in the capsule with them.

Of course, he could fix that. She wanted the big romantic gestures, right?

After climbing into a cab, Tyler pulled out his phone and found the number of the agency that handled special events on the Eye. By the time they reached the busy plaza and long, winding queue, he'd arranged for a private go-around.

The London Eye was massive, dominating the landscape along the river. It seemed ridiculous to call the large white structure with its space-age pods a Ferris wheel, but he supposed that was what it was.

As they approached the VIP entrance he'd been directed to, a small woman with short brown hair and an immaculate black suit greeted them. "Mr. Dixon? I'm Mary, your personal London Eye hostess. We have your private capsule waiting for you."

Amelia looked at him with surprise lighting her eyes. She'd obviously gotten too used to tuning out his phone conversations, assuming they were all about work. She hadn't paid a bit of attention to the intentionally vague yet still decipherable discussion he'd had with the Eye offices. He hadn't been trying to make it a surprise, but he was pleased to see she hadn't anticipated it.

"A private capsule?" she asked with a wide grin. "Really?"

Tyler smiled and gestured for her to go ahead of him and follow behind Mary. They bypassed the hundreds of people lined up and were escorted onto the next available capsule.

"Your three-hundred-and-sixty-degree maps are on the bench. Enjoy the ride," Mary said before the capsule was closed and locked.

"Off we go," Tyler said as the glass bubble moved up and away from the platform. He followed Amelia to the far side of the car overlooking the Thames. The sun was just setting, and the blazing orange-and-red sky illuminated the boats traveling up and down the river and the cars crossing the bridges beside them. The Parliament building, Big Ben and Westminster Abbey beyond it glowed brightly in the evening light. Turning to look the opposite direction, he recognized other famous buildings, like the Gherkin and the Shard, against the skyline.

It was an amazing view at any time of day, but Tyler was certain he'd hit the jackpot tonight. Not only was it the perfect time, but he had a beautiful woman there with him. She had been resistant to coming on this trip at first, especially since he'd planned it as a surprise and gone around her, as she'd put it, but she'd really warmed up to the idea. He'd been to London enough that he didn't get the surge of excitement when he saw one of the famous landmarks. With Amelia here, he was experiencing the city anew. It made him want to take her with him everywhere he went, and if he couldn't do that, he'd rather stay at home and send one of his employees instead.

Amelia's back was to him as she gazed out at the panorama before them. Her red hair was pulled up today, revealing the long line of her neck. He wanted to lean in to her and place a kiss against her sensitive skin. He wanted to hear her gasp with surprise and moan softly as the sensations he coaxed from her rushed through her body.

Stepping up behind Amelia, he leaned in and grasped the railings on each side of her. He rested his chin on her shoulder, breathing in the scent of her.

"It's beautiful," she whispered.

"You're beautiful," Tyler countered, and wrapped his arms around her waist. She leaned back against him, sighing with contentment as their tiny bubble rose higher and higher around the wheel. The view was spectacular, but the longer they spent pressed against each other, the less interested Tyler was in the landscape.

He swept a stray strand of red hair out of the way and pressed his lips to her skin. Amelia gasped and tilted her head to the side to give him better access. He moved across her throat, teasing her with his lips, teeth and tongue. She held still, only her rapid draws of breath giving away her building arousal. His desire for her was harder to disguise. The minute he touched her, the blood rushed to his extremities and he was overwhelmed by the throbbing need to possess his wife.

His wife. Funny how he'd come to think of her that way in only a few short weeks. He'd gotten used to spending the evenings with her, watching her cook and testing her new recipes. He liked falling asleep with her in his arms and waking up to her grumpy morning face. Tyler needed Amelia to fall in love with him. He couldn't bear to lose all this in a week's time.

Just as they crested the top of the Eye, he slipped a hand beneath her coat and cupped one large breast. He could feel the nipple form into a hard peak beneath his touch, straining through the fabric to reach him. Amelia arched her back as he stroked her flesh, pressing her round backside into the firm heat of his desire.

Tyler groaned aloud, the sound echoing in the capsule. He was overcome by the driving need to touch her, bury himself in her and lose all rational thought in loving her. But damned if they weren't four hundred feet in the air, enclosed in a clear bubble with tourists on both sides of them and a closed-circuit camera recording their every movement. It was the most seemingly private yet agonizingly public scenario he could've possibly put them in.

Amelia turned in his arms to face him as they started descending back toward the ground. She slipped her arms around his neck, lacing her fingers together at the nape. She did look beautiful today. And this was an amazingly romantic moment. And yet he couldn't stop from voicing the concerns that had been plaguing him for over a week. They had to get past this.

"Amelia?" he said, his voice near shaking with adrenaline and need.

"Yes?"

"Will you love me?" he asked.

A seductive smile curled her lips. "Absolutely."

Tyler softly shook his head. She'd answered too quickly, so he was certain she misunderstood. "That's not what I meant," he corrected. Amelia had given him her body, but it wasn't enough. He wanted more. He wanted to break through her walls and topple all her misconceptions about love. He knew her well enough to know he couldn't force his way into her heart. She had to let him in. "Will you give me your heart?"

Her eyes widened, her mouth falling open without words.

"I want this to work between us, Amelia. I want you to fall in love with me, so we can have a family and all the wonderful things you've always dreamed of. But you have to stop fighting it. Are you ever going to let yourself fall in love with me?"

There was a long silence, a painful one, but when she finally did speak, it made him yearn for the quiet again.

"You're asking me to give you something with nothing in return."

It was Tyler's turn to look at her with wide-eyed surprise. "What do you mean?"

"Through this whole thing, you've been on a mission to make *me* fall in love with *you*—and you're succeeding, even if you don't feel that way. But you're right, I am holding back, and it's because I get the feeling that *you're* not letting yourself fall in love with *me*. You had it rough with Christine. I know that. Breaking off the engagement a week before the wedding was just cruel, especially if she knew she'd had doubts about the two of you. She hurt you. You wouldn't ever talk about it, but I can tell by the way you changed after that. All work, all the time."

He didn't like talking about what happened with Christine, even with Amelia. Talking about it meant that he would have to face his first big failure in life. To talk about how he couldn't measure up, no matter what. He'd rather just pretend it hadn't happened. "I have a business to run," he argued.

"So do I. That's no excuse. You're just hiding away. You might have lost her, but in the process, I almost lost you, too. You buried yourself in your work, flying so much the flight attendants know you by name. But you need to clip those wings of yours if we're going to make this work. I think both of us are trying so desperately to protect our hearts, so afraid this isn't going to succeed and we're going to lose everything we have.

"I will let myself fall in love with you, Tyler," she continued, "but you have to let yourself do the same."

Tyler swallowed hard, hearing the truth in her words but not knowing quite how to address it. He had held a part of himself back, and he still wasn't certain he could give all of himself the way he had before. It was a scary prospect, even as desperately as he wanted the life they could have together. But they'd never have the chance if he didn't give in. Or at least, let her think that he had.

"You're right," he said, forcing himself to smile at her reassuringly. "From now on, no holding back. I will let myself love you and you will let yourself love me."

A brilliant smile lit her face. Before he could react, her lips met his. He was happy to close his eyes and lose himself in the physical contact that had been his comfort these past few weeks. This was the kiss that was supposed to mark the change in their relationship for the better. They were giving in, and he needed to make her believe his words.

He pressed into her, pushing her back to mold her

against the concave wall of the capsule. Her mouth was soft and welcoming in juxtaposition to his hard advance. His tongue forced its way into her mouth, demanding she give him more, and she gladly complied. She pressed her breasts against his chest and met his every advance.

How had he been so blind to this for so long? Amelia was perfect for him in so many ways. She knew just how to touch him, just how to handle his every mood. She wasn't afraid to call him on his crap. And when it came down to it, he'd never been as attracted to a woman in his life as he was to her. From the first day he laid eyes on her freshman year, he'd known he was hers, be they friends or lovers. When they'd decided on friends, he'd shelved the attraction and kept his distance. Why, even now, he was resistant to let go. The minute he gave in to how badly he wanted her everything would fall apart.

At that unnerving thought, he pulled away. The moment their lips parted, the lights of the Eye illuminated and they were suddenly surrounded by its haunting blue glow. Amelia looked up at him, the lights and shadows highlighting the contours of her delicate features. Her smile was devoid of the pink lipstick she'd had on when they entered the Eye.

"Let's go back to the hotel," Amelia said, her voice breathy.

"You don't want to go to dinner?" he asked.

"No," she replied adamantly. "Take me back to the hotel right now or risk me doing something scandalous to you in this plastic bubble where everyone can see us."

As appealing as that sounded, Tyler could see the loading platform approaching below. They wouldn't have enough time to start anything interesting—or at least not to finish it—before the cops arrested them both.

"To the hotel it is."

* * *

The moment they touched back down on solid earth, they rushed to get a cab to the hotel. Amelia's heart was racing in her chest the entire way there, and when they pulled up outside the Landmark Hotel, she felt a tightness, like a vise closing down on her rib cage.

It wasn't making love to Tyler that made her anxious. She had a thirst for him that never seemed to be satiated. It was their conversation on the Eye that worried her. She'd told him that she sensed he was afraid to give himself fully to the relationship, but there was more to it than just fear. Yes, he might be worried about losing their friendship or afraid of getting hurt again, but there was something else. He'd never seriously pursued her before now. Not once in all these years. But the moment a baby had come into the picture, Tyler had been ready to swoop in and claim her as his own.

Which raised the painful question she didn't really want to face—was Tyler only here for the baby?

Did he really want them to fall in love, or did he just want Amelia to love him enough to stay in the relationship for the sake of their child? She had a miserable track record—she knew that. If not for the baby, she probably wouldn't have let their relationship go on this long, in truth. She would've found some reason why it wouldn't work. But now she was having feelings for Tyler. Real feelings that went far beyond friendship. Far beyond loving him, but not being *in love* with him.

But she didn't get the same vibes from Tyler. It felt more like…an obligation, despite him telling her he was going to stop holding back.

Amelia shuddered at the thought. She never wanted anyone to be with her just because he thought he had to be. Tyler was attracted to her—there was no doubt of that—but could they have more?

The thoughts weighed heavy in her mind, even as they made their way through the stunning eight-story atrium of the hotel. She barely saw it, or any of the other remarkable features about their historic, hundred-year-old hotel. It wasn't until they reached their suite that Amelia pushed the doubts out of her mind, just as she pushed Tyler's suit coat over his shoulders. As they had nearly every night since they'd shared a home, she wanted to lose her worries in Tyler's arms.

His jacket fell to the floor along with her own blue coat. Tyler pulled her into his arms and kissed her until she was nearly breathless. "I've never wanted a woman as badly as I want you tonight," he said, his voice low and rough.

Amelia's anxiety faded at the sound of his voice. It wasn't all about the baby. His desire for her was real enough. She gave him a wicked, knowing grin and tugged at his tie. They shed clothing as they made it through the seating area to the large ivory-draped bed. Tyler whipped back the duvet and the flat sheet, then slipped out of his pants and eased onto the bed. Their make-out session on the Eye had certainly fired up his engine, and he was clearly ready for a long, exhilarating drive.

Kicking out of her heels, Amelia didn't waste any time joining him in the bedroom. She'd been feeling a little feisty when she'd packed for this trip. Beneath her modest dress today, she'd opted for a lacy black demibra with matching panties and garter belt. The sheer black silk stockings were topped with lace that contrasted sharply with her pale skin.

Tyler's mouth dropped open when her dress fell to the ground and she exposed the sexy lingerie she'd kept hid-

den all day. She did a little twirl, showcasing the revealing thong cut of the panties before slipping her thumbs
beneath the sides and sliding them down her legs. She'd
worn them outside the garter belt just for this reason. "Do
you mind if I keep the rest on?" she asked innocently.

A frantic shake of his head was all she received in
reply. Approaching the bed, she crawled slowly across
it, putting the brakes on his rapid-fire seduction. When
she reached the hard-carved muscles of Tyler's bare ab-
domen, she threw one leg over his torso and straddled
him. The movement immediately brought their most sensitive parts into contact, and the sensation brought a gasp
of pleasure to her lips and a wicked smile to her face.

"All day?" He groaned. "You've been wearing that
all day?"

"Mmm-hmm," she hummed, reaching for the pins
holding up her hair. When she removed the third and
final one, her red curls spilled down over her shoulders,
and she shook them out to great effect.

Tyler's palms slid up her silky thighs, running his fingertips over the silver snaps of the garters and lacy tops
of the stockings. "I…" he began, but Amelia brought a
finger to his lips to quiet him.

They had done enough talking for today. There had
been too many emotions and too much angst. Right now
she just wanted to lose herself in making love to him. He
wanted her to let go, and tonight, she would.

Rising up onto her knees, Amelia planted her hands
on the pillows on both sides of Tyler's head. Her breasts
nearly tumbled from their confines as she moved, but
he was quick to offer his hands to support them. As he
kneaded her flesh, she slowly moved back, finding his
firm heat and easing the length of him inside her hot,
aching body.

Sitting up, Amelia rocked her hips forward, the pleasure of the moment forcing her eyes shut. It was better that way, so she kept them closed. With her eyes shut, she could focus on the feeling of Tyler's hands cupping her breasts and teasing her nipples through the lace. She could absorb every powerful sensation as she moved her hips and forced the length of him deeper inside her body. She could hear Tyler's murmurs of encouragement, her own soft gasps, the faint squeak of the bed as she moved…

But most of all, she could focus on the feeling deep in her chest. It was there, as she gave herself to Tyler, that she really opened up. He'd asked her tonight to let him in, to allow herself to love him, so she would. As though she'd turned the key in a rusty, old lock, she opened herself up to the emotions she'd held at bay for so long.

It was a stunning moment when the feelings hit her. The warmth of love heated her from the inside out, with tears forming in the corners of her eyes. But along with the feeling was a revelation she'd never expected—she not only loved Tyler, but she always had. No other man would ever meet her stringent qualifications because no other man could be Tyler. He was her better half, the part she'd always searched for and failed to find because she'd refused to look in the most obvious of places.

And now she was giving herself to him, heart and soul.

"Amelia…" Tyler groaned, bringing his hands to her hips. His palms cupped the lace-covered curve of her rear, guiding her movements, and she knew neither of them would be able to last much longer.

She placed her hands on his chest, one covering the rapid tattoo of his heart. Moving more forcefully, she quickly drove herself to the edge. When her climax came, her whole body shook with the strength of it. Every nerve lit up; every muscle tensed. She cried out to the dim room, gasping for breath.

Tyler rode out her orgasm, then pressed his fingers hard into her soft flesh and drove into her from beneath until he shouted his own pleasure.

Unable to hold herself up any longer, Amelia collapsed against him. She buried her face in his neck, their bodies both trembling with the power of their release. She kept her hand over his heart as they lay there, feeling the beat slow along with their breaths.

She had given Tyler her heart. It was too late for her to consider fighting the feelings anymore. She just didn't have the strength. The thirty days would be up soon after they returned to Nashville, and she knew what her answer would be. She wanted to stay with him and start their family together.

The only problem was that Amelia wasn't entirely sure if she would ever have Tyler's love. He would stay for their child. She knew him well enough to know that. But that big fantasy of love she'd always dreamed of? That still seemed out of reach.

She couldn't have it when only one of the people had fallen in love.

Ten

"London was amazing," Amelia said to her coworkers seated around the conference room table of From This Moment. It seemed like forever since she'd been in the office, although it had just been a week. As Natalie had insisted, she didn't come in over the weekend. She'd been right about the jet lag. Friday, she'd nodded off whenever she had a quiet or still moment. "I take back every ugly thing I said about Tyler."

"I told you," Gretchen said. "What was the best part of the trip?"

"That's a hard one. The food was great. Seeing all the historic landmarks was nice, too. I think I ate my weight in scones."

"Has your morning sickness gone away?" Bree asked.

"Actually, yeah." She hadn't felt anything even close to queasiness since they'd gone to London. She'd had more energy, too, which had been nice to have on the trip. "I was so happy to be able to eat. Our hotel was beautiful. Everything there is so different, yet familiar. Well, aside from driving on the other side of the road. I very nearly got hit by cabs two or three times because I looked the wrong way before crossing the street. They even have big painted letters on the street that say 'look right' for idiots like me."

"You're probably not the only one to nearly get hit," Natalie noted.

"What about the lovin'?" Bree asked with a sneaky smile. Amelia could tell she wasn't the least bit interested in discussions of scones or old churches. "You've got a look about you today—a rosy, well-loved look."

"Bree!" Amelia complained, but she couldn't help smiling. Things had changed between her and Tyler in London. Once they'd both agreed to let down their barriers, their physical and emotional connection had become stronger than it had ever been. She still had a mountain to climb where Tyler and his emotions were concerned, but they'd made significant progress. "I do think we've had a bit of a breakthrough in the relationship."

"Are you in love?" Gretchen asked, perking up in her chair. "He has until Wednesday to make it happen, and judging by the fact that you can't stop smiling, I think Tyler was successful."

"I think he was, too," Amelia admitted.

"Have you said it to him?"

Amelia wrinkled her nose. "No. I want to wait until we reach the end of the thirty days and make it official. Besides, I've never said that to a man before. I'm a little nervous."

"Make him say it first," Natalie noted, her eyes never leaving her tablet.

That probably wasn't a bad idea. She still had her worries and reservations about how Tyler felt. Outwardly, he hadn't given her any reason to doubt he had feelings for her, but she couldn't shake it.

"Oh, I have gifts!" Amelia announced. "Hold on." She scuttled back to her office and returned with three goodie bags. Each held a Union Jack tin of buttery shortbread cookies, a canister of English breakfast tea and a sleeve of French macarons she'd bought at the Ladurée bakery inside Harrods department store.

Everyone was cooing over their gifts when Amelia's phone started to ring. She looked down to see her sister's number. That was odd. She and her sister weren't particularly close. Whitney took more after their mother, and they didn't see eye to eye on very much. They rarely talked on the phone unless it was a special occasion like a birthday or a holiday, and even then, it was a stilted conversation. The women around the table were closer to sisters than her biological one.

Amelia hit the button to dismiss the call. She would call Whitney back when the staff meeting was done. She'd already avoided too much of her work duties around here lately.

"I thought you guys might like them," she said, feeling her phone buzz with a voice mail message. Before she could say anything else, a text from her sister popped up.

Call me right now!

Amelia sighed. "Do you guys mind if I step out for a minute and call my sister back? She seems to be freaking out. I'm sure my parents have just done something to set her off."

"Sure, go ahead," Natalie said. "I'll just start going

over the weekend wedding with them. We can talk about how the catering went when you get back."

Amelia slipped out of the room and went to her office. A discussion with her sister meant sitting—and eventually taking some pain medication for the headache it would inevitably set off. She pulled a bottle of Tylenol out of her drawer and swallowed a couple with her bottle of water. Her lower back was already bothering her today, so she might as well take some pain relievers and kill two birds.

The phone rang only twice before her sister picked up. "You're married?" Whitney nearly squealed in her ear. "And I find out on Facebook. And pregnant, too! Are you kidding me? I know we aren't super close, but you could at least have done me and our parents the courtesy of telling us this directly before it hit the internet."

Amelia was so stunned by her sister's sharp accusations, she didn't know how to respond at first. It actually took her a moment to even process what she was going on about. Facebook? How the hell had any of that information gotten on Facebook? Of course she would've told her family, when she was ready to. Someone had just beaten her to the punch. She swallowed hard and tried to collect the wild emotions that had just been jump-started in her veins. "What are you talking about, Whitney?"

"A woman named Emily posted, and I quote, 'So excited to hear that my little brother Tyler has settled down and started a family with his best friend, Amelia. We've been waiting years for those two to get together. And a baby! So exciting!'"

There were no words. Her sister's fury was nothing compared to the hot blades of anger running through her own veins. He'd told his family. And his sister had put it on Facebook, tagging her so her own family and friends could see it.

They'd had an agreement. No one was supposed to know until they decided what they were going to do. Things had been going so well. The trip to London was amazing. She had finally let go of the last of her reservations and let herself fall in love with her best friend. There was absolutely no reason to go behind her back and tell his family.

Why would he do such a thing? Was he afraid that when the thirty days were up, she was going to walk away? Tyler was the kind of man who won at all costs. Was this his backup plan? A way of strong-arming her into doing what he wanted in the end? Did he think she would be coerced into staying with him if all their friends and family knew they were married and having a baby?

"Amelia!" her sister shouted through the phone when she didn't get a response. "What the hell is going on? Is it even true?"

There was no point in lying about it. That would just cause more confusion and lead to more phone calls. "Yes, it's true. I'm sorry I didn't call, but I didn't expect the news to get out before I could talk to everyone about it. Listen, I can't talk right now, Whitney."

Amelia hung up the phone and turned off the ringer. She was certain her sister would immediately call back and demand answers, but she wasn't ready to give anyone anything—aside from giving Tyler a piece of her mind.

Grabbing her purse from the bottom drawer of her desk, she got up and headed for the door. The short drive back to the house only served to make her angrier, especially when she rounded the fountain out front of their ridiculously big home.

Standing in the driveway, looking up at the massive

house, she realized this place was a metaphor for their entire relationship. Everything had been his way since the moment he arrived in Nashville. They didn't divorce because he didn't want to. They were dating because he insisted on it. They drove around in his car, moved into the house he chose, took the trips he needed to take, even when she had to work.

He knew just how to dangle the carrot to get her to go along with the way he wanted things to be. But this time he'd gone too far. She stomped up the stairs and through the living room to the keeping room, where Tyler had his desk and computer. He was happily typing away on his laptop, his mind probably focused on rubies and diamonds, giving no thought at all to what he'd done.

"You know," she started to speak, her voice trembling with anger she could barely contain, "I thought we had an agreement."

Tyler looked up, his pale eyes wide with sudden concern. "What? What's wrong, Ames?"

She held up her hand to silence him. "We went into this with just a few ground rules, but they were important ones. One rule was that we would give it thirty days, and if necessary, we'd part friends. Another was that we'd live together in this house the whole time. But the most important of all was our agreement that no one would know we were married and pregnant until we were ready to tell them. No one, Tyler! How could you do this?"

Tyler's expression hardened for a moment, his eyes unfocused as he seemed to be trying to piece things together. "What do you mean, how could I—"

"Facebook!" she shouted. "Of all the places."

"Facebook?" His eyebrows drew together in a confused frown. "I don't even have a Facebook account."

"Well, you know who does? My sister. And my

mother. And apparently, your bigmouthed sister Emily, who just announced to God and country that we eloped and we're having a baby."

The color instantly drained from Tyler's face as he processed her words. "Emily posted that on Facebook?"

"Yep," she said. A quick check of her account had confirmed that, plus a few more details that made it all the worse. She hadn't logged in since she'd gotten back from London, but there the post was, big as day, with lots of likes and congratulatory messages for the happy couple. It was when she saw the responses from her own friends, people who didn't even know Tyler, that she realized she'd been tagged in the post. "And Emily tagged me so it showed up in the news feed of everyone I'm friends with, too. The cat is out of the bag in a big way, so thanks a lot."

"Oh, no." Tyler groaned and covered his face with his hands. Now *he* was the nauseated one. He knew it. He knew he shouldn't have said a word to Jeremy. Now it had come back around to bite him. "Amelia, I had no idea that was going to happen."

She crossed her arms over her chest and narrowed her gaze at him in disbelief. "You told your gossipy sister the biggest possible secret and actually expected her to keep it? Are you insane? You should know better than that."

"No," Tyler insisted. "I never would've told Emily, and for that very reason. I told my brother. *Only* my brother. And it was almost a month ago, right after we got the house. He was needling me about why I was moving down here and wouldn't let it go. I told him in confidence. He was the only person I told. If my sister found out, it's Jeremy's fault."

"No, Tyler," Amelia corrected with a sharp tone. "It's

your fault. You're the one that told our secret when you knew you shouldn't. I don't understand why you would do that."

"I told you why!" He stood up from his seat and his fists pounded into the top of his oak desk to emphasize his answer. "I wanted someone in my family to know where I was, because unlike your neurotic crowd, I actually like my family. I chose Jeremy because I thought he would be the least likely to pry, but I was wrong and I ended up having to tell him. I assure you that he and I are going to have a long talk about keeping confidences."

Amelia shook her head and planted her hands on her hips. She winced slightly and squeezed her eyes shut, not responding immediately.

"It was an accident," Tyler continued. "I'm sorry that it got out, but we're only a few days away from telling everyone anyway. Of course, I didn't want my family to find out on the internet, but there's not much we can do about it now. The sooner we stop fighting, the sooner we can start calling everyone and doing damage control."

"And tell them what, Tyler?"

Tyler opened his mouth but paused. "What do you mean, tell them what?"

"What are we telling them? The thirty days aren't up. We haven't declared our undying love for one another. You haven't proposed. None of this is wrapped up in a neat bow yet. Tell the truth, Tyler. You leaked this to your family because you were afraid you weren't going to get your way."

"You think I did this deliberately? To what? Blackmail you into staying with me?"

"You always get your way, no matter what. The clock will be up come Wednesday. Falling in love so quickly is nearly impossible. Were you nervous that you might not succeed this time? There's nothing like taking out a little insurance policy to make sure you still got what you wanted."

Somehow this whole scenario seemed to be his doing. Why? Because he didn't want to raise his child bouncing between two homes like a Ping-Pong ball? Because he was willing to sacrifice his own personal needs to do what was best for everyone? That made him the bad guy? The big manipulator, pulling all the strings, tricking her into moving into a beautiful house and going on expensive trips. He was such a bastard.

Tyler chuckled bitterly and shook his head. He was tired of handling her with kid gloves. "And what makes you think that *any* of this is what *I* wanted?"

Amelia opened up her mouth to argue, but the sharp tone of his words silenced her. He watched as her cheeks flushed red and glassy tears rushed into her eyes. The words had been harsh, and he knew it, but he couldn't keep them from flying from his mouth.

"You think I'm just like your father, trying to manipulate and browbeat you into getting my way. Well, guess what? This isn't what I would've chosen, either. I came to Nashville to get a divorce, and instead I got a whole damn family and a life a thousand miles away from my business and my home. I've tried to make the best of a bad situation, but you make it really hard, Amelia. You want to talk about telling the truth? Here's a dose of honesty for you—you're a coward!"

"A coward?" she gasped, taking a stumbling step back as though he'd slapped her.

"Yes. You tell people you believe in love and that you want it so desperately, but you'll use any excuse to avoid any relationship with potential. You use the guise of looking for this mythical, perfect love to reject anyone that tries to love you."

"You don't know anything about me and my relationships," Amelia said through her tears.

"I know everything about you. Remember, I'm your best friend, not the latest guy you've tried on like a pair of shoes and cast aside when you decided they don't fit. I know you better than you know yourself. I thought we had something good going between us. I thought that in a few days we would be telling our parents some good news. But you're such a chicken, you're grasping at the tiniest excuse to destroy this relationship and throw all the blame on me."

"I am not! You broke our agreement."

Tyler shook his head. "You're so deep in denial, you can't even see it. The only reason you've even given our relationship half a shot is because of the baby."

"Then that makes two of us, Tyler. That's the only reason you're here, so don't be so self-righteous. I—" Amelia paused, her eyes widening with fear, but they weren't focused on him. She gasped and doubled over, clutching her lower belly. "Oh, no," she cried.

Tyler rounded his desk and ran to her side, clasping her shoulders to offer support. "Are you okay? What is it?"

"Something's not right. I think I'm—" she started, and then groaned. "Help me to the bathroom, will you?"

He helped Amelia to the master bathroom, waiting patiently outside the door. It wasn't until he heard her agonized sobs that his stomach sank and he realized what was happening. She was having a miscarriage.

"Come on, we'll get you to the hospital right now," he shouted through the door.

"I just need to call my doctor."

"No. We're going to the hospital first. Let them tell us to go home."

When she came out a moment later, her skin was as white as paper and covered in a thin sheen of sweat. He could see her hands shaking as she gripped the door frame to come out. She was in no condition to be walking around. He grabbed a blanket from the bed and wrapped her in it, then swept her up off her feet. He carried her out to his car and loaded her into the passenger seat. He didn't stop to lock the door or worry about anything other than getting Amelia to the hospital as quickly as he could. St. Thomas West wasn't far; hopefully they could make it in time to save the baby. If they could.

Tyler's heart was racing in his chest as he flew through the streets. This couldn't really be happening. It just couldn't. She'd said this baby was what was keeping them together and she was right, but only to a point. The baby wasn't the glue that held them together, but it was the steel beam that reinforced them so that even strong winds couldn't knock them down. It was what gave him hope that they could make it. It was what made her stay even when she had reservations.

And now, he was certain, they were losing that. What would happen to them? Would this relationship spiral out of control without the child to anchor them? Would the loss bring them closer together or rip them apart? Tyler didn't know.

He occasionally stole a glance at Amelia as they drove. She was bent over in the seat, curled up against the door with her eyes closed. She was biting her lip, holding back tears of pain and fear. Even with the blanket, she was trembling. It broke his heart to see her that way.

Especially knowing that it was all his fault.

He had ruined everything. He'd opened his big mouth

and betrayed her trust. He'd used her own harsh, hurtful words as an excuse to lash back at her and say the most horrible things he could think of. And now she was losing their baby.

Tyler whipped around the corner to enter the emergency area. Coming to a stop, he threw the car into Park and leaped out. Scooping Amelia into his arms, he rushed through the front door. "Please!" he shouted to the women at the front desk. "Please help, I think my wife is losing our baby."

A nurse rushed into the lobby with a wheelchair. Tyler stood helplessly as Amelia was transferred to the chair and taken away. "Please wait here, sir," another nurse told him. "We'll take you back as soon as we can."

Tyler's knees gave out and he slipped down into one of the waiting room chairs. He wished to God he *could* go back—back in time so he could keep this from happening.

Eleven

"There was nothing you could have done, nothing you did to cause this. About ten to fifteen percent of pregnancies fail in the first trimester."

"The baby was fine at our first appointment. The doctor even said he had a strong heartbeat," Tyler argued with the doctor even though he knew it wouldn't change the outcome.

Amelia was lying silently in her hospital bed, recovering from the procedure she'd undergone shortly after arriving at the hospital. Tyler didn't know all the details, but the end result was the same. No more baby.

"At this stage, a lot changes in two or three weeks. And from the sound of things," the doctor said, "the baby stopped growing at around seven weeks, and it just took this long for your body to deal with it."

Tyler frowned. "How can you know that?"

"Ms. Kennedy said her morning sickness had suddenly ceased and she had more energy. This early in the pregnancy, that's a big sign that the baby is no longer developing."

"So it wasn't anything that happened today...?" Tyler's voice trailed off. He didn't want to outright ask if the emotional upheaval he'd put his wife through had caused her to lose the baby, but that had been the question tormenting him all afternoon.

"No, no. This was just nature dealing with a problem. But the plus side is that there's no reason why you two can't try again. Take some time to recover from this, give your body a few months and then you can give it another try. Just because you miscarried this time doesn't mean it will happen again. You don't have any of the risk factors, Ms. Kennedy, so I wouldn't worry."

"Thank you, Doctor," she said at last. It was the first time Amelia had spoken since she'd greeted the doctor and told him how she was feeling.

"Well, everything else seems to be okay, so the nurse will be around shortly with your discharge paperwork and a few prescriptions to help with the discomfort. Take it easy for a few days. Feel free to have a glass or two of wine to help you unwind, just don't overdo it until your symptoms fully clear up. If there are no other questions, I'll get out of your hair." When they didn't speak up, the doctor shook Tyler's hand and then slipped out of the room.

Tyler slumped down into the chair beside her bed, not certain what to do now. He felt completely helpless, and he hated that. She'd accused him of always being in control, of always getting his way, and she was right. He didn't like it when he couldn't fix things, and this was one thing he simply could not fix.

How quickly things had changed. A few weeks ago,

neither of them had even considered having a child, much less together. And now that the child was gone…he felt as though a part of him had been ripped away. He knew that it was a piece of him that he could never get back.

At this point, he didn't even know what to say to Amelia. She was his best friend, and he'd never felt the awkward lack of words when he was with her. But now, he wasn't sure where they stood. He was fairly certain that she wouldn't want to try getting pregnant again. Where did that leave them? Their last real words to one another before the miscarriage had been cutting and painful. He wasn't even entirely sure he would walk out of the room with a best friend, much less a wife.

"Tyler?" Amelia said at last.

"Yes?" Tyler leaped up from his chair to stand at the rail of her hospital bed. She seemed so small with the oversize hospital gown and all the wires and tubes hooked up to her. Her color was better now, but that wasn't saying much. The faint gray circles under her eyes spoke volumes. She might be healthy, but she was not fine. "Can I get you something?"

"No." She shook her head and winced slightly. "I'm okay."

"How are you feeling?"

"Better than I was," she said, attempting a small smile, but it didn't make it to her eyes. "Tyler…I want you to go home."

"I'm not going home without you. The doctor said you'll be released shortly."

"You don't understand. I want you to go home to New York."

Even though a part of him had been anticipating this eventuality, he didn't expect the painful blow to his midsection that accompanied it. It was excruciating, worse than anything he'd experienced, even his breakup with Christine a week before their wedding. "Amelia—" he began, but she held up her hand.

"Tyler, please. You were and are my best friend. But we never should've been anything more than that. We made a mistake and compounded it by trying to force ourselves into a different mold for the sake of our baby. I'm sorry that all this happened and that I put you through this, but now it's done. Things have worked out the way they were meant to. Without a baby, there's no reason for us to continue on."

Tyler tried to swallow the lump that had formed in his throat, but it remained stubbornly lodged there as he struggled to breathe.

"If you don't mind," she continued in his silence, "I'll stay in the house a few more days until we can arrange the movers to put my things back in my apartment."

"We don't have to make any quick decisions. Give yourself a few days."

Amelia sighed and reached out to pat his hand. "Tyler, you and I both know we don't need a few days. We were ending it this morning before everything else went wrong. Now we just don't have to face the endless custody complications and awkward eventuality of seeing each other with other people. You can travel the world without worrying about me and the baby at home. I can go back to my little apartment and continue my quest for love. This is the way it needs to be."

Tyler felt his grief morph in his veins to a low, simmering anger. She'd been angry with him this morning, yes, but if they had finished that fight, he would've seen to it that it was just a fight. Couples fought from time to time; it didn't have to put an end to the whole relationship. She was using the Facebook leak as an excuse to push him away, just as she was using the miscarriage to push him away. Whenever she got close to anyone, she panicked.

"This wasn't just about the baby, Amelia. Look me in the eye and tell me you don't have feelings for me. Tell me you're not in love with me and I'll walk right out the door."

Her dark gaze flicked over his face for a moment, and she looked intently into his eyes. "I'm not in love with you, Tyler."

She was lying. He could tell she was lying. Her fingers were rubbing anxiously at the blanket, the same way she used to fidget with a pencil or pen in class. But why would she lie about something like that? About something so important?

Tyler took a deep breath and sighed, the fight draining out of him. Even if she did love him, for whatever reason, she didn't want him. Nothing had changed over the years. She hadn't wanted him when they were sixteen and she didn't really want him now. The last thing Tyler wanted to do was force himself on a woman who didn't want to be with him. This wasn't the first time he'd fallen short where a woman was concerned. If she wanted him gone, he'd go. He had work in New York. A life there. An apartment. If there wasn't a reason to be in Nashville, he didn't want to stay another minute.

"Okay," he said with a sigh of resignation. "If that's what you want. I'll let the real estate agent know we'll be out in a week or so and arrange the movers."

"I've called Natalie to come pick me up."

Tyler looked up at her. She didn't even want him to drive her home? "Okay. Well, then, if there's nothing else I can do for you, I won't subject you to my presence any longer."

"Tyler…" Amelia began with a coddling tone he wasn't in the mood to hear.

"No, it's fine. You want me gone. I'm gone." He reached down and squeezed her hand, his eyes not able to meet hers. He didn't want to see conflict there. That might give him hope, and if he knew Amelia well enough, he knew there was no hope. "Have your lawyer draw up the divorce paperwork and send it on when you're ready. Feel better."

With those last words hanging in the air between them, he slipped into the hallway and let the door shut behind him. There, he slumped against the wall and dropped his head back, hard. His chest was so tight he could barely breathe, his hands aching to reach out for her and pull her into his arms. But he wouldn't. He would forfeit for the first time in his life, because that was what she wanted.

And in that moment, he realized it was because he loved her enough to give her what she wanted, even if it killed him to do it.

Amelia had thought their house was large with the two of them in it. Tyler had taken his personal things, some clothes and his laptop before she came home from the hospital. The rest, she assumed, the movers would pack up. The house had hardly been full before, but Tyler's absence made it just that much emptier. When she was alone, it was like being locked in the Metropolitan Museum of Art at night. Room after room surrounded by eerie silence and unfamiliar shadows.

The first night there alone hadn't bothered her as much, but she hadn't really been alone. Natalie had picked her up from the hospital and all the girls had met her at the house with reinforcements. They'd piled up in the bed and had pizza, wine and copious amounts of chocolate while watching a couple of sappy chick movies. It was an excellent distraction, and crying during the movies had been a much-needed outlet for all the emotions she hadn't allowed herself to process yet.

Tonight was her first night by herself. Gretchen had offered to come by, but Amelia had shooed her away. She could use some time by herself, and really, she was used to being alone. She'd always lived on her own. She wasn't sure how living with Tyler for only a few weeks could make it feel as though somehow he'd always been there.

He was back in New York now. He had texted her that much. Other than that, he had thankfully left her in peace. When she'd told him to leave, she hadn't been sure he was going to. She'd seen the resistance in his pale blue eyes, the curl of his hands into fists at his sides. He'd wanted to fight, and for a moment, deep inside, she'd hoped he would. She'd lied when she said she didn't love him, but she wasn't about to admit to something like that when he wouldn't do the same. If Tyler truly cared about her, and hadn't just been sticking it out for the baby's sake, he would've told her no. He would've proclaimed that he loved her and he wasn't going anywhere no matter what.

But he'd just walked away, confirming her worst fear. And breaking her heart.

She'd lain in her hospital bed and sobbed after he'd left, only pulling herself together when she'd heard the nurse coming. Amelia had managed to hold the fragile pieces of herself together since then, but it was hard. In one day, she'd lost the man she loved, her best friend, her husband and their child. Despite the promises they'd made, Natalie was right. She really didn't think their friendship would survive this, and that was what hurt the most. She had never felt so alone in her whole life.

Amelia was standing in the kitchen, attempting to replicate Tyler's hot cocoa, when she heard the buzzer on the gate. She made her way over to the panel by the door, where the screen showed a fuzzy image of her grandmother waiting impatiently to be let in.

She had made the obligatory call to her parents and her sister the day before to tell them what was going on. One of them must have passed along the information to her grandmother and had dispatched her from Knoxville as soon as she could finish curling her hair.

Amelia swallowed hard and pressed the button that would open the gates. She unlocked the front door and left it ajar as she ran back to the kitchen and pulled the milk off the stove before it boiled over. By the time she got back to the foyer, her paternal grandmother, Elizabeth Kennedy, was standing in the doorway.

The woman had recently celebrated her eightieth birthday, but you wouldn't know it to look at her. Amelia was a clone of her grandmother. Elizabeth's flame-red hair was as bright as Amelia's, but maintained now by a fine salon in Knoxville. Her dark eyes saw everything, with the thin curl of her lips giving away her wry sense of humor. She was sharp as a tack, as nimble as ever and drove her old Buick around like an Indy driver.

The moment her grandmother saw her, she opened her arms up and waited. In an instant, whatever threads that were holding Amelia together snapped. She rushed into her grandmother's arms and fell into hysterical tears.

"I know, I know," Elizabeth soothed, stroking Amelia's hair and letting her tears soak through her sweater. When Amelia finally calmed down, her grandmother patted her back and said, "Let's go to the kitchen, shall we? I think a time like this calls for a warm drink and something sweet. I, uh…" She looked through the various doorways. "Where is the kitchen? This place is enormous."

Amelia chuckled for the first time in a long while and took her grandmother's hand, leading her through the maze of halls and rooms to the kitchen. Elizabeth's eyes lit up when she saw the kitchen, reminding Amelia of her first day in the house. "It's beautiful, isn't it?"

Her grandmother nodded. "It's amazing." She went around opening drawers and investigating. "If this is any indication of the rest of the house, I'm moving in."

"It's available for rent," Amelia said with a sad tone in her voice. "The current occupants will be out by the end of the week."

Elizabeth spied the pot of cocoa on the stove. "You sit down. I'm going to finish this cocoa and you're going to tell me what's going on."

Amelia did as she was told, climbing gingerly onto a stool and watching her grandmother cook the way she had as a child. Her grandmother had passed along her love of cooking to Amelia. Most of her childhood they lived apart, but she had looked forward to summers spent with her grandparents and visits at Christmas. It was her favorite time of year.

Elizabeth restarted the cocoa, stirring it with a spoon before going into the pantry. She came out a moment later with peanut butter, cornflakes and Karo Syrup, making Amelia's eyes light up with delight.

"Cornflake cookies?"

Her grandmother smiled. "Of course, baby. Now, what is this I hear from your father about you getting married to that little boy you used to run around with?"

Amelia took a deep breath and started at the beginning. She told about the elopement in Vegas, the pregnancy and the whirlwind romance that followed. She ended the tale with its new, sad conclusion. "And now he's gone, and once I'm out of this house, it will be like none of it ever happened."

Her grandmother placed a steaming mug of cocoa and a plate of still warm and gooey cornflake cookies on the counter in front of her. "I doubt that," she said. "From the sound of things, nothing is ever going to be the way it was before." She pushed up her sleeves and started scrubbing the pans in the sink.

"Just leave those, Grandma. We have a lady for that."

Elizabeth scoffed at the suggestion. "I think better when I'm working in the kitchen. So what are you going to do now? Move back to your apartment?"

"Yes," Amelia answered. "Until my lease is up. Then I think I might buy a townhouse, something with a little more space, although not as much as we have here."

"And what about you and Tyler?"

Amelia shrugged and shoved a cornflake cookie in her mouth to avoid the question awhile longer. "I'm hoping we can still be friends. Obviously we're not meant to be together romantically. I knew from the beginning he wasn't my big love. I was just hoping I was wrong."

"Big love?" her grandmother said with a frown drawing her wrinkled brow together. "What kind of nonsense is that?"

"The big, grand love. The kind of romance that you and Grandpa have. The kind that moves mountains and lifts spirits and makes you certain that you can weather anything with that person at your side. The love that makes you happy to wake up to that person every day. I should've known I couldn't achieve that in thirty days. I mean…how long did you and Grandpa date before you got married?"

Elizabeth considered the question for longer than

Amelia expected her to. Her lips twisted together in thought before she finally planted her palms on the counter. "A week."

Amelia sat bolt upright in her chair. "What?"

"Now, don't you go running around telling people that. No one knows. Your granddaddy and I met when I was working at the university bookstore. He was there studying to be a lawyer. I thought he was so handsome, but I was too shy to speak to him. One day, he asked if I would join him for the football game on Saturday. We went for ice cream. We went out for breakfast," she said with a naughty smile, "and the following Friday, we ditched classes to elope at the courthouse."

This was not the story Amelia had been told all her life. "What about the big church wedding? I've seen the pictures!"

"That happened a year later. We kept our marriage a secret and told our families and friends we were dating. Months down the road, we announced that he had proposed, and we set the wedding day for our first anniversary. No one but your grandpa and I ever knew the truth until now."

Amelia didn't even know what to say. How was it even possible? "But you and Grandpa have the perfect love! The great romance I've always strived for. How could you have possibly known he was the right man for you, your soul mate, in just a week?"

Elizabeth sighed and made her way around the counter to sit at a bar stool beside her. "There is no such thing as a perfect love, Amelia, just like there is no such thing as a perfect person. Your grandpa and I had to work very hard on our relationship. Maybe even harder than other people, because we wed so quickly. There were times I wanted to hit him with a frying pan because he kept leaving his slippers where I could trip over them. There were times I'm certain your grandpa wished he'd taken me on a couple more dates before he proposed. But we made our decisions and we made the best of it."

The cornflake cookies felt like lead in her stomach. It was as if she'd just been told the truth about the Tooth Fairy, the Easter Bunny and Santa all over again.

"In the end, yes, marrying your grandfather was one of the best decisions I ever made. I acted on instinct, on passion, and I was right. If I had overthought it, we probably never would've married. We had ups and downs like any couple, but I don't regret a minute of the time we've spent together."

Tyler's words popped into her mind. *We might end up being totally incompatible, and if we are, we end it and you can go back to your quest for the White Buffalo.* The White Buffalo. Magical. Rare. A fantasy. She'd spent the past ten years of her life chasing a myth and she was the last to realize it.

"I think part of this is my fault," Elizabeth admitted. "When you were little, I filled your head with romantic stories, treating our marriage like one of your fairy-tale books. When you were older, I never thought to go back and tell you differently. I guess I imagined you'd grow up and shelve those fantasies with Cinderella and her glass slipper."

"No," Amelia spoke at last. "No, it isn't your fault. You were right, you were telling a little girl stories. When I grew up, I should've realized that there's no such thing as perfection. When I think about all the men I've driven out of my life because they weren't just so... I feel awful."

"Honey, it's possible that none of those men would've been right for you anyway. But I wonder about this last one. It sounds to me as if he loves you very much."

Amelia perked up in her seat. "What makes you say that?"

"The way you described him. The way he did so much for you, even when you didn't want him to. I know that sort of thing can make a girl like you crazy, but you have to understand why he does it. Moving here on a dime, getting this house, doing everything in his power to make you happy, comfortable and safe… Those aren't the actions of a man who feels obligated because of the child. Those are the actions of a man so desperately in love with a woman that he will do anything and everything to see her smile."

Amelia shook her head. She wished her grandmother was right, but it just couldn't be true. "He's not in love with me, Grandma. He left. He wouldn't have walked out if he'd loved me."

"I thought you loved all the fairy tales with the big romantic gestures? *The Little Mermaid*, *The Gift of the Magi*, *Beauty and the Beast*… In each of those stories, the character sacrifices the most valued thing in their life for the one they love. If you think Tyler left because he didn't care, you're a fool. He left, and gave you up, because he thought that was what you wanted."

Amelia felt the dull ache of regret start to pool in her stomach. Was it possible she had driven away the man who loved her, the man she loved, because she was too blind to see the truth?

And more important…would he ever forgive her?

Twelve

Tyler hesitated only a moment before turning the knob and opening the front door of the home he used to share with Amelia. He could see the lights on in the kitchen, but the rest of the house was dark and empty. "Amelia?" he called, hoping not to startle her. "Hello?"

No one answered, so he traveled down the corridor to the kitchen. Amelia was standing at the counter, her wary eyes watching him as he came in. Apparently she'd heard him but hadn't had anything to say. Or didn't know what to say. Either way, she wasn't about to leap into his arms and kiss him. That was disappointing. At the same time, she hadn't immediately thrown him out either, so he'd count his blessings.

"Hi," he said.

"Hi."

She looked better than she had at the hospital. Her color was vastly improved and she didn't look nearly as tired. Her hair was pulled up into a ponytail, a casual look that went well with her little T-shirt and jeans. The rest of her was anything but casual. Her whole body was stiff. She had a bottle of wine clutched with white-knuckled intensity in one hand, the opener in the other.

"Would you like some wine?" she offered. "I was just about to open it."

"Sure, thanks. Let me—" he started, and then stopped. His instinct was to offer to open it, but that was the wrong tactic with Amelia. She hadn't wanted to be helped with everything when she was pregnant; she certainly wouldn't want to be coddled when she wasn't. "I'll get some glasses," he said instead.

He went to the cabinet and fetched two glasses. By the time he returned, Amelia had the bottle open. He held them by the stems as she poured them each a healthy serving.

"Would you like to go sit outside?" she asked. "It's been a pretty warm day. It would be a shame to move out of here without at least taking advantage of the back-yard once."

"Okay." Tyler followed her through the door to the backyard he hadn't set foot in since he toured the home with the real estate agent. There was a kidney-shaped pool and hot tub with a waterfall to one side. A fire pit was surrounded by stone benches just off the patio. To the right was a large stretch of lawn that would've been perfect for a swing set someday.

The thought brought a painful pang to the back of his mind. Since he'd left the hospital, he'd done the same thing Amelia accused him of doing after his breakup with Christine—he'd thrown himself into his work so he didn't have to think about everything he'd lost. He'd grabbed his computer and a suitcase full of clothes and toiletries and hopped the first plane back to New York. He'd bypassed his empty apartment and gone straight to the offices, where he'd worked until he was blurry eyed and hallucinating at his computer screen. The next morning, he got up and did it again.

Today, he'd woken up missing the warmth of her body only inches away on the mattress beside him. He'd wanted to make her a smoothie and kiss her as she headed out the door. Then he'd realized he was a bigger coward than he'd accused her of being. He got back on a plane to Nashville and came straight to the house to tell Amelia how he felt. Which he would do. Any second now. If he could just figure out *how* to tell Amelia how he felt.

She'd already rejected him once. He wasn't too excited to stick his neck back out again and get his head chopped off, but he knew he had to. He'd regret this for the rest of his life if he didn't.

Amelia strolled out to the stone fire pit and sat down on one of the benches. Tyler resisted the urge to give her personal space and sat right beside her. He leaned forward and turned on the switch the agent had shown him, and there was suddenly a raging fire in the gas fireplace. It was just enough to take the mid-March chill out of the air.

"Nice," Amelia said, leaning in to warm her face. "As much as I complained, I am going to miss this place. It's going to be hard to go back to my tiny, plain apartment after this. We never even got to use the movie theater."

Tyler nodded, but the words fighting to get out of him made it hard for him to focus on conversation. "How are you feeling?" he asked.

"Okay. I'm still sore and achy, but I'll live," she joked with a small smile. "How are you?"

Tyler sighed. That was a loaded question, or at the

very least, a loaded answer. "I am…a little numb. A little overwhelmed. Sad. But mostly, I'm feeling guilty."

"You shouldn't feel guilty, Tyler. It wasn't anybody's fault."

"I know. But there are plenty of other things that I am responsible for. I told my brother about us when I shouldn't have. I said things to you that were hurtful. And I walked away from you when every fiber of my being was screaming at me to stay."

He could sense Amelia stiffening beside him. She hastily took a sip of her wine before she responded, "I told you to go," she said, her voice flat and emotionless.

"You did. But since when have I ever done what you've told me to do?"

Amelia snorted softly, covering her mouth with her hand to smother it. "Practically never."

"Exactly. I picked the wrong damn time to start doing things your way."

"Hey, now—" Amelia started in a sharp tone, but Tyler cut her off.

"I didn't come back to argue, Amelia."

She looked at him with large dark eyes, taking in every detail of his face as though she were trying to catalog it, memorize it somehow. "Then why did you come back, Tyler?"

Tyler took a deep breath. "I came back to tell you that I'm going to be breaking our agreement."

Her auburn eyebrows drew together in confusion. "What do you mean, breaking our agreement?"

"Well," he began, "when all this started, we agreed that when the thirty days were up, if both of us were in love, we would get married. But if one of us still wanted a divorce…we would part as friends."

Amelia swallowed hard and focused her gaze on the

glass in her lap. "So you've come to tell me we're not going to be friends any longer?"

"No. I've come here to tell you that divorce is off the table."

Amelia nervously chuckled, a tone of disbelief in her lyrical laughter. "I think I've heard this out of you before. A couple weeks ago, in fact. And look where it got us."

"That was completely different. The last time, it was because we were having a baby and I thought it was the right thing to do. This time, we're not getting a divorce because I am in love with you. And *you* are in love with *me*, even if you don't want to admit to it."

Amelia's mouth dropped open, a soft gasp escaping her lips. "You *what*?"

"I love you," he repeated. "And I'm not going to let you run away from this. I can't just stand idle while you try to ruin everything we have together. I tried to just sit back and let you lie to yourself and to me, but I can't do it anymore."

Tyler set his wine on the ground and turned on the bench until he was facing her. He scooped up her hand and cupped it between his own. "I love you, Amelia. And I loved you long before there was a baby, even before our wild night in Las Vegas. I've realized that I've loved you since study hall and shared lunches on the lawn by the football stadium. I've loved you since the day you called me over to the empty seat beside you in freshman English and introduced yourself. You were the most beautiful, sweet, loving creature I had, or have, ever met in my whole life."

"How could you have been in love with me all these years?" she argued. "You never said anything. You never acted like you had feelings for me."

"I didn't fully realize it. All these years, I knew that

I loved you as a friend. I didn't allow for the possibility of anything more than that. But the feelings were there, simmering under the surface. Every time I dated a woman and something just didn't click. Every time I saw your number come up on my phone and my heart leaped a little in my chest. Christine knew it, but somehow it took the possibility of losing you forever to make me see the difference."

Tyler slipped onto the patio on one knee and looked up at her. "You're everything to me, Amelia. And I want you to marry me."

"We're already married, Tyler."

"I know," he said with a wicked smile that curled his lips. "But my wife once told me that if I loved her and wanted to stay married, I'd have to propose again—properly—so we could have the big romantic church wedding with our family and friends."

Tyler reached into his coat pocket and pulled out the same black velvet jewelry box he'd offered to her the night they eloped. He opened the box to display the eight-carat diamond they'd used at their first wedding ceremony. Once they'd moved into the house, she'd given it back to him. At the time, she either didn't think they would make it, or if they did, he wouldn't want her to have such a large, expensive piece. She was wrong on both counts.

"I gave that back to you," Amelia frowned. "That was never intended to be my ring. You were supposed to sell that to a dealer in LA so it could become one of the Kardashians' engagement rings."

"Whether or not that's what I intended when I bought it, a fact is a fact. This is my wife's ring, so it belongs to you. Even if I went shopping for a new one, I wouldn't be able to beat it. I've come across larger stones, flashier stones, well-known stones, but this one is the most perfect specimens of diamond I've ever had in my possession. It's flawless and colorless. The cut is perfect, allowing the diamond to truly shine. It's a classic beauty, just like you, and it belongs on your finger. No one else's."

Tyler felt an unexpected nervousness in his stomach. He'd already proposed to Amelia once. They were already married, as she'd pointed out. But this was different. The last time was a joke that went too far, an adventure they'd never expected. This time was for real. He loved her. He wanted to spend the rest of his life with her. He swallowed the anxiety rising in his throat and looked up into her eyes. "Amelia, will you marry me?"

Amelia didn't know what to say. She was stunned. Well and truly stunned. This was not at all how she'd expected this day, or even this conversation, to go. When she'd heard Tyler's voice in the hallway, there had been a moment of elation, followed by panic, with caution bringing up the rear. Her conversation with her grandmother had given her a lot to think about. She had been on the verge of pouring a glass of wine to gather her courage to call Tyler. To tell him that she'd lied and she did love him.

Then, suddenly, he was standing in their kitchen and she didn't know what to think. He probably hadn't come all this way to fight. Or to get his things. The movers could do that. She figured he wanted to talk in person, without the emotions of the hospital and the miscarriage fueling the discussion. At best, she'd been hopeful they could stay friends. She'd never dared or dreamed for more.

But a marriage proposal?

"I don't know what to say," she said with a stunned shake of her head.

Tyler frowned. "I'll give you a hint. The key word is *yes*, quickly followed by *I love you, Tyler*. We'll try this again. Amelia, will you marry me? Okay, now it's your turn."

Amelia smiled. He was right. She felt it. She wanted this. All she had to do was say it. "Yes, Tyler, I will marry you."

"And?" he pressed with a hopeful grin.

"And...I love you. Very much."

Tyler slipped the ring onto her finger and kissed her knuckles before standing up and pulling her into a gentle embrace. Amelia melted into the safety and comfort of his arms, a place she'd thought she might never be able to return to. She tipped her head up to kiss him, pressing her mouth against his soft lips. The moment they made contact, she felt a rush of excitement run through her body. The thrill of new love, the delight of finally experiencing the moment she'd always dreamed of. His proposal was all she'd ever hoped for and more, because it was Tyler. The man who knew her better than anyone. The man who could make her laugh, make her smile and even make her cocoa.

She had always fantasized about perfection. It didn't get any more perfect than this.

Breaking away, Amelia clung to his neck, burying her face in the lapel of his suit coat and breathing in the warm scent of his skin. She sighed in relief as he held her, grateful she hadn't lost him with her foolish fears.

"You know what?" he asked. "It's Wednesday. Day thirty."

Amelia smiled up at him. He was right. Everything had ended just the way it was supposed to. "It looks as though we've made it. It's kind of hard to believe it, but a lot has happened in the past month."

"It certainly has. And one of the things I've learned over the past few days is that I don't want to keep this a secret. We need to call our families. Tonight. We can't make that same mistake twice."

"You're right. But let's wait a little while longer so I can bliss out in this moment."

"Okay. And I'm sure after that, we start planning the big wedding you've always dreamed of. Do you still have that giant notebook?"

Amelia shrugged. "I do, but you know, I've done a lot of thinking since you left. The idea of that isn't as appealing anymore. My big wedding plans were focused on everything but starting off a new life with the man I love. I'd rated cake and flowers over the groom. I guess it's because I was planning a wedding when I wasn't in love yet. Now that I am, I don't think I need all that anymore. We're already married. We love each other. I think that's all I need."

One of Tyler's eyebrows raised curiously at her. "You say that now, and it's sweet, but I know you'll regret it later. One day, ten years down the road, we'll have an argument and you'll throw out there that we eloped in Vegas and you were wearing black and you never got to have your dream wedding. Somehow it will be all my fault. You'll be a total Momzilla when our daughter gets married as you try to live the dream you lost. No way. We're having a wedding. I insist."

Amelia twisted her lips in thought. "Okay, then. Maybe we can come up with something in between. Not quite as grand an affair as I have in my notebook, but one with a white dress, a pastor that doesn't look like Elvis and our friends and family there to share the moment with us."

Tyler smiled and pulled her into his arms. "That

sounds like the perfect wedding to me. Plan whatever you like. All I ask is that you don't make me take dance lessons."

Amelia laughed aloud. Tyler was a confident, powerful businessman, but he had zero rhythm. "I've seen you dance before, Tyler. No amount of lessons is going to help."

"Hey!" He laughed. "Okay, you're right. Just tell me when to show up and what to wear."

"It's so easy for men."

Tyler laughed. "That's because we're far more interested in the honeymoon."

Amelia laughed, then felt the light moment fade. When she looked up into his pale blue eyes, she felt the urge to tell him everything. Why she'd done what she'd done. Why she'd lied. "Tyler..." she began, running her fingers through his messy blond hair. "I'm so sorry for how I've acted. I was terrified of being in love with you and not knowing if you felt the same way. I just couldn't believe that you were here because you loved *me*, so I convinced myself it was just because of the baby."

"That's my fault," Tyler admitted. "I was afraid, too, so I tried to focus on the baby because no matter how you and I felt about each other, the child was going to be a part of my life. I felt things for you that I'd never felt for another woman, but I was waiting for the other shoe to drop. I thought that if I kept my feelings locked inside, when you pushed me away, it wouldn't hurt as badly."

Amelia winced. "And I did push you away. I fulfilled your biggest fear."

"And it didn't hurt any less by keeping my secret. It probably made it worse. I should've just said it right there in the hospital room and not cared what you might say. If I'd told you I loved you and I wasn't going to let you push me away, would you have still told me to go back to New York?"

She wasn't sure. Would she have believed him? She didn't know if her heart had been strong enough in that dark moment to take the risk. "It doesn't matter," she replied. "We can't change the past, and I think this happened the way it needed to. Being apart helped us both realize how much we love each other and want to be together. Sometimes that's what it takes."

"I know it made me realize I hate my apartment in New York. I can run my business from here just as easily as I do there. I really don't want to give up this house. I know it's too big, but..."

"We'll work on filling it up," Amelia said with a smile. She didn't want to get rid of the house, either. It would take some time, but eventually it would be filled with children and laughter and life, and it wouldn't feel so large and empty. Losing the baby had made her realize how badly she really did want children. Searching for the perfect mate had put that dream on hold. The doctor said they should wait a few more months, but when it was time, she wanted to try again.

"You know, I grew up with five brothers and sisters crammed into a three-bedroom, two-bath apartment. We've got thousands of square feet to work with here. If you want to fill this place up, we can fill it up."

"Sounds like a challenge," Amelia laughed.

"I don't know," Tyler warned. "For a girl so focused on perfection, you may find a house full of kids to be a very messy prospect."

"I've decided that perfection isn't so perfect after all. While you were in New York, I had a much-needed and enlightening conversation with my grandmother."

Tyler looked at her with surprise. "The one with the perfect, long-lasting marriage I'll never live up to?"

"The one I *thought* had a perfect marriage. To make a long story short, I had apparently been given the romantic fairy-tale version for little girls. But in reality, I think I got what I wanted anyway. I've always dreamed of having a marriage like hers and, ironically, we've gotten pretty close to achieving that. At least the start. We've just got fifty-some odd years of togetherness to go."

Tyler smiled and kissed her again. "I can't wait."

Epilogue

Four months later

It was happening. The day Amelia had been waiting for since she was five years old had arrived, and sooner than she'd expected.

When a late-summer wedding was postponed, she and Tyler had jumped on the chance to book their moment in the chapel. From there, it was months of excitement and planning. While she had toned down the event, once she started putting together their wedding, there were some details she found she just couldn't skimp on.

Her gown was the most beautiful dress she'd ever worn, a dazzling ivory-and-crystal creation. Her veil was long, draping down her back and spreading across the gray carpet. The pastor was reading a passage about love and the bonds of marriage as Amelia stood on the raised platform and looked into the eyes of the man she loved.

Turning briefly toward the crowd that filled the chapel of From This Moment, she could easily pick out the faces of the family and friends who had joined them here today. It was just the way she envisioned it—the important people in her life witnessing this important moment.

For years, Amelia had planned a wedding with no groom in mind. But looking into Tyler's eyes, she knew that he was the most important part of this day. More important than a beautiful dress or a fancy cake.

They had arranged this wedding because he'd wanted her to have the moment, but it wasn't necessary. The key ingredients—him and her—had been there at their first wedding. The only difference was going through the ritual and repeating the words with love and tears making their voices tremble as they spoke. The words meant so much more this time.

"And now, I pronounce you man and wife. You may kiss the bride."

Tyler pulled her into his arms, a smile spreading across his remarkably clean-shaven face. Amelia felt her heart skip a beat in her chest when he looked at her that way. She hoped and prayed he would look at her like that for the rest of their lives.

"I love you," Tyler whispered.

"I love you, too. And," she added with a smile, "I'm pregnant."

His eyes widened for a moment before an excited grin changed his whole face. "Really?"

"Yes, really."

His lips pressed to hers in an instant, and she melted into him. The hundreds of people around them faded away. The roar of applause was just a faint buzz in the background, the flash of Bree's camera no match for the fireworks going off beneath her eyelids. She felt a thrill run down her spine and a warmth spread through her body. It wasn't until the pastor cleared his throat that they pulled apart. "Later," the pastor assured them. A rumble of laughter traveled through the audience.

Amelia blushed as her sister, Whitney, handed back her bouquet. She slipped her arm through Tyler's, and they turned to face the crowd and their new, exciting future together.

"Ladies and gentleman, I'd like to present Mr. and Mrs. Tyler Dixon."

Arm in arm, they marched down the aisle of scattered rose petals to start their life together. As they stepped through the doorway as man and wife, she realized this was the moment she'd dreamed of. Not the wedding, but the beginning of their life together. At last, they had a happily-ever-after for them both.

* * * * *

If you loved this novel, pick up the first book in the
BRIDES AND BELLES *series from*
Andrea Laurence,
SNOWED IN WITH HER EX
Available now!

"I hope you'll let Davy and me show our appreciation by buying you breakfast, Dr St. Sebastian."

"Thanks, but I've already had breakfast."

No way Mike was letting this gorgeous creature get away. "Dinner, then."

"I'm, uh, I'm here with my family."

"I am, too. Unfortunately." He made a face at his nephew, who giggled and returned the exaggerated grimace. "I'd be even more grateful if you give me an excuse to get away from them for a while."

"Well…"

He didn't miss her brief hesitation. Or her quick glance at *his* left hand. The white imprint of his wedding ring had long since faded. Too bad he couldn't say the same for the inner scars. Shoving the disaster of his marriage into the dark hole where it belonged, Mike overrode her apparent doubts.

"Where are you staying?"

She took her time replying. Those exotic eyes looked him up and down.

"We're at the Camino del Ray," she said finally, almost reluctantly. "It's about a half mile up the beach."

Mike suppressed a smile. "I know where it is. I'll pick you up at seven-thirty."

* * *

The Texan's Royal M.D.
is part of the Duchess Diaries series—Two royal
granddaughters on their way to happily ever after!

THE TEXAN'S
ROYAL M.D.

BY
MERLINE LOVELACE

Published in Great Britain 2015
by Mills & Boon, an imprint of Harlequin (UK) Limited,
Eton House, 18-24 Paradise Road, Richmond, Surrey, TW9 1SR

© 2015 Merline Lovelace

ISBN: 978-0-263-25249-1

51-0215

Harlequin (UK) Limited's policy is to use papers that are natural, renewable and recyclable products and made from wood grown in sustainable forests. The logging and manufacturing processes conform to the legal environmental regulations of the country of origin.

Printed and bound in Spain
by CPI, Barcelona

A career Air Force officer, **Merline Lovelace** served at bases all over the world. When she hung up her uniform for the last time she decided to combine her love of adventure with a flair for storytelling, basing many of her tales on her own experiences in uniform. Since then she's produced more than ninety action-packed sizzlers, many of which have made the *USA TODAY* and Waldenbooks bestseller lists. Over eleven million copies of her books are available in some thirty countries.

When she's not tied to her keyboard, Merline enjoys reading, chasing little white balls around the fairways of Oklahoma and traveling to new and exotic locales with her handsome husband, Al. Check her website, merlinelovelace.com, or friend her on Facebook for news and information about her latest releases.

To Neta and Dave: friends, traveling buds and the
source of all kinds of fodder for my books.
Thanks for the inside info on research
grants and nasty bugs, Neta!

Prologue

I seem to have come full circle. For so many years my life centered on my darling granddaughters. Now they're grown and are busy with lives of their own. Quiet, elegant Sarah has an adoring husband, a blossoming career as an author and her first child on the way. And Eugenia, my carefree, high-spirited Eugenia, is the wife of a United Nations diplomat and the mother of twins. She fills both roles so joyously, so effortlessly.

I do wish I could say the same of Dominic, my impossibly handsome great-nephew. Dom still hasn't adjusted to the fact that he now carries the title of Grand Duke of Karlenburgh. I've caught him rolling his shoulders as though he itches for his previous life as an undercover agent. Then his glance strays to his wife and his restlessness fades instantly. Natalie's so demure, so sweet and so startlingly intelligent!

She quite astonishes us all with the depth of her knowledge of the most arcane subjects—including the history of my beloved Karlenburgh.

These days I live vicariously through Dom's sister, Anastazia. I'll admit I played shamelessly on our distant kinship to convince

Zia to reside with me during her pediatric residency in New York City. She's only a few short months away from finishing the grueling three-year program. She should be feeling nothing but elation that the end is in sight. Yet I sense that something's troubling her. Something she doesn't wish to talk about, even with me. I shan't force the issue. I don't condone unwelcome intrusiveness, even by the most concerned and well-meaning. I do hope, however, that the vacation I've engineered for the family over the coming holidays eases some of the worry Zia hides behind her so bright, so lovely smile.

From the diary of Charlotte,
Grand Duchess of Karlenburgh

One

Zia almost didn't hear the shout over the roar of the waves. Preoccupied with the decision hanging over her like an executioner's ax, she'd slipped away for an early-morning jog along the glistening silver shoreline of Galveston Island, Texas. Although the Gulf of Mexico offered a glorious symphony of green water and lacy surf, Zia barely noticed the ever-changing seascape. She needed time and the endless, empty shore to think. Solitude to wrestle with her private demons.

She loved her family—her adored older brother, Dominic; her great-aunt Charlotte, who'd practically adopted her; the cousins she'd grown so close to in the past few years; their spouses and lively offspring. But spending the Christmas holidays in Galveston with the entire St. Sebastian clan hadn't allowed much time for soul-searching. Zia only had three more days to decide. Three days before she returned to New York and…

"Go get it, Buster!"

Sunk in thought, she might have blocked out the gleeful shout if she hadn't spent the past two and a half years as a pediatric resident at Kravis Children's Hospital, part of the Mount Sinai hospital network in New York City. All those rewarding, gut-wrenching hours working with infants and young kids had fine-tuned Zia's instincts to the point that her mind tagged the voice instantly as belonging to a five- or six-year-old male with a healthy set of lungs.

A smile formed as she angled toward the sound. Her sneakers slapping the hard-packed sand at the water's edge, she jogged backward a few paces and watched the child who raced through the shallows about thirty yards behind her. Red haired and freckle faced, he was in hot pursuit of a stubby brown-and-white terrier. The dog, in turn, chased a soaring Frisbee. Boy and pet plunged joyously through the shallow surf, oblivious to everything but the purple plastic disc.

Zia's smile widened at their antics but took a quick downward turn when she scanned the shore behind them and failed to spot an adult. Where were the boy's parents? Or his nanny, given that this stretch of beach included several glitzy, high-dollar resorts? Or even an older sibling? The boy was too young to be cavorting in the surf unsupervised.

Anger sliced into her, swift and icy hot. She'd had to deal with the results of parental negligence far too often to view it with complacency. She was feeling the heat of that anger, the sick disgust she had to swallow while treating abused or neglected children, when another cry wrenched her attention back to the boy. This one was high and reedy and tinged with panic.

Her heart stuttering, Zia saw he'd lunged into waves to meet the terrier paddling toward shore with the Frisbee clenched between its jaws. She knew the bank dropped off steeply at that point. Too steeply! And the undertow when the tide went out was strong enough to drag down full-grown adult.

She was already racing back to the boy when he disappeared. She locked her frantic gaze on the spot where his red hair sank below the waves, crashed into the water and made a flying dive.

She couldn't see him! The receding tide had churned up too much sand. Grit stung her eyes. The ocean hissed and boiled in her ears. She flung out her arms, thrashed them blindly. Her lungs on fire, she thrust out of the water like a dolphin spooked by a killer whale and arced back in.

Just before she went under she caught a glimpse of the terrier's rear end pointed at the sky. The dog dove down at the same instant Zia did and led her to the child being dragged along by the undertow. She shot past the dog. Grabbed the boy's wrist. Propelled upward with fast, hard scissor kicks. She had to swim parallel to the shore for several desperate moments before the vicious current loosened its grip enough for her to cut toward dry land.

He wasn't breathing when she turned him on his back and started CPR. Her head told her he hadn't been in the water long enough to suffer severe oxygen deprivation, but his lips were tinged with blue. Completely focused, Zia ignored the dog that whined and pawed frantic trenches in the sand by the boy's head. Ignored as well the thud of running feet, the offers of help, the deep shout that was half panic, half prayer.

"Davy! Jesus!"

The small chest twitched under Zia's palms. A moment later, the boy's back arched and seawater spewed from his mouth. With a silent prayer of thanksgiving to Saint Stephen, patron saint of her native Hungary, Zia rolled him onto his side and held his head while he hacked up most of what he'd swallowed. When he was done, she eased him down again. His nose ran in twin streams and tears spurted from his eyes but, amazingly, he gulped back his sobs.

"Wh...? What happened?"

She gave him a reassuring smile. "You went out too far and got dragged in by the undertow."

"Did I…? Did I get drowned?"

"Almost."

He hooked an arm around his anxious pet's neck while a slowly dawning excitement edged out the confusion and fear in his brown eyes. "Wait till I tell Mommy and Kevin and *abuelita* and…" His gaze shifted right and latched on to something just over Zia's shoulder. "Uncle Mickey! Uncle Mickey! Did you hear that? I almost got drowned!"

"Yeah, brat, I heard."

It was the same deep baritone that had barely registered with Zia a moment ago. The panic was gone, though, replaced by relief colored with what sounded like reluctant amusement.

Jézus, Mária és József! Didn't this idiot appreciate how close a call his nephew had just had? Incensed, Zia shoved to her feet and spun toward him. She was just about to let loose with both barrels when she realized his amused drawl had been show for the boy's sake. Despite the seemingly laconic reply, his hands were balled into fists and his faded University of Texas T-shirt stretched across taut shoulders.

Very wide shoulders, she couldn't help but note, topped by a tree trunk of a neck and a square chin showing just a hint of a dimple. With her trained clinician's eye for detail, Zia also noted that his nose looked as though it had gotten crosswise of a fist sometime in his past and his eyes gleamed as deep a green as the ocean. His hair was a rich, dark sorrel and cut rigorously short.

The rest of him wasn't bad, either. She formed a fleeting impression of a broad chest, muscular thighs emerging from ragged cutoffs, and bare feet sporting worn leather flip-flops. Then those sea-green eyes flashed her a grateful look and he went down on one knee beside his nephew.

"You, young man," he said as he helped the boy sit up,

"are in deep doo-doo. You know darn well you're not allowed to come down to the beach alone."

"Buster needed to go out."

"I repeat, you are *not* allowed to come down to beach alone."

Zia shrugged off the remnants of the rage that had hit her when she'd thought the boy was allowed to roam unsupervised. She also had to hide a smile at the pitiful note that crept into Davy's voice. Like all five- or six-year olds, he had the whine down pat.

"You said Buster was my 'sponsibility when you gave him to me, Uncle Mickey. You said I had to walk him 'n feed him 'n pick up his poop 'n…"

"We'll continue this discussion later."

Whoa! Even Zia blinked at the *that's enough* finality in the uncle's voice.

"How do you feel?" he asked the boy.

"'Kay."

"Good enough to stand up?"

"Sure."

With the youthful resilience that never failed to amaze Zia, the kid flashed a cheeky grin and scrambled to his feet. His pet woofed encouragement, and both boy and dog would have scampered off if the uncle hadn't laid a restraining hand on his nephew's shoulder.

"Don't you have something you want to say to this lady?"

"Thanks for not letting me get drowned."

"You're welcome."

His uncle kept him in place by a firm grip on his wet T-shirt and held out his other hand to Zia. "I'm Mike Brennan. I can't thank you enough for what you did for Davy."

She took the offered hand, registered its strength and warmth as it folded around hers. "Anastazia St. Sebastian. I'm glad I got to him in time."

* * *

The sheer terror that had rocked Mike's world when he'd spotted this woman hauling Davy's limp body out of the sea had receded enough now for him to focus on her for the first time. Closer inspection damn near rocked him back on his flip-flops again.

Her wet, glistening black hair hung to just below her shoulders. Her eyes were almost as dark as her hair and had just the suggestion of a slant to them. And any super-model on the planet would have killed for those high, slash-ing cheekbones. The slender body outlined to perfection by her pink spandex tank and black Lycra running shorts was just icing on the cake. That, and the fact that she wasn't wearing a wedding or engagement ring.

"I think he'll be all right," she was saying with another glance at now fidgeting Davy, "but you might want to keep an eye on him for the next few hours. Watch for signs of rapid breathing, a fast heart rate or low-grade fever. All are common the first few hours after a near drowning."

Her accent was as intriguing as the rest of her. The faint lilt gave her words a different cadence. Eastern European, Mike thought, but it was too slight to pin down.

"You appear to know a lot about this kind of situation. Are you an EMT or first responder?"

"I'm a physician."

Okay, now he was doubly impressed. The woman pos-sessed the mysterious eyes of an odalisque, the body of a temptress and the smarts of a doc. He'd hit the jackpot here. Nodding toward the colorful umbrellas just popping up at the restaurant across the highway from the beach, he made his move.

"I hope you'll let Davy and me show our appreciation by buying you breakfast, Dr. St. Sebastian."

"Thanks, but I've already had breakfast."

No way Mike was letting this gorgeous creature get away. "Dinner, then."

"I'm, uh, I'm here with my family."

"I am, too. Unfortunately." He made a face at his nephew, who giggled and returned the exaggerated grimace. "I'd be even more grateful if you give me an excuse to get away from them for a while."

"Well…"

He didn't miss her brief hesitation. Or her quick glance at *his* left hand. The white imprint of his wedding ring had long since faded. Too bad he couldn't say the same for the inner scars. Shoving the disaster of his marriage into the dark hole where it belonged, Mike overrode her apparent doubts.

"Where are you staying?"

She took her time replying. Those exotic eyes looked him up and down. Lingered for a moment on his faded T-shirt, his ragged cutoffs, his worn leather flip-flops.

"We're at the Camino del Rey," she said finally, almost reluctantly. "It's about a half mile up the beach."

Mike suppressed a smile. "I know where it is. I'll pick you up at seven-thirty." He gave his increasingly impatient nephew's shoulder a squeeze. "Say goodbye to Dr. St. Sebastian, brat."

"Bye, Dr. S'baston."

"Bye, Davy."

"See you later, Anastazia."

"Zia," she said. "I go by Zia."

"Zia. Got it."

Tipping two fingers in a farewell salute, Mike used his grip on his nephew's T-shirt to frog-walk him up the beach.

Zia tracked them as far as the row of houses on stilts fronting the beach. She couldn't believe she'd agreed to dinner with the uncle. As if she didn't have enough on her mind right now without having to make small talk with a complete stranger!

Arms folded, she watched the terrier jump and cavort alongside them. The dog's exuberance reminded her all too forcefully of the racing hound her sister-in-law had hauled down to Texas with her. Natalie was nutso over the whip-thin Magyar Agár and insisted on calling the hound Duke—much to the chagrin of Zia's brother, Dominic, who still hadn't completely adjusted to his transition from Interpol agent to Grand Duke of Karlenburgh.

The duchy of Karlenburgh had once been part of the vast Austro-Hungarian Empire but had long since ceased to exist anywhere except in history books. That hadn't stopped the paparazzi from hounding Europe's newest royal out of the shadows of undercover work. And Dom had retaliated by sweeping the woman who'd discovered he was heir to the title off her feet and into the ranks of the ever-growing St. Sebastian clan. Now Zia's family included an affectionate, übersmart sister-in-law as well as the two thoroughly delightful cousins she and Dom had met for the first time three years ago.

And, of course, Great-Aunt Charlotte. The regal, iron-spined matriarch of the St. Sebastian family and the woman who'd welcomed Zia into her home and her heart. Zia couldn't imagine how she would have made it this far in her pediatric residency without the duchess's support and encouragement.

Two and a half years, she thought as she abandoned the rest of her morning run to head back to the condo. Twenty-eight months of rounds and call rotations and team meetings and chart prep and discharge conferences. Endless days and nights agonizing over her patients. Heartbreaking hours grieving with parents while burying her own aching loss so deep it rarely crept out to haunt her anymore.

Except at moments like this. When she had to decide

whether she should continue to work with sick children for the next thirty or forty years…or whether she should accept the offer from Dr. Roger Wilbanks, Chief of the Pediatrics Advanced Research Center, to join his team. Could she abandon the challenges and stress of hands-on medicine for the regular hours and seductive income of a world-class, state-of-the-art research facility?

That question churned like battery acid in her gut as she headed for the resort where the St. Sebastian clan was staying. With the morning sun now burning bright in an achingly blue Texas sky, the holiday sun worshippers had begun to flock down to the beach. Umbrellas had flowered open above rows of lounge chairs. Colorful towels were spread on the sand, occupied by bathers with no intention of getting wet. Patches of dead white epidermis just waiting to be crisped showed above skimpy bikini bottoms, along with more than one grossly distended male belly.

Without warning, Zia's mind zinged back to Mike Brennan. No distended belly there. No distended *anything*. Just muscled shoulders and roped thighs and that killer smile. His worn flip-flops and ragged cutoffs suggested a man comfortable with himself in these high-dollar environs. Zia liked that about him.

And now that she thought about it, she actually liked the idea of having dinner with him. Maybe he offered just what she needed. A leisurely evening away from her boisterous family. A few hours with all decisions put on hold. A casual fling…

Whoa! Where had that come from?

She didn't indulge in casual flings. Aside from the fact that her long hours and demanding schedule took so much out of her, she was too careful, too responsible—all right, just too fastidious. Except for one lamentable lapse in judgment, that is. Grimacing, she shrugged aside the memory of the handsome orthopedic surgeon who'd somehow neglected to mention that his divorce was several light-years from being final.

She was still kicking herself for that sorry mistake when she keyed the door to the two-story, six-bedroom penthouse. Although it was still early morning, the noise level had already inched toward the top of the decibel scale. Most of that was due to her cousin Gina's almost-three-year-old twins. The lively, blue-eyed blondes acted like miniatures of their laughing, effervescent mother...most of the time. This, Zia could tell as shrieks of delight emanated from the living room, was most definitely one of those times.

An answering smile tugged at her lips as she followed the squeals to the living area. Its glass wall offered an eye-boggling panorama of the Gulf of Mexico. Not that any of the occupants of the spacious living room appeared the least interested in the view. They were totally absorbed with the twins' attempts to add blinking red Rudolph noses to the fuzzy reindeer antlers and jingle-bell halters already adorning their uncles. Dominic and Devon sat cross-legged on the floor within easy reach of the twins, while their dad, Jack, watched with diabolical delight.

"What's going on here?" Zia asked.

"Thanta's coming," curly-haired Amalia lisped excitedly. "And..."

"Uncle Dom and Dev are gonna help pull his sled," little Charlotte finished.

The girls were named for the duchess, whose full name and title filled several lines of print. Sarah's and Gina's were almost as long. Zia's, too. Try squeezing Anastazia Amalia Julianna St. Sebastian onto a computer form, she thought as she paused in the doorway to enjoy the merry scene.

No three men could be more dissimilar in appearance yet so similar in character, she decided. Jack Harris, the twins' father and the current United States Ambassador to the United Nations, was tall, tawny haired and aristocratic.

Devon Hunter's hard-fought rise from aircraft cargo han-
dler to self-made billionaire showed in his lean face and
clever eyes. And Dominic…

Ahh. Was there anyone as handsome and charismatic as
the brother who'd assumed legal guardianship of Zia after
their parents died? The friend and advisor who'd guided
her through her turbulent teens? The highly skilled undercover agent who'd encouraged her all through college and
med school, then walked away from his adrenaline-charged
career for the woman he loved?

Natalie loved him, too, Zia thought with an inner smile
as her glance shifted to her sister-in-law. Completely, un-
reservedly, joyously. One look at her face was all *anyone*
needed to see the devotion in her warm brown eyes. She occupied one end of a comfortable sofa, her fingers entwined
in the collar of the quivering racing hound to prevent him
from joining the reindeer brigade.

Zia's cousins sat next to her. Gina, with a Santa hat
perched atop her tumble of silvery blond curls and candy-
cane-striped leggings, looked more like a teenager than
mother of twins, the wife of a highly respected diplomat and
a partner in one of NYC's most successful event-hosting
enterprises. Gina's older sister, Sarah, occupied the far end
of the sofa. Her palms rested lightly on her just-beginning-
to-show baby bump and her elegant features showed the
quiet joy of impending motherhood.

But it was the woman who sat with her back straight and
her hands clasping the ebony head of her cane who caught
and held Zia's eye. The Grand Duchess of Karlenburgh was
a role model for any female of any age. As a young bride
she'd resided in a string of castles scattered across Europe,
including the one that guarded a high mountain pass on the
border between Austria and Hungary. Then the Soviets in-
vaded and later brutally suppressed an uprising by Hungarian patriots. Forced to witness her husband's execution,

Charlotte had made a daring escape by trekking over the snow-covered Alps with her newborn infant in her arms and a fortune in jewels hidden inside the baby's teddy bear. Now, more than sixty years later, she'd lost none of her dignity or courage or regal bearing. White haired and paper skinned, the indomitable duchess ruled her ever-growing family with a velvet-gloved fist.

She was the reason they were all here, spending the holidays in Texas. Charlotte hadn't complained. She considered whining a deplorable character flaw. But Zia hadn't failed to note how the vicious cold and record snowfall that blanketed New York City in early December had exacerbated the duchess's arthritis. And all it took was one mention of Zia's concern to galvanize the entire St. Sebastian clan.

In short order, Dev and Sarah had leased this six-bedroom condo and set it up as a temporary base for their Los Angeles operations. Jack and Gina had adjusted their busy schedules to enjoy a rare, prolonged holiday in South Texas. Dom and Natalie flew down, too, with the hound in tow. The family had also convinced Maria, the duchess's longtime housekeeper and companion, to enjoy an all-expenses-paid vacation while the staff here at the resort took care of everyone's needs.

Zia hadn't been able to spend quite as much time in Texas as the others. Although Mount Sinai's second- and third-year residents were allowed a full month of vacation, few if any ever strayed far from the hospital. Zia hadn't taken off more than three days in a row since she began her residency. And with the decision of whether to accept Dr. Wilbanks's offer weighing so heavily on her mind, she wouldn't have dragged herself down to Galveston for a full week if Charlotte hadn't insisted. Almost as if she'd read her mind, the duchess looked up at that moment. Her gnarled fingers tightened on the head of her cane. One snowy brow lifted in a regal arch.

* * *

Ha! Charlotte had only to look at Zia to guess what the girl was thinking! That she was so old and decrepit, she needed this bright Texas sunshine to warm her bones. Well, perhaps she did. But she also needed to put some color back into her great-niece's cheeks. She was too pale. Too thin and tired. She'd worn herself to the bone during the first two years of her residency. And worked even more the past few months. But every time Charlotte tried to probe the shadows lurking behind those weary eyes, the girl smiled and fobbed her off with the excuse that exhaustion just was part of being a third-year resident in one of the country's most prestigious medical schools.

Charlotte might not see eighty again, but she wasn't yet senile. Nor was she the least bit hesitant where the well-being of her family was concerned. None of them, Anastazia included, had the least idea that she'd engineered this sojourn in the sun. All it had taken was some not-quite-surreptitious kneading of her arthritic knuckles and one or two few valiantly disguised grimaces. Those, combined with her seemingly offhand comment that New York City felt especially cold and damp this December, had done the trick.

Her family had reacted just as she'd anticipated. Within days they'd sorted through dozens of options from Florida to California and everywhere in between. A villa on the Riviera and over-water bungalows in the South Pacific hadn't been out of the mix, either. But they'd decided on South Texas as the most convenient for both the East and West Coast family contingents. Within a week, Charlotte and Maria had been ensconced in seaside, sun-drenched luxury with various members of the family joining them for differing lengths of time.

Charlotte had even convinced Zia to take off the whole of Christmas week. The girl was still too thin and tired, but at least her cheeks had gained some color. And, the duchess noted with relief, there was something very close to a sparkle in her eyes. Even more intriguing, her glossy black hair was damp and straggly and threaded with what looked suspiciously like strands of seaweed. Intrigued, she thumped her cane on the floor to get the twins' attention.

"Charlotte, Amalia, please be quiet for a moment."

The girls' high-pitched giggles dropped a few degrees in decibel level, if not in frequency.

"Come sit beside me, Anastazia, and tell me what happened during your run on the beach."

"How do you know something happened?"

"You have kelp dangling from your ear."

Zia patted both ears to find the offending strand. "So I do," she replied, chuckling.

The lighthearted response delighted Charlotte. The girl hadn't laughed very much lately. So little, in fact, that her rippling merriment snagged the attention of every adult in the room.

"Tell us," the duchess commanded. "What happened?"

"Let's see." Playing to her suddenly attentive audience, Zia pretended to search her memory. "A little boy got sucked in by the undertow and I dove in after him. I dragged him to shore, then administered CPR."

"Dear God! Is he all right?"

"He's fine. So is his uncle, by the way. Very fine," she added with a waggle of her brows. "Which is why I agreed to have dinner with him this evening."

Two

As Zia had anticipated, the announcement that she'd agreed to dinner with a total stranger unleashed a barrage of questions. The fact that she knew nothing about him didn't sit well with the overprotective males of her family.

As a result, the whole clan just happened to be gathered for pre-dinner cocktails when the doorman buzzed that evening and announced a visitor for Dr. St. Sebastian. Zia briefly considered taking the coward's way out and slipping down to wait for Brennan in the lobby. But she figured if he couldn't withstand the combined firepower of her brother, cousins and the duchess, she might as well not waste her time with him.

She was waiting at the front door when he exited the elevator. "Hello."

"Hi, Doc."

Wow, Zia thought. Or as some of her younger patients might say, the man was chill! The easy smile was the one she remembered from this morning, but the packaging was completely different. He'd traded his cutoffs and flip-flops for black slacks creased to a knife edge, an open-necked blue oxford shirt and a casually elegant sport coat. The tooled leather boots and black Stetson were a surprise, however.

Like most Europeans, Zia had grown up on the Hollywood image of cowboys. Tom Selleck in *Last Stand at Sabre River*. Matt Damon in *All The Pretty Horses*. Kevin Costner in *Open Range*. Living in New York City for the past two and a half years hadn't altered her mental stereotype. Nor had she stumbled across many locals here in Galveston who sported the traditional Texas headgear. It looked good on Brennan, though. Natural. As though it was as much a part of him as his air of easy self-assurance and long-legged stride. It also lit a spark of unexpected delight low in her belly. The man was primo in flip-flops or cowboy boots.

She did a mental tongue-swallow and asked about his nephew. "How's Davy?"

"Sulking because he got cut off from TV and videos for the entire day as punishment for skipping out of the house."

"No aftereffects?"

"None so far. His mother's patience is wearing wire thin, though."

"I can imagine."

"My family's having drinks on the terrace. Would you like to say hello?"

"Sure."

"Be prepared," she warned. "There are a lot of them."

"No problem. My Irish grandfather married a Mexican beauty right out of a convent school here on South Padre Island. You haven't experienced big and noisy until you've been to Sunday dinner at my *abuelita*'s house."

Now that he'd mentioned his heritage, Zia could see traces of both cultures. The reddish glint in his dark chestnut hair and those emerald-green eyes hinted at the Irish in him. What she'd assumed was a deep Texas tan might well be a gift from his Mexican grandmother. Wherever the source, the combination made for a decidedly potent whole!

As she led him to the terrace that wrapped around two sides of the condo, she was glad she'd decided to dress up a bit, too. She spent most of her days in a lab coat with a stethoscope draped around her neck and her rare evenings off in comfortable sweats. She had to admit it had felt good to slither into a silky red camisole and a pair of Gina's tight, straight-leg jeans with a sparkling red crystal heart on the right rear pocket. Gina had also supplied the shoes. The lethal stilettos added three inches to Zia's own five-seven yet still didn't bring her quite to eye level with Mike Brennan.

She'd clipped her hair up in its usual neat knot, but Sarah had insisted on teasing loose a few strands to frame her face. And Dom's wife, Natalie, contributed the twisted copper torque she'd found in a London shop specializing in reproductions of ancient Celtic jewelry. Feeling like Cinderella dressed by three doting fairy godmothers, Zia slid back the glass door to the terrace.

The twelve pairs of eyes that locked on the new arrival might have intimidated a lesser man. To Brennan's credit, his stride barely faltered as he followed Zia onto the wide terrace.

"Hey, everyone," she announced. "Say hello to Mike—"

"Brennan," Dev finished on a startled note. "Aka Global Shipping Incorporated." He pushed to his feet and thrust out his hand. "How're you doing, Mike?"

"I'm good," he replied, obviously as surprised as Dev to find a familiar face at this family gathering. "You're related to Zia?"

"She and my wife, Sarah, are cousins."

"Five or six times removed," Zia added with a smile.

"The degree doesn't matter," Sarah protested. "Not among the St. Sebastians." She aimed a quizzical glance at her husband. "How do you two know each other?"

"Mike here is president and CEO of Global Shipping Incorporated, the third largest cargo container fleet in the US," Dev explained. "We contract for, what? Eight or nine million a year in long-haul shipping with GSI?"

"Closer to ten," Brennan responded.

Zia listened to the exchange in some surprise. In the space of just a few moments her sun-bronzed beach hottie had morphed to cool cowboy dude and now to corporate exec. She was still trying to adjust to the swift transitions when Dev threw in another zinger.

"And now that I think about it, doesn't your corporation own this resort? Along with another dozen or so commercial and industrial facilities in the greater Houston area?"

"We do."

"I'm guessing that's why we got such a good deal on the lease for this condo."

"We try to take care of our valued customers," Brennan acknowledged with a grin.

"Which we certainly appreciate."

Devon's positive endorsement might have carried some weight with outsiders. The two other males on the terrace preferred to form their own opinions, however. Skilled diplomat that he was, Gina's husband, Jack, hid his private assessment behind a cordial nod and handshake. Dominic was less reserved.

"Zia told us your young nephew almost drowned this morning," her brother said, his dark eyes cool. "Pretty careless of your family to let him go down to the beach alone, wasn't it?"

Brennan didn't try to dodge the bullet. A ripple of remembered terror seemed to cross his face as he nodded. "Yes, it was."

Aiming a behave-yourself glance at her brother, Zia introduced her guest to Gina, Maria and Natalie, who kept a firm hand on the collar of the lean, quivering hound eager to sniff out the new arrival. The twins regarded him from the safety of their mother's knee, but Brennan won giggles from both girls by hunkering down to their level and asking solemnly if that was a tree sprouting from Charlotte's head.

A giggling Amalia answered for her sister. "No, thilly. Those are antlers."

"Oh! I get it. She's one of Santa's reindeer."

"Yes," Charlotte confirmed as she held up two fingers, "and Santa's coming to Texas in this many days!"

"Wow, just two days, huh?"

"Yes, 'n it's our birthday, too!" She uncurled another finger. "We're going to be this many years."

"Sounds like you've got some busy days ahead. You guys better be good so you'll get lots of presents."

"We will!"

With that ringing promise producing wry smiles all around, Zia led Mike to the snowy-haired woman ensconced in a fan-backed rattan chair. He swept off his hat as Zia made the introduction.

"This is my great-aunt, Charlotte St. Sebastian, Grand Duchess of Karlenburgh."

Charlotte held out a blue-veined hand. Mike took it in a gentle grip and held it for a moment. "It's a pleasure to meet you, Duchess. And now I know why Zia's last name seemed so familiar. Wasn't there something in the papers a couple of years ago about your family recovering a long-lost painting by Caravaggio?"

"Canaletto," the duchess corrected.

Her eyelids lowered and her expression turned intensely private, as it always did when talk drifted to the Venetian landscape her husband had given her when she'd become pregnant with their first and only child.

"Would you care for an aperitif?" she asked, emerging from her brief reverie. "We can offer you whatever you wish. Or," she added blandly, "a taste of one of the finest brandies ever to come out of the Austro-Hungarian Empire."

"Say no and make a polite escape," Gina warned. "*Pálinka* is not for the faint of heart."

"I've been accused of a lot of things," Brennan responded with a crooked grin. "Being faint of heart isn't one of them."

Sarah and Gina exchanged quick, amused glances. Downing a swig of the fruity, throat-searing brandy produced only in Hungary had become something of a rite of passage for men introduced into the St. Sebastian clan. Dev and Jack had passed the test but claimed they still bore the scorch marks on their vocal chords.

"Don't say you weren't warned," Zia murmured after she'd splashed some of the amber liquid into a cut-crystal snifter.

Mike accepted the snifter with a smile. His dad and grandfather had both been hardworking, hard-living longshoremen who'd worked the Houston docks all their lives. Mike and his two brothers had skipped school more times than they could count to hang around the waterfront with them. They'd also worked holidays and summers as casuals, lashing cargo containers or spending long, backbreaking hours shoveling cargo into the holds of cavernous bulk carriers. All three Brennan sons had been offered a coveted slot in the International Longshore and Warehouse Union after they'd graduated from college. Colin and Sean had joined, but Mike had opted for a hitch in the navy instead, then used his savings and a hefty bank loan to buy his first ship—a rusty old tub that made milk runs to Central America. Twelve years and a fleet of oceangoing oil tankers and container vessels later, he could still swear and drink with the best of them.

So he tossed back a swallow of the brandy with absolute certainty that it couldn't pack half the kick of the corrosive rotgut he'd downed in and out of the navy. He knew he was wrong the instant it hit the back of his throat. He managed not to choke, but his eyes leaked like an old bucket and he had to suck air big-time though his nostrils.

"Wow!" Blinking and breathing fire, he gave the brandy a look of profound respect. "What did you say this is?" he asked the duchess between quick gasps.

"Pálinka."

"And it comes from Austria?"

"From Hungary, actually."

"Anyone ever tried to convert it to fuel? One gallon of this stuff could propel a turbocharged two-stroke diesel engine."

The smile that came into the duchess's faded blue eyes told Mike he'd survived his initial trial by fire. He wasn't ashamed to grab a ready-made excuse to dodge another test.

"I've made reservations at a restaurant just a couple of blocks from here," he told her. "Would you like to join us for dinner?" He turned to include the rest of the family. "Any of you?"

Charlotte answered for them all. "Thank you, but I'm sure Zia would prefer not to have her family regale you with stories about her misspent youth. We'll let her do that herself."

Once in the elevator, Mike propped his shoulders against the rear of the cage dropping them twenty stories. "Misspent?" he echoed. "I'm intrigued."

More than intrigued. He was as fascinated by this woman's stunning beauty as by the dark circles under her eyes. She'd tried to conceal them with makeup but the shadows were still visible, like faint bruises marring the pearly luster of her skin.

"I guess *misspent* is as good a description as any," she replied with a laugh. "But in my defense I only tried to operate on the family dog once. My brother, unfortunately, didn't get off as easily. I subjected him to all kinds of torture in the name of medicine."

"Looks like he survived okay."

He also looked decidedly less than friendly. Mike didn't blame the man. He and *his* brothers had threatened bodily harm to any male who let his glands get out of control while dating one of their sisters.

God knew Mike's glands were certainly working overtime. Despite those faint shadows under her eyes, Anastazia St. Sebastian was every man's secret fantasy come to life. Slender, graceful and so sexy she turned heads as they crossed the marble-tiled lobby and exited into the six acres of lush gardens at the center of the Camino del Rey complex.

The vacation complex was only one of several projects Mike's ever-expanding corporation had invested in to help restore Galveston after Hurricane Ike roared ashore in September 2008. The costliest hurricane in Texas history, Ike claimed more than a hundred lives and did more than $37 billion in damage all along the Gulf. Parts of Galveston were still recovering, but major investments like this beautifully landscaped luxury resort were helping that process considerably.

A frisky ocean breeze teased Zia's hair as she and Mike wound past the massive Neptune fountain the landscape architect had made the focal point of the gardens. Beyond the statue were two tall, elaborately designed wrought-iron gates that gave directly onto the beach. On the opposite side of the garden, a set of identical gates exited onto San Luis Pass Road, the main artery that ran the length of Galveston Island.

"I made reservations at Casa Mia," Mike said as he took her elbow to steer her through the gates. "Hope that's okay."

"This is my first trip to Galveston. I'm more than happy to trust the judgment of a local."

Temperatures in South Texas during the summer could give hell a run for its money. In the dead of winter, however, the balmy days and sixty-five-degree evenings were close to heaven…and perfect for strolling the wide sidewalk that bordered San Luis Pass Road. Smooth operator that he was, Mike casually shifted his hold from Zia's elbow to her forearm. Her skin was warm under his palm, her muscles firm and well-toned. He used the short walk to fill in the essential blanks. Found out she was born in Hungary. Did her undergraduate work at the University of Budapest. Graduated from medical school in Vienna at the top of her class. Had offers from a half-dozen prestigious pediatric residency programs before opting for Mount Sinai in New York City.

She elicited the same basics from him. "Texas born and bred," he admitted cheerfully. "I traveled quite a bit during my years in the navy, but this area kept pulling me back. It's home to four generations of Brennans now. My parents, grandparents, one brother and two of my three sisters all live within a few blocks of each other."

She eyed the ultraexpensive high-rises crowding the beachfront. "Here on the island?"

"No, they live in Houston. So do I, most of the time. I keep a place here on the island for the family to use, though. The kids all love the beach."

"And you're not married."

It was a statement, not a question, which told Mike she wouldn't be walking through the soft evening light with him if she had any doubts about the matter.

"I was. Didn't work out."

That masterful understatement came nowhere close to describing three months of mind-blowing sex followed by three years of growing restlessness, increasing dissatisfaction, angry complaints and, finally, corrosive bitterness. Hers, not his. By the time the marriage was finally over Mike felt as though he'd been dragged through fifty miles of Texas scrub by his heels. He'd survived, but the experience wasn't one he wanted to repeat again in this lifetime. Although…

His psyche might still be licking its wounds but his head told him marriage would be different with the right woman. Someone who appreciated the dogged determination required to build a multinational corporation from the ground up. Someone who understood that success in *any* field often meant seventy- or eighty-hour workweeks, missed vacations, opting out of a spur-of-the-moment junket to Vegas.

Someone like the leggy brunette at his side.

Mike slanted the doc a glance. One of his sisters was a nurse. He knew the demands Kathleen's career made on her and on the other professionals she worked with. Anastazia St. Sebastian had to have a core of steel to make it as far as she had.

His curiosity about the woman mounted as they turned onto a side street. A few steps later they reached the Spanish-style villa that had recently become one of Galveston's most exclusive spots. It sat behind tall gates with no sign, no lit menu box, no indication at all that it was a commercial establishment. But the hundreds of flickering votive lights in the courtyard drew a pleased gasp from Zia, and the table tucked in a private corner of the candle-lit patio was the one always made available to the top officers and favored clients of Global Shipping Incorporated.

"Back to subjecting your bother to all kinds of medical torture," he said when they'd been seated and ordered an iced tea for the doc and Vizcaya on ice for Mike, who sincerely hoped a slug of white rum would kill the lingering aftereffects of *pálinka*. "Did you always want to be a physician?"

"Always."

The reply was quick but not quite as light as she'd obviously intended. Mike hadn't survived all those summers and holidays in the bare-knuckle world of the docks without learning to pick up on every nuance, spoken or not.

"But….?" he prompted.

She flashed him a look that ran the gamut from surprised to guarded to deliberately blasé. "Med school's been a long and rather grueling slog. I'm in the homestretch now, though."

"But…?" he said again, the word soft against the clink of cutlery and buzz of conversation from other tables.

The arrival of the server with their drinks saved Zia from having to answer. She hadn't shared her insidious doubts with anyone in her family. Not even Dominic. Yet as she sipped her iced tea she felt the most absurd urge to spill her guts to this stranger.

So why *not* confide in him? Odds were she'd never see the man again after tonight. There were only a few days left on her precious vacation. And judging from Dev's comments about Global Shipping Inc., its president and CEO had a shrewd head on his shoulders. Granted, he couldn't begin to understand the demands and complexities of the medical world but that might actually be a plus. An outsider could assess her situation objectively, without the baggage of having cheered and supported and encouraged her through six and a half years of med school and residency.

"But," she said slowly, swirling the ice in her tall glass, "I'm beginning to wonder if I'm truly right for pediatric medicine."

"Why?"

She could toss out a hundred reasons. Like the overwhelming sense of responsibility for patients too young or too frightened to tell her how they hurt. The aching helplessness when faced with children beyond saving. The struggle to contain her fury at parents or guardians whose carelessness or cruelty inflicted unbelievably grievous injuries.

But the real reason, the one she'd thought she could compensate for by going into pediatric medicine, rose up to haunt her. She'd never talked about it to anyone but Dom. And even he was convinced she'd put it behind her. Yet reluctantly, inexplicably, Zia found herself detailing the old pain to Mike Brennan.

"I developed a uterine cyst my first year at university," she said, amazed that she could speak so calmly of the submucosal fibroid that had changed her life forever. "It ruptured during winter break, while I was on a ski trip in Slovenia."

She'd thought at first that she'd started her period early but the pain had become more intense with each hour. And the blood! Dear God, the blood!

"I almost died before they got me to the hospital. At that point the situation was so desperate the surgeons decided the only way to save my life was to perform an emergency hysterectomy."

She fell silent as the waiter materialized at their table to take their order. Mike sent him away with a quiet, "Give us some time."

"I love children," Zia heard herself say into the silence that followed. "I always imagined I'd have a whole brood of happy, gurgling babies. When I accepted that I would never give birth to a child of my own, I decided that at least I could help alleviate the pain and suffering of others."

"But…"

There it was. That damned "but" that had her hanging from a limb like a bird with a broken wing.

"It's hard giving so much of myself to others' children," she finished, her voice catching despite every attempt to control it. "So much harder than I ever imagined."

Her doubt and private misery filled the silence that spun out between them. Mike broke it after a moment with a question that cut to the core of her bruising inner conflict.

"What will you do if you don't practice medicine?"

"I'll stay in the medical field, but work on another side of the house."

There! She'd said it out loud for the first time. And not to her brother or Natalie or the duchess or her cousins. To a stranger, who didn't appear shocked or disappointed that she would trade her lifelong goal of treating the sick for the sterile environment of a lab.

Like all third-year residents at Mount Sinai, she'd been required to participate in a scholarly research project in addition to seeing patients, attending conferences and teaching interns. Worried by the seeming increase in hospital-acquired infections among the premature infants in the neonatal ICU, she'd searched for clues via five years' worth of medical records. Her extensive database included the infants' birth weight, ethnic origin, delivery methods, the time lapse to onset of infections, methods of treatment and mortality rates.

Although she wouldn't brief the results of her study until the much anticipated annual RRP—Residents' Research Presentation—her preliminary findings had so intrigued the hospital's director of research that he'd suggested an expanded effort that included more variables and a much larger sample base. He'd also asked Zia to conduct the two-year study under his direct supervision. If the grant came through within the next few months, she could start the research as her spring elective, then join Dr. Wilbanks's team full-time after completing her residency.

"The director of pediatric research at Mount Sinai has already asked me to join his staff," she confided to Mike.

"Is that as impressive as it sounds?"

A hint of pride snuck into her voice. "Actually, it is. Dr.

Wilbanks seems to think the study I've been working on as a resident is worth expanding into a full-fledged team effort. He also thinks it might warrant as much as a million-dollar research grant."

"That *is* impressive. What does the study involve?"

Lord, he was easy to talk to. Zia didn't usually discuss topics such as Methicillin-resistant Staphylococcus aureus, aka MRSA, with someone not wearing scrubs. Especially during a candlelit dinner.

As the incredibly scrumptious meal progressed, however, Brennan's interest stimulated her as much as his quick grasp of the essentials of her study.

She couldn't blame either his interest or his intellect for what happened when they left the restaurant, however. That was result of a lethal combination of factors. First, their decision to walk back along the beach. Zia had to remove her borrowed stilettos to keep from sinking in the sand, but the feel of it hard and damp beneath bare feet only added to her heightened perceptions. Then there was the three-quarter moon that traced a liquid silver path across the sea. And finally the arm Mike slid around her waist.

She turned into his kiss, fully anticipating that it would be pleasant. A satisfying end to an enjoyable evening. She *didn't* expect the hunger that balled in her belly when his mouth fused with hers.

He felt the kick, too. Although his hat brim shadowed his eyes when he raised his head, his skin was stretched tight across his cheeks and there was a gruff edge to his voice when he asked if she'd like to stop by his place for coffee or a drink.

Or…?

He didn't have to say it. Her pulse kicking, Zia knew the invitation was open-ended. "Don't you have company?

Davy and…" She searched her memory. "And Kevin and their mother?"

"Eileen took the kids back to town this afternoon. I suspect she won't let either of them close to the water for the next five years. She wants to thank you personally, by the way. She told me to be sure and get your phone number." Laughter rumbled in his chest. "I promised I would."

Zia hesitated for all of three seconds before digging her cell phone out of her purse. "I'll text my family and tell them not to wait up for me."

Three

The brief detour to Mike's place should have allowed plenty of time for Zia's common sense to reassert itself. *Would* have, if he hadn't taken her arm again to steer her toward a barely discernible path through the dunes. His hand was warm against her skin, his body close—too close!—to hers in the silvery moonlight.

The beach house on stilts he conducted her to was obviously new. Gleaming a pale turquoise in the moonlight, it sat on a high rise that gave it an unobstructed view of both the Gulf of Mexico and the lights of Houston gleaming in the far distance. The thick pilings looked as though they went down a mile, and white-painted storm shutters framed every window.

When Mike ushered her up the stairs to the front landing and keyed the door lock, Zia still had time to defuse the situation. Once inside, she could have drifted to the wall of windows overlooking the Gulf. Could have contemplated the moon's reflection on the dark, restless sea. Could have accepted his offer of an after-dinner brandy or coffee. Against every increasingly strident warning issued by her clinical, careful self, she ignored the view and declined a drink. Weeks of stress, indecision and near exhaustion got lost in a rush of biological need. For what was left of the night, she didn't want to think. Didn't want to do anything but give herself up to the hunger pulsing through her in slow, liquid rolls.

And Brennan didn't waste time repeating the offer. Tugging off his hat, he skimmed it carelessly toward the nearest chair and cupped her face in his palms.

"You are *so* gorgeous."

His thumbs brushed her cheeks, her lower lip. An answering need turned his forest-glade eyes as dark and restless as the sea. Zia felt another wild leap as she sensed the iron control that held him back. He was leaving it to her to dodge the bullet hurtling at them in warp speed…or step in front of it. She chose option B.

Dropping the stilettos she'd carried into the house, she hooked her arms around his neck. "So are you."

"Me? Gorgeous?" He looked startled, then amused. "Not hardly, darlin'."

The drawl came slow and rich, and the laughter in his eyes raised goose bumps of delight. That, and the quick, confident way he claimed her mouth. He was much a man, this Michael Brennan.

Very much a man, as she discovered when he lowered his hands to her waist and drew her into him. He hardened against her hip even as his lips moved over hers with dizzying skill. He'd been married, she remembered, and had learned well how to stoke a woman's fire. She was panting when he raised his head. Eager for his touch when he fumbled the clip from her hair. The heavy mass tumbled free, and Brennan buried his hands in it, holding her steady while he explored her mouth again.

With every nerve in her body alive and clamoring, Zia conducted her own avid exploration. Her palms planed his broad shoulders. Her fingers found the lapels of his sport coat. She peeled it back, forcing him to break contact long enough to wrestle free of it. He reached for her again but felt compelled to offer a gruff caveat.

"Just so you know, I don't make a habit of trying to finesse women I've just met into bed."

"Nor," she murmured, her acquired New York twang slipping away a little more with each word, "do I allow myself to be finessed."

The blood of her Magyar ancestors thrummed hot in her veins. She felt as wild as the steppes they'd swept down from on their fast, tireless ponies. As fierce as winds that howled through the mountains and valleys they'd eventually settled in.

"But tonight I shall make an exception, yes?"

"*Hell*, yes!"

He scooped her up almost before the words were out of her mouth. Cradling her against his chest, he headed in what she assumed was the direction of the bedroom. She used the short trip to attack the buttons on his crisp blue shirt.

She got the top two open and was nipping at the cords in his neck when he elbowed a door open. She gained a vague impression of wide-plank floorboards, sparse furnishings and framed posters of ships filling one wall. Then he was lowering her to a king-size bed covered in thin, buttery-soft suede.

Mike shed his shirt, boots and jeans with minimal motion and maximum speed. A real trick, considering that every drop of blood had drained from his head and was now pooled below his waist. He couldn't believe he'd managed to get the exotic, intriguing doc in his bed, but he sure as hell wasn't about to give her time for second thoughts.

Yet he dredged up enough self-control to strip her slowly, item by tantalizing item. The silky camisole. The thigh-hugging jeans with the sparkly red heart that had drawn his eyes to her butt every time she'd walked in front of him. Her half bra and thong were mere scraps of lace and easily disposed of. Then he made the near fatal mistake of pausing to drink in the sight of her long, slender curves. She gleamed like alabaster against the pearl-gray bedcover. Her hair spilled across the suede, as silky and erotic as the dark triangle at the apex of her thighs. Mike almost lost it then. Probably would have, if he hadn't gritted his teeth and held back the raging tide with the promise of exploring every slope and hollow of that luscious body.

Thank God he kept an emergency supply of condoms in the nightstand. The cache was a year old. Maybe more. With the demand for super-container ships skyrocketing and his fleet expanding almost faster than he could keep up with it, Mike hadn't had all that many opportunities to dip into this private stash. He intended to make up for those missed opportunities now, though.

If he could find the damned things! Muttering a curse under his breath, he rifled through the drawer. Where the devil had all this junk come from? With another muffled curse, he finally resorted to dumping the contents on the bed. Two dog-eared paperbacks, a handful of loose change, a spare set of keys, several socks and a plastic fire truck tumbled out.

Zia pushed up on one elbow and eyed the hook and ladder. "I've seen all kinds of sex toys during my years in med school," she said with a grin. "Some were put to rather remarkable use. But that's a new one."

"Dammit, I told Kevin and Davy to stay out… Ah! Thank God." He gave a huff of relief and held up two foil packets. "I caught the boys making water balloons out of them four or five months back but was sure I'd salvaged a few."

Four or five months back? Zia digested that little tidbit of information as he used his teeth to rip into one of the packets. Brennan must not bring many female friends to his beach house. The thought surprised her. And added another bubble to the cauldron that erupted into a furious boil at the sight of him sheathing himself.

He made quick work of it. A snap, a roll, and he tumbled her back onto the suede. He followed her down, bracing himself on his elbows to kiss her again. And again. And again. Her mouth. Her throat. Her aching breasts. Her quivering belly. When he eased a hand between her thighs, Zia went taut as a bow.

Yes! This was what she needed. What both her mind and her body craved. This wild pleasure. This dizzying spiral of excitement that contracted the muscles low in her belly. With each kiss and stroke of his busy fingers, the spasms got tighter, faster.

"Wait."

She clenched her jaw, tried to clamp down on the soaring sensations.

"Mike. Wait." She scrunched deeper into the velvety suede and reached for him. "Let me… Oh!"

Before she could do more than wrap her fingers around his rock-hard length the sensations spun into a white-hot core. Groaning, Zia gave up trying to stop the climax that shot up from her belly. She couldn't have held back if she'd wanted to. It came at her like an out-of-control freight train.

Neck arched, spine bowed, she rode it to the last shuddering sigh. When she collapsed onto the covers and opened her eyes, she saw Brennan watching her.

"Sorry," she murmured. "It's, ah, been a while."

"Oh, sweetheart." He was still hard and rampant against her hip. His shoulders were still taut, his tendons tight. Yet his grin contained nothing but smug male satisfaction. "You wouldn't be sorry if you had any idea how glorious you just looked."

Zia had studied human sexuality and the reproductive

process, of course. She could put a name to each stage of her body's response. Desire. Arousal. Lubrication. Orgasm. Satisfaction. She also knew the female of the species could generally repeat the cycle faster than the male. Still, she was surprised at *how* fast. All it took was for Mike to lean down and feather his lips over hers. The kiss was so tender—and such a contrast to the tension still locking his muscles—that Zia kicked into high gear again.

He filled her. Stroked her. Pushed her to another peak. She hung on this time and refused go over the edge without him.

Gasping and limp with pleasure, Zia knew she should get up, get dressed and go home. *Should* drifted into *later* when Mike defied conventional science by proving he could repeat the cycle after only a minimal break.

If the first round was fast and urgent, the second round was exquisitely slow. So slow, Zia had more than enough time to explore his hard, muscled body. The corded tendons, the washboard ribs, the flat belly, the five-inch scar on his left shoulder. She'd set enough stitches during her ER rotation to know a knife wound when she felt one.

"How did you get this?"

"Hmm?"

He shifted, obviously more interested her body than his own

"This scar?" she persisted. "How'd you get it?"

"It was just a slight misunderstanding."

"Between?"

"Me and a one-eyed, foul-breathed Portuguese. He was a pumper on the tanker I shipped out on the summer before my senior year in high school."

"And?"

"Let's just say Joachim didn't appreciate smart-assed

kids pointing out he hadn't grounded himself before opening the feed nozzle. Now…"

His hands cupped her butt and scooted her up a few
inches.

"Let's get back to more important matters."

Zia hadn't planned to zone out. Grabbing twenty or thirty
minutes to recharge in the residents' lounge had pretty much
become a way of life. All she'd intended was a brief cat-
nap between the sheets with her head nestled in the warm
angle between Brennan's neck and shoulder. So when she
blinked awake to a blaze of sunlight spilling through the
wide windows she gave a small yelp.

"Oh, no!"

She jerked upright and pushed her hair out of her eyes. A
quick glance around confirmed her hazy impressions from
last night. The flooring *was* wide oak planking polished
to a rich sheen. One wall *did* sport a collection of framed,
poster-size photographs of oceangoing vessels. And she
huddled amid a welter of silky cotton sheets topped by a
cloud-soft suede cover. Naked. With what felt like a good-
size patch of beard burn on her left cheek.

Oh, for heaven's sake! She was an adult. Responsible
and unattached. She had no reason to feel guilty or uncomfortable about explaining a whisker scrape to her family.
Or the fact that she'd spent the night with an interesting,
attractive man.

A man who evidently knew his way around a kitchen.
She discovered that after she'd made a trip to the bathroom,
scrambled into her clothes and followed the scent of frying
bacon. Mike had a small feast laid out on a glass-topped
breakfast table with a breath-knocking view of the Gulf.
Her surprised glance slid over the juice, sliced melon and
basket of croissants to lock on a tall carafe.

With a melodramatic groan, she made her presence

known. "Please tell me that's coffee," she begged, nodding to the carafe.

Mike angled around, spatula in hand, and grinned. "It is. Help yourself."

She did, but one sip had her gasping. "Good Lord!"

"Too strong?"

"Strong doesn't begin to describe it. This makes the black tar in the resident's lounge taste good by comparison."

"Sorry. I try to remember not everyone likes navy swill. Guess I didn't water it down enough. Why don't you run another pot?"

"That's okay. I'll just doctor this one."

Several ounces of milk and two heaping spoons of sugar made the coffee marginally more palatable. Sipping cautiously, Zia leaned her hip against the marble-topped island and watched the man work. She couldn't help noting how his faded University of Texas T-shirt molded his broad shoulders and his chestnut hair showed glints of dark red in the morning sunlight. She also noticed that he wielded the spatula with easy confidence.

The bacon cooked, he drained the grease and swiped the pan with paper towels before offering her a choice. "I've got the makings for a Spanish omelet and French toast. We can do either or both."

"You don't need to go to all that trouble. I'm fine with just coffee and a roll."

"I'm not," he countered, a smile in those sexy green eyes. "We burned up the calories last night. I need sustenance. So…omelet or French toast or both?"

"Omelet. Please."

Zia settled onto one of the stools lined up at the island, a little surprised she didn't feel even a trace of morning-after awkwardness. Not that the absence should surprise her. Mike Brennan had proved an easy, attentive companion at dinner last night. She'd opened up to him about doubts and worries she hadn't even shared with Dom yet.

Which reminded her...

She'd carried her purse into the kitchen with her. She fished out her cell phone, so glad she'd sent that text last night so Dom wouldn't have the police out searching for her maimed and mutilated body. She skimmed over the list of messages and saved them to be read later before sending a brief text saying she'd be home soon. That done, she refilled her coffee cup and watched a master at work.

"Where did you learn to cook?" she asked, marveling at his chopping, browning and omelet-flipping skills.

"That one-eyed Portuguese I told you about? Joachim Caldero? He pulled doubled duty as pumper and cook. Bastard jumped ship in Venezuela. Since I was the junior crew dog aboard, the captain stuck me with galley duty." He slid the first omelet onto a plate and poured the remaining egg mixture into the frying pan. "It was either dish up canned pork and beans all the way back to Galveston or teach myself a few basic skills."

She admired the perfect half oval. "Looks like you learned more than the basics."

"I added to my repertoire over the years," he admitted with a shrug. "My ex-wife wasn't into cooking."

Or anything else that didn't involve exclusive spas and high-end boutiques. Mike didn't look back often. Nor did he wallow in regrets. But as he added diced peppers and onions to the second omelet, he had to force the memory of his soured marriage out of his head. The outing took surprisingly little effort with this stunning, dark-haired beauty watching him with admiring eyes. Playing to his audience, he flipped the omelet into a perfect crescent and let it firm before sliding it onto a plate.

"Bring your coffee," he instructed as he added bacon strips to each plate and led the way to the breakfast table.

* * *

Mike already knew he wanted more time with Dr. Anastazia St. Sebastian. Arranging a follow-up assignation turned out to be a challenge, however.

"I need to spend time with my family," she said when he proposed getting together later. "It's Christmas Eve," she added when the significance of the day failed to register with Mike.

"Oh, hell. So it is."

No way he could duck the mandatory family gathering. With its dense Hispanic concentration, the four-block area of Houston where his grandmother lived still clung to the old ways. The entire Brennan clan would gather at her house this afternoon for food and games. Come dusk, they'd troop outside to watch the traditional *posada*. Local teenagers had been chosen to portray Mary and Joseph, and the whole parish would follow with lit candles and paper lanterns.

After the procession, it was back to his *abuelita*'s to hoist the star-shaped piñata. The seven-pointed star held all kinds of religious significance, most of which Mike had forgotten. There were devils in there. He remembered that much. They had to be beaten out with a stick, with the reward being the candy that showered down on shouting, squealing kids. After that came a feast of gargantuan proportions. Tamales, *atole, buñuelos*, and *ponche*—the potent hot drink brewed from spiced fruits.

Then the Irish portion of Mike's heritage would take over. He would accompany his parents and assorted siblings to midnight Mass. Go home with them for the inevitable last-minute toy assembly and gift-wrapping. And crash until the entire clan reconvened at his parents' house Christmas morning for an orgy of present opening followed by the traditional turkey dinner.

Mike had always enjoyed the nonstop celebrations. Even when his ex-wife was at her worst. Jill had alienated everyone in the family, but she'd never managed to destroy their enjoyment in the traditions they celebrated year after year.

Tradition was one thing, Mike thought as he eyed the woman seated across the table. Anastazia St. Sebastian was another. He'd met her less than twenty-four hours ago. Still, he would cheerfully abandon any and all family rituals for a chance to spend another evening with her.

Oh, hell! Who was he kidding? He wanted more than an evening. He wanted another entire night. Or two. Three.

"What about tomorrow? After all the presents have been opened and everyone's feasted? You might need a break from the family. I know I will."

"Tomorrow's full. It's Christmas and the twins' birthday."

"The day after?"

He was pushing too hard. He knew it. But he hadn't gotten where we was today by conceding defeat without a fight. And he still had an ace in the hole.

"Actually, I have an ulterior motive for wanting to see you again."

Her inky-black brows drew together. "Ulterior?"

He could see her turning that over in her mind. Maybe wondering if she'd walked into something here. She had, but Mike didn't want to scare her off.

"Last night at dinner you told me a little about the research you're doing. I'd like to know more."

The groove in her forehead deepened. "Why?"

"GSI has an entire division dedicated to studying and implementing technological improvements. Most of our efforts focus on the petroleum and shipping industries, of course, but we've funded research in other areas, as well."

"Medical research?"

He leaned forward, all business now. "We were part of a study last year to look at the exposure of crew members to carcinogenic agents on the decks of crude oil tankers.

It assessed the effects of the lead chromate paint used in cargo holds. I've also got my people looking at ways to contain the spread of norovirus. It doesn't hit only cruise ships," he admitted wryly.

"But I'm looking specifically at MRSA and its rate of incidence in newborn infants."

"You might be interested to know two Galveston seamen sued the owners of the *Cheryl K* for two million dollars a few years back. They claimed the owners failed to inform them of an allegedly high presence of bacteria on the vessel. Both seamen became infected with MRSA."

Mike had actually forgotten about that incident until Zia mentioned the virulent virus last night. He'd hit the internet this morning, though, and was now armed with specific details.

"The men reportedly suffered multiple infections to their extremities, backs and other parts of their body. Their suit accused Cheryl K Inc. and its namesake ship of general maritime negligence, unseaworthiness and failure to pay maintenance and cure."

He'd snagged her. He saw the interest spark in her eyes and slowly, carefully reeled her in.

"If you could squeeze out an hour or so, you could talk to the head of our Support Division. He's the one who manages our technology and research divisions."

"I would love to but I fly back to New York on Friday."

"Then we'll have to do it today or tomorrow."

"You wouldn't make your man come in on Christmas Eve!"

"Actually, he's my brother-in-law. Trust me. Rafe will grab at any excuse to escape the chaos for an hour or two."

She chewed on her lower lip, obviously torn. "How about I call you after I talk to my family and see what the plans are?"

"That works." He grabbed a pen and scribbled his cell

phone number on a napkin. Once she'd tucked it in the pocket of her jeans, he pushed away from the table. "If you're ready, I'll walk you back to the resort."

"You don't need to do that."

"Sure I do." He took her hand and tugged her out of her seat. "I also need to do this."

She came into his arms so easily, so naturally. The satisfaction that gave Mike didn't come close to the jolt that hit him when she tipped her head and returned his kiss, though. The taste of her, the feel of her, raised an instant, erotic response in every part of his body. And the little purr in her throat damned near doubled him over.

He spent the entire walk back to the resort plotting ways to delay Dr. St. Sebastian's return to New York.

Four

Zia key-carded the condo's main entrance and braced herself for the inquisition ahead. To her profound relief, the male half of the St. Sebastian clan had already departed for a round of golf. The females were lingering over cups of coffee and tea before a girding up for a final shopping foray. The adult females, anyway. The twins, Gina informed Zia before she pounced, were down at the resort's kiddie playground with Maria and the hound.

"So tell us! Was Brennan as yummy in bed as he is in person?"

"Really, Eugenia." The duchess sent her granddaughter a pained look. "Do try for a little more refinement."

"Forget refinement," Sarah interjected, crossing her hands over her belly. "We want details."

Even Natalie endorsed the demand, although she prefaced it with a solemn promise *not* to share those details with Dom.

"There's not much to tell," Zia answered, grinning. *"Vidi, vici, veni."*

Despite her bubbly personality and careless tumble of curls, Gina was no dummy. She picked up immediately on the variation of Caesar's famous line and gave a hoot of delight.

"No way you're getting away with just that, Zia Mia. We need more than 'I saw, I conquered, I came.'"

"Eugenia!" The duchess issued a distinct huff. "If Anastazia wishes to explain why she spent the night with a complete stranger, she will."

"I didn't intend to," Zia admitted with a sheepish grin as she dropped into an empty chair. "We had a lovely dinner and talked about…about all kind of things."

The duchess didn't miss the brief hesitation. Charlotte cocked her head, her shrewd gaze intent on her great-niece's face, but kept silent. She disapproved of casual sex with all its inherent dangers and complications. Not that she hadn't indulged in one or two liaisons during her long years as a widow. The brief affairs couldn't erase the pain of losing her husband, of course, but they had helped to lighten it.

Just as last night appeared to have lightened some of the shadows in her great-niece's eyes. Seeing the smile that now filled them, Charlotte gave the absent Mike Brennan her silent stamp of approval.

"Then after dinner," Zia continued, "when we were walking home in the moonlight, he kissed me."

Gina pursed her lips in a long, low whistle. "That must have been some kiss."

"It was. Believe me, it was."

That produced several moments of silence, which the irrepressible Gina broke with a snicker. "So you tumbled into bed and did the happy dance. What happens now? Are you and Mike going to see each other again?"

"He wants to. But it's Christmas. Like me, he's got family obligations. And I'm flying back to New York Friday morning, so…"

"So nothing! Much as we love you, cousin of mine, we'll

understand if you decide to absent yourself for a couple of hours. Or," she added with a wicked grin, "nights."

"Thanks," Zia said wryly. "Nice to know I won't be missed. But there's no point in getting together with Mike again, as hunky as he is. He's based here in Texas, I'm in New York. For the next few months, anyway. After that..."

"After that, you'll stay in the States," Gina finished firmly. "Your family lives here. Dom and Natalie, all of us. And you're already getting offers from children's hospitals all across the country. Any of them would be lucky to have a physician with your smarts. Who knows?" she added with a gleam in her blue eyes. "You may end up here in Houston. So, yes, you should most definitely steal away with the hunk for another few hours."

To everyone's surprise, it was the duchess who settled the matter. She'd picked up on Zia's vague reference to the future and watched her face during Gina's declaration. Folding her hands on the top of her cane, she held her great-niece's gaze.

"If I've learned nothing else in my eighty plus years, Anastazia, it's that one must trust one's instincts. As you must trust yours."

She knew, Zia realized. Maybe not the exact parameters of the decision she'd been struggling with. But the duchess had obviously guessed something was weighing on her heart. Chagrined, Zia leaned over and kissed the papery skin of her cheek.

"Thank you, Aunt. I will."

Mike answered on the second ring. He didn't try to hide his satisfaction when she told him she'd like to take him up on his offer to learn more about his company's research programs.

"I can slip away for a few hours today if that doesn't mess up your plans for Christmas Eve."

"Not at all. I was just about to shut down the beach house and head into Houston. I'll pick you up."

"Then you'll have to drive all the way back out to the island."

"Not a problem."

Maybe not, but Zia had some serious showering and makeup repairs to attend to. "Also not necessary," she said firmly. "I've got a whole fleet of rental cars at my disposal. Give me the address of your corporate offices and a good time to meet you there."

Zia pulled into the underground parking lot of the steel-and-glass tower housing the corporate headquarters of Global Shipping Incorporated a little before two that afternoon. Following Mike's instructions, she found the GSI guest parking slots and took the elevator to the three-story lobby dominated by a monster Christmas tree. Bubbling fountains and a rippling stream cut through a good half acre of marble tile, serenading her as she checked in at the security desk.

The uniformed guard wished her happy holidays and checked her ID. "I'll let Mr. Brennan know you're here," he said, handing her a bar-coded guest pass. "Take the first elevator on the left. It'll shoot you right to the GSI offices."

"Thanks."

The express elevator opened to a reception area with an eagle's-eye view of the Houston skyline. An electronic map of the world took up one entire wall, with flashing lights designating GSI's ships at sea. Zia's eyes widened at the array of green and amber dots. The legend beside the map tagged the green dots as cargo ships and the amber ones as oil tankers.

She was trying to guesstimate the total number when Mike emerged from an inner office accompanied by the individual she presumed was his brother-in-law. Both wore jeans and open-necked shirts but the similarity stopped there. Where Mike was tall, tanned and green-eyed, the man with him had jet-black hair, a pencil-thin mustache and a smile that emitted at least a thousand kilowatts of wow-power.

"Hello, Zia."

They strode forward to greet her, presenting a double whammy of pure masculinity.

"This is Rafe Montoya, GSI's VP for Support Systems. The poor guy's married to my sister Kathleen."

"It's a pleasure to meet you, Dr. St. Sebastian."

"Please, call me Zia."

"Zia it is." He took her hand in both of hers. "The whole family's still shaken over Davy's near miss yesterday. You have our deepest gratitude."

"I'm just glad I was there."

"So are we." Releasing her hand, he cut right to the reason they'd congregated in the empty office building. "I understand you're an expert in bacterial infections."

"Not an expert, by any means, but I'm compiling statistical data on the increasing incidence of infectious diseases in newborn infants."

"A disturbing trend, certainly. As is the increasing incidence of both bacterial and viral infections among crews at sea. Would you like to see some of the data we've collected?"

"Very much."

"I set up my laptop in Miguel's office."

"Miguel?" she echoed as Mike gestured to the set of double doors leading to the inner sanctum.

"Miguel, Mick, Mickey, Mike, Michael. I answer to any and all."

"Don't forget your sisters' favorite," his brother-in-law interjected, pitching his voice to a reedy falsetto. "Mike-eee."

With a good-natured grimace, Mike-eee ushered her

into a spacious, light-filled office. It was surprisingly un-cluttered. The desk was a slab of acrylic on twin, bow-shaped arcs of bronze. A matching conference table was positioned beside the windows to take advantage of the distant view of Houston's busy docks. Above the credenza that ran the length of one wall was another map, this one depicting global shipping lanes. The computer-generated routes crisscrossed cobalt-blue oceans in a spaghetti tangle of neon red, gold, green and black.

Zia noted with interest the eclectic collection of items Mike had obviously picked up in his travels. An elaborately carved boomerang that looked big enough to take down an elephant occupied a triangular frame made of some exotic wood. A three-foot-high Maori tiki god painted persim-mon red sat on a pedestal, his face screwed into a ferocious grimace and his tongue stuck out, presumably to deride would-be enemies. And standing in a corner like a fourth attendant at the meeting was a tan canvas dive suit topped by a dented brass helmet.

"I made coffee," Mike told Zia, "but there's tea or soft drinks or water if you'd prefer."

"Water would be great, thanks."

"Wise decision," Montoya commented as he powered up his computer. "Miguel's coffee has the flavor and con-sistency of bilge water."

"I had a sample this morning," Zia replied, laughing. "It would certainly rank up there with some of the bile we resi-dents down to stay awake during a thirty-six-hour rotation."

Montoya hiked a brow but he was too well mannered to follow up on her admission that she'd shared morning coffee with his brother-in-law. Instead, he tapped a couple keys on his laptop. The computerized wall map faded to a blank screen.

"As you can imagine, the health of the crews that man our ships is an ongoing concern. The IMO—International

Maritime Organization—has set guidelines for conducting pre-sea and periodic fitness examinations for all crewmembers. Despite this medical screening, however, we've noted disturbing trends in recent years.

"Part of that stems from the fact that seamen constitute a unique occupational group. Their travel to different parts of the world exposes them to infections and diseases at a rate comparable only to that of airline crews. And, like airline crews, they generally remain in port for relatively short time periods."

"But wouldn't a short turnaround mitigate their risk of exposure?"

"You'd think so, but that doesn't prove to be the case. In fact, seafarers report an incidence of certain diseases eight to ten times higher than the international average."

Montoya brought up the first slide. Its no-nonsense title—Infectious Diseases—riveted Zia's attention instantly.

"GSI maintains a database of all medical issues that impact our crews, but I extracted the data Mike indicated you might be particularly interested in."

The title slide gave way to a series of graphs that tracked GSI's reported incidents of HIV, malaria, hepatitis A, B and C, and tuberculosis against the international average. As Montoya had warned, the numbers were significantly higher than those Zia was familiar with.

"Although GSI is below the maritime average in every category, we're concerned by the worldwide upward trend in both malaria and tuberculosis. As a result we've funded or contributed heavily to a number of research projects targeting those diseases."

The next slide listed five studies, the company or institute that conducted them and the dollars GSI had contributed. The string of 0's on each study made Zia blink.

"Mike said you're focusing specifically on MRSA-related incidents," Montoya commented.

"That's right."

"We track that data, too."

She leaned forward, her interest riveted once again as he brought up the next slide. It showed the number of MRSA incidents by year and then by ship.

"Damn," Zia muttered. "You're seeing an across-the-board increase, too."

"Unfortunately."

"That's one nasty bug," Mike put in.

"Yes, it is. And becoming more and more resistant to antibiotics."

"Which is why we'd be interested in the results of your study," Montoya continued.

Startled, Zia started to protest that she'd focused on the very controlled world of neonatal nurseries. She couldn't imagine an environment farther removed from a massive container ship or oil tanker until she stopped, backed up and thought about it for a moment. The grim fact was that MRSA was on the rise in hospitals, nursing homes, homeless shelters, military barracks and prisons. All places where people were crowded and confined. Crews on ocean-going vessels certainly fell into that category.

"I'd be more than happy to share my findings, as limited as they are."

GSI's chief executive officer and VP for Support Systems exchanged a glance.

"Mike mentioned the possibility you might expand your research," Montoya said. "If so, GSI might be in a position to help with a grant."

Zia's jaw sagged. No way she would have imagined that a casual dinner date with a near stranger could lead to funding for the kind of in-depth study Dr. Wilbanks had talked to her about.

"Are you serious?"

"Very much so. We'd have to see a proposal that includes

all the standard criteria, of course." He ticked them off with knowledgeable ease. "A comprehensive rationale for the study. An assessment of the resources required. A detailed budget for the initial start-up, along with an estimated budget for the entire project. Biographical sketches of the people on your team, what you hope to accomplish and so on."

"Right."

Her mind whirled. Global Shipping Inc. had just made the question of whether she should switch from hands-on medicine to research ten times more difficult. Up to this point the possibility of participating in a major research effort with big-dollar funding had been just that—a possibility. Suddenly it had moved into the realm of probable. *If* she chose to go in that direction.

"Would you make me copies of these slides?"

She needed to study the data and think about the possibility of cross-fertilization with her research.

"Certainly."

He hit a key on his laptop. A sudden whir sounded from the printer on the sleek credenza behind Mike's desk. While he went to retrieve the copies, Montoya extracted a slim case from his shirt pocket.

"Here's my card. Please let me know if and when you're ready to put your proposal together. I'll be happy to take a look at it and provide input from this end."

Zia nodded, her mind still churning, and slipped his business card into her purse.

"Now, if you'll excuse me, I'd better get back to *abuelita*'s before the kids have Kate pulling out her hair." He shut down the laptop and tucked it under his arm. "It was good meeting you, Zia. Mike explained that you're pressed for time, but if you can squeeze out another hour or two I know the rest of the family would like to meet you, too."

"Particularly Davy's mom," Mike added. "Eileen called

just before you arrived with explicit instructions to bring you by the house if at all possible."

"Well…"

Zia checked her watch, surprised to find the session with Rafe Montoya had lasted a mere forty minutes.

Sarah, Gina and Natalie hadn't left to go shopping until almost noon. They'd taken the twins with them to give Maria and the duchess some downtime. Zia suspected both women were on the balcony, their feet up and eyes closed for an afternoon snooze.

The men would have finished their golf game by now but would no doubt hit the clubhouse before returning to the condo. Nothing formal was planned until this evening, when the family would follow the age-old Hungarian custom of celebrating *Szent-este*, or Holy Evening, with carols and a Bethlehem play using nativity figures.

Once the girls were in bed, the adults would indulge in a little stronger Christmas Eve cheer. Tomorrow would bring church services, the extravagant Christmas buffet at the resort's tony restaurant and the twins' birthday party later in the day. If Zia was going to meet the other members of the Brennan family, it had to be this afternoon.

"I guess I could stop by for a quick visit," she told Mike.

"Great." He grabbed his hat and settled it low on his forehead. "Everyone's congregated at our grandmother's house. It's only a few miles from here."

"I'll follow you."

Those few miles took them out of the canyon of downtown skyscrapers into what was once obviously a working-class neighborhood of small stucco houses. Property values must be shooting up, though, as newer and much larger residences appeared to be replacing the older homes.

Red, pink and white oleander bushes defined front- and backyards, while hundred-year-old live oaks dripping with

Spanish moss formed dense canopies. A heavy Hispanic flavor showed in storefront signs and churches with names like Our Lady of Guadalupe and Saint Juan Diego. Mike turned onto a tree-lined street and pulled up behind a string of vehicles parked curbside in the middle of the block. Zia parked behind him and got out, careful to avoid a hot-pink bike lying on its side in the middle of the sidewalk.

"This'll be Teresa's," Mike said as he whisked the bike up and out of the way. "She's Davy and Kevin's sister and the bane of their existence, the way they tell it. Here, let's go around to the patio. Everyone's usually out back."

As they followed a winding path, Zia admired the skillful way the original one-story stucco house had been expanded. The stone-fronted second story added both living space and architectural interest, while a glassed-in sunroom extended the first floor and brought the outdoors in.

"Does your grandmother live here alone?"

"She did until recently. My youngest sister and her new baby have moved in while her husband's in Afghanistan. We're negotiating with *abuelita* what'll happen when Maureen moves back out."

"How many brothers and sisters do you have again?"

"Three sisters, three brothers. Between them they've produced fifteen offspring…so far. And from the sound of it," he added, cocking his head as high-pitched shrieks of laughter emanated from the rear of the house, "they're pretty much all here."

Even with that warning, the noise and sheer size of the crowd in the backyard made Zia blink. Three little girls clambered in and out of a plastic castle while two others and a toddler made good use of a swing set. Several boys of varying ages played a game of tag with two joyously barking dogs. One was a large mixed breed, the other the small wirehaired terrier Zia remembered from yesterday morning. His owner, Davy, appeared to be suffering no aftereffects from his dunking as he raced after an older, near carbon copy, who had to be his brother, Kevin.

Additional family members crowded the glass-topped tables and lounge chairs set under a pergola draped with red and green lanterns. Kids occupied one table, adults another, both groups involved in noisy board games. The rhythmic beat of "Feliz Navidad" rose above the dogs' barking, shrieks of laughter and buzz of conversation. The music pulsed through a screen door that must lead to the kitchen, Zia guessed as she breathed in the tantalizing scents of roasting pork and spicy chipotle marinade.

One of the board players glanced up and caught sight of the newcomers. Pushing away from the table, the brunette jumped out of her chair and rushed across the lawn.

"Mike called and said you were stopping by, Dr. St. Sebastian. Thank you!" Disdaining formalities, she enveloped Zia in a fierce hug. "Thank you so much!"

"I'm just glad I was in the right place at the right time."

"Me, too! I'm Eileen, by the way. Eileen Rogers."

"And this is her husband, Bill," Mike said, introducing yet another of his brothers-in-law. This one didn't come anywhere close to either Mike *or* Rafael Montoya on the hotness index, but his warm brown eyes signaled both sincerity and a keen intelligence.

"You have my thanks, too, Dr. St. Sebastian. From the bottom of my heart."

"You're welcome. Both of you. And please, call me Zia."

"That's short for Anastazia, right?" Eileen hooked arms with her son's rescuer. "I looked you up on the internet," she admitted as she tugged Zia toward the others. "You're Hungarian, graduated from med school in Vienna and are just about to finish a residency at Mount Sinai."

"I think Zia knows her pedigree," Mike drawled from behind them.

Eileen ignored him. "You're also the sister of the yummy

Grand Duke of Karlenburgh, whose face was plastered all over the tabloids last year. Kate, Maureen and I all drooled over his picture."

"Thanks," her husband said with a mock groan. "Just what the rest of us mere mortals needed to hear."

His comment almost got lost in a chorus of excited shouts. The kids—all ten or twelve or fifteen of them— had noticed the newcomers' arrival. Like a human tsunami, they surged past Zia and Eileen emitting shrill squeals.

"Uncle Mickey! Uncle Mickey!"

They swamped him. Literally. Hung on his arms and wrapped around his legs. He crab-walked past the two women with kids dangling from every extremity. Zia laughed, but Eileen's chuckle ended on a low, almost inaudible mutter.

"Damn that bitch."

Zia sent her a startled glance. "Excuse me?"

"Sorry." Color rushed into the other woman's cheeks. "I shouldn't have let that slip out. It's just…"

"Just what?"

Eileen bit her lip, her gaze on the shrieking tangle of humanity a few yards ahead. "Mike is so good with them. With all of them. He'd make such a fantastic father."

A sudden, queasy sensation hit Zia. She had a feeling she knew where this was going. Her stomach muscles clenched, preparing to ward off the blow that Eileen Rogers delivered like a roundhouse punch.

"I probably shouldn't air our family's dirty laundry, but…" Eileen's voice flattened. Hardened. "It broke our hearts when his bitch of an ex-wife announced she didn't want children. Broke Mike's heart, too, although he would never admit it."

Five

Mike could sense the change in Zia. The signs were subtle—a slight dimming of the smile in her exotic eyes, just a hint of reserve in her responses to his family's boisterous welcome. He shouldn't have been surprised, given how many there were of them!

Interesting, though, that he'd become so attuned to this woman's small nuances after only one night together. He did his best to wipe the erotic mental images out of his head as he introduced her around. Her every move got to him, though. Each time she hooked a strand of hair behind her ear or bent to catch something someone said or just glanced his way, Mike felt a tug. And each tug only increased his determination to get to know Anastazia St. Sebastian a whole lot better.

She renewed her acquaintance with Davy and his terrier before Mike introduced her to his parents. He could see her relaxing a little as they welcomed her. It would be hard not to relax around Eleanor and Big Mike Brennan, given that they were two of the most unpretentious and genuine people on God's green earth. And, of course, Zia had snatched their grandson from the treacherous waters of the Gulf. That put her right at the top of their list of can-do-no-wrong human beings.

The shamrock-green eyes Big Mike had passed to six of his seven of his children beamed his gratitude. "You need anything, Doc, anything at all, you just call. What Mickey here can't do for you, Eleanor or I or one of the others will."

Zia looked a little overwhelmed by the offer but accepted it graciously. "Thank you."

She connected with Mike's middle sister, too. Not surprising, since the two women shared a common bond. Jiggling her nine-month-old on her hip, Kate expanded on that link. "I don't know if Mickey told you that I'm a cardiovascular surgical nurse at St. Luke's, here in Houston."

"He mentioned that you're a nurse, but not your specialty. Cardio's a tough area."

"It can be," Kate admitted cheerfully. "My husband, Rafe, said you're doing a research study on MRSA. Obviously, I have a vested interest in hospital-acquired infections. I'd love to sit down and talk with you about your study sometime. Maybe we could do lunch after the craziness of the holidays?"

"I wish we could. Unfortunately, I'm flying home to New York the day after tomorrow."

"Too bad." Her gaze turned speculative. "My brother hasn't shown much interest in any of the women Eileen and Mo and I have thrown at him the past three years. Not enough to bring them home to meet the family, anyway. You've obviously made an impression."

"Obviously," Mike's youngest sister chimed in, joining the group. Like Kate and most of the other Brennan siblings, Maureen had inherited their father's shimmering green eyes, but her red hair was at least a dozen shades lighter and brighter than the others'.

As though uncomfortable with the turn the conversation had taken, Zia smiled and redirected it. "I understand your husband's in the military."

"That's right. He's army, despite Colin and Mickey's attempt to browbeat him into going navy."

"Colin being the most obnoxious of my brothers," Mike warned with a grin as he shepherded Zia toward the men waiting their turn. "Right after Sean and Dennis."

He made quick work of the intros to the rest of the clan. Brothers, sisters-in-law, kids all got a brief acknowledgment before Mike whisked Zia away to meet the clan's matriarch.

Consuela Brennan's unlined skin and calm black eyes belied her age. To Mike's admittedly biased minds, his grandmother still exuded an aura of quiet beauty and the convent-bred serenity that had captivated his rough-and-tumble Irish grandfather so many years ago.

"So you are the one who saved our little Davy." She framed Zia's face with her palms. "I lit a candle this morning to thank God for His grace in bringing you into our lives. I will light another each day for a year."

"I…uh…thank you."

"And now, I think, you should sit here in the shade with Eleanor and me and tell us about your country. Miguel says you're from Hungary. I must confess I know little about it."

Zia chatted with Consuelo and Eleanor Brennan for a good twenty minutes or more. The mother- and daughter-in-law were very different in both age and interests but shared an absolute devotion to each other and to their families. Under any other circumstances, Zia would have thoroughly enjoyed getting to know them better.

Yet she couldn't help sneaking an occasional side glance, observing Mike interact with his siblings and in-laws. Noting, as well, how his nieces and nephews all seemed to adore him. Cries of "Uncle Mickey, watch me!" and "Come push me, Uncle Mickey!" peppered the air. Each shout, every giggle and squeal of delight, seemed to reinforce his sister Eileen's earlier comment. Mike Brennan would make a fantastic father.

The thought twisted like a small knife in Zia's chest. She shrugged the familiar pain aside as she said her goodbyes and wished everyone merry Christmas but it was still there, buried deep, as Mike walked her to her car.

"You have a wonderful family," she said, smiling to cover the ache. "I thought mine was big and lively, but yours wins the prize."

"They keep life interesting."

She fished out the keys of the rental and clicked the lock, but Mike angled between her and the door.

"I want to see you again, Zia. Sure you can't slip away again tonight or tomorrow?"

She wanted to. God, she wanted to! With him leaning so close, his smile crinkling the tanned skin at the corners of his eyes, his body almost touching hers, all she could think of was how his hands had stroked her. How he'd kissed and teased and tormented her. How she'd given more of herself to this man in one night than she'd ever given before.

She had a sneaking suspicion she could fall in love him. So easily. He was smart, handsome, fun, unpretentious and devoted to his family...which was the one thing she *couldn't* give him.

"I'm sorry, Mike. I need to spend tonight with my family. And tomorrow isn't just Christmas, it's also the twins' birthday. Gina wants to make a big deal of it since the girls won't have any of their friends from preschool to play games and blow out candles with, so we'll all be doubly..."

He laid a finger on her lips. "Leave it to me. I'll find a way to make it happen."

Not if she didn't answer her phone or return his calls. Trying to convince herself it was better to cut the cord now, before they got in any deeper, Zia shook her head. "Best to just say goodbye now."

He looked ready to argue the point but gave in with a shrug.

"Okay."

Bending, he brushed his lips over hers. The first pass was light, friendly. The second set her heart thumping against her sternum.

"Goodbye, Zia. For now."

He didn't call to press the issue. Although Zia had made up her mind to end things between them before they could really get started, she had to admit she was surprised. Okay, maybe a little miffed.

She spent Christmas Eve enjoying the twins' almost giddy eagerness over Santa's imminent arrival and the fact that they would share their birthday with Baby Jesus the next day.

The evening blended so many traditions, old and new. With her eye for color and genius for party planning, Gina made the most of all of them. The tree, the carols, the twins' construction-paper daisy chains draped like garlands at the windows. Stockings hooked above the marble fireplace for every member of the family, the hound included. White candles giving off just enough heat to gently turn the five-tiered nativity carousel, a reminder of the duchess's Austrian roots and a precious memento from Sarah and Gina's childhood.

They celebrated the Hungarian side of the St. Sebastian heritage, as well. Zia and Natalie spent a fun hour in the kitchen baking *kiffles*, the traditional Hungarian cookie made from cream cheese dough and filled with various flavors of pastry filling. Delicate and sinfully rich, they made a colorful holiday platter in addition to supplying the required treat to leave for Santa.

The highlight of the evening was the Bethlehem play orchestrated by Zia and Dom. The original folk tradition went back centuries, when children dressed in nativity costumes would go from house to house. Carrying a crèche, the young shepherds and wise men accompanying Joseph and Mary would sing and dance choreographed versions of the birth of Christ. Their performance would be rewarded with a treat of some kind at each house.

The tradition had gone through many different variations over the centuries. Most Bethlehem plays these days were performed at churches or schools. So Dom and Zia had to improvise costumes and staging and conscript the other adults for various roles. The performance delighted the twins, however. So much so that everyone was exhausted by the time Gina and Jack finally got them to bed.

The next morning the hyper-excited twins roused everyone before seven, the hound included. Gina and Jack were determined the girls should experience all the joy of Christmas morning, so their follow-up birthday celebration wasn't planned until late that afternoon…a timetable Mike Brennan exploited very nicely.

The call came after the family returned from church services and had all trooped down to the resort's elegant restaurant for the Christmas buffet. They were waiting to be seated when Dev's cell phone pinged. He checked caller ID and shot Zia a glance before answering.

"Hey, Brennan. What's happening?" He listened a moment, his brow hiking. "Yeah, she's right here."

To everyone's surprise, he handed the phone to Gina instead of Zia. She took it with a bewildered look. "Hi, Mike. Yes," she said after a brief pause. "Around four."

Another pause, punctuated by a wide smile.

"The twins would love that! If you're sure it's not too

much trouble. Yes. Yes, by all means! Great! We'll see you then."

Grinning, she hung up and addressed a phalanx of questioning faces. Her brightest smile went to Zia. "How sweet of you to tell Mike that you couldn't pass up the girls' birthday party to see him again."

"I…well…"

"So he's coming to the party," she said happily. "With a piñata and a pony and a half-dozen nieces and nephews, all close to the girls' age. He said he knew the twins' friends were all back home, so he thought they might like to share their special day with new ones."

Zia could only stare at her, openmouthed, and left it to the girls' father to inquire drily how they were supposed to accommodate a pony in the condo.

"Mike suggested we have the party in the play area. He's already spoken to the resort manager. The entire playground is ours for the duration." She hunkered down to address her wide-eyed daughters. "What do you say, girls? Do you want pony rides and a piñata at your party?"

Amalia stamped both feet and clapped her hands enthusiastically. "Yeth!"

Wide-eyed, serious Charlotte had to ask, "What's a piñata?"

By six-thirty that evening, Zia's suspicion that she could fall in love with Mike Brennan had solidified into certainty. She'd never met any man more suited to a brood of nosy, lively children. Children she could never give him, she reminded herself with a slice of pain.

And then, when the last of the kids had driven off with their respective parents and Zia's family had retreated to the condo, it was just her. Just him.

The salt breeze fluttered the ruffles of the cinnamon-colored overblouse she'd changed into along with jeans and a pair of sandals more suitable to a playground party. Mike had changed, too, and was once again in his beach persona of shorts and flip-flops. Trying to decide which version she liked best, Zia ached to lose herself in the smile she saw in his eyes.

"Thank you. You made this day so special for the twins. For all of us."

"It's not over yet." He tilted his head toward the surf rustling against the deserted shoreline. "Walk with me?"

Zia's precise mind tabulated an instant list of reasons not to let this man burrow deeper into her heart. Just as quickly, she countered them with the same arguments she'd trotted out yesterday. She was leaving tomorrow. Flying back to cold, snowy New York. She'd most likely never see him again. Why not make the most of these stolen hours?

"Sure."

As they tracked a path of side-by-side footsteps in the damp sand, his hand folded around hers. His grip remained loose, his voice easy as they swapped stories from their childhood and tales of Christmases past. By contrast, a tight, delicious tension gathered in the pit of Zia's stomach. It had knotted into a quivering bundle of need by the time the pale turquoise silhouette rose above the dunes directly ahead.

"I know you must be tired," Mike said as they approached the beach house, "but I don't want the day to end. How about we have that drink I offered last night but we never quite got around to?"

"A drink sounds good."

He'd closed the shutters after Zia had left yesterday morning. No light spilled through them as they took the path through the dunes and mounted the zigzagging staircase. Once inside the beach house, she sniffed the faint scent of trapped salt air. Mike made quick work of folding back the shutters protecting the French doors in the high-ceilinged living room, though, and opened them to let in the sea breeze.

"Would you like coffee or something a little stronger?"

"No offense, but your coffee should be registered with the EPA as a class II corrosive."

"True." Grinning, he acknowledged the hit. "But ironic coming from the woman whose great-aunt serves *pálinka* to unsuspecting guests."

"I tried to warn you."

"Yeah, you did. I think I have a less explosive brandy."

The banter was relaxed, the Courvoisier he poured into two snifters as smooth as sin. And with each sip, the need to touch him grew more critical. She fought the urge, determined to stretch their time together for as long as possible, and carried her drink out to the deck.

The wraparound, multilevel deck was banded by a railing of split boards spaced close enough to keep young nieces and nephews from wiggling through and plunging to the dunes below. The top rail was wide and flat and set at just the right height for adults to lean their elbows on. Zia took advantage of the ledge, cradling the heavy snifter in both hands while she absorbed the vista of foaming surf and the sky purpling out over the Gulf.

"You know," Mike mused as his elbows joined hers on the weathered shelf, "the NMC is working on a program that would allow mariners to upgrade or renew their credentials on demand from any cyber location in the world."

She angled to face him, not sure where he was going with that conversational gambit. "NMC?"

"Sorry. The National Maritime Center. It's a US Coast Guard agency, under the auspices of the Department of Homeland Security. The center is responsible for credentialing US mariners. The process is complicated and time-consuming now, but the NMC's new program would let crews access the system electronically, just like they access their bank accounts or withdraw cash from an ATM."

"Sounds reasonable."

"GSI provided input into the initial system architecture."

"Oh-kay."

She still couldn't guess where this was heading, especially with the swiftly falling darkness painting Mike's face in shadows.

"NMC's presenting a status update briefing at the Maritime Trades Association's executive board meeting in mid-January. I was supposed to be in Helsinki and hadn't planned to attend but now I'm thinking I might. The meeting's in New York. Not," he added with an exaggerated drawl, "that I need an excuse to come callin'."

She wasn't expecting the sudden zing of excitement at the prospect of seeing him again. It took every ounce of Zia's resolve to squelch it.

"I've enjoyed our time together, Mike, as brief as it's been. But..." She pulled in a breath. "I don't think it's a good idea for us to try to build on it."

"Funny, I think it's a hell of an idea."

She had a dozen convenient excuses she could have thrown out. She was supervising four interns, conducting team meetings, examining patients, doing chart reviews—and all this less than two weeks away from presenting the results of her research study. She also owed Dr. Wilbanks an answer when she got back to New York.

But dealing with patients and anxious relatives had taught Zia it was best to be honest. She usually softened a harsh truth with sympathy, but sometimes it was stark and unavoidable. This was one of those times.

"I like you, Mike. Too much to let either of us get in over our heads."

"Okay, that needs a little more explaining."

"The other evening, during dinner, I told you about… about the skiing trip in Slovenia that ended in disaster."

Now it was his turn to look as though he wasn't sure where the conversation was going. "I remember."

"I watched you with your family yesterday. With my family today. You're so good with the children." She dragged in another breath and carefully centered her snifter on the broad ledge. "You don't need to get involved with a woman—*another* woman—who isn't going to give you any."

"Well, Christ! Which one of my loving sisters told you about…?" He shook his head, exasperated. "Never mind. It doesn't matter. What does matter is that we're a long ways yet from getting in over our heads."

"Which is why I say…" She caught her accent slipping and forced a correction. "Why I *said* we should stop now, before either of us gets hurt."

He angled his head, studying her in the deepening twilight. She couldn't see the expression in his eyes, only the purse of his lips as he weighed her comment.

"How about we strike a deal here?" he said after several long moments. "I'll tell you if and when I approach the hurting stage, and you do the same."

Rendben! Oké! She'd warned him. Made it perfectly clear they could never become serious. So…

"All right."

"All right?"

"I accept the deal." She hooked a hand behind his neck, tugged him down to her level. "And just to seal the bargain…"

Mike was careful not to let his quick, visceral triumph flavor the kiss. He hadn't lied. He *was* a long way yet from getting in over his head. But he was navigating in that direction and had no intention of charting a different course. Zia St. Sebastian fascinated and challenged and aroused him in ways he hadn't been fascinated or challenged or aroused in a long, long time.

Her revelation the other night at the restaurant that she couldn't have children had given him pause for maybe ten, fifteen seconds. It had also brought back some bitter memories. Right up until he reminded himself there was a whole passel of difference between *couldn't* and *wouldn't*.

Zia wasn't Jill. The two women might have been bred on different planets. Different universes. And right now, all Mike wanted to do was revel in those differences. Like the way Zia's mouth molded his with no coy pretense of having to be coaxed. The fit of her tall, slender body against his, so perfect he didn't have to stoop or contort to cant her hips into his. The lemony scent of her shampoo, the smoky taste of Courvoisier on her lips, the way the skin at the small of her back warmed under his searching fingers when he tugged up the hem of her blouse. Every touch, every sensory signal that raced along his snapping nerves, made him raw with wanting her.

He managed to keep from tugging the ruffled blouse over her head and baring her to the night. But he did circle her waist and perch her on the wide ledge. The move put her nose just a few inches above his and gave him easy access to the underside of her chin.

"You know," he said as he nibbled the tender skin, "you're a hard woman to please. I had to call a dozen stables before I found someone who would deliver a pony this afternoon."

"That was your idea, not mine," she reminded him, threading her fingers through his hair. "And totally unnecessary, I might add. The piñata and kids were more than enough. But I appreciate the trouble you went to."

"Yeah, well, since you brought it up…"

"*You* brought it up."

"I'm talking about your appreciation."

"Is that right?" She used her hold on his hair to tilt his head back. "What about it?"

"Well, it just seems to me there are a number of ways you might show it."

Her eyes glinted with amusement. "Just what did you have in mind, cowboy?"

He answered her question with a quick barrage of his own. "What time's your flight tomorrow?"

"Eleven-twenty."

"From Houston Hobby or George Bush Intercontinental?"

"Houston Hobby."

"And how long will it take you to pack?"

"Thirty minutes. Maybe less. *Why*?"

"Hold on." He settled his hands on her hips and pretended to conduct a series of rapid mental calculations. "Okay, the way I figure it we have fifteen and a half hours. Should be just enough time for me to go through my entire repertoire of moves and send you back to New York a happy woman."

"Good Lord!" The amusement bubbled into laughter. "Fifteen and a half hours going through your repertoires and I won't be able to walk, much less board a plane."

Which was pretty much the idea. Mike didn't share that thought, choosing instead to scoop her off the rail and into his arms.

"Better call back to the condo," he suggested as he carried her, still grinning, into the house. "Your brother wasn't looking all that friendly this afternoon."

"Are you worried what Dom might think?"

"More what he might do," Mike admitted wryly. "Which is probably exactly the same thing I would if any of *my* sisters spent fifteen and a half hours engaged in the kind of activity I have planned for you, Doc."

<u>Six</u>

Zia slept for the entire flight from Houston to LaGuardia. Hardly a surprise, given that Mike had made good on his promise to keep her busy for an astonishing portion of their stolen interlude.

When she exited the terminal, the icy air hit like a slap in the face. Luckily, she'd worn her UGGS and fleece-lined parka on the flight down to Texas. They protected her now while she stood in the taxi line, but the howling wind sliced into the tiger-striped leggings Gina had given her for Christmas and her nose dripped like a faucet by the time she tumbled into a cab.

After a week of sun-washed beaches and balmy days, the dirty slush and nasty gray sky should have been a shock to her system. Yet as the taxi rattled over the Robert F. Kennedy Bridge and headed for Manhattan's Upper West Side, the hustle and bustle of her adopted city grabbed her. She loved its pulsing rhythm, its cultural diversity, its kitsch and class. Of course, her perceptions were skewed by the fact that she now lived in one of the city's most famous apartment buildings.

As the cab pulled up at the entrance to the Dakota, Zia couldn't help thinking how much the multistory Victorian-era complex reminded her of her native Budapest. Gabled and fancifully turreted, the Dakota stood out from the modern structures crowding it on three sides and drew the eye with the same regal dignity as the iconic spires of Hungary's parliament building.

Charlotte St. Sebastian had purchased her fifth-floor, seven-room apartment after an odyssey that included her escape from the Soviets and short stays in both Vienna and Paris. Her title and the jewels she'd converted to cold, hard cash had won her acceptance by the Dakota's exclusive enclave that over the years had included such luminaries as Judy Garland, Rudolph Nureyev, Leonard Bernstein, Bono and John Lennon, who was tragically murdered just steps from the front entrance.

Zia knew the duchess had almost been forced to sell her apartment not long ago. The apartment and her determination to educate her granddaughters in the manner she insisted was commensurate with their heritage had drained her resources. Bad investments by her financial advisor had sucked away most of the rest.

When Sarah married her handsome billionaire, she'd known better than to offer to pay her grandmother's living expenses. The duchess's pride would never allow it. But Charlotte *had* allowed Dev to sink what little remained of her savings in several of his wildly successful business ventures. And Gina's husband, Jack, had added to the duchess's financial security with investments in blue-chip stocks. Charlotte could now live in splendid luxury for the rest of her life.

This development pleased the uniformed doorman who made his stately way to help Zia from the taxi almost as much as it did the St. Sebastians. Sarah and Gina considered Jerome one of the family. He'd treated them to candy and ice cream during their schoolgirl years, scrutinized their high school dates with steely eyes, attended their weddings and delighted in the lively twins.

He'd taken Zia under his wing, too, when Charlotte had invited her to live at the Dakota. As kind as he was dignified, Jerome had acquainted the new arrival with such intricacies as subway schedules, jogging paths and the best pastrami this side of Romania. Which is why Zia made sure she paid the cab fare even before the driver pulled up at the curb. There was no way she would keep Jerome standing in the icy wind.

"Welcome home, Doctor."

He would no more think of dropping her title than he would Lady Sarah's or Lady Eugenia's. But his smile was warm and welcoming as he held the door and ushered her into what was once the *porte cochère.*

"How was your Christmas?"

"Wonderful."

"And the duchess? Maria? They're enjoying being out of this ice and snow?"

"Very much so, although I suspect they'll be happy to come home after another two weeks of sun and sand."

"I suspect so, too. And if I may be so bold," he added as he escorted her to the bank of elevators, "may I say it's good to see you smiling again."

"Was I so glum before?" Zia asked, startled.

"Not glum. Just tired. And," he said gently, "somewhat troubled."

Jézus, Mária és József! Was she so transparent? Surely she did a better job of sublimating her inner self when working with patients.

"You hid it well," the doorman hastened to assure her. "But a keen eye and an ability to assess character comes with this job." He paused, searching her face. "Did you find the solution to whatever was distressing you in Texas?"

She had to hide a smile at the slight but unmistakable

emphasis on the last word. New York born and bred, Jerome would find it hard to believe the answer to anyone's problems couldn't be found right here in the city. And to tell the truth, Zia wasn't quite sure how those stolen hours with Mike had lifted some of the weight of the decision that still hung over her like an executioner's ax, but they had. They most definitely had.

"Not the solution, perhaps," she said as the elevator door pinged open, "but a very potent antidote."

Propping the door with one hand, she took her bag in the other and leaned in to kiss the doorman's cheek.

"Just so you know," she added, "the antidote plans to make a trip to New York in the next week or so. His name's Brennan. Michael Brennan."

"I'll be sure to ring the apartment the moment Mr. Brennan arrives," Jerome replied with a twinkle in his eyes.

Strange, Zia thought as she keyed the front door and let herself into the black-and-white-tiled foyer. She still faced a wrenching decision. Yet now opting for research instead of hands-on medicine didn't feel like such a traitorous act. The possibility of a substantial grant from GSI to underwrite that research had given it impetus. She could be part of a team that pinpointed sources of deadly infections. Reduced risks to hospital patients. Saved lives.

First, though, she had to draft the proposal Rafe Montoya had outlined. She'd get on the computer, she decided as she dropped her bag in her bedroom and went to the bathroom. Right after she'd soaked long enough to ease her aching hip and thigh and calf muscles. Mike Brennan, she acknowledged with a rueful grin, had given her a lesson in anatomy unlike any she'd taken in med school.

She was at the hospital early the next morning. Those residents who'd worked through Christmas greeted her return with relief.

"Hope you're rested and ready to go," Don Carter warned. Happily married and totally stressed, he couldn't wait to shed his stethoscope for a long-anticipated New Year ski trip to Vermont. "We've been slammed with the usual spike in heart attacks and acute respiratory failures."

Zia nodded. Contrary to the popular misperception that the sharp increase in holiday deaths was driven by substance abuse, family-related homicides or depression-driven suicides, she now knew other significant causes came into play. A major contributing factor was that people who felt ill simply put off a trip to the hospital, choosing instead to be with their families over Christmas or New Year's.

Holiday staffing was also an issue, especially at Level 1 trauma centers, where seconds could mean the difference between life and death. Recognizing that fact, Mount Sinai's various centers, schools and hospitals paid careful attention to staff levels during this critical period.

Even with the controlled staffing, however, the holidays kept everyone hopping. Zia quickly fell back into the hectic schedule of morning team meetings, patient exams, family-centered rounds, chart reviews, one-on-ones with her interns and day-end team sessions. She still had two weeks in the Pediatric Intensive Care Unit before she completed that rotation. And, as they always did, these desperately ill kids tugged at her heart. Some cried, some screamed, but others showed no reaction to the catheters and IVs and high-dosage drugs that made them groggy or nauseous or both.

This was particularly true of the five-month-old admitted the second day after Zia's return. The infant lay listless and unmoving, his skin sallow and his eyes dull. She said nothing while one of her interns read aloud the admitting physician's chart notations. Nor did she offer an opinion or advice while he examined the patient under his parents' worried eyes.

When her small group had adjourned to the hall outside the nursery however, she quizzed the intern. "Did you note any anomaly in Benjamin's penis?"

She always referred to her patients by first name to insure neither she nor her students ever forgot they were treating living, breathing humans.

"I...uh..." The intern looked from her to his fellow students and back again. "No."

"It appeared elongated to me. Combined with his low birth weight and failure to thrive, what does that suggest to you?"

The intern bit his lip and searched his memory. "Low-renin hypertension?"

The genetic defect was rare and difficult to diagnose. She didn't blame the intern for missing it on the first go-around.

"That's what it looks like to me. I would suggest you have the lab measure his renin level and compare it to his aldosterone."

"Will do."

"If the ratio's too low, as I suspect it may be, let's get a consult from the Adrenal Steroid Disorders group before we discuss his condition with his parents."

Relief and respect reverberated in the fervent reply. "I'll take care of it."

Jézus! Had she ever been that young? Ever that terrified of doing more harm than good?

Of course she had.

That thought stayed with her as she crossed the catwalk connecting the Kravis Children's Hospital with the tower housing the school of medicine's research center. As head of the world-renowned facility, Dr. Wilbanks and his staff occupied a suite of offices with a bird's-eye view of Central

Park. Zia confirmed her appointment with the receptionist, then stood at the windows to admire the landscape. From this height, the frozen reservoir, rolling fields and bare-branched trees were a symphony in gray and icy white.

The buzz of the intercom brought her around. The receptionist listened for a moment and nodded to Zia. "Dr. Wilbanks will see you now."

Roger Wilbanks's physical stature matched his reputation in the world of pediatric research. Tall, snowy haired and lean almost to the point of emaciation, he greeted Zia with a burning intensity that both flattered and intimidated.

"I hope you've come to tell me you've decided to join our team, Dr. St. Sebastian."

"Yes, sir, I have."

As soon as the words were out, a thousand-pound boulder seemed to roll off Zia's shoulders. This was right for her. She'd known it somewhere deep inside for months but hadn't been able to shake the feeling that she would be abandoning the youngest, most helpless patients.

That guilty sense of desertion, of turning her back on her young patients, was gone. Part of that was due to Dr. Wilbanks's validation of her initial research. And part, she realized, was due to Mike Brennan. He'd triggered an interest in a world outside of pediatric medicine. She was light-years from expanding her research to the wider population of ships' crews and prison populations, but Mike had opened whole new vistas that gave the sterile environment of a lab new, exciting dimensions.

The possibility GSI might contribute to her research sparked an interest on the part of Dr. Wilbanks, as well. "Global Shipping Incorporated?" he echoed, his brows soaring above his rimless half-glasses. "They suggested they might fund a study of hospital-acquired infections in newborn infants?"

"They're interested in any research that might pinpoint

sources of infection. Apparently MRSA is as much a worry in the maritime world as it is in hospitals."

His brows remained at full mast while Zia walked him through the paper copies of the slides Rafe Montoya had printed out for her. The chart listing the studies GSI had funded or contributed to proved especially riveting. By the time she finished, she could almost see the dollar signs gleaming in her mentor's eyes.

"When do you present your current study to the faculty?" he asked.

"The second week in January. I don't have a specific day or time yet, but…"

"I'll take care of that. In the meantime, you need to get to work on a proposal for an expanded study. I'll have one of the senior research assistants work with you on that. You also need to talk to someone in the comptroller's office. Unfortunately, requesting and acquiring grants has become a complex process. So complex we often use the services of consultants. The comptroller will help you there. In the meantime, you can count your work with us as an elective and complete your residency on schedule."

He pushed away from his desk and came around to lay a collegial hand on her shoulder.

"I don't need to tell you research is the heart and soul of medicine, Dr. St. Sebastian. The public may hail Albert Sabin and Jonas Salk as the heroes who conquered polio, but neither of those preeminent scientists could have developed their vaccines without the work done by John Enders at Boston's Children's Hospital. God willing, our research into the molecular genetics of heart disease, the pathogenesis of influenza and herpes and, yes, the increasing incidence of MRSA among newborns, will yield the same profound results."

Zia couldn't have asked for a more motivational speech. Or a more ringing endorsement of her shift to full-time research. Buoyed by the increasing certainty she'd made the right decision, she traded hours with another resident so she could have dinner with Natalie and Dom the evening they flew in from Texas.

They'd come back a week before the duchess and Maria were scheduled to return. The New Year celebrations were over, the slush had morphed to grime, and the city shivered under an Arctic blast. Hunched against the cold, Zia took a cab to their apartment in the venerable old 30 Beekman Place building. It was less than a block from UN Headquarters, where Dom was still trying to adjust to his mission as cultural attaché.

The tenth-floor condo boasted plenty of room for entertainment and a million-dollar view of the Manhattan skyline. More important, as far as Natalie was concerned, it was only steps from a dog run, where she and the liver-and-white-spotted Magyar Agár exercised twice a day.

Natalie and the hound were just returning from their evening constitutional when Zia climbed out of the cab. The whipcord-lean hound greeted her ecstatically, Natalie with a hug and a smile.

"I was so surprised and excited when you called and told us you were switching to pediatric research," her sister-in-law said. "I hope you get as much fulfillment from your field as I do from mine."

"I hope so, too." She had to ask. "How did Dom react to the news that I won't be practicing hands-on medicine?"

"Oh, Zia! Your brother wants whatever you want." Her brown eyes brimmed with laughter. "You could dance naked down Broadway and Dom would flatten anyone who so much as glanced sideways at you. And speaking of dancing naked…"

She hit the elevator button and spun in a slow circle to unwind the leash wrapped around her calves.

"Mike Brennan stopped by the resort before we left."

"Why?"

"He *said* he wanted to talk to Dev about a fleet of new cargo ships his company is thinking about acquiring. But he and Dom spent quite a bit of time out on the balcony, one-on-one."

This was news to Zia. She and Mike had iMessaged each other a few times. Like most texts, they were short and only hinted at the activities cut off by her departure from Houston. Yet they also managed to convey an unsaid but unmistakable desire to pick up where they'd left off. None of Mike's iMessages had mentioned a one-on-one with her brother, however.

"How did they get along? Was any blood spilled? Bodily harm inflicted?"

"Let's just say your brother isn't making any more 'Cossack-y, I'll carve out his liver with a saber' noises."

Zia had to smile. Dom talked a good game. She couldn't count the number of dates she'd had to bring by the house so he could scope them out. Or the friends he'd subjected to intense and, to them, nerve-racking scrutiny. Yet he'd always respected Zia's intelligence and, more important, her common sense. He'd never interfered or second-guessed her choices. Not an easy task for the older brother who'd raised her from her early teens.

"By the way," Natalie said casually as the elevator arrived and the hound dragged her inside, "we expect you to bring Mike to dinner when he's in New York for that conference he's suddenly decided to attend."

"How did you…?" Laughing, Zia followed her sister and the hound into the elevator. "Never mind."

The two women exchanged a wry smile. Dominic St. Sebastian might have put his days as an undercover agent behind him. He kept a hand in the business, however. Or at least a finger.

* * *

Zia didn't exactly count the days until Mike showed up in New York. She was too busy with rounds and teaching and preparing the presentation of her MRSA study to the faculty and her fellow residents. In between, she snatched what time she could to work on the proposal for the expanded study.

Per Dr. Wilbanks's instructions, she used National Institutes of Health guidelines to draft the proposal. The first step was to describe the greatly expanded research project and what it was intended to accomplish. After that she interviewed prospective team members, detailed their credentials and ran her choices by Dr. Wilbanks for approval. Once she had the team lined up, she used their collective expertise to refine the objectives and nail down the resources required. They also put together a projected budget for the estimated life of the study. The "one million, two hundred thousand" bottom line made Zia gulp.

It caused the school's assistant comptroller to suck a little air, too. A busy, fussy type with salt-and-pepper hair and a string of framed degrees on her office wall, the financial guru felt compelled to deliver a lecture about the acquisition and disbursement of grant monies.

"I'm sure you understand that we have to be very careful, Dr. St. Sebastian. Especially with a grant in the amount you're requesting. We have an excellent record here at Mount Sinai, I'm very happy to say. But recent audits by the National Institutes of Health have uncovered waste and, in some cases, outright fraud at other institutes."

"That's why I'm here, Ms. Horton. I want to be sure we do everything by the book."

"Good, good." She glanced over the figures in the proposed budget again. "I doubt you'll pull in half of what you're requesting."

She hesitated, her lips pursed.

"We use the services of two excellent consulting firms that specialize in searching out and securing grant monies. I'll give you the contact information for both, but in this tight economy…"

She shook her head discouragingly. Zia debated whether to tell her about the GSI connection. She decided to wait until the expanded study had been approved and the hunt for funding actually got under way.

A few clicks of the assistant comptroller's keyboard produced a printed list of "grant consultants." Zia tucked it in the black Prada messenger bag Gina and Jack had given her for Christmas. It was exactly the right size to carry her iPad mini, her phone and all the paraphernalia she needed for work.

The dollars were still on her mind when she emerged from the subway at 72nd and Broadway just after seven o'clock. The Arctic cold front had finally blown itself out, but the air was still frosty enough for her to keep her head down and her shoulders hunched as she hurried the two blocks to the Dakota.

Jerome had gone off duty at six. The new night doorman, whose name Zia had to struggle to recall, intercepted her on the way to the elevators. "Excuse me, Doctor. A courier delivered this for you a short time ago."

With a word of thanks, she examined the plain white envelope he handed her. The outside contained only her name. The inside, Zia discovered with a delighted grin, contained an IOU for one carriage ride through Central Park, redeemable tonight or anytime tomorrow. Her pulse skipping, she dialed Mike's number.

"When did you get in?"

"A couple of hours ago."

"Why didn't you call me?"

"I knew you were working. So what's the deal? Are you up for a carriage ride?"

"It's freezing out there!"

"I'll keep you warm."

The husky promise sent a shiver of delight dancing down Zia's spine. She tried to remember if she'd seen any carriages during her dash from the subway. The new mayor had vowed to ban them, citing traffic safety and animal protection issues. She didn't think the ban had gone into effect but didn't remember noticing any carriages on the street.

"Why don't we decide what we'll do when you get here?"

"Fine by me. I'll grab a cab. See you shortly."

"Wait! How shortly?"

Too late. He'd already disconnected. She headed for the elevator again and keyed the door of the duchess's apartment with a fervent prayer she had time for a shower and to do something with her hair.

She didn't. The intercom buzzed while she was soaping herself down. She almost missed it over the drum of the water. Would have if she hadn't kept an ear tuned for it.

"Damn!"

She grabbed a towel but left a trail of wet footprints as she dripped her way from the bathroom to the hall intercom. "If that's Mr. Brennan, send him up."

"Yes, ma'am."

Back in the bedroom she yanked her closet doors. She was reaching for the comfortable sweats she spent most evenings in but stopped with her hand in midair. When she answered the front door a few moments later, she was wearing only the towel and a smile.

He, on the other hand, was wearing leather gloves, a charcoal cashmere overcoat and his black Stetson. Tipping the brim back with two fingers, he gave a low whistle.

"If this is how you New York City gals answer the door," he drawled as his gaze made a slow, approving circuit from her neck to her knees and back again, "I'll have to make a few more executive board meetings."

"I'm only a temporary resident," she reminded him.

"So this is a Hungarian custom?"

"Actually, it is. Public baths have been popular in my country for several thousand years. The Romans loved to luxuriate in the bubbling hot springs in and around Budapest."

"That so?" He waggled his brows in an exaggerated leer. "You have to hand it to those Romans."

Laughing, she backed into the foyer. "Are you going to just stand there and gawk or do you want to come in?"

"I not sure I can move. I'm a little weak at the knees."

"Mike, for heaven's sake! I'm getting goose bumps in places no woman should. Come in."

Seven

For the next forty minutes the towel proved superfluous. So did Mike's overcoat, suit, shirt and tie.

He'd intended to display a little couth this time. Show Zia his smooth, sophisticated side as opposed to the bare-foot beach bum and everyone's favorite uncle. The two of them had been so pressed for time in Galveston, so surrounded by their loving but in-the-way families. Despite having stolen her away for two memorable nights, he hadn't had time to show her that he could be as comfortable in her world as he was in his own.

Time wasn't the only issue that had factored into his decision to go for more suave and less hot and hungry. As every one of his sisters had tried to hammer home to their brothers and spouses, women need romance. Wooing. Candles and flowers and, yes, heart-shaped boxes of chocolates.

Mike had considered various strategies to up the romance quotient on the flight from Houston. New York offered all kinds of possibilities. A carriage ride in the park, an elegant dinner for two at the latest in spot, a Broadway show. He'd even been prepared to man up and take her to a concert or opera if she'd preferred.

Then she had to open the door and drain every drop of

blood from his head. He'd damned near had a coronary right there in the hall. The hour that followed would remain etched in Mike's mind for the next hundred years.

Now they were lazing side by side on a sofa angled to catch the heat of a roaring fire, both of them more or less fully clothed. She was in warm, well-washed sweats and fuzzy slippers. He'd pulled on his shirt, pants and shoes. He liked the way her head rested on the arm he'd stretched across the back of the sofa. Was glad, too, that they'd decided to order Chinese instead of going out in the cold. Empty cartons littered the coffee table and surrounded a half-consumed bottle of California cabernet.

Mike played with a strand of her hair and let his appreciative gaze roam the elegant room. The duchess's salon, as Zia had termed it, featured parquet floors, antiques and a ceiling so high it was lost in the shadows. Flames danced in a fireplace fronted with black marble, and a tiny Bose Bluetooth speaker filled the room with the haunting strains of a rhapsody. Liszt's "Hungarian Rhapsody No. 5," Zia had informed Mike. One of nineteen he'd composed based on folk music and Gypsy themes.

"This is nice," he announced, wrapping a finger around the silky strand of hair. "Much better than a carriage ride. We'll have to go that route next time I'm in New York, though."

She tipped her face to his. The firelight added a rosy glow to her cheeks but didn't do anything for the shadows under her eyes. Mike found himself wishing he could banish them by keeping her in bed for the next week or month or decade.

"Is this a horse fetish," she wanted to know, "or just a Texas thing?"

"Neither. My secretary pulled up a list of the ten most romantic things to do in New York."

"You're kidding."

"Nope. A carriage ride through Central Park was near the top of the list."

"Not in January!"

The laugh accompanying the protest was easy, natural. But when she tugged her hair free of his loose hold and sat up to retrieve her wineglass, he could feel the subtle withdrawal.

Well, hell! He'd overplayed his hand. The doc had let it be known back in Galveston she didn't want to get in too deep, too fast. Yet he'd just pretty well let drop that *he* was already in up to his neck.

With deliberate nonchalance, he redirected the conversation. "How's the proposal coming?"

The ploy worked. Groaning, she dropped back against the sofa.

"I had no idea getting a major research project approved was such a complicated process. I'm on the third draft of the proposal now and have yet to finalize the lab protocols. And I still have to meet with one of the consultants the hospital recommended. Evidently there's a whole subspecialty of 'grant professionals' out there who make their living seeking out and securing funding for studies like this."

Mike nodded. "We've worked with a few of them."

"I'm going to make an appointment tomorrow. If nothing else, they can give me a reality check on the dollar figures."

"Want me to take a look at them?"

"Would you?" She hesitated and bit her lip. "Or would that be a conflict of interest? If we come to GSI for funding, I mean."

He flashed her a grin. "Not unless you intend to skew your study to show that GSI operates the cleanest, most bacteria-free ships at sea."

"Not hardly." She laughed again, once more relaxed. "I don't even know how I got interested in the incidence of

MRSA aboard ships in the first place. Wait! Yes, I do! You and Rafe reeled me with all those statistics."

Some women were wowed by money, Mike thought wryly. Others by extravagant romantic gestures. The way to Anastazia St. Sebastian's heart, apparently, was through a germ.

"Get your draft and let me take a look."

She pushed off the sofa and retreated down a tiled hall. When she returned, she flipped on the overhead lights, killed the music and deposited a thick file secured by a paper clip on the coffee table.

"I'm assuming you're not interested in the list of publications or bibliography."

"You assume right. Let me see the description of facilities and resources, then we'll take a look at the budget."

Nodding, she slid off the paper clip. "The research center at Mount Sinai is state-of-the-art. We'll use the computers there to collect and analyze data. Also to test samples."

"Good."

"Here's the estimate of start-up costs and first-year operating budget, broken out by personnel, equipment and overhead. The second and third pages project the costs out for an additional two years, assuming the initial results warrant continuation."

As Mike skimmed the neat columns, her commentary took on a hint of nervousness.

"I ran the figures by the hospital's assistant comptroller. She sucked some serious air when she saw the bottom line. That's when she suggested I talk to a grant professional."

"I'm not surprised. One-point-two million isn't exactly chump change in today's environment." He flipped to the next page, studied the numbers, returned to the summary. "You may want to take another look at your ratio of direct to indirect costs in year two. You show a shift to more field sampling at that point, so your direct costs will increase more than you project here."

Frowning, she leaned in for another look. "Damn! You're right. I've worked these numbers until I was cross-eyed. How did I miss that?"

"Because you worked the numbers until you were cross-eyed."

"Yet you caught it on the first pass."

"Unfortunately, I spend most of my time these days looking at numbers and not nearly enough with salt spray in my face."

He lazed back against the sofa, enjoying the way the firelight shimmered against the glossy black of her hair.

"Which brings me to another item on the top-ten list. Not as romantic as a carriage ride in Central Park maybe, but a lot more exciting."

"Mmm." The deep crease between her brows told him she was still crunching her numbers. "What's that?"

"Next month's Frostbite Regatta, hosted by the New York Yacht Club. A friend of mine is a member. He and his wife have been inviting me… Correction. They've been *daring* me to come up and help crew for years. I'll tell them I will if I can bring along a third mate."

He had her full attention now. Incredulous, she glanced from him to the draped windows and back again.

"Let me get this straight. You're inviting me to go sailing? On the open sea? In *February*?"

"Actually, we'd be sailing Long Island Sound, not the open sea but…" He rubbed his chin and appeared to give the matter some thought. "I can see how that might not appeal as much as the midwinter races in Kauai. I'd rather do those, too, if you can get away for a week."

"Kauai, like in Hawaii? Oh, Mike! You know I can't. I've got too much going on right now."

"Yeah, I figured that was out. But circle Saturday, February thirteenth, on your calendar. That's the date of the Frostbite Regatta. And as an added incentive, everyone who survives the regatta will rig themselves out in long gowns or tuxes for the big Valentine bash at the 44th Street Clubhouse that evening."

She was getting that cautious look again. Pulling back. He could feel her retreating into herself. Away from him.

"I don't know my February schedule yet."

"No problem. Just give me a call when you do and we'll plan accordingly." He kept it easy, casual, and made a show of looking at his watch. "I'd better head back to the hotel."

"But you..." She stopped, restarted more slowly. "You could stay here."

"I've got two fat notebooks to review before the board meeting tomorrow morning. Besides..." He brushed a fingertip under the sooty-black lower lashes of her left eye. "You look whipped. Get some sleep, and I'll see you tomorrow evening. We'll go out for dinner, this time."

He shrugged into his suit jacket and pulled on his overcoat before issuing a final word of warning. "Just don't answer the door in a towel again. My system can't take another shock like that."

Zia flipped the locks behind him and shuffled slowly back down the tiled hall. She wasn't sure her system could take another shock like the one that had hit her when she'd opened the door, either.

The jolt of delight had come fast and cut deep. She shouldn't have ignored that warning. Shouldn't have engaged in the silly exchange about the Romans and laughed at his admission of going all weak at the knees. And she most definitely shouldn't have enticed him into bed again. Not that he'd required much enticing.

She wandered back into the salon and gathered the empty cartons to carry to the kitchen. The possibility she'd worried about in Galveston was now looking all too probable. She'd thought then she could fall in love with Mike Brennan. She knew now it was more than a mere possibility.

The old hurt, the one buried deep in her heart, sent out a familiar stab of pain. Dropping the cartons in the trash, Zia flattened both hands on the kitchen counter and fought back.

Why *not* take the tumble, dammit? Why *not* let herself start imagining a future that included Mike? He knew she couldn't have children. She'd shared that agonizing reality with him their first night together. She still couldn't quite believe she'd opened up to a stranger the way she had but even then, when they'd only known each other for a few hours, he'd called to something inside Zia. His humor, the intelligence behind his easy smile, his obvious affection for his nephew and Davy's for him...

Her raging inner debate stopped dead. As her flattened palms curled into fists, all she could hear was an echo of his sister's bitter revelation. Mike's ex-wife refused to give him children...and had broken his heart in the process.

"A francba!"

Thumping the counter with her fists, she whirled and stalked out of the kitchen.

She woke the next morning prey to the same wildly conflicting emotions. She wanted to have dinner with Mike that evening. She even wanted to be crazy stupid and go sailing with him in the dead of winter, then feel his hands and his mouth and his body covering hers in the coming weeks and months. Years!

Yet wanting wasn't enough. Was it?

What about Mike? His needs, his desires? Did she have the right, the incredible selfishness, to tie his future to her past?

She was still torn between waiting and wanting when

she hit the hospital. As always, she sublimated her personal life to the hectic routine. Team meetings, patient exams and family-centered rounds consumed most of her morning, but she used a late lunch break to review the list of consulting firms the assistant comptroller had given her yesterday. As much as she hated to divert any of her project's potential funding to consultants, their success rates in securing that funding overcame her initial reluctance.

The head of the first firm she contacted was out of town until the following week. His office manager offered to set up an appointment with an assistant but given the amount of money involved, Zia opted to wait for the main man.

She tried the second firm, Danville and Associates, and was put through to the boss himself. As brief as their conversation was, Zia's description of her proposal fired Thomas Danville's interest.

"Sounds like you've done a lot of preliminary work, Dr. St. Sebastian." He spoke fast, his words staccato and filled with energy. "But one of the key services we provide is a thorough scrub before a draft proposal goes final. We're very skilled at nuancing research projects to make them more salable to private foundations and corporations."

Judging by the successes posted on their website, Zia could believe it. But given the interest Mike and Rafe Montoya had already expressed, did her proposal need nuancing?

Danville sensed her hesitation and jumped on it. "You have some reservations about working with a consultant, right? Understandable. Look, why don't we get together and I'll explain exactly what we can do for you?"

"It'll have to be soon. I want to get this in the works."

"Not a problem. In fact…I'm having dinner with another client at La Maison tonight. It's just a few blocks from the hospital. I could swing by and meet with you beforehand.

Or, better yet, you could join us for dinner. Get a firsthand testimonial from a satisfied customer."

"I'm sorry, I have other plans for dinner tonight."

"Drinks, then. It'll be easier to talk at the restaurant than at the hospital."

That was true enough. Her beeper never seemed to stop going off here at work.

"What time do you finish your shift?" Danville asked.

He was certainly persistent. Probably not a bad trait for a grant professional.

"I should be done by seven."

"Perfect. That'll give us an hour before my other client arrives. I'll see you then."

Feeling as though she'd just been swept along on a high-energy tide, Zia tried to reach Mike. She guessed he was still in his board meeting and sure enough, her call went to voice mail.

"About dinner tonight. I'm getting together with a grant consultant at seven o'clock at La Maison on East 96th. He's hooking up with another client at eight, so you could meet me then and we'll go from there."

Mike wasn't in the best of moods when the Maritime Trades Association executive board meeting finally adjourned.

The US Coast Guard had presented an excellent update on their new electronic credentialing program. Mike and most other ship owners hailed it as a welcome advance, one that would allow the crews manning their ships to apply for recertification via any computer in any country in the world.

Unfortunately, someone had gotten to the reps from the Seafarers International Union. Citing growing concerns over government surveillance of electronic communications, they'd dug in their heels. They wanted a detailed account of built-in safeguards to protect personal, medical and psychological information. Not an unreasonable demand but the resulting exchange was as exhaustive as it was acerbic. As if any system could guarantee 100 percent protection, Mike thought grimly as he retrieved his voice mails.

When he spotted Zia's name and number in his recent calls list, his gut tightened. She wanted to cancel dinner. He would bet money on it. The woman was so wary, so cautious. So damned worried about this baby thing. As if his interest in her depended on her reproductive abilities!

Thinking he might have to step up his campaign to convince her otherwise, Mike hit Play. His gut unkinked as he listened to her invitation to meet her at La Maison. He checked his watch and saw he had just enough time to go back to his hotel to shower. Better scrape off his five-o'clock shadow, too, he thought, scrubbing a palm over his chin. What he had planned for Dr. St. Sebastian tonight involved some very sensitive patches of skin.

Mike had been in business long enough to know as many deals were cut over drinks or dinner as they were in boardrooms. He hadn't thought twice about Zia meeting this consultant at what turned out to be a very small, very elegant restaurant on the Upper East Side…right up until he walked into the dimly lit bar and he spotted the slick New Yorker in the thousand-dollar suit crowding her space. Ignoring the fact that his own suit and tie had been hand tailored in Italy, Mike started toward them.

The consultant caught sight of him first. In one narrow-eyed glance he assessed the newcomer's style, size and attitude. As a result, he didn't need either Zia's warm greeting or the quick, proprietorial kiss Mike dropped on her lips to understand he was skirting dangerously close to territorial waters. He acknowledged as much with a cool smile when he stood to shake hands.

"Good to meet you, Brennan. We were just talking about you."

"That right?"

"Zia…Dr. St. Sebastian…says your corporation is a source of funding for her research project."

"A *potential* source," she corrected, shooting Mike an apologetic glance. "Actually, I was relating some of the statistics you and Rafe shared about the rate of MRSA incidents among ships' crews."

"A correlation worth exploring," Danville said smoothly.

Too smoothly. Mike concealed his instinctive dislike behind a polite nod.

"I agree. I've reviewed Dr. St. Sebastian's draft proposal, but my VP for Support Systems will have to do an in-depth analysis of the final before he brings a recommendation for funding before our board."

"Of course."

Zia picked up on the chill in the air. Her brows rose, but her smile stayed in place as she rose and hooked her coat off the back of her chair.

"I appreciate you squeezing in time to meet with me, Tom. I'll email the draft proposal to you tomorrow."

"I'll look for it."

Yeah, Mike just bet he would. He didn't comment, though, until he had Zia in a cab and she turned to him with an exasperated look.

"What was that all about?"

"I didn't like the guy."

"Obviously. Care to tell me why?"

"He was too smooth. And he was poaching. Or trying to."

"Poaching? What on earth do you…? Oh."

"Yeah. Oh."

Her mouth opened. Closed. Opened again. "Please tell me you're not serious."

The irritation he'd clamped down on in the restaurant gathered a whole new head of steam. Dammit all to hell! He backed off every time Zia turned all wary and skittish. Folded himself almost in half trying not to push her into something she wasn't ready for. There was only so much a man could take, however.

"Sorry, sweetheart. I'm dead serious."

"I don't believe this. I assumed... I thought..."

She broke off, shaking her head in disgust. Mike should have let it go at that point. Given them both time to cool down. Perversely, he fanned the fire.

"You thought what?"

"I thought this Texas cowboy stuff was just another layer! One of the many that make up Michael slash Mike slash Uncle Mickey."

He had to smile. "You forgot Miguel. He's in there, too. Probably the most anachronistic part of the mix."

"Anachronistic?" Ice dripped from every syllable. "Or chauvinistic?"

"They're pretty much the same thing where I come from."

"And that's supposed to make me feel better?"

"No," he replied, realizing too late that he needed to tread carefully, "it's not supposed to do anything but put you on notice."

Her chin came up. A dangerous glint lit her dark eyes. "Of?"

Mike knew it was too soon. He'd intended to give her time. Calm her doubts. Let her get used to the course he was steering. But the angry set to her jaw told him he'd just run out of windage.

"Remember the deal we made back in Galveston?"

Anger gave way to the wariness that hit him like a right cross. "I remember," she said cautiously. "Do you?"

"Every word. I said I would tell you if and when I approached the hurting stage."

He reached for her hand. She resisted but he folded it between both of his. Was that a slight tremor in her fingers or the hammer of his own pulse? He didn't know, didn't care.

"I'm there, Zia. I'm in love with you, or so close it doesn't matter."

The admission came easy and felt so right he asked himself why the hell he'd waited this long. He got his answer in the quick flare of panic in the dark eyes locked on his face.

"Mike, I…uh…"

"Relax." He forced a grin. "This isn't a race. Doesn't matter who gets where first. And," he said when the panic didn't subside, "you don't need to come up with an appropriate response right this minute. You've got a whole month to think it through."

"A whole month?"

"Okay, three weeks and some change. Until the Frostbite Regatta," he added in answer to her blank look.

"Holy Virgin!" Her expression went from blank to incredulous. "You're not really planning to participate in that insanity, are you?"

"Not unless you do. Although I have to say…" His grin widened. Curling a knuckle under her chin, he tipped her face to his. "My sisters all insist I look pretty hot in a tux."

Her disbelief melted into a reluctant laugh. "Do they?"

"Word of honor." He puffed out his chest. "Be a shame if you didn't get to see me in all my splendor."

"And I can't do that without freezing my ass off aboard a sailboat as it cuts through the icy waters of Long Island Sound?"

"Nope. That's the deal. You, me, wind and waves." His voice softened. Caressed. Challenged. "C'mon, Doc. Live dangerously."

Eight

Despite her unrelenting schedule, Zia was thrilled when the duchess and Maria finally returned from their Texas sojourn the last week in January. She'd rattled around in the empty apartment during her hours off for well over a month. The week in Galveston and Mike's brief visit had provided welcome diversions. She'd also had lunch or dinner with her brother and Natalie several times during the interval. But she was ready for the companionable presence of the duchess.

Thankfully, the vicious Arctic cold and damp that had caused Charlotte's bones to ache so badly had loosened its grip on the city. The temperature hovered at a balmy forty degrees the evening Charlotte, Maria, Gina and the twins arrived home. Jack was in Paris for some high-level diplomatic meeting, while Sarah and Dev had flown back to LA.

That left Dom and Natalie and Zia to greet the remainder of the Texas contingent when they drove in from the airport. The three St. Sebastians waited in the lobby with Jerome, who'd lingered an additional forty minutes after his shift ended to greet the travelers.

"We can't stay," Gina said as she hopped out of the limo to distribute hugs all around, including a big one for the delighted doorman. "The girls are tired and cranky. I need to get them home to bed. I'll see you this weekend, Grandmama, after you've rested and recovered."

She hopped back in and left it to the welcoming committee to escort the duchess inside. Zia noted with some concern that Charlotte leaned heavily on her cane as they crossed the lobby. So did Jerome. The doorman and Zia exchanged a speaking glance but neither wanted to spoil the homecoming by commenting on her uneven gait.

Yet after everyone else had dispersed and it was just the duchess and Zia settling in for a chat before the fire, Charlotte's first concern was for her great-niece. When Zia delivered the aperitif her aunt insisted on, the duchess's paper-thin skin of her palm stoked her cheek.

"I hoped to find the shadows under your eyes gone, Anastazia."

"It's been crazy here, Aunt Charlotte. I've been so busy."

"I can imagine." She accepted the snifter Zia handed her. "How did your presentation to the faculty go?"

"Great! Fantastic! Really, really good!"

Chuckling, the duchess hefted her glass in a salute. "Tell me."

Trying not to sound too self-congratulatory, Zia gave a quick recap of the nerve-racking session in front of the faculty and her fellow residents.

"They all found the statistics detailing the increase in Methicillin-resistant Staphylococcus aureus infections in neonatal facilities sobering."

"I should think so!"

"And no one challenged my correlation between the increasing number of MRSA incidents and staffing levels in neonatal intensive care units. Or," she added with deliberate nonchalance, "the need for more intensive study of MRSA in controlled environments similar to NIC units."

"Such as crew compartments on seagoing vessels?"

She shot the duchess an incredulous look. Charlotte chuckled and took a sip of her brandy. "Don't look so astonished. Mike Brennan paid me several visits after you left."

"He did?"

"He did. I suspect," she added drily, "he holds the mistaken impression I wield as much influence over my family as his *abuelita* does over his."

The comment struck Zia the wrong way. She couldn't believe Mike hadn't told her about these visits. Or that he might be conducting some kind of an end run by enlisting the duchess to exert her influence.

"Is that what he did? Ask you to plead his case for him?"

"Of course not. He's too intelligent for that. We discussed your research proposal...among other things."

"*What* other things?"

The abrupt demand had the duchess lifting a haughty brow. Skewered by that regal stare, Zia issued a quick apology.

"I'm sorry. It's just...Mike didn't tell me he'd spoken with you when he was here a few weeks ago."

"I'm not surprised," Charlotte returned. "Reading between the lines, I gather the time you two have spent together has been..." She paused. "Shall we say, intense."

Coming from the duchess, the delicate wording put spots of heat in Zia's cheeks. She took a few moments to regain her composure by downing a healthy gulp of *pálinka*. "I guess that's as good a description of our time together as any," she admitted.

The duchess's eyes might be clouded with age but they lingered on Zia's face with disconcerting shrewdness. "The man's in love with you, Anastazia. Or so close to the edge you could push him over with a single poke." Her voice softened, and her face folded into fine lines. "Why aren't you poking?"

"It's complicated."

"Tell me."

"I…"

"Tell me, dearest."

The quiet command broke the dam. Abandoning her chair, Zia dropped to her knees beside the duchess. The private pain she'd shared with no one but her brother—and Mike Brennan!—spilled out in quick, disjointed phrases.

"I had a hysterectomy. When I was in college. They had to do it to save my life. And now…now I can't have children."

She dropped her forehead. The words came more slowly now, more painfully.

"You saw Mike. He loves kids. He's terrific with them. He deserves someone who can give him the family he—"

"Bull!"

Zia's head jerked up. "What?"

"You heard me," the duchess retorted. "That's total and complete bull."

Her eyes snapping, she took her great-niece's chin in a firm grip.

"Listen to me, Anastazia Amalia. You're a sensitive, caring physician and a brilliant researcher. Far more important, you have a wonderful man who's in love with you. You should be grabbing at the future with greedy hands. Instead you're wallowing in self-pity. Stop it," she ordered briskly. "Now! This very instant!"

Zia reared back, or tried to. Charlotte refused to release her chin. Their eyes locked, faded blue and liquid black. One woman with a lifetime of great joy and great sorrow behind her, another just embarking on that perilous, exhilarating journey.

She was right, Zia realized with a crush of self-disgust. She'd been so worried about what she and Mike *couldn't* have that she'd refused to let herself focus on everything they *could*.

"Okay," she said on a shaky laugh. "I'm done wallowing."

"Good." The duchess didn't release her firm hold. "Now be honest with me. Do you love him?"

She couldn't deny it any longer. Not to Charlotte. Not to herself.

"Yes."

"Ahh." The quiet sigh feathered through the duchess's lips. Her cheeks creasing in a smile, she gave her great-niece's chin a little shake. "Then put the poor man out of his misery! Tell him how you feel."

"All right! I will."

The duchess released her grip but not her tenacious hold on the subject under discussion. "When?" she demanded.

Surrendering, Zia sank back on her heels. "He's flying in to New York for Valentine's weekend. He wants to take me sailing. In something called the Frostbite Regatta."

"Good heavens. That sounds perfectly dreadful."

"Exactly what I said!"

"Then again," Charlotte mused as she reached for her brandy and took a delicate sip, "I seem to recall that a sailboat rocking on a choppy sea can be rather erotic. If you're curled up in a bunk with the right person, of course."

Zia didn't share the duchess's musings with Mike when he called later that night to make sure the travelers had all returned home safely. She did, however, tell him that Charlotte had mentioned his visits.

"I enjoyed getting to know her a little better. She's a fascinating woman."

"She said pretty much the same thing about you."

"Not only fascinating, but very discerning." He let that hang for a moment before changing the subject. "So, where are you on your proposal?"

"It's signed, sealed and delivered. The research center's executive review committee meets tomorrow."

If...*when*...they gave the expanded study their stamp of approval, Danville and Associates would go out for funding. And if the financial gods were kind, the project would be up and running within weeks.

"Let me know what the committee decides," Mike said.

"I will."

"And I'll see you soon. I'm flying into New York the afternoon of the twelfth. I want to make sure we have time to suit you up for the regatta the next day."

"Right," she said slowly.

"You're not chickening out, are you?"

"What if the boat tips over? Do you know how quickly we could succumb to hypothermia?"

"Not gonna happen, Doc. It's been a while since I exercised my sea legs, but sailing's like riding a bicycle. It's easy once you learn the ropes."

"Oh, that's reassuring! You might be interested to know ERs treat more than three hundred thousand kids for bike injuries every year."

"Crap." He paused, no doubt thinking of his hyperactive nieces and nephews. "That many?"

"That many."

He mulled that over for a few moments before tossing out the one argument she couldn't counter. "I guess you'll just have to trust me to take care of you."

"I guess so. I'll see you on the twelfth."

Zia was conducting chart reviews with her interns when Dr. Wilbanks buzzed with word that the executive review committee had green-lighted her proposal.

"Congratulations," he said in his brusque way. "You're the first resident to have a study of this scope and magnitude approved. Who are you working with to secure funding?"

"Danville and Associates."

"Have we used them before?"

"They were on the list Ms. Horton gave me."

"Then I suggest you get with them as soon as possible and tell them to start the ball rolling."

"Yes, sir."

Zia made the call as soon as Dr. Wilbanks disconnected. Tom Danville added his congratulations, along with the suggestion that Zia come to his office so she could meet the others on his staff. She checked her schedule and set the appointment for three the following afternoon.

Danville and Associates occupied a suite of offices on the thirty-second floor of Olympic Tower on Fifth Avenue. Zia stepped out of the elevator into a sea of Persian carpets and gleaming mahogany. She cringed a little at the thought that the cost to maintain these expensive surroundings came from the commissions Danville and Associates made off proposals like hers. She'd included their commission in her budget but still...

A smiling receptionist confirmed her appointment and reached for her phone. "We've been expecting you, Dr. St. Sebastian. I'll let Tom know you're here."

Danville appeared a moment later. Zia wasn't intimately familiar with men's apparel, but the European in her had no trouble identifying the leather loafers and silk tie as Italian.

His eyes bright and brimming with high-voltage energy, he escorted her to his office. "I had my people scrub your proposal. They've lined up a hit list of potential funding sources. I think you'll be impressed."

He made quick work of the intros. Two men, one woman, all dressed as expensively as their boss. And all sporting very impressive credentials, Zia knew, from her study of Danville and Associates' website.

Elizabeth Hamilton-Hobbs took the lead. A trim brunette in a black Armani suit and a butterscotch silk blouse, she held a BS and a master's from the Wharton School of Business. Zia's field might be medicine, but even she knew Wharton was private, Ivy League and one of the top-ranked business schools in the US.

"My colleagues and I are very impressed with your proposed research project, Dr. St. Sebastian. You're investigating a dangerous trend impacting medical facilities, but you left room to explore other occupational areas, as well. As a result—"

"As a result," Tom Danville jumped in, scrubbing his upper lip in his eagerness, "we have the perfect in with the big shipping companies like MSC, COSCO and GSI. Also with state and federal agencies looking at the spread of infectious disease among their prison populations."

Hamilton-Hobbs waited for him to finish before continuing her presentation "We've prepared a target list of private corporations and health-oriented foundations. Now that your study's been approved, we'll get the solicitations in the works and—"

"Dr. St. Sebastian doesn't want to hear 'in the works,'" Danville huffed, scrubbing his upper lip again. "Neither do I."

Zia went cold. Stone-cold. She didn't need the quick glance the brunette exchanged with her colleagues to guess what lay behind it.

Their boss was flying high. Soaring. That wasn't his upper lip he was itching. That was the underside of his nose.

An irritated septum was one of the classic symptoms of cocaine snorting, right along with the fever-bright eyes and hyperactivity. Zia couldn't believe she'd missed the warning flags at their first meeting. She didn't miss them now, however. Danville must have cut a line right before she arrived.

Her glance shot from him to Hamilton-Hobbs. The other woman had to have seen the dawning realization and disgust in her client's expression. She held Zia's gaze with a steely one of her own.

"I'll be handling the solicitations personally, Dr. St. Sebastian. They'll go out this afternoon, and I promise I'll follow up on each one myself."

When Zia hesitated, the brunette laid her professional reputation on the line.

"Danville and Associates has one of the highest success rates in the country. I guarantee we'll secure the one-point-two million you require for your study."

Medicine, Zia had learned, was knowledge multiplied by experience compounded by instinct. So was life. She could get up, walk out and start over again with the next grant professional on the comptroller's list. Or she could trust Elizabeth Hamilton-Hobbs.

She nodded. Slowly. Not bothering to disguise her reluctance. "I want to be kept in the loop. Please copy me on each solicitation you send out and every response you receive."

Danville voiced an instant objection. "We'll send you weekly status reports. That's our standard policy. But we don't…"

His subordinate cut him off with a knife-edged smile.

"Not a problem, Dr. St. Sebastian. I'll keep you in the loop every step of the way."

Elizabeth held to her word. She cc'd Zia on every solicitation that went out and forwarded copies of every response that came in. In a remarkably short space of time, Danville and Associates secured more than eight hundred thousand dollars from three foundations and four private corporations....including a quarter million promised by GSA over the projected two-year life of the study.

Rafe Montoya called Zia personally with the news. He caught her at work, busy preparing for the weekly discharge conference. It was one of Children's Hospital's most popular sessions. Attended by faculty and staff alike, the conference focused on patients with unusual diagnoses or diseases difficult to treat. One of Zia's patients would be discussed at this session—a five-year-old who'd presented with retinitis pigmentosa, mental retardation and obesity. She'd tested him for a dozen different possibilities before diagnosing the extremely rare Bardet-Biedl Syndrome. She was preparing to lead the discussion of his case, but took Rafe's call eagerly.

"Thought you might want to know GSI's executive board voted unanimously to help underwrite the study."

"Really? That's fantastic!"

She couldn't resist a little happy dance. The gleeful two-step set her stethoscope bobbling and her interns gaping. But when the initial thrill subsided, she had to ask.

"Just out of curiosity, how many members of GSI's executive board are related to the CEO?"

"Seven of the twelve," Rafe admitted with a chuckle. "If it makes you feel any better, though, the remaining five all have extensive backgrounds in the shipping industry. Your proposal struck a chord with them, Zia. Especially after I dropped a casual reminder of the multimillion-dollar MRSA suit brought by the crew of the *Cheryl K.*"

"Thanks, Rafe. I really appreciate your support. I'll do my damnedest to make sure our research justifies GSI's investment."

"That's all we can ask. And it wasn't just me pushing this," he added. "Mike's been behind this project from the start. Okay, not just the project. He believes in you, Zia."

* * *

Rafe's ringing endorsement was still front and center in Zia's mind when Mike called to advise her of his arrival time on February twelfth. He caught her in the hospital cafeteria. She'd missed lunch and had dashed down to grab a frozen yogurt and a much-needed break. She was just dousing the creamy ice-cream substitute with chocolate sprinkles when her cell buzzed. She fished the iPhone out of the pocket of her white coat and balanced it between her shoulder and ear while signing the chit for her yogurt.

"Wheels down at five-fifteen," Mike announced as Zia carried her treat to an empty table. "I'll be at my hotel by six-thirty. Seven at the latest. Plan on dinner at eight, with several hours of uninterrupted quality time to follow. Or," he said with a husky laugh that raised shivers of anticipated delight, "quality time first and dinner to follow. Your choice, Doc."

"Wrong," she countered with a quick lick of her spoon.

"Which part?"

"The choice part. Anyone who can squeeze a quarter-of-million dollars out of his board of directors to study germs deserves first pick."

It was a joke. A lighthearted attempt to thank him for his support. Yet Zia sensed instantly the joke had fallen flat.

"Is this something we need to talk about?" he asked. "Our personal relationship vis-à-vis our professional responsibilities? I don't have a problem keeping them separate, Zia."

"Neither do I. I was just kidding, Mike. Although…"

Now that it was out there like the proverbial elephant in the room she couldn't ignore it.

"Is it really possible to separate them? Would you have endorsed my study if you didn't…if we weren't…"

"Lovers?" he supplied when she fumbled for the right word. "Friends? Acquaintances?"

"Involved."

That was greeted with a dead silence that thundered in Zia's ears, drowning out the rattle of the trays two candy stripers had just placed on the cafeteria's conveyor belt.

"Okay," Mike said after that pregnant pause. "Looks like we're going to have to sit down and have a long talk about tax credits and incentives for corporations to invest in research and development. They vary greatly at national, state and local levels."

"I know that."

"Did you also know Texas possesses four of this country's busiest deep-water ports? Galveston, Beaumont, Houston and Corpus Christi."

"No," she replied, a little put off by the lecturing tone.

"Houston is the tenth busiest port in the *world* in tonnage. So yes, GSI invests heavily in research we think may positively impact our industry and, oh, by the way, earns us almost as much in tax breaks as our original investment. Does that answer your question?"

"No," Zia snapped back, annoyed now. "I know how much GSI invests in research. Rafe briefed me on the figures in your office, yes?"

She could hear her accent thickening, feel the temper stirring behind it.

"My question was…and still is…would you have supported this particular project if you and I were not *involved*?"

"Dammit, woman, is that the best you can up with to describe where we are together?"

He still hadn't answered her question, but he now singed the airways. She gripped the phone and started to bite back. Would have, if she hadn't remembered her recent conversation with the duchess.

She owed Mike the truth. She might have given it if he hadn't just come down on her with both feet. Gritting her teeth, she forced a cool reply.

"Do you not think this is something we should discuss in person?"

"No," he shot back, as irritated now as she was. "I told you I wouldn't push you. I also remember saying this isn't a race. But I think I need some indication of whether you're even on the track."

"Jézus, Mária és József!" Goaded, she spit out the truth she'd owned up to so recently. "I love you! There! Is that what you wish to hear?"

The pause this time was longer. Moments instead of seconds.

Embarrassed by her heated outburst, Zia glanced around to see if any of the other cafeteria customers had tuned in. None had, and despite her simmering irritation she found herself holding her breath until a slow drawl came across the airwaves.

"Oh, yeah, darlin'. That's exactly what I wanted to hear. Maybe not quite in that tone, but I'm not complaining."

She could hear the laughter in his voice. And something deeper, something that locked her breath in her chest.

"Care to repeat it?" he asked, a caress in each word. "Without the attitude this time?"

How in God's name did he do this? Spark her temper one moment and make her melt the next? Sighing, Zia stabbed her spoon into the melting yogurt.

"I love you."

"There now. That wasn't so hard, was it?"

"Yes, it was! I was going to wait until this weekend to tell you, in the proper setting."

"Aboard a sailboat while we're freezing our asses off?"

"No, you fool. Before that. Or at the ball afterward."

She gave a hiccuping laugh. "I hadn't nailed down the specifics."

"Tell you what. You decide on the venue and we'll do this again in person. Deal?"

A smile spread across her heart. "Deal."

Nine

To Zia's infinite relief, she didn't get to experience the thrill of chopping through the icy waters of Long Island Sound. A front rolled in Friday afternoon, bringing with it a dense fog. Every airport on the East Coast shut just hours before Mike's private jet was scheduled to land. He had to divert to Pittsburgh and wait it out.

The impenetrable mist continued to blanket New York well into Saturday morning, forcing the yacht club to postpone their Frostbite Regatta. The Valentine Ball, however, remained on schedule for that evening. Mike promised he'd arrive by plane, train or rental car to escort her to the big bash.

The duchess took advantage of the delay to arrange a shopping expedition. Zia had already called Gina to ask if she could borrow one of her many gowns, but Charlotte dismissed that with a wave of one hand. "Nonsense. You have a very distinct style, quite different from Gina's."

"I've lived in white coats and sweats for almost three years," Zia protested. "If I had a distinctive style, it's dead and buried."

"Then we shall have to resurrect it."

Conceding defeat, Zia buzzed down and asked Jerome

to hail a taxi. It was waiting curbside when the two women emerged into the gray, drizzly afternoon a little past one o'clock.

The doorman opened the rear door with a flourish. "Where shall I tell the driver to take you, Duchess?"

"Saks Fifth Avenue."

"Of course."

The cabbie zipped through the light weekend traffic and pulled up less than thirty minutes later at the mecca for shoppers with discriminating tastes and the money to indulge them. Saks's flagship store first opened in 1924 and now covered an entire city block. Its seventh-floor café looked down on the spires of St. Patrick's Cathedral. Every floor above and below offered an array of tempting, high-end goods.

Charlotte had been forced to dispense with the services of a personal shopper during the lean years. Since Sarah married and her husband had taken over management of the family's finances, however, she was once again able to indulge in one of life's more decadent luxuries.

The ponytailed personal attendant had been alerted by a phone call from Jerome and was waiting curbside to help his clients out of the cab. "What a delight to see you again, Duchess."

"And you, Andrew."

"How may I assist you today?"

"This is my great-niece, Dr. Anastazia St. Sebastian. She requires a ball gown, shoes and an appointment at the salon."

"A pleasure to meet you, Dr. St. Sebastian." The shopper measured Zia's lithe figure and distinctive features with something approaching ecstasy. "I'm sure we can find just what you're looking for."

Mere moments later he had them ensconced in a private viewing room on the fifth floor. Crystal flutes shared a silver tray with iced champagne and bottles of sparkling water.

"May I ask if you have a particular style or color in mind?" Andrew asked as he poured champagne for Charlotte and a Perrier for Zia.

"No frills," the duchess pronounced. "Something sleek and sophisticated. In midnight blue, I think. Or..." She cocked her head, assessing Zia with the discerning eye that had once filled her closets with creations from the world's most exclusive designers. "Red. Shimmering, iridescent red."

"Oh, yes!" Andrew almost clapped his hands in delight. "With her ebony hair and dark eyes, she'll look delicious in red. Emily! Madeline!" A snap of his fingers made the two waiting saleswomen jump. "What do we have that might fit the bill?"

"It's Valentine's week," the older of the two women reminded him. "We're swimming in red."

"Well, show the duchess and Dr. St. Sebastian what we have."

The women disappeared and returned mere moments later with an array of designer originals. Each, Zia noted, was more expensive than the last. Not that she was particularly concerned about the price tag. Charlotte had flatly refused to let her contribute to household expenses for the past two and a half years. She'd insisted instead that her great-niece's company in the big, empty apartment was more than enough recompense. So Zia had banked her entire salary and could well afford to splurge on something outrageously expensive.

She tried several designs and labels, but the moment she slithered into a tube of screaming scarlet, she knew that was the one. The front bodice was cut in a straight slash from shoulder to shoulder. The back, however, plunged well below her waist. And every step, every breath, set off tiny pinpricks of light from the sparkling paillettes woven into the fabric.

Three-inch stilettos and a clutch bag in silver completed the ensemble, but the duchess wasn't done. After high tea at the seventh-floor café with its magnificent views, the two women hit the salon. They emerged three hours later. Charlotte's snowy hair was arranged in a regal upsweep. Zia wore hers caught high behind one ear with a rhinestone comb, falling in a smooth black wing over the other.

It was almost six when they returned home. Mike had called to let Zia know he'd made it into the city okay and would pick her up at seven. That left a comfortable margin to freshen up, shimmy into her gown and apply a little more makeup than her usual swipe of lip gloss. She was adding mascara to her thick lashes when the duchess tapped lightly on her bedroom door.

"Oh, my dear!" Charlotte's blue eyes misted a little as she had Zia perform a slow pirouette. "You've inherited the best of the St. Sebastian genes. There's Magyar in your eyes and high cheekbones, centuries of royal breeding in your carriage. You do the duchy of Karlenburgh proud, my dear."

Charlotte's praise stirred a glow of pride. Zia had indeed inherited a remarkable set of genes. The fierce Magyars who'd swept down from the steppes on their ponies…the French and Italian princes and princesses who'd married into the St. Sebastian family in past centuries…the Hungarian patriots who'd fought so long and so hard to throw off the Soviet yoke… They'd all contributed to the person she was. She felt the beat of their blood in her veins and a wash of surprise when the duchess pressed a small velvet box into her hand.

"These are part of your heritage, and my gift to you."

Zia flipped the lid on the box to reveal a pair of ruby

earrings nested in black velvet. Each red oval dangled from a smaller but similarly cut diamond.

"Oh, Charlotte! They're beautiful. I'll certainly wear them tonight, but I won't keep them. You should give them to one of the twins."

"I've managed to preserve a few pieces for my great-grandchildren. And Dev, clever boy that he is, has helped me reclaim some I was forced to sell over the years. These," she said with a sniff of disdain, "were apparently purchased by an extremely vulgar Latvian plutocrat for his mistress. I didn't ask Dev how he recovered them, although I understand Jack had to step in and exercise some rather questionable behind-the-scenes diplomatic maneuvering. Now," she finished firmly, "they're yours. Let's see how they look on you."

Zia thought they looked magnificent.

So did Mike when he arrived a few moments later.

When Zia met him at the door, what looked like an acre of pleated white shirtfront and black tuxedo filled her vision. He carried his overcoat over his arm, his hat in his hand and an awed expression on his face.

"Wow. You, Dr. St. Sebastian, are stunning."

"It's the earrings." She bobbed her head to set the rubies dancing. "Charlotte gave them to me, insisting they're part of my heritage."

"Trust me," he growled when she turned to precede him through the foyer, "it's not the earrings. You sure that dress won't get us both arrested?"

She was laughing when she left him to say hello to the duchess while she fetched her wrap…and thoroughly surprised for the second time that evening when she exited the lobby to find a black carriage with bright yellow wheels drawn up at the curb. The driver wore a top hat and voluminous red coat. A jaunty red plume decorated his horse's headpiece.

Zia came to a dead stop. "You've *got* to be kidding."

"Nope. I decided to do it up right this evening."

"You do know it's February, right? There's still frost on the ground."

"Not to worry. Natalie sent along a warm blanket. And your brother provided this." He fished a thin silver flask out of his pocket and held it up with a smug grin. "It's not *pálinka*, but Dom guarantees it'll warm the cockles of your heart. Whatever the hell those are," he added as he took her elbow to help her climb aboard.

"The ventricles," Zia murmured while he settled beside her. "From the Latin, *cochleae cordis*. When did you see Natalie and Dom?"

"Right before I came to pick you up." He draped the blanket over her knees and settled his hat on his head before stretching an arm across her shoulders to keep her close for added warmth. "All right, Jerry. Let's go."

The driver nodded and checked over his shoulder for traffic before clicking to his horse. Still slightly dazed to find herself clip-clopping down Central Park West, Zia felt compelled to ask.

"Did you stop by Natalie and Dom's just to pick up a blanket and brandy?"

"Pretty much. Although *abuelita* suggested it would be a smart move to let your brother know I intended to ask you to marry me. I wasn't too keen on the idea," he admitted with a grimace. "At best, Dominic considers me a half step above a freebooter. But I figured I…"

"Wait! Back up!"

"To what? Freebooter? It's an old Dutch term for pirate." He attempted to look innocent but the gleam in his eyes gave him away. "Or do you mean the part of about telling Dom I intend to propose?"

"You know very well that's what I mean!"

"Well, I have to say His Grace wasn't all that happy about his sister hooking up with a lowlife Texas wharf rat. But after some abject begging on my part and several comments from Natalie about *his* lifestyle prior to marriage, Dom conceded it was your decision."

Zia's mind whirled with images of swashbuckling pirates and Dom assuming his haughtiest grand duke demeanor and Mike trying his best to appear abject. She was still trying to sort through the kaleidoscope when he used the arm draped across her shoulders to angle her into a close embrace. His breath warmed her cheek, and his eyes smiled down into hers.

"Why look so surprised? What did you think was going to happen after you threw that bombshell at me over the phone?"

"I *thought* we were going to talk about it this weekend, at a time and venue to be decided."

"We could talk, I suppose, but it makes more sense to me to cut right to the chase. I love you. You love me. What else matters, Anastazia Amalia Julianna St. Sebastian?"

"Did Dom make you memorize all my names?"

"No, that was Natalie. Your sister-in-law," he added with a touch of awe, "is a powerhouse packed in a very demure, very deceptive package. I'm not sure I want to get her and my sisters in the same room at the same time. The males on both sides of our respective family trees might never recover."

A thousand questions had swirled through Zia's mind. Where would they live? How would marriage affect her appointment to Dr. Wilbanks's research team? When, if ever, would she return to her homeland? But his comment about family trees pushed everything else out of her head.

"We *do* need to talk, Mike." She threw a quick glance at the driver and dropped her voice. "We're making a life decision here and I don't even know how you feel about adoption. Or fostering. Or using a surrogate or…or not having children at all."

"Look at me."

His eyes lost their teasing glint and he, too, lowered his voice to give her gut-wrenching worry the seriousness it demanded.

"I'm good with *any* of those options, Zia. As long as we make the decision together."

"But your family…your sisters…"

"This isn't about them. It's about us. You and me, spending the rest of our lives together. I want to sail the Pacific with you and show you my world. Tag along behind you at the hospital to learn more about yours. When and if we decide to bring children into the world we create together, we'll figure out the best way to do it. All that's required at this moment is a simple 'yes.'"

The old hurt, the sense of loss Zia had carried since that long-ago ski trip, was still buried deep in her psyche. She suspected it would never fully disappear. But a burgeoning joy now overlaid the ache. The duchess was right. She had to reach out and grab the future with both hands.

Literally *and* figuratively. Sloughing off her doubts, she hooked both hands in the lapels of Mike's overcoat and tugged him closer. "Yes, Michael Mickey Miguel Brennan. Yes."

When he moved in to seal the deal with a kiss, Zia knew she would always remember this snapshot in time. Whatever came, whatever the future he'd sketched for them brought, she would feel February's nip. Hear the horse's hooves clacking on the cold pavement, the carriage wheels rattling out their winter song.

Then he surprised her with another memory to tuck away and savor. This one included a jeweler's box. Her second of the night, Zia thought with a wild thump of her heart. She raised the lid, her fingers a little shaky, and gasped when the pear-shaped diamond caught the glow of the streetlamps.

"I had to guess at your ring size," he confessed as he plucked the ring out of its nest and eased it over her knuckle. "The fit looks pretty good to me, though."

Not just the fit. The size and clarity and the fact that it adorned her finger had Zia swinging between delight and disbelief. She'd met this man less than two months ago and now wore his ring. It was only a symbol. A *very* expensive token. Yet it shouted to the world she and Mike intended to make a life together. She'd never appreciated the awesome power of symbols before.

She tucked her hands under the blanket and fingered the ring throughout the ride. The raised mounting and sharp, V-shaped prong protecting the pear's pointed tip had almost drawn blood by the time they arrived at the New York Yacht Club.

Hemmed in on three sides by towering skyscrapers, the club was a bastion of old Manhattan now immortalized as a National Historic Landmark. Light poured from the huge windows fronting West 44th Street. Fashioned to resemble the elaborate transoms of Spanish galleons, the windows gave tantalizing views of an immense interior room lined with scale models of members' yachts.

Hundreds of scale models, Zia discovered after she and Mike had checked their coats and joined the glittering crowd. Thousands! Some with sails furled, some in full rigging. They were mounted on lit shelves that filled almost every inch of the fantastic room's walls, leaving space only for a monstrous white marble fireplace decorated with tridents and anchors and an oval painting of a ship in full sail. Zia rested her arm lightly in the crook of Mike's arm and craned her neck to take in all the nautical splendor.

"Mike!"

A short, sturdy fireplug of woman with iron-gray hair and leathery skin cut through the crowd. A distinguished and much taller gentleman trailed in her wake.

"That's Anne Singleton," Mike advised as the woman plowed toward them. "Her husband and I served in the navy together."

Zia appreciated the brief heads-up, especially after Anne latched on to Mike's lapels and hauled him down for a loud, smacking kiss. She broke the lip-lock but hung on to his tux.

"Can't believe we finally got you up here to the Frostbite Regatta and the damned thing gets postponed! Promise you'll come when we reschedule."

"We'll see."

"If you're done with him, Annie, mind if I say hello?"

The mild exposition came from the man Zia assumed must be Singleton's husband. His wife relinquished her hold and used the brief interval while they shook hands to inspect Zia from head to toe. All of a sudden she let out an earsplitting whoop.

"He did it!" Her leathery face creased into a wide grin. Eyes alight, she jabbed an elbow into her husband's side. "Harry! He did it!"

"I see," he replied, wincing.

Zia didn't, until Mike explained. "After cooling my heels so long in Pittsburgh this morning, I wasn't sure I'd get here in time to pick up the ring. Tiffany's said they would courier it to my hotel, but just to be safe I called Anne and asked her to pick it up, then meet me at the airport."

"Which I was so thrilled to do! You have no idea how many women I've tried to hook this man up with in the past three years. I've run through every one of my single, divorced and widowed friends, the *daughters* of those friends, the *friends* of those..."

"I think she's got the picture, Anne."

"Oh hush, Harry! You paraded a few past him, too. Remember that bottle blonde you invited to the races in Newport? Worst weekend of my life," his wife confided with a shudder. "The woman had a laugh that could strip the paint from a steel hull."

"True," her husband conceded good-naturedly.

They were so different, Zia thought. One so tall and elegant in his tux, the other wearing what was probably a ten-thousand-dollar designer original with complete disregard for the way it hitched up on one shoulder and bunched around her sturdy hips. Yet the affection between them was obvious and heartwarming.

"I'm Harry Singleton, Dr. St. Sebastian. I don't know if Mike told you, but he and I go way back."

"Please call me Zia. And, yes, he mentioned that you served in the navy together."

"Did he also mention that he saved my ass when I went overboard in the Sea of Japan during Typhoon Ito?"

"No."

She threw Mike a questioning glance, but Anne Singleton waved an impatient hand. "You can bore her with your war stories later. Right now we need to toast this momentous occasion."

She detached Zia from Mike, caught her arm and hauled her toward a table groaning with crystal and china bearing the yacht club's distinctive insignia etched in gold. Two other couples lingered by the table, cocktails in hand. While her husband signaled to one of the hovering attendants, Anne introduced Zia to their obviously close circle of friends.

"That's Alec, former conductor of the Lincoln Center Orchestra," she said, stabbing a finger at each of the four in turn. "Judy, his wife and the lawyer you want if you're ever charged with tax evasion. Helen, mother of five and the world's greatest cook. Dan, who's yet to miss one of

Helen's meals. Okay, now listen up, crew. This is Zia St. Sebastian. She and Mike are about to hook the bight."

Zia's puzzled look generated grins all around and several equally unintelligible phrases.

"Fit double clews," Harry supplied, his eyes twinkling.

"Get spliced," the retired conductor put in.

"Also," Judy drawled, "known as getting hitched." She rounded the table and took both of Zia's hands in hers. "I know protocol says you're supposed to congratulate the man in this situation, but I think everyone at this table will agree you've won a real prize."

Zia didn't need to hear Mike's low groan to know his friends had acutely embarrassed him. She, on the other hand, was delighted to discover yet another dimension to his multi-faceted personality. A side of him this group obviously cherished. A side she was suddenly, voraciously eager to explore.

The rest of the evening passed in whirl of color and music. The seven-course dinner was a gourmand's delight. The live band provided dreamy music during and after the meal. What kept Zia laughing, though, were the personal recollections that grew more incredible and less believable as the night progressed. Interestingly, there was only one mention of Mike's previous plunge into stormy matrimonial waters. It was couched in an obscure nautical term that dropped Zia's jaw when Anne whispered a translation.

Her sides were still aching when she and Mike collapsed in the backseat of a taxi well past one in the morning. By unspoken consent they went to his hotel. And, again by mutual consent, they called the duchess the next morning to ask her permission for a family gathering at the apartment later that afternoon.

Natalie and Dom showed up. So did Gina and Jack and the twins. Maria made a special trip in, and even Jerome managed to pop up for a quick glass of champagne.

After the toasts and hearty congratulations, Dom engineered a few moments alone with Zia. They stood at the windows overlooking Central Park, two foreigners with unbreakable ties to America…and Americans.

"This is what you want?" he asked softly in their native Hungarian.

"Yes."

"It's not easy to blend two worlds, two nationalities."

"You and Natalie don't seem to have had any problems."

"We haven't," Dom agreed, his gaze drifting to his wife. "But Natalie is altogether unique."

"So is Mike."

His glance came back to Zia. The love in his eyes flooded her heart. "Then I wish you all the joy that I've found, little one."

"Thank you."

An hour later, Zia kissed Mike goodbye. She hated to see him go. This separation loomed so much larger than their previous weeks apart. It also resurfaced her concerns about where they'd live and how they'd merge their very different careers.

"We'll work it out."

"Before or after we're married?"

"Whenever."

"Mike…"

Her snort of exasperation made him smile, but his eyes turned dead serious as he curled a knuckle under her chin.

"We Texicans are thickheaded as hell, darlin'. Stubborn, too. But I've been down this road before. Nothing and no one matters to me more than you do. We'll work out the minor details."

Mike made pretty much the same declaration to his family when he returned to Houston and announced his engagement. Eileen took considerably more convincing than the rest. Probably because she'd seen him at his lowest point after his divorce.

Mike hadn't been happy then, when his sister had tracked him to one of Houston's sleaziest waterfront dives. And he wasn't happy now, when she marched into his office unannounced and uninvited. It didn't faze his sister that he was on a teleconference with Korea. She planted a hip on the corner of his desk, crossed her arms and waited.

"I like Zia," she said the moment he disconnected. "I do! And I get down on my knees every night to thank God she was there to drag Davy out of the undertow. But you've known her for what? Six weeks?"

Mike set his jaw, but she ignored the warning.

"That's two weeks less than you knew The Bitch before you waltzed her to the altar."

"Eileen…"

"I don't want to see you hurt again, Mike. None of us do." Tears filmed her eyes. "Please tell me you know what you're doing."

The tears took the sting from his anger. He pushed out of his chair and came around to drape an arm across her shoulders.

"Jill was heat and hunger and lust. Zia's…" He searched for the impossible words to describe her. "Zia's what you and Bill have," he said finally. "What Kate and Maureen and our parents and *abuelita* all found. What I need."

His sister heaved a resigned sigh. "Since you put it that way…"

He thought he was home free after that. Right up until the middle of March, when Rafe came into his office just hours after Mike's return from a three-day meeting in Seoul. A frown creased his brother-in-law's forehead and his dark eyes telegraphed trouble. Still, Mike wasn't prepared for his uncharacteristically hesitant opening salvo.

"You remember the bottom line on Zia's MRSA study?"

"One point two mil and some change." A knot formed low in Mike's belly. He'd worked with Montoya long enough now to read his VP for Support System's unspoken signals. "Why?"

Rafe scowled at computer printouts in his hand and framed a slow, careful reply. "The change seems to have multiplied since the original proposal. And I'm damned if I can figure out why."

Ten

With Rafe's words hanging heavy in the air, Mike got out from behind his desk. "Let's take this to the conference table. You need to show me exactly what's got you concerned."

The table was a slab of thick glass supported by a bronze base. It seated twenty and had hosted too many high-level negotiations and contract signings for Mike to count. Those billion-dollar deals weren't on his mind as Rafe spread out his pencil-annotated reports, however. What concerned him was a specific project that GSI had helped fund to the tune of a quarter-of-a-million dollars.

"The study's direct costs track," Rafe said, spreading out a series of documents. "Zia's initial report accounts for every hour her team spent refining their objectives and setting up their base of operations. Ditto expenses for supplies and equipment, hours logged on the center's computers and fees paid to their outside funds consultant."

Mike frowned as he skimmed the fees charged by Danville and Associates. The total was on the high side, but not out of the ballpark compared to those charged by other firms that specialized in securing and managing grant monies. He just couldn't get past his instinctive and purely personal gut reaction to Danville himself.

"The discrepancy's in the indirects," Rafe was saying as he flipped several pages.

Well, hell! Mike had warned Zia to check her indirects. They were tricky at best. A soft area encompassing overhead expenses like administrative support, utilities and depreciation for buildings and equipment. Usually the parent institution—in Zia's case Mount Sinai's school of medicine—negotiated with the United States Department of Health and Human Services every four years or so to determine its indirect cost rate. Unfortunately, those negotiations weren't based on any hard-and-fast mathematical formula. They had to take into consideration such intangibles as the school's academic standing, salary levels of their professors compared to other institutions, and so on.

"As you know," Rafe said, echoing his thoughts, "indirect rates can vary anywhere from twenty to forty percent depending on the reputation of the institution involved. And even when HHS agrees to a rate, there's still considerable flex in the process."

He flipped to another printout. This one showed the amounts contributed by private foundations and corporations.

"Not all of Zia's investors funded her indirects at the same percentage. These two didn't fund the indirects at all."

Mike zeroed in on a single entry. "But GSI did."

"Yes, we did. We also approved the formula the university uses to determine how much of the money we send them goes into their general operating fund and how much goes back to Zia's project."

Rafe paused and stroked a fingertip along his pencil-thin mustache. An unconscious habit, Mike knew. One that suggested he'd damned well better sit up and pay attention.

It also usually indicated he wouldn't like what his VP for Support Systems was going to say next.

"That redistribution doesn't happen automatically. The project manager has to request it."

"What are you telling me? Zia hasn't requested her indirects?"

"Yeah, she has. Or rather, the agency managing her project funds has."

"Danville and Associates."

"Right. But…" Rafe frowned at his penciled notes. "As best I can tell, they're using a different formula than the one we approved."

Mike bit down on a curse. Whatever the discrepancy—*if* there was one—this was Zia's project. When she signed her name on the bottom line of her proposal, she'd accepted full responsibility for how the money expended on the project was used.

"I'm sure Zia can explain the difference," he said with a shrug.

He checked his watch, saw it was almost three-thirty New York time and pulled out his cell phone. When his call went to her phone's voice mail, he left a message asking her to call him back, then tried the number she'd given him for her new work area at the research center. That call was answered by one of the other researchers working the project.

"Dr. Elliott."

After more than a month of communicating with Zia via email, FaceTime and phone—and one very eye-opening visit to the research center—Mike was now on a first-name basis with most of his fiancée's team.

"Hi, Jordan. This is Mike Brennan. I'm trying to reach Zia."

"She's still at lunch. I expected her back before now but it's a working session. Must be running longer than expected."

"Must be."

"I'll be happy to take a message. Or you could contact Danville and Associates. I'm sure Tom's secretary can tell you where he and Zia are having lunch."

Mike didn't skip a beat, but he could feel his fist tightening on his phone. "Just ask her to give me a call, would you?"

"Sure thing."

"Thanks."

He cut the connection and gave Rafe a quick update. "She's having a late lunch. Why don't you leave your notes and I'll go over them with her when she calls back?"

"Sure. In the meantime, I'll keep scrubbing the numbers."

Mike pushed away from the conference table but didn't return to his desk after Rafe left. Jamming his hands in his pants pockets, he faced the windows and stared unseeing at the haze belched out by Houston's millions of vehicles and dozen or so oil refineries. ExxonMobil's Baytown facility—the world's largest—processed more than five hundred thousand barrels a day. It also contributed heavily to GSI's profit margin. Even from where he stood, Mike could see two GSI tankers negotiating the bays and bayous leading to Exxon's giant facility. Yet the sight of their distinctive green-and-white hulls barely registered on his consciousness. He was still trying to understand his gut-level reaction to hearing Zia had yet to return from an extended lunch with Tom Danville.

Hell! What was the matter with him? He wasn't some Neanderthal. A throwback to the Middle Ages, jealously guarding his property. What he was, he reminded himself, was ass over end in love with a smart, savvy professional woman. One who couldn't be more different from his ex-wife if she tried. And yet...

He still remembered Jill's reaction when he'd told her

he was filing for divorce. He'd be a long time erasing the memory of her face as it twisted into a mask of fury. Or the string of affairs she'd tossed at him in retaliation. Or her snarling admission that she'd counted the hours until he'd left on another of his endless business trips. Or her shouted obscenities when he'd walked out the door for the last time.

Mike had never told anyone about that sorry scene. Not his family. Not his friends. Maybe because he knew the debacle was as much his fault as Jill's. He *had* used his rapidly expanding business interests as an excuse to escape her endless complaints. He *had* picked up more than one subtle hint that there might be more to his wife's jaunts to Vegas than casinos and high-end malls. And he'd experienced nothing but relief when their marriage was finally over.

What he had now, with Zia, represented the opposite end of the spectrum. From the moment he'd met her on the beach at Galveston, he'd felt nothing but admiration for her dedication, her brilliance, her unshakable belief that her research might make a difference. And, yeah, the woman inside those sweats and lab coats was pretty spectacular, too.

Now her research could be in trouble. Rafe hadn't come right out and mentioned fraud or mismanagement. He didn't have to. Mike didn't believe in the old saw that money was the root of all evil, but he'd seen it corrupt too many people too often. His jaw set, he whirled and strode to the outer office.

"Clear my schedule for the rest of the week, Peggy. I'm going to New York."

"Tomorrow?"

"This afternoon—or as soon as they can get the Gulf-stream turned around."

The jet would have to be serviced after the flight back from Seoul and a new crew called in. Mike would be lucky to be in the air by five, in New York by ten Eastern time. Although he wasn't jet-lagged from the Korea trip, he knew the time warp would hit with a vengeance somewhere over

Ohio. He should probably wait until tomorrow to fly but couldn't shake the need to work through this problem— whatever it was—with Zia.

Half a continent away, Zia was prey to the same itchy feeling of impatience. Against her better judgment, she'd yielded to Tom's argument they could get more done at a restaurant than at his office, where his phone rang incessantly and other clients demanded his attention. She'd also accommodated his busy schedule by agreeing to a late lunch.

His solo appearance at this cozy French bistro on Broadway and 58th had irritated her no end, however. So had his insistence that they eat before getting down to the nitty-gritty. She'd picked her way through half of her Salad Niçoise but now pushed her plate to the side and voiced her annoyance.

"I've communicated directly with Elizabeth Hamilton-Hobbs for the past month. She's my primary contact at your firm. I don't understand why she couldn't make this meeting."

"That's one of the reasons I wanted this face-to-face." Danville dabbed his mouth with his napkin and folded his expression into unhappy lines. "I know how well you and Elizabeth connected. But...well...I had to let her go."

"What! When?"

"This morning."

Zia jerked back, her shoulders slamming the padded booth. She'd worked so closely with Elizabeth these past weeks! Had come to appreciate the woman's droll sense of humor almost as much as her business acumen. When GSI approved that quarter-million-dollar grant, Zia and Elizabeth had celebrated with a bottle of Chilean Malbec. And when the rest of the funding came through, they'd treated each other to an orgy of Godiva chocolate. Now she was gone?

"What happened? Why did you let her go?"

"I really can't…" Danville paused and scrubbed a finger under his nose. "I'm sorry, Zia. I have to follow certain rules of confidentially in situations like this."

"Situations like *what*, dammit?"

"I can't say. I really can't. But I can tell you this. From now on I'll manage your funding personally."

Oh, sure! Like she was going to trust a crackhead to oversee her project's finances? She started to tell him so but pulled up short when she remembered the contract she'd signed with Danville and Associates.

How binding was it? Did she have an out? Any grounds to terminate? She'd better find out, and fast.

Grabbing her purse and hooded wool jacket, she squeezed out of the booth. "I'm not happy about this, Tom."

"Neither am I. I trusted Elizabeth."

He rose and helped her on with her coat. Zia murmured her thanks and raised her left hand to tug her hair free of the hood. The sight of her engagement ring sparked a now-familiar refrain.

"I hope your fiancé knows what a lucky bastard he is."

"I hope so, too."

He caught her hand and angled it so the pear-shaped diamond caught the light. "If any your project funding falls through," he said with a cynical twist of his lips, "you could always hock this."

She tugged her hand free and pinned him with an icy stare. "Let's hope it doesn't come to that. For *both* our sakes."

"Whoa!" He held up both palms. "Just kidding, Doc."

He'd damned well better be! Her mind churning, Zia left the restaurant and headed for the subway stop on the corner. A quick glance at her phone showed a short list of missed calls, including one from Mike. She decided to wait until she was back at the hospital to return it along with the others.

She exited the subway at Lexington and 96th and cut

over to Mount Sinai's four-block campus. Spring was still just a vague hope. Trees and bushes had yet to put out any buds and the hospital's brick-and-glass towers looked stark against the unforgiving sky.

The sounds and smells of the Children's Hospital greeted her. She'd finished her neonatal ICU rotation and now spent the majority of her time in the research center. The familiar scent of antiseptic followed her as she hurried past the labs with their gleaming equipment and ongoing experiments to the modular unit set up to house the MRSA study. The only member of the team present at the moment was Jordan Elliott, a microbiologist with a specialty in infectious diseases. Petite and vivacious, she glanced up from her computer and flashed a smile.

"Hey, Zia. How was lunch?"

"Long. Unproductive. Worrying."

"Huh?"

"Elizabeth Hamilton-Hobbs isn't with Danville and Associates anymore."

"You're kidding! When did that happen?"

"This morning, evidently. Tom wouldn't tell me why he and Elizabeth parted ways. It's some kind of confidentiality thing." Frowning, Zia shed her coat and hooked it over the back of her chair. "I need to review our contract with Danville and see what our options are."

Jordan's brows lifted but she didn't comment. This wasn't her first research study. She knew funding was a complex and multilayered process. Even more complicated with outside sources like GSI in the mix. Which reminded her...

"I almost forgot. Mike called. He wants you to call him back."

"I will," Zia promised, her gaze locked on the contract scrolling up on the computer screen.

The legalistic phrasing didn't reassure her. If she was interpreting it correctly, the only way out of the contract was if Danville and Associates failed to meet one of their stated objectives. Elizabeth had aced them all so far, not least of which was soliciting and securing every penny Zia had requested.

Only a fraction of those funds had been disbursed to date, though. Just what they'd needed to cover the start-up. Computers, furniture, subscriptions to medical and commercial databases, the first month's salaries for team members…six pages worth of direct costs. The total looked ginormous to Zia, but she knew it would climb even higher when they factored in the indirects.

With a moue of disgust, she clicked through the dizzying array of figures again before listening to her messages. The one from Mike requested a callback. He didn't answer his cell, though, so she tried his office.

"Hi, Peggy. It's Zia. I'm returning Mike's call."

"Sorry, Zia. He's already left for the airport."

"Left? I thought he just got back."

"Didn't he let you know? He's on his way to New York. They should be wheels up, um, right about now."

Surprised and delighted, Zia thanked her and tried Mike's cell again. The call went through this time, although about all she could hear was the roar of revving engines.

"I just heard you're headed this way," she shouted over the noise. "What's the occasion?"

"Do we need one?"

"I can barely hear you."

"I said… Never mind. Hang loose and I'll call you back when we're airborne."

Mike waited for the sleek ten-passenger executive jet to slice through the haze and hit open sky to make the return call. When he picked up his phone, however, the instrument buzzed in his hand and Rafe's office number popped up on the screen. He took his brother-in-law's call and had his world rocked for the second time that day.

"Have you talked to Zia?" Montoya wanted to know.

"Not yet. We've been playing telephone tag. I was just about to call her back."

"You may want to hold off on that."

The reply turned Mike's insides cold. "Why?"

"Remember I told you I was going to keep scrubbing the numbers on her indirects."

"What'd you find?"

"A disbursement code that wasn't in the original proposal. It's buried in a subset of indirects relating to utilities. But instead of linking to the university's general operating fund, the code links to a separate bank routing number."

Mike's knuckles turned white where they gripped the phone. "Bottom line this for me, bro."

"That's just it. I can't. When I tried to trace the routing number, I hit a wall. Or more precisely, a damned near impenetrable firewall."

"Oh, hell. It's a blind?"

"That's what I'm thinking."

Rafe fell silent. Mike knew there was more, though. When his brother-in-law sank his teeth into something, he didn't let go.

"You said damned near impenetrable. Did you get in?"

"No, but I did poke around enough to generate a call from a friendly FBI agent."

"Christ!"

"He's with what used to be the white-collar-crimes division, Miguel. He wanted to know why we're digging into that particular account."

"Did you tell him I'm on my way to New York? That I plan to check into this very issue myself?"

"Yeah, I did. He says he needs to talk to you first. In fact, he offered to fly up from DC tomorrow and meet you in New York. I told him I'd check with you and see if that's how you want to handle it."

Mike scrubbed a hand across his jaw. He could feel the jet lag from his trip to Seoul crawling over him now. Combined with the tension Rafe had just piled on, he felt as though he'd been hit with a pile driver.

"Mike?"

"Yeah, I'm here. Set up the meeting."

Before returning Zia's call he signaled the steward. The Gulfstream crew didn't normally include a cabin attendant on short hops within the States. Graham hadn't checked out after the transatlantic flight, however, and at this moment, Mike was happy to make use of his services.

"Would you bring me a Scotch, Gray? Neat."

"Sure thing."

The Glenlivet went down with its usual smoky fire, but the heat didn't dissipate the cold spot in Mike's stomach. Whatever way he looked at it, he couldn't see a good ending to what was smelling more and more like fraud.

Although he didn't for a second believe Zia had a hint of anything questionable in the works, she was the project manager. She'd put the proposal together. She'd signed off on the grant solicitations. She was responsible for proper distribution of funds. At the very least, a fraud investigation would hang a cloud over her project. At the worst, her reputation in the tight-knit world of pediatric research would take a hit. Not the best way to kick-start a new career.

Mike tossed back the rest of his Scotch, powered up his phone and hit the speed-dial number for Zia's cell.

"Sorry it took so long to get back to you. I had another call."

"No problem. So how was Korea?"

"Busy and productive. GSI's going to acquire six new Triple-E class super-containers over the next three years."

"Super-containers, huh? I'm getting a mental picture

of hundreds of those shipping containers piled one on top of each other."

"Try thousands. Eighteen thousand, to be exact."

"On each ship?" she asked incredulously.

"On each ship."

"Okay, I'm officially impressed." She paused before changing the subject. "I'm really glad you're flying in to-night, Mike. Something's come up. I'd like to talk to you about it."

"Personal or otherwise?"

"Otherwise."

Hell! He had to ask. "Is this related to your working lunch with Tom Danville?"

"How did you know about lunch?"

Surprise and just a hint of wariness colored the question. She obviously hadn't forgotten Mike's reaction to Danville when they'd met at La Maison.

Or was it something else?

No, dammit! He was letting this FBI business spook him! Whatever the hell was going on, there was no way Zia could be involved. Deliberately, he put a shrug in his reply.

"Jordan mentioned where you were when I called ear-lier."

"Oh." Another pause. "What time do you think you'll be in?"

"Late, I'm afraid. After midnight."

"You have to be dead, considering you were on the other side of the world this morning. Get some sleep tonight and I'll take off early tomorrow afternoon to welcome you home in style."

"Define style," he said with a smile, relaxing for the first time since Rafe's call.

"We could do the ballet," she teased, well aware of how he felt about it. "Or the opera. Or maybe just snuggle in with a pizza and a movie."

"Now you're talking. Your place or mine?"

"Well…" Her voice dropped to a provocative purr. "The duchess doesn't particularly care for pizza."

"This is sounding better by the moment."

She laughed and agreed. "Where are you staying this time?"

"Let me check." He pulled up the travel docs Peggy had loaded to his phone. "The W New York."

"Okay, here's the deal. I'll call you when I'm on the way with pizza. You pick the movie. But nothing X-rated," she instructed sternly. "Maybe not even R. We wouldn't want to overstimulate your poor, jet-lagged brain."

"Can't happen, kid. You walk into the room and my brain shuts down anyway. All that's left is pure, unadulterated…"

"Lust? Greed?"

"I was going to say love, but lust and greed are right there in the mix, too."

He disconnected, still smiling. Rafe's call a few minutes later wiped the smile off his face and put the kink back in his gut.

Eleven

"It's set," Mike's brother-in-law announced tersely. "Tomorrow, 9:00 a.m., at the FBI's New York office. Ask for Special Agent Dan Havers."

"Got it. Although I've got to tell you, Rafe, I don't like keeping Zia in the dark about all this."

"I understand, but…"

"But what?"

"I'm beginning to think there's more to the situation than we suspect, Miguel. I can't see a DC-based FBI agent jumping on a plane and meeting you in New York just to talk about fifty thousand in misdirected grant money."

"I've been having those same thoughts," Mike admitted grimly. "They're the only reason I didn't tell Zia about this FBI contact. The more I can find out from this guy tomorrow, the better I can help her navigate through whatever the problem is."

"Keep me in the loop, too."

"Will do."

Mike had the steward pour him another Scotch and nursed it for the rest of the flight. He nursed more than a few doubts, as well. He knew he was setting himself up for some potentially tense moments with Zia if he told her about the FBI meeting after the fact. But he also knew he was in a better position to elicit information than she was at this point. GSI was only one of several corporations contributing to the MRSA study but it had provided significant funding. Naturally Mike would want to investigate any apparent anomalies in the distribution of those funds. Especially if the person ultimately responsible for the disbursement was his fiancée.

The FBI would view Zia in a more cautious light. She was a foreign national in the United States on a work/study visa. What's more, she had close ties to some very high viz personalities. Jack Harris, Gina's husband, was the US Ambassador to the UN. And Sarah's husband, Dev, operated half the damned civilian transports in the country.

Then there was the duchess. And, Mike thought with an inner grimace, the grand duke. He didn't know much about Dominic's years as an undercover agent for Interpol. Just enough to appreciate that the FBI might be understandably wary of crossing agency lines. Looking at it from that angle made Mike feel marginally better about his 9:00 a.m. meeting.

Any delusion that the FBI was the least bit concerned about Zia's personal situation or connections shattered ten minutes after Special Agent Dan Havers met Mike in the lobby of the FBI's New York office at 26 Federal Plaza.

Havers was an athletic-looking thirty-six or -seven, with wrestler's shoulders and a tree-trunk neck that strained his white shirt and navy suit jacket. The lines etched deep around his eyes suggested white-collar crime was something other than sport, however.

"Thanks for coming in, Brennan."

Mike took the hand Havers thrust out and braced for a bone cruncher that didn't come.

"Let's get you ID'd and badged. We've got a conference room reserved. We'll talk there."

They kept small talk to a minimum until Havers ushered Mike into the twenty-third-floor conference room. Four others—two men, two women—were waiting his arrival. Three clustered around the coffee and pastries at the far end of the room. One stared moodily through the blinds at the Manhattan skyline.

Mike's chest got tighter with each introduction. One of the women was Havers's New York counterpart, a special agent working white-collar crime. The other was from the International Operations Division. The two men were from the Counterterrorism Division.

"Coffee?" Havers asked. "A bagel or Danish, maybe?"

"I'm good."

"Okay, then let's get to it."

The group drifted to the table. Mike claimed a seat with his back to the windows. It was a small power play, just one of the many any negotiator worth his salt might employ, but it gave him the advantage of facing away from the bright sunlight.

He didn't derive much satisfaction from the maneuver. Not when he faced two counterterrorism agents. They left it to Havers to lay whatever cards they intended to share on the table.

"Here's the deal, Brennan. Your guy Montoya set off all kinds of alarms with his probe into that blocked account yesterday. We had to decide fast what to do about it. Especially when Montoya said you were on your way to New York. So we ran both of you through our computers. Every wrinkle, every wart."

"Find anything interesting?"

"Montoya is an open book. You read more like a tabloid."

"That so?"

"We know about the knife fight with the Portuguese cook when you were a ten-dollar-a-day deckhand," Havers commented. "We know about the navy medal you were awarded after diving into the Sea of Japan to save a crewmate who'd been swept overboard. We know you bought a rust bucket after you got out of the service and parlayed it into a multinational corporation. We know about your friends, your family, the divorce."

"What's your point?"

"My point is we wouldn't be talking to you today unless we knew we could trust you."

"Right now I can't say I feel the same. Cut to the chase. What's this all about?"

Havers angled his bull-like neck a few degrees to the right and nodded to one of the counterterrorism agents. Sandy haired and squinty eyed behind his wire-rim glasses, the other agent took the lead.

"What this is about is a guy named Thomas Danville and his five-thousand-dollar-a-week habit, which he feeds by skimming from his clients."

Mike felt his insides go tight but kept his voice even. "And?"

"And how this guy Danville buys his drugs from an international consortium. One that just happens to be headed by a terrorist organization whose stated goal is to wipe Israel—and its evil ally, the United States—off the face of the earth. You've heard of Hezbollah?"

Mike didn't alter his expression, didn't blink, but they'd just confirmed his worst-case scenario. Zia had gotten caught up in something a whole lot deeper and uglier than fraud.

"Yes, I've heard of Hezbollah."

"Then you might also have heard it has a substantial connection to the Mexican cartel Los Zetas. Two years ago we got an indictment in absentia against one of the middlemen acting on behalf of Hezbollah, a Lebanese drug lord by the name of Ayman Joumaa. Bastard conspired to smuggle more than 9,000 tons of cocaine into the US. In the process, he laundered over $250 million for the cartels.

"Look," he continued. "We don't give a shit about Danville. He's small change. Wouldn't even constitute a blip on our radar except for this drug connection. Nor would we be talking to you this morning if you hadn't started nosing around one of Danville's blind accounts. We need you to back off, Brennan. Now. Today."

Havers picked up the ball again. "We've been tracking Danville ever since one of his employees tipped us to his extracurricular activities. Problem is, he fired that employee yesterday."

Mike's eyes narrowed. "So you're worried Danville could be spooked."

"He could be," Havers conceded. "Though that's not all bad. Spooked guys make mistakes. Sometimes they run. Sometimes they turn to their big, bad pals for something to calm their jittery nerves."

"And sometimes," Mike said coldly, "they take innocent people down with them."

"Exactly. That's why we need you to back off. We've got taps on Danville's home, office and cell phones. We'll know if and when he makes a wrong move. Let us handle him, Brennan. Don't get in the middle of it."

"You're welcome to him. Like you, I don't give a shit about Danville. I do, however, care about—"

"Your fiancée. Yeah, we know."

Havers pursed his lips, as if debating whether to continue. The act didn't fool Mike for a moment. He sensed what was coming. Still, it hit hard.

"Danville and Dr. St. Sebastian enjoyed a three-hour lunch yesterday. According to one source, they got real close. Some might say cuddly."

Mike's reply came fast and flat. "For someone who wants my cooperation, you just went in exactly the wrong direction. This meeting is over."

He shoved back from the table and strode for the door. Havers had to scramble to catch up with him.

"Hold on, Brennan!"

He reached for Mike's arm. A low, savage warning halted his hand in midair.

"You really don't want to do that."

"Okay." He dropped his arm. "Look, I obviously pushed the wrong button there. I'm sorry."

Mike didn't bother to respond, just made for the elevator.

"Brennan! Wait. I have to escort you out."

He tried again to apologize but the elevator arrived too quickly. All he could do was follow Mike inside and ride down in silence. When they hit the lobby, though, he reached into his suit pocket.

"Here's my card," he said as they approached the security checkpoint. "Call me if there's anything else you want to talk about."

Mike came within a breath of telling him where he could shove the stiff, sharp-edged cardboard. He swallowed the urge, stuck the card in his wallet and tossed his visitor's pass on the security desk.

He used the rest of the morning to work the fury out of his system. A brutal workout in the hotel's exercise center helped. A long session in the steam room sweated out the rest. Showered and under control, he called Rafe with an update. His brother-in-law listened without interruption. At the end his only comment was a succinct and very graphic curse.

"Yeah," Mike drawled. "My sentiments exactly."

"How much of this are you going to tell Zia?"

"All of it."

"The FBI okay with that?"

"I didn't ask."

"I guess you probably didn't need to. They have to know you're not going to let her get in any deeper with this bastard Danville."

Let, Mike acknowledged wryly after he'd hung up, was the wrong verb. If he'd learned nothing else from living with three sisters and a moody ex-wife, it was to be extremely careful with that particular verb.

He shoved his hands in his pockets and wandered across the sitting room of his twentieth-floor suite. The wall-to-wall window offered an unimpeded view of One World Trade Center and, farther out, the Statue of Liberty. Mike let his gaze drift from one to the other, thinking of the jihadist pumping drugs into the United States, determined to destroy it one way or another. Thinking, too, of the thousands of little people caught in his poisonous web.

Like Danville.

And this employee Danville had reportedly fired.

And Zia.

Now him.

He'd charged right in, suspecting there was more to that blind account than mismanagement or misdirection of funds, and firing up like an Aegis missile when Havers and company confirmed it.

The more he thought about that visceral reaction, the more it bothered him. He didn't want to admit it sprang from that crack about Zia and Danville getting cuddly. He couldn't get around the implanted image, though. Not after Zia's wariness when Mike had told her he knew about the long lunch. Which, he remembered grimly, had come right on the heels of her saying she needed to talk to him. Maybe she already knew about Danville skimming his client's funds. Or maybe...

Christ! He had to stop chasing his tail like this. He'd

wait for Zia, talk it out with her, lay what he knew on the line and get it behind them both.

So he was more than ready when she called a little past three o'clock. "I'm just getting ready to leave the hospital. Are we still on for pizza and a movie?"

"I am if you are."

"Good. I skipped lunch so I'm starved. There's a John's Pizzeria right around the corner from the W. I'll call ahead and have a large regular crust waiting for pick up, all hot and gooey. What do you want on it?"

"Everything but anchovies or anything that resembles fruit."

"Got it. See you in forty-five minutes or so. In the meantime, you could check out the movies. I'm in the mood for something light and silly."

"Light and silly it is. See you soon."

Smiling in anticipation, Zia hit the off button and grabbed her coat.

"Pizza and a movie, huh?"

She glanced up to find Jordan Elliott smirking across the top of her computer terminal. The microbiologist's eyes reflected both mischief and envy.

"Sounded more like a little afternoon delight to me."

"What happens at the W, stays at the W."

"Oh, sure! Rub it in. You know very well the closest I've come to sex in the past month is watching bacteria multiply in a petri dish."

"I also know," Zia shot back, "there's a certain radiologist who's offered to fix that problem. Several times."

"Ugh. I'd rather cozy up to the bacteria. Hang loose a sec. I need to go over to the Infectious Diseases center. I'll walk out with you."

They exited the school of medicine and took the sidewalk that cut diagonally across Mount Sinai's sprawling campus. Spring was still weeks away, although the afternoon sun offered a hint of warmer temperatures and a sudden burst of greenery.

Zia was just about to peel off and make for the subway when her phone buzzed again. It was a text message from Tom Danville.

"It's Danville," she told Jordan, skimming the message. "He needs to talk to me ASAP about Elizabeth."

The two women exchanged quick glances. The Wharton School of Business grad's firing had shocked them both. Maybe now they'd discover what was behind it. When Zia called Danville, however, he didn't want to talk over the phone.

"It's an extremely sensitive issue. I need to discuss it with you in private."

"I don't have time now, Tom. I'm on my way to an appointment downtown."

"It'll just take a few minutes. You really need to know the mess Elizabeth's landed us both in."

She hesitated, chewing on her lower lip. "Where are you now?"

"At the office."

"All right. I'm just leaving the hospital. I'll swing by there on my way downtown."

Mike expected Zia by four. At four-thirty he hit the speed-dial number for her cell phone. When the call went to voice mail, he tried her office.

Her associate picked up and responded with a throaty chuckle when he identified himself. "Hi, Mike. Don't tell me you and Zia have already, uh, finished your pizza."

"We might have, if she'd showed up with it."

"She's not there? Wait. Scratch that. Of course she's not, or you wouldn't be calling."

"So she's not still at the hospital?"

"She left a couple of hours ago. I walked out with her, in fact."

"Did she take the subway?"

"That was the plan, but she got a call from Tom Danville. He said he needed to talk to her privately, right away, so she told him she'd swing by his office on the way downtown."

"I'll call you back."

"Wait! What's—"

He stabbed the end button and did a Google search for Danville and Associates. His jaw was tight and the cords in his neck as taut as hawsers. He knew what he would hear even before Danville's secretary confirmed that her boss had left the office several hours ago.

"Was Dr. St. Sebastian with him?"

"No," she replied in some surprise. "I'm looking at Tom's schedule now. He didn't have an appointment with her. Shall I—"

Mike slammed the phone down to search his wallet for Special Agent Havers's card. The FBI agent answered on the third ring.

"Havers."

"This is Brennan. Where are you?"

"On my way to the airport, getting ready to head back to DC. Why?"

"My fiancée was supposed to meet me at my hotel an hour ago. She hasn't showed."

"Have you—"

"She was on her way," Mike cut in savagely. "An associate walked out with her. The same associate just informed me that Zia got an urgent call from Danville. He needed to talk to her. Privately. At his office. But he left, and she never showed."

The pregnant silence that followed torqued his jaws so tight he could feel his teeth grinding.

"Listen to me, Havers. She's not having an affair with Danville. Nor is she in any way involved in his schemes."

When the agent still didn't reply, Mike pulled out every ace in the deck.

"My next call is to Dr. St. Sebastian's brother. He won't hesitate to tap his former sources at Interpol. Then I'm contacting Ambassador Harris at the UN. Then…"

"Hang up. Sit tight. Wait for me to call you back."

Mike's lips curled back in a snarl. "The hell I will. I'm going to hold on the line while you do the following. First, you contact your pals in the New York office. Second, you have them run a GPS trace on Danville's mobile phone. Third, you tell me where the bastard is."

"We warned you this morning to stay out of this, Brennan. We'll handle it."

"Call your pals, Havers. Now!"

Twelve

Zia just had to wait him out.

She'd stopped kicking herself for agreeing to meet Danville at his office. Gotten past the surprise of finding him in the lobby and ushering her into the elevator, only to send it down to the parking garage instead of up to his office. She'd also worked through her shock when he'd pulled out a small, lethal-looking pistol and aimed it at her heart.

Once her stunned mind reengaged, she'd recognized the signs. The fever-bright eyes. The agitation. The desperation. She'd seen it in patients, read about it in hundreds of case studies. Danville was in the panic stage. It usually set in several hours after the user's last hit. He would feel himself coming down and go frantic with the need to make sure he could score another hit.

If he didn't have a supply on hand, he'd beg, borrow or steal for it. Patients had reported pawing through their own and their parents' houses for something, *anything*, to pawn or sell. Others had robbed convenience stores, fast-food restaurants, even busy mall stores. The withdrawal is so intense, the craving so frantic, that they work themselves into a frenzy of need.

Danville was there. Jerky. Desperate. Paranoid. As he

forced her to get behind the wheel of the flashy red Porsche parked in his assigned slot, he kept mumbling they would kill him.

"Who, Tom? Who's going to kill you?"

"Drive! Just drive!"

She did. Up Madison Avenue, across 106th, down 2nd Avenue, with the pistol jammed into her side the entire time. She'd tried to talk him down. Tried to calm and soothe and assure him she'd get him help, but he was still locked in that hard, panicky shell. Checking his watch constantly. Flinching at every sound, every distant siren or screech of tires. And phones. Zia's. His. The buzzing must have ricocheted around in his mind like a loose ball bearing.

She'd considered crashing the Porsche into a street sign or traffic light, but she couldn't take the chance the airbags would explode in Danville's face before he pulled the trigger. So she'd followed his instructions until her shoulders ached with tension and her mind screamed with the need to do something, anything, to end the situation.

"There! Turn in there!"

She had to brake to take the ticket from the automatic dispenser at the entrance to the underground garage. Two lanes over, a bored attendant sat in his booth with his back turned so he could service exiting vehicles. Zia willed him to turn around, begged him to send just one glance her way. When he remained facing the other direction, she calculated her chances of yanking the door open and throwing herself out. Not very good with Danville's pistol bruising her ribs.

"Go down to the bottom level," he rasped at her.

She followed the winding ramp down five increasingly less crowded levels. The last was almost deserted.

"Pull into that space. The one beside the pillar."

The concrete column was square and fat but not difficult to maneuver around with so many empty spaces. Zia barely had time to wonder why he'd chosen that particular slot before she realized the pillar screened them from the security camera mounted in the corner.

Danville had been here before. Used this same parking slot. The realization hit like a balled fist to her chest. Fighting for calm, she cut the engine and angled toward him. He twisted in his seat, too, planting his back against the door, pulling the gun back with him. The bruising pressure on her ribs eased, but the barrel was still terrifyingly close.

"What now, Tom?"

"We wait."

She let her hand drop to her thigh, clenching and unclenching her fist as though driven by nerves. Which she was! But if she could keep him talking, keep his eyes on her face, she might be able to inch her hand into her tote, finger her iPhone, tap 911. The bag was in the space between their seats, just behind the gearshift console. So damned close.

"What do we wait for?"

"Not what. Who." He shot another look at his expensive watch. "They'll come," he muttered, more to himself than her. "Now that I can pay, they'll call off the dogs and deliver."

His suppliers, she guessed as the knot in her chest pressed hard against her sternum. She flattened her palm, eased it over the outside of her thigh.

"You cannot do this." She spoke evenly, slowly, but she could hear the American accent she'd acquired over the past two and a half years slipping away. "You cannot kidnap me, make me drive to this place, and think to get away with it."

Anger and a smirking bravado leaped into his face. Not a good mix with the desperation.

"Shows what you know! I've been getting away with it for years. Five thousand from one client, ten K from another. Eighty, a hundred thousand a year funneled into a special account the auditors never got a whiff of until that bitch started sniffing around it."

"Are you...? Are you speaking of Elizabeth?"

"Yes, Elizabeth." His lips curled back in a sneer that didn't quite match the fear and paranoia behind it. "She sicced the FBI on me. My...my associates found out about it. I don't know how. But they took care of her and now I have to cut and run. Today. Tonight."

Zia's stomach heaved. She'd ascribed his frenetic mood and barely controlled panic to crack. Now she knew it was due to something much worse, much uglier.

"How do you mean, they 'took care of her'?"

"It doesn't matter. She doesn't matter. *That's* what matters."

His gaze dropped like a stone and locked on the hand she'd slipped closer to her bag. For a frozen instant Zia thought he'd detected her cautious moves. Then she realized he'd focused on her engagement ring.

"I can't go back to my place. The FBI is probably watching it. I don't dare use my laptop or phone or credit card to withdraw the cash I need to pay my associates. But I can use that." He made a short, choppy motion with the gun. "Take it off."

"This is all you want from me?" she asked incredulously. "The ring?"

"Take it off."

She played the fingers of her right hand over the pear-shaped diamond. The faceted stone sat high in its mount. The surface was smooth, the tip sharp against her nervous fingers.

"You can have it, Tom. It is only a stone. Then will you let me go?"

He wouldn't meet her eyes, wouldn't answer her question. She knew then he would feed her to the dogs as cold-bloodedly as he had Elizabeth.

He had not the courage to do it himself, Zia thought on a burst of contempt. The men he waited for. They came not just to bring him the cocaine he craved. They would dispose of yet another problem female for him.

She twisted the band, tugged it toward her knuckle, pretended to have trouble getting it over the joint. "It's too tight. I...I meant to have it sized but have not had time."

"You'd damned well better get it off," he snarled, "or my friends will do it the hard way."

"So they are now your friends?" She couldn't keep the disgust from her voice as she twisted the band again. "A moment ago they were merely associates."

"It's none of your business wh—"

He broke off, his head cocking. Above the jackhammering of her heart, Zia caught the rumble of an engine. A vehicle was descending from the level right above them. A large, heavy vehicle.

"About damned time," Danville muttered, glancing over his shoulder at the ramp.

This was her chance! Her only chance! She didn't stop to think. Didn't weigh the odds. Fired by fear and utter desperation, she flayed out her arm and knocked the gun barrel aside. The violent action triggered an equally violent response. Shots exploded inside the sports car. One. Two. With blinding flashes. Concussive waves of sound. The searing burn of nitrate and the nauseous stink of sulfur.

Even before the shock waves died, Zia whipped her arm back. Ears ringing, eyes streaming, she curled her fist and put every ounce of her strength into a blow aimed for Danville's face. The force of it sank the sharp tip of her diamond deep into his left eye.

His eyeball exploded almost as violently as the shots had. Vitreous solution spewed in a clear arc. Blood gushed as Zia wrenched her wrist down and ripped through the lower lid. Howling, Danville dropped the pistol and slapped both hands to his eye.

She scrabbled for the gun with her bloody hand, but it

had fallen behind her seat. Not daring to wait another second, she shoved her door open and lunged out onto the oil-stained concrete. Her ears screaming, her cheek burning, she took a dizzy second or two to reorient herself. God help her if she ran up the down ramp and met Danville's *associates* head-on.

The brief hesitation proved a fatal mistake. A huge black SUV with darkened windows careened off the ramp less than thirty yards away. Zia whirled, then felt a scream rise in her throat when she saw Danville had crawled out of his car. Using the roof of the Porsche, he dragged himself upright. One hand still covered his oozing eye. The other gripped the pistol he'd recovered from the floor of the car.

Then everything happened in a blur. The SUV streaked by. Zia jumped back, barely avoiding its fender. It fishtailed to a screeching halt, and she dodged for the concrete pillar. Before she reached it, the SUV's passenger door flew open and Mike launched himself at the Porsche.

Danville whirled to meet this new threat, but the eye injury threw off his aim. The bullet hit the pillar just inches from Zia's head. Vicious bits of concrete bit into her still-burning cheek as the two men went down on the far side of the Porsche.

When Zia raced around the rear of the car, Mike was slamming his fist into Danville's already bloody face. She couldn't hear a thing above the screaming in her ears, but she saw his nose flatten and more blood gush through the shattered cartilage. Then a big, bull-like man rushed up and kicked the pistol away.

"Brennan! Enough."

He caught Mike's arm and hauled him off the now-unconscious Danville. Chest heaving, Mike shoved to his feet and spun around.

"Zia! Jesus!"

She saw his lips move but heard only a muted echo of

his words. She clung to him, her heart pumping fear and relief in equal measures until he caught her arms and gently eased her away. An oozy mix of blood and vitreous fluid now splotched the front of his saddle-tan leather jacket.

"Are you hurt?" His gaze raked her, searching for injuries. "Zia, tell me where you're hurt."

She saw his lips moving again, heard the words as a tinny echo this time and shook her head. "I'm okay. This...." She had to gasp for breath. "This is Danville's blood."

And some of her own, she realized as she fingered the bits of concrete embedded in her cheek. Her hand came away filthy with body fluids and gunpowder residue.

The hulking man next to Mike said something. He was huge, with a loud, rumbling voice that was completely drowned out by the squeal of tires as what looked like an entire fleet of black-and-white patrol cars screeched down the ramp and onto their level.

She grabbed Mike's lapels and shouted to make herself heard. "Danville was expecting his...his suppliers. Here. Any moment."

"Hell!"

The next thing she knew she was being bundled into the back of a squad car.

"Get her out of here," the big man barked at the uniformed officer behind the wheel, then shouted to two others. "And get this bastard to a hospital. Then the rest of you disperse. Now! Tune to my frequency for additional instructions."

The ringing in Zia's ears had subsided enough for her to distinguish his roared commands. She also heard the one he threw at Mike.

"You go with the doc, Brennan. This is our operation."

"It was." His mouth grim, Mike scooped up Danville's

pistol. In one smooth move, he hit the release, popped out the magazine and snapped it back in. "It's mine now."

The squad car Zia had been thrust into sped past the openmouthed booth attendant and took up a position a block away. Then they waited.

The ringing in her ears had lessened in volume but now had a sharp, shrill pitch. Tinnitus, she diagnosed. Not a concern in and by itself, but the accompanying numbness and tingling could signal a possible perforation of the middle ear. She fisted her hands and tried to ignore the metallic pinging while she waited. It couldn't have been more than a half hour but it felt like five before the radio squawked.

"Operations terminated. Four men in custody. All other units will be back in service."

"It's over?" she asked the uniformed officer.

"Yes, ma'am."

"Please, take me back to the garage."

He put the car in Park at the entrance and Zia waited anxiously for Mike to emerge from the dark tunnel. The moment she spotted him, she hammered on the Plexiglas partition.

"Let me out!"

Light-headed with relief, she threw herself at Mike for the second time that afternoon. As before, he held her gently. Too gently. She ached for the feel of his arms around her, but he eased her away and frowned at her cuts and powder burns.

"We need to get you to the ER."

"I'm…I'm supposed to wait and give a statement."

"The authorities can come find you."

By the time they reached the hospital her tinnitus had subsided to a bearable level. Enough, anyway, that she could hear the ER physician's diagnosis when he confirmed her own.

"You've sustained sensorineural damage in both ears.

The numbness and tingling in your right ear indicate moderate to severe nerve irritation. The ringing in your left may be temporary, but you should consult an audiologist as soon as possible."

"I will."

He rolled his stool back, looking as tired at the end of his long shift as Zia had so often felt. "We need to clean the debris from your cheek and swab it. Then, I'm told, the FBI wants to talk to you. There's an agent waiting outside."

She nodded but turned a surprised face to Mike after the door to the exam room closed behind the ER physician. "Did he say FBI?"

"Yeah, he did."

"How did the FBI get involved?"

"It's a long story. I'll tell you later."

The big, burly man from the SUV identified himself as Special Agent Dan Havers. He spent a good forty minutes walking Zia through her ordeal, from Danville's call to his gut-wrenching admission in the garage.

"He said that?" Havers demanded. "He said his friends had 'taken care' of Elizabeth Hamilton-Hobbs?"

Sick at heart, she could only nod. The FBI agent gestured for her to go on. She related the rest of the conversation, the momentary distraction of the vehicle on the floor above, her frantic swipe at Danville's arm, the ring she'd stabbed into his eye.

"Jesus!"

Havers shot Mike a quick glance but he didn't see it. His face was set in savage lines and his gaze had dropped to the gore still staining Zia's left hand. She couldn't tell whether he was pleased the engagement ring had proved so lethal or shocked she'd used it as a weapon.

She got her answer when he reached for her hand and

eased the ring over her knuckle. Face grim, he tossed it into the plastic-lined trash can beside the gurney.

"Hey!" Havers grabbed a glove from the box mounted on the near cabinet and shoved his beefy fist into it. "That's evidence. We need to preserv—"

"Preserve whatever you want. Then you can toss the thing in the East River, for all I care. Come on, Zia. I'm taking you home."

After a brief stop at the front desk to sign the necessary paperwork, he hustled her into a cab. Her ears were still tinny and every street sound seemed magnified a hundred times over. Still, she tried to dissuade him from calling ahead to alert the duchess.

When he insisted, the call resulted in exactly the chain reaction Zia feared. Charlotte alerted Dominic and Natalie, who arrived at the Dakota mere moments after Zia and Mike. Gina and her husband had been en route to a black-tie charity event and showed at almost the same time, Jack in his tux and Gina dripping sapphires. The duchess had even called Sarah, who'd begged for an update as soon as Zia and Jack explained everything.

The concern, the questions, the straining to separate their voices from the high-pitched ringing in her ear proved too much for Zia. With a pleading look, she turned to Mike.

"I need to wash and change. You tell them what happened."

Her departure left a stark silence in the sitting room. Mike squared his shoulders and faced her family. They were arrayed in a semicircle, Dom and Jack standing, Gina on the sofa holding Natalie's hand, the duchess in a high-backed chair gripping the head of her cane. Even Maria had come in from the kitchen to hear the details. All wore almost identical expressions of shock and concern.

Mike debated briefly where to start, then jumped right

to the heart of the issue that concerned them most—Zia's abduction.

"I don't know if Zia told you that she was working with a consultant to secure and manage the funding for her grant."

"Yes," Dom said shortly. "We know about that."

"Turns out this consultant—Thomas Danville—was skimming from his clients' accounts to support a cocaine habit. Evidently Danville was obtaining his coke from thugs working for a drug cartel with direct links to a known terrorist organization."

"What cartel?"

"Los Zetas. Which supposedly has ties to—"

"Hezbollah," Dom supplied, his jaw working. "And through them to Iran."

Hissing, he spit out something in Hungarian that whipped the duchess's head around. She said nothing, however, as he continued in a low growl.

"The Iron Triangle of Terror. And Zia got caught in the middle of this?"

"One of Danville's associates—a woman by the name of Elizabeth Hobbs—evidently became suspicious and contacted the authorities. Danville's suppliers got wind of it somehow and…"

A muscle worked in the side of Mike's jaw. He had to force himself to continue.

"According to Danville, his pals took care of Hobbs. At that point he panicked. He knew the authorities had to be on to him, tapping his phones, tracking his finances. He planned to skip the country but needed cash. And, apparently, another fix."

The grim account didn't get any easier with telling. An iron band seemed to tighten around Mike's chest as he finished in short, terse bursts.

"Danville contacted Zia. Arranged to meet her around three this afternoon. He pulled a gun on her, then forced her to drive to an underground garage. He intended to parlay her engagement ring into cash and coke. She used it instead to put out the bastard's eye."

The silence this time ranged from stunned to incredulous to furious. Gina broke it by pounding a clenched fist on her thigh. "I wish she'd jammed it down his throat!"

"Zia's face," the duchess put in. "The blood on her clothes. She was injured?"

"Danville got off a couple of shots at close range. One hit a concrete pillar mere inches from Zia's face, and her ears are still ringing from the percussive impact. The doc at the ER diagnosed the ringing as tinnitus but wants her to schedule an appointment with an audiologist for a more thorough check."

The family looked from one to another, still stunned, still processing the incredible information.

"Why didn't you call me?" Dom wanted to know. "Or Jack?"

"There wasn't time."

"The hell there wasn't. You just told us my sister went missing in midafternoon. You had hours to get hold of us. Unless…" Dom's eyes narrowed. "What *aren't* you telling us, Brennan?"

The razor-edged question brought Jack Harris out of his chair. Frowning, he stood shoulder to shoulder with his wife's cousin. "Cut the bull, Brennan. What do you know that we don't?"

Tension raced like a tsunami through the room. The force of it stiffened the duchess in her high-backed chair and caused her to rap out an imperious command.

"Sit down!"

She enforced the order with a vigorous thump of her cane. The solid whack pivoted the men around. Three bristling males who'd stormed or stolen their way into her heart. Jack so tall and tawny haired and sophisticated.

Dominic, her great-nephew, the grand duke, so dark and dangerous looking. And Michael, with his wide shoulders braced for battle and his green eyes refusing to yield so much as an inch.

Charlotte couldn't have asked for a more impressive set of genes to infuse the St. Sebastian family line. She wouldn't admit that to them, of course, any more than she would permit them to behave with such a lamentable lack of manners in her presence.

"I must ask you not to ruffle your feathers and scratch the dirt like fighting cocks in my sitting room. Sit down. Now, if you please."

They obeyed. Slowly. Reluctantly. Charlotte tipped her chin and waited until they were seated to pin Mike with a cool stare.

"I, too, would like an explanation of why it took so long for Zia's family to be apprised of the danger she faced from this...this Danville person. Why didn't she tell us?"

"She didn't know the full extent of it until he abducted her this afternoon."

"But you knew?" The duchess's snowy brows arched. "You must have, to have enlisted the FBI's aid so quickly."

"An agent contacted GSI yesterday," Mike admitted, his jaw working. "I met with them this morning."

"A fenébe is!" Dominic shoved to his feet again, his eyes blazing. "You knew about Danville, and yet you let Zia walk into his trap?"

"I didn't let—"

"What was she?" His fists balled. "Bait? A lure to bring the bastard crawling out of the woodwork?"

"No."

Mike understood the man's fury. The same anger boiled in his gut. He should've told Zia about the call from the FBI last night. Failing that, he should've insisted she accompany him to Havers's office this morning. Instead, he'd kept his damned mouth shut and she'd ended up fighting for her life. He'd never forgive or forget that monumental error in judgment.

Neither would Zia's brother. St. Sebastian moved on Mike, ignoring the duchess's gasp and his wife's quick word of warning.

"The FBI needed her, didn't they? To help nail their terrorist. *You* needed her, to recover your quarter million."

The charge was absurd. St. Sebastian knew that as well as everyone else in the room. Yet Mike didn't argue. Just waited for the punch *he* would have thrown if it had been one of his sisters in that dim, cavernous garage.

St. Sebastian ached to deliver it. Mike saw the primal urge in the man's bunched shoulders, read it in the flared nostrils. Then Dominic's dark eyes shifted to the right.

Mike followed the look and saw Zia standing in the arched entrance to the sitting room. She'd scrubbed her hands, combed back her hair and changed into sweats. Confusion and disbelief chased across her face.

"Did I hear right? The FBI contacted you *yesterday*? And you didn't tell me?"

Thirteen

Mike had only himself to blame for Zia's close brush with death. He couldn't escape that burden and didn't try. It sat like a stone on his chest as he related the sequence of events that had led him to the FBI.

First, Rafe's discovery of the overpayment of indirects. Then their suspicion funds were being diverted to a blind account. Mike's abrupt decision to fly to New York to discuss the discrepancy with Zia. Rafe's call relating the grim news that his probe had resulted in a call from the FBI. The request for Mike to meet with the agent this morning in New York.

His audience listened in stony silence. Zia, the duchess, Dom and his wife, Gina and her husband. The St. Sebastians had closed ranks, protecting their own, shutting him out. Mike's family would have done the same.

"I could have told you about it last night," he said to Zia. "I started to. Then…"

"Then?"

The single word was edged with ice.

"Then I played the odds," Mike admitted with brutal honesty as she entered the room. "I figured they had to know your background. I figured they'd also know yours," he said, meeting Dominic's stare head-on. "Europe's newest royal. Cultural Attaché to the UN. Former undercover agent. You think the Bureau didn't consider the possibility Interpol might come crashing down on them?"

His gaze shifted, pinned Jack Harris.

"Then there's you, Ambassador. Doesn't take a genius to grasp the political fallout if word leaked that the FBI was asking questions about your wife's cousin. And you, Duchess. You've become a celebrity. Again," he amended as her chin tilted.

"What has my aunt's status or that of anyone in my family got to do with your decision to talk to the FBI and not me?" Zia asked coldly.

"I thought they would talk to me more openly without all the heavy guns your family could bring to bear. The plan was to scope out the extent of the threat before I told you about it."

"*Would* you have told me if Danville hadn't abducted me and forced your hand?"

"Yes! Hell, yes!"

"How do I know that?" The frost didn't leave her voice, thick now with her native accent. "How do I know you do not think to protect me always? How do I know you won't shield me from everything that is dangerous or cruel or merely unpleasant?"

He opened his mouth, snapped it shut again. He wanted to assure her that he was modern enough, mature enough, to respect her as both an adult and a professional. Yet he couldn't deny the instincts imprinted in his DNA. Or was it RNA?

Hell, who cared? All Mike knew was that he was driven by the same need to shield his mate as every other living creature. He'd be lying if he denied it, so he pulled in a breath and spoke straight from his heart.

"I love you, Zia. I respect your drive and can't even begin

to appreciate your intelligence. But I'll always, *always*, try to protect you from harm."

That was met with dead silence. Mike thought he detected a glimmer of understanding in Jack's eyes, maybe even Dom's. The duchess looked cautiously noncommittal. But Zia had heard enough.

"I can't speak more about this now." She lifted trembling fingers to her bruised and cement-pitted cheek. "My face hurts and I still hear tinny cymbals in my ear. I'll call you, yes?"

When she turned away, Mike stretched out a hand. "Zia..."

"I'll call you!"

She whirled and left the room. To Mike's surprise, Dom rose and crossed slowly to where he stood. His dark eyes, so like his sister's, held marginally less hostility than they had before.

"I understand why you did what you did. I don't like the results, but I understand."

Mike snorted. "Can't say I'm real happy with the results, either."

"I know my sister. She won't be pushed or prodded. Give her time. Wait for her to call."

"And if she doesn't?"

"Then I would advise you to go back to Texas and forget her."

Yeah, Mike thought as he gathered his stained leather jacket and made for the door. Like that was going to happen.

Zia emerged from her bedroom into the stillness of the night, enveloped in the familiar comfort of her sweats and fuzzy slippers. An *un*familiar and unrelenting sense of loss sat like a stone on her chest as she negotiated the darkened apartment and shuffled into the kitchen. She flipped on the lights and filled the teakettle. While she waited for the water to heat, she rested both palms on the counter and stared blindly at the backsplash.

Her parents' death had shattered her. If not for Dom, she might still be mired in grief. He'd been her anchor then, and again during those long days after she'd nearly died herself. He'd buried his pain to help her work through hers. Brought her slowly, inevitably back to an appreciation of the joys life had to offer.

Yet Zia sensed—she *knew*—she couldn't turn to her brother to ease this hurt. He wouldn't understand how deep it cut. He couldn't. Although Dom would never admit it, he was every bit as possessive and territorial as any of their sword-wielding ancestors. Luckily he'd married a woman with the smarts and humor to tame those atavistic tendencies.

But Zia didn't want to "tame" her chosen mate. She wanted an equal. Was sure she'd found one. The realization Mike regarded her as someone to be coddled and protected blasted crater-sized holes in that erroneous assumption.

"Are you making tea?"

Lost in her thoughts, Zia hadn't heard the duchess's cane tracking toward the kitchen or the gentle swish of the swinging door. Her great-aunt stood on the threshold. She was wrapped in the fleecy blue robe Sarah had given her for Christmas and leaned heavily on her cane.

"I'm so sorry. Did I wake you?"

"Unfortunately not," Charlotte replied drily. "Sleep becomes extraneous when one reaches my age. May I join you?"

"Of course. The water's about to boil. Shall I make a pot of decaffeinated Spiced Chai?"

"Yes, please."

With the ease of long familiarity, Zia measured the fragrant tea into the infuser in Charlotte's favorite Wedgwood pot and added boiling water. While the tea steeped and released the tantalizing scent of ginger and cloves and cardamom, she filled a tray with two delicate china cups and saucers, a matching sugar and creamer, napkins, spoons and fresh lemon wedges.

She carried the tray to where the duchess waited in the breakfast room just off the kitchen. During the day, the room's ivy-sprigged wallpaper, green seat cushions and tall windows seemed to reflect Central Park at its joyous summer best. Even this late on a cold March night, the room served as a cheerful beacon in the gloom.

"There's something so soothing, so civilized about tea," Charlotte mused as she stirred milk into her cup. "Especially after such a brutal day."

Zia nodded and opted for lemon instead of milk.

"Are your ears still ringing?"

"Not as badly as before."

"And your face? Your lovely face?"

"The cuts will heal."

"Yes, they will." Carefully, the duchess replaced her spoon on the saucer. "Most hurts do, eventually."

"And some go deeper than others." Zia looked up from the dark swirl in her cup. "I'm not a child. Although Dom still tries to play the big brother, I declared my independence some years ago. I respect his concern for my welfare but I don't need him to protect me. I don't need any man to protect me. I thought Mike understood that."

"Forgive me, Anastazia, but that's twaddle."

"Excuse me?"

"Twaddle," the duchess repeated. "You're a physician. You know the male of the species better than most women. Their instincts, their idiosyncrasies. One of which is the belief that they're supposed to beat their chests and protect their females from all poachers."

The duchess's choice of words hit home. Mike had used the same word to describe Tom Danville after their first meeting. The noun ruffled Zia's feminist feathers almost as much now as it had then.

"Of course I know men are driven by primal urges. So are women. That doesn't mean we can't control them." She frowned, surprised by the direction the conversation had taken. "I thought you of all people would understand how I feel. You're the bravest, most courageous woman I know. You would never let someone wrap you in cotton wool and shield you from the realities of life."

"Oh, but you're wrong! You can't imagine how many times I wished for that cotton wool. For someone to block at least a little of the ugliness. And," she added with a sigh, "share the beauty."

"So what are you suggesting? That I should let Mike decide what to block and how much to share?"

"You must *both* decide. That's what marriage entails. Learning to respect each other's wants and needs and boundaries. It doesn't happen overnight."

"It certainly didn't happen today."

"Oh, Anastazia." The duchess stretched out a hand and folded it over Zia's. "I believe Michael only intended to… how did he phrase it? Scope out the threat. I also believe he planned to tell you as soon as he'd done that. Don't you?"

"I… Yes."

"And, my dear, I think you're forgetting one rather salient fact." She gave Zia's hand a brisk pat. "You're hardly a weak, helpless female. You didn't sit around and wait to be rescued. You incapacitated your attacker and escaped."

Those terrifying moments in the garage replayed in Zia's mind. Each graphic sequence, every desperate move. Including the heart-stopping seconds when Mike lunged across the Porsche.

"That's not entirely true," she said slowly. "I did incapacitate Danville and managed to get out of the car, but he still had his gun. Mike wrestled it away from him before he pounded the bastard into the pavement."

"He did that? Good for him!"

"He didn't tell you?"

"No."

Zia's surprise must have shown on her face.

"I suspect," Charlotte said drily, "he was more prepared to accept the blame for what happened than any credit." She let that sink in for a moment, then grasped her cane. "It's late and you've had a horrific day. You should get some rest."

"I will, I promise. As soon as I finish my tea."

"All right. Sleep well, dearest."

When the quiet thump of her cane faded, the apartment settled into silence. Zia cradled her cup in both hands and breathed in the last whiff of ginger and cloves from her cooling tea. The final moments in the garage kept playing and replaying in her mind.

"Dammit!"

Cutting off the mental video, she pushed away from the table.

The call dragged Mike from a restless doze. He'd hit the rack an hour ago and spent most of that time with his hands behind his head, staring up at the ceiling. After what seemed like hours, he'd finally drifted off.

When his cell phone buzzed he fumbled it off the nightstand. The number marching across the incoming display had him swinging his legs over the side of the bed and jerking upright.

"Zia? All you all right?"

"No. We have to talk."

"Now?"

"Yes, now. What's your room number?"

"My…?" He shook away his grogginess. "You don't need to come all the way downtown. I'll come there."

"Too late. I'm in the lobby. What's your room number?"

"Twelve-twenty."

"Got it. Now tell security to keycard the elevator for me."

After Mike gave his okay, Zia came back on the phone with a crisp, "I'm on my way up."

He pulled on his jeans, his thoughts grim. She'd told him to wait for her call. It had come a hell of a lot sooner than he'd anticipated. Too soon, his gut told him. She was still angry, still hurt. And very possibly suffering a delayed reaction to the traumatic events of the afternoon. He'd have to be careful, measure every word, or he'd screw this up worse than he already had.

He shagged a hand through his hair and made a quick trip to the bathroom. He barely had time to splash water on his face before she rapped on the door to his suite. He flicked the dead bolt, prepared for a kick to the gut when he saw her cut-and-bruised cheek. He *wasn't* prepared for the red-and-white cardboard carton she balanced on the palm of her hand.

"No anchovies or anything resembling fruit," she announced as she sailed past him with the carton held high. "I hope you have wine or beer in your minibar."

He stammered for a moment but finally managed, "I'm pretty sure there's both."

"Then I'll take wine. Red, not white."

She plopped the carton onto the counter that separated the living area from a small kitchenette and flicked on the overhead lights. The canned spots illuminated both the cuts and the determination in her face.

Mike was damned if he could interpret her confusing signals. Pizza and that lethal "we need to talk." Wine and utter resolve. Still wary, he uncorked a red and filled two wineglasses. She accepted hers with a cool word of thanks.

Ah, hell! He'd never been one for sailing at dead slow speeds. Might as well get the water roiling. Raising his glass, he tipped it toward hers.

"What should we drink to?"

She thought that over long enough to have him sweating.

"To us," she finally answered, "with certain caveats."

He brought his glass down. Slowly. Carefully. "I think I'd better hear what those caveats are before we drink to them."

"Smart man." She deposited her wine on the counter beside the pizza box and folded her arms. "Okay, here's the deal. I love you. You love me. But, as you no doubt learned from your previous marriage, love isn't always enough."

She had that right. Although Mike now wondered if he'd ever really loved Jill. Whatever he'd felt for her had certainly come nowhere close to this driving need to keep Zia in his life.

"So what do you propose?"

"First of all, no more scoping out situations on your own. No more independent threat assessments. We need to talk things out. Everything! The big issues, the little annoyances. Our families, our dreams, our fears."

"You want to talk all that out tonight?"

He was half teasing, half scared she meant it. Thankfully, his question elicited a muffled laugh.

"I supposed we can stretch out the discussion period."

The reluctant laugh told Mike he hadn't totally blown it. He moved closer, relief washing through him. "Stretch it out for how long?"

"Ten years?"

"Not long enough."

"Thirty?"

"Still too short." He caged her against the counter and felt himself falling into those dark, exotic eyes. "I'm thinking forty or fifty."

"Hmm," she murmured, sliding her arms around his neck, "that sounds about right."

A raw, gaping hole had ripped open when he'd almost lost her—literally and figuratively. She filled that emptiness now. The feel of her, the taste of her, was like coming home.

Sighing, she rested her forehead against his chin. "I was so terrified this afternoon."

"Who wouldn't be in that situation?"

"I wasn't scared for me! Well, yes, for me but for you, too. My heart stopped when you threw yourself at Danville."

"I was just the cleanup crew. You did the hard work."

She shuddered, and Mike wished savagely that he could have another ten minutes alone with Danville.

"You know," he said, to take her mind off the horror of the afternoon, "there's something we need to discuss that can't wait ten or twenty years."

She tipped her head back. "What's that?"

"When and where we're getting married. I vote for city hall, this weekend."

"This weekend!"

"As soon as we can get the license and blood tests done," he confirmed. "Your friends at the hospital lab ought to be able to help us out there."

"But city hall…"

"Or St. Patrick's or the chapel at your hospital or the top of the Empire Building. You pick the place, I'll take care of the arrangements."

"You can't! I mean, we can't. Gina would have a fit."

"What's she got to do with it?"

"Gina's an event coordinator! She does only a few select events now that she has the twins, but she's still one of the best in the business."

"Fine. Ask Gina to arrange it. For this weekend."

She leaned back in his arms. "This is your idea of talking things out?"

"Well..." He tried to sound apologetic but couldn't pull it off. "Pretty much."

"I'll get together with my cousin," she said, holding his eye sternly, "and come up with a list of options for us to discuss. You. Me. Together."

Mike had no problem with that. He'd achieved his primary objective of getting her mind off the horror of this afternoon. Even more important, he had her thinking when, not if.

"Fine. Now let's talk about whether we're going to eat pizza or go to bed. You. Me. Together."

She melted into a smile. "Bed. Now. End of discussion."

Fourteen

Gina pulled out all the stops and coordinated two separate events.

The first was a May wedding that took place in Galveston a week after Zia completed her residency. They did it Texas style, with Mike's male relatives and friends in either formal Western wear or Spanish-style suits. The women wore lacy dresses in a rainbow of colors. Even the New York contingent got in the spirit of things, with the duchess looking especially regal in a tall ivory comb and exquisite white lace mantilla purchased for the occasion.

The Camino Del Rey resort erected a portable pavilion that stretched from the dunes almost down to the water's edge. Filmy bows with sprays of bluebonnets decorated the white chairs. Long, fluttering white ribbons tied additional clusters of bluebonnets to the pavilion's tall poles.

Mike's three brothers stood shoulder to shoulder with his brothers-in-law. His three sisters joined Gina and Sarah and Natalie on the other side of the dais. Little Amalia and Charlotte made prim, dainty flower girls, in direct contrast to the fidgeting, reluctant ring bearers, Davy and his brother, Kevin.

Mike's parents and *abuelita* sat with the duchess in the

front row of seats. Aunts, uncles, cousins, friends and acquaintances of both families filled the rest. But Mike had
eyes for no one but his bride when she walked down the
aisle on the arm of her brother.

She'd caught her ebony hair back and crowned it with a
garland of white roses, but the sea breeze played with the
ends. The glossy black tendrils danced around her face as
she and Dom matched their steps to Franz Liszt's "Liebe-
straum No. 3." Or maybe it was one of his nineteen rhap-
sodies. Mike figured he'd learn which was which in the
next ten or twenty or thirty years.

Then he took Zia's hand in his and refused to let his
gaze linger on the spot where she'd worn the diamond.
She hadn't wanted another engagement ring. Just the wide
gold band he'd had inscribed with what had become their
personal mantra. With a smile in his heart, he recited the
words to her now.

"You. Me. Together. Forever."

Gina coordinated a second event that took place less
than a week later, just before the start of Zia and Mike's
extended honeymoon trip to all her favorite haunts in Hungary and Austria. This event took place on a rocky prom-
ontory guarding a high Alpine pass between those two
countries, with the ruins of Karlenburgh Castle forming a
dramatic backdrop.

The number of people in attendance was considerably
smaller than the Galveston event. Just Zia and Mike. Dom
and Natalie. Sarah and Gina and their husbands. The twins,
bundled against the cool mountain air. And the Grand
Duchess of Karlenburgh.

It was the first time she'd returned to her homeland since
she'd fled it more than sixty years ago. She stood alone,
both hands resting on the head of her cane, the ruins behind her, the sun-dappled valley far below. She didn't seem

to notice the wind that molded the skirt of her pale green traveling suit to her hips and fluttered the scarf she wore around her neck in a fashionable double loop. Her gaze was fixed on the distant horizon. Her family could only guess what she saw in those lacy clouds.

"She must be remembering the first time she came here as a bride," Gina murmured, maintaining a firm grip on Amalia while Jack kept Charlotte corralled. "She was so young. Barely eighteen. And so much in love."

"Maybe she's thinking of the balls she and our grandfather held here," Sarah said softly. "How I wish we had a photo or portrait of her in sables and the St. Sebastian diamonds."

"Or she may be remembering Christmases past," Dom put in quietly. "The last time Natalie and I were here, we talked to an old goatherd. He still remembered the tree-lighting ceremony in the magnificent great hall. Everyone from the surrounding villages was invited."

Zia folded her hand into her husband's, aching for the woman she'd come to love so fiercely. Zia and Mike were just beginning their life together. So much of Charlotte's was past and shrouded with sadness.

The duchess's eyes drifted shut for a few moments. Her right hand lifted a few inches, moving in a small, almost imperceptible wave. Then she regripped the ebony head of her cane and squared her shoulders. When she turned to face her family, her chin was high and her eyes clear.

"Thank you for talking me into returning to Karlenburgh. I shall always remember this moment and I'm more grateful than you can ever imagine that I was able to share it with all of you. Now for pity's sake, let's go down to the village. I could use a good, stiff *pálinka*."

Epilogue

What an amazing summer this has been. My darling Sarah
has given birth to the most exquisite baby girl. Dev is beyond
thrilled and sends me detailed and rather exhaustive reports
on her gurgles, her burps, her every hiccup. Gina and Jack stood
as her godparents, then just weeks later Natalie and Dom announced that they, too, would be adding to the ever-increasing
St. Sebastian clan.

Anastazia and Michael are so very busy with his business
and her work. Her research, I'm quite pleased to note, has expanded to such an extent that she travels extensively to other
universities and hospitals around the country—most often to
University General Hospital in Houston, I must note.

She and Michael talked about starting a family. I took great
care not to insert myself into that discussion, of course. But
it couldn't have been more than three weeks later that Maria
called, frantic with the news that she'd found a toddler wan-
dering down her street wearing only a soiled diaper. Anastazia
rushed over immediately to examine the child. It's a crack baby,
as addicted to drugs as its mother must have been when she

abandoned him. The authorities took custody of the child and Anastazia has become his fierce and very protective advocate. I suspect it won't be long before she becomes his mother.

When I look back at all these astonishing events I realize yet again what a rewarding life I live. I wake every morning eager to see what the day will bring. And every night before I drift to sleep I let my gaze linger on the Canaletto hanging in my bedroom. The painting takes me back to Karlenburgh—the sorrows, the joys, the memories I'll hold in my heart forever.
From the diary of Charlotte,
Grand Duchess of Karlenburgh

* * * * *

If you loved THE TEXAN'S ROYAL M.D.,
pick up the other stories in
the DUCHESS DIARIES series
from USA TODAY bestselling
author Merline Lovelace

A BUSINESS ENGAGEMENT
THE DIPLOMAT'S PREGNANT BRIDE
HER UNFORGETTABLE ROYAL LOVER

Available now

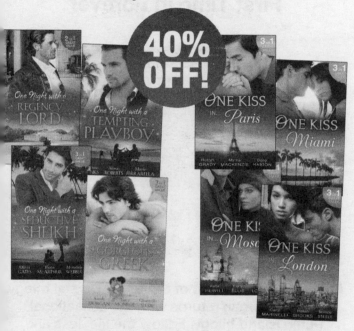

MILLS & BOON®

Why not subscribe?
Never miss a title and save money too!

Here's what's available to you if you join the
exclusive **Mills & Boon Book Club** today:

- *Titles up to a month ahead of the shops*
- *Amazing discounts*
- *Free P&P*
- *Earn Bonus Book points that can be redeemed against other titles and gifts*
- *Choose from monthly or pre-paid plans*

Still want more?
Well, if you join today we'll even give you
50% OFF your first parcel!

So visit **www.millsandboon.co.uk/subs**
or call **Customer Relations on 020 8288 2888**
to be a part of this exclusive Book Club!

MILLS & BOON®

Desire™

PASSIONATE AND DRAMATIC LOVE STORIES